Temptation *in* Regency Society

MARGARET McPHEE

MILLS &
BOON

Published in Great Britain 2014
by Mills & Boon, an imprint of Harlequin (UK) Limited,
Eton House, 18-24 Paradise Road, Richmond, Surrey, TW9 1SR

TEMPTATION IN REGENCY SOCIETY
© 2014 Harlequin Books S.A.

Unmasking the Duke's Mistress © 2011 Margaret McPhee
A Dark and Brooding Gentleman © 2011 Margaret McPhee

ISBN: 978-0-263-25015-2

052-0615

Harlequin (UK) policy is to use papers that are natural, renewable and recyclable products and made from wood grown in sustainable forests. The logging and manufacturing processes conform to the legal environmental regulations of the country of origin.

Printed and bound
by CPI Group (UK) Ltd, Croydon, CR0 4YY

Margaret McPhee loves to use her imagination—an essential requirement for a trained scientist. However, when she realised that her imagination was inspired more by the historical romances she loves to read rather than by her experiments, she decided to put the ideas down on paper. She has since left her scientific life behind, retaining only the romance—her husband, whom she met in a laboratory. In summer, Margaret enjoys cycling along the coastline overlooking the Firth of Clyde in Scotland, where she lives. In winter, tea, cakes and a good book suffice.

Unmasking the Duke's Mistress

MARGARET McPHEE

For Patricia—
I hope that it's not too saucy for you!

Chapter One

April 1809

Within the large and tastefully decorated drawing room of Mrs Silver's House of Rainbow Pleasures in the St James's district of London, Arabella Marlbrook paced and tried to ignore the feeling of dread that coiled deep in the pit of her stomach.

The black silk dress she was wearing had been made for a thinner woman and clung in an indecent fashion to the curves of her hips and breasts and she was all too aware that she was wearing neither petticoats nor stays. Her skin was like ice to touch, yet she could feel the smear of clamminess upon her palms. And she worried that the black feathers of the mask across her eyes did not obscure her identity well enough.

There were five other women artfully arranged around the drawing room, each one in a different colour and all in attires that made Arabella look positively overdressed.

'Do sit down, Arabella,' Miss Rouge said from where she reclined in her scarlet underwear and stockings upon one of the sofas. 'You are making me quite dizzy. You would do better to save your strength for there'll be gentlemen aplenty and eager tonight. And some of what they'll ask for will be demanding, to say the least.' She gave a sly smile and from behind the bright red feathers of her facemask her eyes looked almost black.

'Leave her be, Alice. Think how you felt on your first night. It is only natural that she is nervous,' said pale pink Miss Rose who was leaning against the mantelpiece so that the flicker of the flames illuminated her legs through the pale pink silk as if she were not wearing a skirt at all. Then she looked across at Arabella. 'You'll be fine, girl. Don't you worry.'

Arabella shot Miss Rose a grateful look, before turning to Miss Rouge, 'Please do not address me by my given name. I thought we were supposed to use the names Mrs Silver told us.' Arabella had no wish for the man she must lie with this night—her stomach turned over again at the thought—to know her true identity. It was vital that not the slightest hint of her shame attach itself to those that she loved.

'It's only a name, Miss Noir, keep your skirt in place!' snapped Miss Rouge.

'Leastways till she gets her gent upstairs!' quipped the small blonde in the armchair who was all in blue. She cackled at the joke and all of the other women, except for Arabella, joined in.

Arabella turned away from them so that they would not see the degree of her humiliation, and moved to stand before the bookcase as if she were perusing the titles upon the shelf. Only when her expression was quite composed did she face the room once more.

Alice, Miss Rouge, was buffing her nails. Ellen, Miss Vert, yawned and closed her eyes to nap upon the day bed. Lizzie, Miss Bleu, and Louisa, Miss Jaune, were engaged in a quiet conversation and Tilly, Miss Rose, was reading a romantic novel.

Arabella studied the décor of the room in an attempt to distract her mind from the prospect of what lay ahead. It was a fine room, she noted, perhaps one of the finest she had seen. The floorboards were polished oak, and covered with a large gold-and-blue-and-ivory Turkey carpet. The walls were a pale duck-egg blue that lent the room a peaceful ambience. In the centre of the ornate plasterwork ceiling was a double-layered crystal-drop chandelier and around the room several matching wall sconces sat against large, elegant looking-glasses so that the light of the candle flames was magnified in glittering excellence. The furniture was mainly oak, all of it finely turned, understated and tasteful.

There were five armchairs, two sofas and a daybed, some of which were upholstered in ivory and duck-egg blue stripes, some in plain ivory and others in a pale gold material that seemed to shimmer beneath the candlelight. On a table in the corner of the room was a vase filled with fresh flowers, the blooms all whites and creams and shades of yellow.

It might have been a drawing room in any respectable wealthy house in London. Arabella marvelled at the contrast between the calm elegance of the décor and the crude reality of what went on within these walls… and was faced once more with the stark truth of what she was here to do.

She dreaded the moment when some gentleman would arrive and buy her 'services.' Indeed, she had to fight every minute not just to walk out the door and keep on walking all the way home. But she knew she could not do that. She knew very well why she was here and the reason she must go through with this.

She closed her eyes and tried to calm the nausea and dread that was prickling a cold sweat upon her forehead and upper lip. A hundred guineas a week, Mrs Silver had promised. A fortune, indeed.

A hundred guineas to sell herself. A hundred guineas to save them all.

Dominic Furneaux, otherwise known as his Grace the Duke of Arlesford, swirled the brandy in his glass while he deliberated over the four cards held in his hand. Then, having made his decision, he drained the contents of the glass in a single gulp and gestured to the banker to deal him another card.

There was an audible intake of air from the smartly dressed men gathered around the Duke's gaming table in White's Gentlemen's Club. The pile of guineas heaped in the centre of the table was high, and most of it had been staked by the Duke himself.

The card was dealt with a flip so that it was placed face up on the green baize before the Duke.

Marcus Henshall, Viscount Stanley, craned his neck to look over the top of the heads of the gentlemen that stood before him.

The Ace of Hearts.

'An omen of love,' someone whispered.

The Duke ignored them. 'Five-card trick. *Vingt-et-*

un.' He smiled lazily as if he cared and laid his cards upon the table for all to see.

'Well, I will be damned, but Arlesford has the very luck of the devil!' someone else exclaimed.

There was laughter and murmurs and the scrape of chairs against the polished wood of the floor as his friends threw in their cards and got to their feet.

'What say you all to finding ourselves some entertainment of a different variety for what remains of the night?' Lord Bullford said.

The suggestion was met with raucous approval.

'I know just the place,' Lord Devlin chipped in. 'An establishment in which the wares are quite delicious enough to satisfy the most exacting of men!'

More laughter, and lewd comments.

Dominic watched as Stanley made his excuses and left, rushing home to his wife and baby. He felt a pang of jealousy and of bitterness. There was no woman or child awaiting Dominic. Indeed, there was nothing in Arlesford House that he wanted, save perhaps the cellar of brandy. But that was the way he wanted it. Women were such faithless creatures.

'Come on, Arlesford,' drawled Sebastian Hunter, only son and heir to a vast fortune. 'We cannot have you celebrating all alone.'

'When have I ever celebrated alone?' Dominic asked with a nonchalant shrug.

'True, old man,' said Bullford, 'But I will warrant the pleasures to be had in the house of paradise to which Devlin will take us will beat that offered by whichever little ladybird you have waiting for you in your bed.'

Dominic's smile was hollow. He had his share of women; indeed, he supposed that he truly did merit the title of rake that London bestowed upon him. But there was no ladybird waiting in his bed; there never had been. Dominic did not bring women home. He visited the beds of those women who understood the game and walked away afterwards. He gave them money and expensive gifts, but never anything of himself, nothing that mattered, nothing that could be hurt. And he was always discreet.

He had no notion to visit the establishment of which Devlin spoke. He glanced around the table, taking in how loud and bawdy and reckless was the mood of his friends. Too foxed and excited to exercise any morsel of discretion, young Northcote more so than the others. As if to prove his point Northcote accepted the bottle of wine that Fallingham offered and drank from its neck, so that some of the ruby-red liquid spilled down his chin to stain the boy's cravat and shirt.

'Arlesford is on his best behaviour. Wants to impress Misbourne and his daughter. Nice little heiress and even nicer big dowry!' shouted young Northcote.

The party hooted and cheered.

'Since you obviously appreciate her merits, Northcote, you may have her. I have no intention of being caught in parson's mousetrap, as well you know.'

Fallingham sniggered. 'Old Misbourne doesn't think so. There is a hundred-guinea stake in the betting book in here that the Duke of A. will be affianced to a certain Miss W. before the Season is over.'

Dominic felt his blood run cold. 'A fool and his money are soon parted. Someone is about to be a hundred guineas lighter in the pocket.'

'Au contraire,' said Bullford. 'Misbourne was overheard discussing it in this very club. He is very deter-

mined to have you marry his daughter. Thinks it is some sort of matter of honour.'

'Then Misbourne has misunderstood both honour and me.' Dominic did not miss the meaningful glance Hunter threw him at Bullford's words. Unlike the others, Hunter knew the truth. He knew what Dominic had come home to find in Amersham almost six years ago, and he understood why Dominic had no wish to marry.

Devlin's eyes flicked to the doorway. 'Speak of the devil! Misbourne and his cronies have just come in, no doubt hoping to engage the prospective son-in-law in a game of cards,' he said with a chuckle.

'Time indeed that we departed for Devlin's house of pleasures,' murmured Hunter.

'And give young Northcote the education that he deserves,' Devlin laughed.

'With the amount Northcote has had to drink I doubt he'll be up for that manner of education,' said Dominic.

'That's monstrous unfair, Arlesford! I'll have you know that my chap is more than capable of standing proud. Indeed, he's stirring even at the thought of it.'

'Prove it,' sniggered Fallingham.

Northcote got to his feet and moved a hand to unfasten the fall on his pantaloons.

'Don't be such a bloody idiot,' snapped Dominic. To which Northcote belched and sat down again.

'You see you'll have to come, Arlesford. Who else is going to stop Northcote making a complete cake of himself?' said Hunter.

'Who indeed?' Dominic arched a brow, but the sarcasm was lost on Hunter.

Northcote was out of his depth in such company,

and dangerously so. Dominic knew he could not just abandon the youngster. He supposed he could endure an evening of flirtation in an upmarket bordello for Northcote's sake.

Dominic followed his friends towards the doorway and walked past Misbourne with only the briefest of nods in the man's direction. As he had told his friends, he had no intention of entering the marriage mart.

Dominic Furneaux had learned his lesson regarding women very well indeed. And so he turned his thoughts away from the past to the rest of the evening that lay ahead.

Mrs Silver gave the women only a few minutes' warning before showing the group of four gentlemen into the room.

Arabella felt the wave of panic go through her. Her stomach revolted and she felt physically sick at the prospect of what she was about to do with one of these men and for money. For one moment the desire to flee was overwhelming. She wanted so much just to run away. But then she remembered why she had to do this. And the memory resolved every trembling nerve in Arabella's body and lent her the strength that she needed. She stilled, took a deep breath and raised her eyes to face the men.

They were all young, not much older than her own four-and-twenty years; all used expensive tailors if their tight-fitting dark coats and pantaloons were anything to go by. Ruddy cheeked and bright eyed, and most definitely the worse for drink, especially the youngest-looking man of the group. She could smell the wine and brandy from where she stood at the farthest side of the room behind the striped sofa, as if the distance and the barrier of the furniture could save her from what lay ahead.

Her eyes began to move over them and she wondered which man would choose her. And the worry struck her that perhaps none of them would and then what would she do? Much as she loathed being here in this awful position, the thought of returning home empty-handed was even worse.

The men looked eager, salivating almost, so that she could not suppress the shudder that rippled through her. She turned her glance to the two taller gentlemen who were only just entering the room to join their friends… and her stomach sank right down to her toes.

It felt to Arabella as if she had just stepped off the edge of a cliff. The breath froze in her throat, her blood turned to ice and her heart hammered so hard and fast that she thought she might faint. She gripped tight to the back of the sofa, oblivious to the fact that her fingernails were digging into the expensive ivory material.

It cannot be. The thought was loud in her mind.

'It cannot be.' The words were barely a whisper upon her lips.

She stared all the harder, sure that she must be mistaken. But there was no mistake. She would have known the tall dark-haired man anywhere, even though she had not seen him in almost six long years.

He had not changed so very much. His shoulders were broader, his body carried more muscle and there were a few more lines of life etched upon his handsome face, but there could be no doubting that the man was most definitely Dominic Furneaux, or the Duke of Arlesford, as he was now.

His expression was one of boredom as he surveyed the room and its inhabitants. He looked as if he had no interest in being here in Mrs Silver's drawing room. His glance passed over her and then shot back to her face.

Please God, do not let Dominic, of all people, recognise her!

Her fingers touched the black feathered mask, checking that it was properly in place, but still he stared at her as if he could see right through it to the face of the woman beneath. His bored expression had vanished to be replaced by one of intense scrutiny.

The pop of the first champagne cork made her jump, but it was not the noise that set the tremor racing throughout her body. She averted her gaze and noticed that Mrs Silver was smiling meaningfully in her direction. Arabella saw the older woman gesture towards the glasses and suddenly remembered that she was supposed to be offering champagne to the gentlemen.

Miss Rouge had already dispensed with the first bottle and one of the men uncorked the second and began to pour. Arabella's hands trembled so much that she feared she would be unable to disguise it, but she knew she could not just stand there staring at Dominic. Perhaps if she busied herself he would stop looking at her with that too-seeing gaze.

She crossed the room towards Mrs Silver and collected two crystal-cut glasses of champagne as she had been told. And all the while her mind was reeling from the impact of seeing Dominic after all this time. She felt panicked, agitated, unable to think straight. She squeezed her eyes shut, trying to marshal her thoughts, struggling to control the shock that was roaring through her veins.

Of all the places to see him again, when she had
learned to live with the weight of that which had almost
crushed her. Maybe he would fix his attention on one
of the other girls. Maybe. But would it be any easier
to stand here and watch him take Miss Rouge or Miss
Vert or any one of the other women upstairs? Could she
feign a smile, pretend a flirtation and go willingly with
another man, knowing that he was here? She shook her
head in an infinitesimal movement of denial. This night
had promised to be the most difficult and degrading
of Arabella's life. Dominic's presence made it nigh on
impossible.

A hand touched against her sleeve and she opened
her eyes to find Mrs Silver looking at her with both
warning and concern.

'One hundred guineas a week,' she mouthed almost
silently. 'Think of the money.'

Arabella gave a tiny nod at the reminder and reined
in her emotions with a will of iron. A deep breath…and
then she turned around.

Dominic was standing right before her.

'Miss Noir, I presume.' His gaze swept slowly over
the transparent dress before coming back to rest upon
her face. 'Arlesford, at your service, ma'am.'

So he did not know her after all. *Thank God!* She
breathed a silent sigh of relief at that small mercy and
steeled her nerves to play the role of a woman she was
not.

'Your Grace.' She forced the words to her lips and
curtsied, but she could not bring herself to smile. Every
bone in her body felt chilled to the marrow, every inch
of her skin cold and bloodless. This was the meeting,
albeit not under such circumstances, she had prayed

so hard first for and then against. All her beliefs that she was over him, that she no longer cared, had been a delusion. She cared so much that it was as if the air had been knocked clean from her lungs.

They stared at one another and for Arabella it was as if the years had rolled back and she was looking at the man she would never manage to forget no matter how hard she tried. She averted her gaze, lest he see even a grain of her riotous emotions in her eyes, and glanced around the room.

The other women were smiling and conversing in coquettish teasing tones, each paired with a single gentleman. From the corner of the room Mrs Silver was looking at Arabella with a look of exasperation. The older woman gestured with her eyes from Dominic to the two glasses of champagne, that Arabella was still gripping for dear life, and back again.

There was no way out, no room for retreat. Arabella held her head high and forced her gaze back to Dominic. 'Would you care for some champagne?'

He ignored her question and studied her with those dark brown eyes that were so disturbingly familiar. The seconds seemed to stretch to minutes as they stared at one another, the champagne seemingly forgotten. But then his eyes darkened and he accepted the glass from her hand.

'I should...' She glanced round for another gentleman to whom she might pass the second glass but all of the men were already drinking and their attentions most definitely engaged in so obvious a manner that made Arabella feel as embarrassed as if she had been an innocent.

'It is for you, I believe,' Dominic said. He paused and

the dark gaze held hers once more before adding, 'Perhaps we can drink our champagne together...upstairs?'

Arabella's heart stumbled and missed a beat before galloping off at full tilt. The breath caught in her throat. The whole world seemed to turn upside down.

She knew what his suggestion meant.

Dominic had chosen her.

Her whole body trembled at the knowledge and she did not know whether it was the worst thing that could have happened or the best. Nearly six years, and yet it was as if her lips still burned from his kisses, her body still tingled from his love-making. To give herself to him again, and for money, flayed her pride more than anything.

Her hand itched to dash the contents of her glass in his face, to shout at him, to refuse him in the cruellest of terms. A vision of him standing there, his face and hair soaked from her champagne, his pride slurred before his friends swam in her mind, and that imagining was the one glimmer of light in the grim darkness of what was happening. But Arabella did not indulge her fantasy; she could not afford to. Even through the force of all that raged within her, she did not forget the stark truth of why she was here at Mrs Silver's House of Rainbow Pleasures. She had her responsibilities.

And she was honest and practical enough to admit to herself that, if she must couple with a gentleman this night it was better that it was Dominic rather than some stranger.

She glanced again at the other men in the room, at their faces glistening with sweat and flushed from drink and the greedy lust and excitement in their eyes. No matter how much she was loathe to admit it, the knowledge that it would be Dominic, and not one of them, was something of a relief, albeit a bitter one.

And if she kept the mask in place he would never know the identity of the woman for whom he was paying. And that at least would make it tolerable.

Arabella swallowed her pride. Her eyes met his. She nodded and turned to lead the way to the room Mrs Silver had shown her.

Within the black-clad bedchamber Dominic could not take his gaze from Miss Noir. He knew that he was staring and still he could not stop. His intention of watching over Northcote had been forgotten the moment he had set eyes on her downstairs in Mrs Silver's drawing room. God help him, but he could no more have turned away from her than stop breathing. It was as if the years had not passed and it was another woman standing before him.

'Is something wrong?' she asked.

Hell's teeth, he thought, but she even sounded like her.

Miss Noir's fingers fluttered nervously around the edges of her mask.

'Forgive my manners, but your appearance stirs memories from my past. You have the very likeness of someone I once knew.' It was the reason he was standing here with her now in the bordello's bedchamber and the very same reason why he should have turned his back and walked away. The pain had returned, and the bitterness, but when he looked at this woman he wanted her with what could only be described as desperation.

He wanted her because she looked like Arabella Tatton.

She did not smile or simper or offer playful seductive words. She did not unlace her bodice or stand before the fire to reveal the outline of her legs or lie upon the daybed with her skirts arranged to show her stockings. Rather her expression was serious, and her manner, for all she tried to hide it, was one of unease. She just stood there and watched him, all calm stillness, yet the white-knuckled clasp of her hands gripping together betrayed that she was not as calm as she was pretending. And beside her on the small occasional table, amidst the coil of dark silken ropes and the feathers and fans, the bubbles sparkled and fizzed within her untouched glass of champagne.

He drained the contents of his own glass in an effort to dampen the strength of emotion the woman's startling resemblance stirred.

'You seem a little nervous this evening, Miss Noir.'

'It is my first night here. Forgive me if I am unfamiliar with the usual etiquette. I...' She hesitated and seemed to have to force the remainder of the sentence, 'I wish only to please you.' Her head was held high and the glint in her eyes belied the subservience of the words. She raised her chin a notch and everything of her stance was as defiant and tense as if she were facing a combatant rather than a man whom she was trying to seduce. 'Do you wish me to undress now?'

He rose, setting his empty glass down next to her full one.

She looked so like Arabella that he felt like he had been kicked in the gut. His blood was rushing too hot, too fiercely. And no matter how hard he tried to suppress them, the memories were as strong and vivid as if all that had happened between them had been only yesterday.

The depth of his desire shocked him for he would have thought his anger at her to have long since tempered that. Yet his body was already hard and throbbing with impatience…as if it really were Arabella standing there. And because she looked so like Arabella, Dominic knew that he would not reject what she offered. He gave not another thought to Northcote and stripped off his tailcoat.

'There is more pleasure for us both if I undress you,' he said, never taking his eyes from hers. Her lashes swept low, not in a teasing manner, but as if she sought to hide something of herself from his scrutiny. He resolved to stop staring. But he could not.

'As you wish.' She walked to stand before him, and the dress she was wearing seemed to accentuate rather than hide the curves of her figure. In this, at least, she differed from Arabella, for although Arabella had been quite as tall as this woman, she had been more slimly built.

Arabella. Her very name seemed to whisper through the silence of the room. And the images were flashing through his mind, of Arabella lying beneath him, of her laughter and her smile; of him burying his face in the golden silk of her hair spread across his pillow, and his mouth whispering words of love upon hers while his hands stroked a caress over the naked satin of her skin.

And for all the anger in his heart, Dominic's body grew harder. With an effort he reined himself back under some measure of control. Arabella Tatton. He despised her. He should walk away from this woman, she, whose resemblance to Arabella had unleashed all that he had hidden away in the dark recesses of his mind. The logical part of his mind knew that with absolute certainty. Yet Dominic did not leave.

Instead, he reached over and untied the laces of her dress, loosening them until the bodice gaped wide to reveal the lush perfect breasts beneath. They nosed at the fabric, the nipples a rosy pink beside the pale perfection of her skin. And when his fingers brushed against them he felt the nipples harden and peak.

He leaned down and touched his lips against the soft skin of first one cheek and then the other, and when he looked through the holes cut within the feathered mask he saw her pupils widen, black as ebony, within eyes that were the same colour as Arabella's, the true clear blue of a sunlit summer sky.

Arabella. The pain was in equal measure to the depth of his desire.

His mouth traced down the slender column of her throat, to kiss each hollow of her collarbone as he eased the dress halfway down her arms. The laces were undone enough to expose her breasts in full and he moved his mouth over them so close yet without touching. Her nipples beaded harder as he caressed them with his breath. Slowly, teasingly he touched his tongue to her.

She closed her eyes and tried unsuccessfully to catch back the rush of breath that escaped her. Beneath his lips he felt the shiver pass right through her.

Very gently, very slowly he laved her, sucked her, measured the weight of each delicious breast within his hands. He could feel the fast hard beat of her heart and, more surprisingly, the slight tremor within her body.

And when he drew back her cheeks were faintly

flushed and behind the mask her eyes were open again, and just for a moment he saw that they glittered with desire before she hid them once more from his view. She slid the rest of her dress from her arms and unfastened the buttons by her waist so that the skirts slithered down her legs to pool upon the floor. She stepped out of the pile of silk, naked save for her high-heeled shoes and stockings, and the mask upon her face.

Miss Noir did not posture to encourage him, not that she needed to. She just stood there, proud and watchful.

Arabella, he wanted to whisper, and even though the name had never left his memory for all of these years past, having this woman who bore so much of her resemblance had slashed the bindings on all of those old wounds. And yet he wanted her more than ever. He wanted her as if she were Arabella herself.

Dominic shrugged off his waistcoat, unfastened his cravat and peeled off his shirt. He saw Miss Noir's gaze move over his chest and down to take in the bulge of his manhood straining in his pantaloons. And when her eyes met his again there was the strangest expression in them, one that he could not quite fathom.

He closed the distance between them and, pulling her into his arms, kissed her as thoroughly as he had wanted to from the moment he had laid eyes on her. She was rigid at first, but then she succumbed to his kisses and melted against him, and it was just like having the real Arabella in his arms. He did not even have to close his eyes to pretend it was her.

He kissed her as if she were the woman that he had loved. He kissed her with all the anguish that was in his soul…and in the answer of her lips he was shocked to feel an echo of how it had been between Arabella and himself. He stilled and eased back that he might look into her eyes but, just as quickly, Miss Noir turned away and bent to unfasten the garters of her stockings.

Dominic stayed her. 'Leave them,' he murmured. 'I want to look at you.'

She misunderstood and took a few steps away, opening up a small distance between them so that he might view her. He could not ignore the invitation, swallowing hard as his gaze swept over the long white legs that rose out of her dark stockings, over the smooth curve of her hips and the small triangle of fair hair that sat between her legs, and the soft feminine belly.

She blushed beneath his scrutiny, as if she were not a well-practised courtesan that rode different men every night of the week, as if she really were his Arabella. His manhood strained all the harder against the fine wool of his pantaloons.

She made no move to unfasten the mask from her face, nor did he ask her to do so, for he had no wish to shatter the illusion that had him standing here in the first place.

He stripped off his clothing and then took her in his arms once more.

Arabella, he mouthed silently against her throat as she wound her arms around his neck.

Arabella, as he carried her to the bed and laid her down. The contrast of her pale naked skin against the black silken sheets seemed to emphasise her similarity to Arabella all the more. He wanted her so much he was aching for her, so much that he could think of nothing else. His body covered hers, one hand thrumming at her nipple as he positioned himself between her legs.

She was open to him, moist and ready, and he was

rock hard as he stroked against her. Everything of her—the scent, the taste, the feel—was so like Arabella that as he slid into her silken heat in his mind it was Arabella he was entering. And when he rode her it was Arabella he was riding until both their breaths were ragged and their bodies were slick with sweat. He rode her until he found the relief of his climax, pulling out of her just before he spilled his seed.

Such exquisite torture.

But the minute that his body was spent he rolled off her, already regretting his decision to come upstairs with her.

She was not Arabella, and all that he had done was tear asunder ill-healed wounds of the past. He felt as empty and alone and unhappy as ever he had been and longed to be gone from this place. Throwing the covers back, he climbed from the bed.

'Thank you,' he said awkwardly, but could not bring himself to use the woman's name. He walked away, found his shirt and pantaloons and pulled them on.

A faint breathy noise sounded from the bed, a noise that sounded suspiciously like a silenced sob.

Dominic looked back at the bed and the woman who lay there so still and unmoving. And as his gaze found hers, she turned quickly away, rolling on to her side to present him with her back, as if she sought to block him out.

His eyes traced the golden tendrils that had escaped from the pile of curls pinned upon her head, over her pale shoulders and down the straight line of her back. Her waist was narrow before the flair of her hips and her perfect bottom.

His fingers froze in the act of fastening the buttons

of his pantaloons. His blood turned to ice. He could not move, could not so much as take a breath. He stared at the fullness of her rounded buttocks, stared at the soft white skin…and the distinctive dark mole upon her right cheek that he remembered so well.

The shock was as explosive as if someone had taken a pistol and shot him at point-blank range. Everything else in the world seemed to diminish. Dominic gaped with utter incredulity, staring at a truth so blatant that he marvelled he had not realised right from the very start.

'Arabella?' His whisper was barely more than a breath, yet it seemed to resonate within the room as loudly as if he had roared it at the top of his voice.

Every line of her body stiffened and tensed, the reaction confirming the suspicion his mind had been too slow to form. He saw the small shiver that rippled through her before she pulled the top cover free and then, holding it against her body to cover her nakedness, climbed from the bed. Only then did she turn to face him.

They stared at one another across the rumpled mess of sheets, and the very air seemed to vibrate with a barely contained tension.

Even now his mind could not accept the enormity of the discovery. Even now he thought she would deny it. But in her silence and stillness there was nothing of denial.

Dominic reached her in an instant. With one hand he pulled her to him, barely noticing that he had displaced the bedcover from her in the process. He was too busy untying the ribbons of her face mask, too busy tearing it from her. Even as she gasped, the black-feathered object tumbled to lie at their feet. And he stared down with horror into the shocked white face of Arabella Tatton, or Arabella Marlbrook as she was now.

Chapter Two

Arabella's naked body was hard against the length of Dominic's, their hips so snug that she could feel the press of his manhood. For a moment the shock of him discovering her was so great that she could do nothing other than stare right back into the eyes of the man she had loved. But then she recovered something of her wits and struggled to free herself.

'Arabella!' He tried to still her.

She hit out at him and tried to escape. But Dominic caught her flailing arms and hauled her back to him, securing her wrists behind her in a grip that was gentle yet unbreakable.

'Arabella.' Quieter this time, but no less dangerous.

'No!' she cried, but Dominic was unyielding. He stared down at her with implacable demand.

'What the hell are you doing here?' His eyes had darkened to a black glower that smouldered within the pallor of his face. And there was about him a simmering, barely contained rage so unlike the man she remembered.

She strove to stay calm, but her breath was as ragged as if she had been running at full pelt and with every breath she took she could feel the swollen tips of her breasts brush against his unfastened shirt.

'At least grant me the honour of allowing me to clothe myself before we have this conversation,' she said with a calmness that belied everything she was feeling.

His gaze dropped to rove over her nakedness with deliberate and provocative measure so that she thought he meant to refuse her but, just as she thought it, she felt his grip loosen and drop away.

She gathered up the black dress from where it lay on the floor and, turning her back to him, quickly garbed herself. She stretched around and tightened the laces of the bodice that she could reach, but had no other option than to leave the remainder loose. The dress gaped from the untied laces, revealing far too much of the pale swell of her bosom. It was the antithesis of respectable clothing, but it was better than facing him naked. She hoisted the neckline of the dress and clutched it in place. Dominic had finished his own dressing and now watched her with eyes burning with a shock that mirrored her own and an unmistakable anger.

'I will ask you again, Arabella,' he said with a quietness that was deadly, 'what are you doing here?'

'The same as any woman does in a place such as this.' She faced him defiantly, and with a determination to hide the shame and wretchedness beneath that façade.

'Whoring.' His voice was harsh.

'Surviving,' she said with as much dignity as she could muster and stared down his contempt.

'And where in damnation is Henry Marlbrook while you are "surviving" in a brothel? What manner of husband is he that you have been reduced to this?' His voice changed, hardened, as he spoke Henry's name and the word 'husband.'

'Do not dare to mention Henry's name.' Arabella would not stand here and hear it.

'Why ever not?' he threw back at her. 'Frightened that I find him and run him through?'

'Damn you, Dominic! He is dead!'

'Then he has saved me the trouble,' he said coldly.

Arabella gasped at Dominic's cruelty and then, before she could think better of it, she slapped him hard across his face. The crack resounded in the room around them and was followed by silence. Even in the soft flickering candlelight she could see the mark her palm had left upon his cheek.

His eyes had been dark before, but now they appeared as black and deadly as the night that surrounded them. But Arabella would not back down.

'You deserved that.' For everything he had done. 'Henry was a good man, a better man by far than you, Dominic Furneaux!'

Henry had been kind.

And Arabella had been grateful.

She saw something flicker in the darkness of Dominic's eyes.

'Just as he was all those years ago,' he said in a chilled voice. 'I have not forgotten, Arabella, not for one single day.'

Neither had she. With those few words all the past

was back in an instant. Of the joy of losing her heart to Dominic, of her happiness and expectations for the future, of the lovemaking they had shared. Lies and illusions, all of it. It had meant nothing to him. *She* had meant nothing to him, other than another notch upon his bedpost. At nineteen she had not understood the base side of men and their desires. At four-and-twenty Arabella knew better.

'You wasted no time in wedding him. Less than four months from what I hear.'

She could hear the accusation in his voice, the jealousy, and it fanned the flames of her ire. 'What on earth did you expect?' she shouted.

'I expected you to wait, Arabella!'

'To wait?' She stared at him in disbelief. 'What manner of woman did you think me?' Did he honestly think that she would have welcomed him back with open arms? That she would have given herself to him again after he had discarded her in such a humiliating way? 'I could not wait, Dominic,' she said harshly. 'I was—' Her eyes sought his.

His gaze was dark and angry and arrogant, every inch the hard, ruthless nobleman she knew him to be.

'You were...?'

She hesitated and felt the pulse in her throat beat a warning tattoo.

'A fool,' she finished. A fool to have believed his lies. A fool to have trusted him. 'You have what you came here for, Dominic. Now be gone and leave me alone.'

'So that you might rush down to Mrs Silver's drawing room to offer a "glass of champagne" to the next gentleman who is doubtless already waiting there.' Contempt dripped from his every word. 'I do not think so.'

How dare he? she thought. *How damnably dare he stand there and judge me after what he has done?* And in that moment she hated him with a passion that was in danger of driving every last vestige of control from her head. She wanted to scream at him and hit him and unleash all of her anger, for all that he had done then, and for all that he had done now. But she hung on to her self-control by the finest of threads.

His eyes held hers for a moment longer and the very air seemed to hiss between them. Then he walked over to stand behind one of the two black armchairs by the fireplace.

'Sit down, Arabella. We need to talk.'

She gave a shake of her head. 'I think not, your Grace,' she said and she was proud that her voice came out as cold and unemotional as his, for beneath it she was shaking like a leaf.

'If it is the money you are concerned over, rest assured that I have paid for the whole night through.' He looked at her with flint in his eyes.

There was a lump the size of a boulder in her throat that no amount of swallowing would shift. She faced him squarely, pretending she was not ravaged with shame, pretending that she was standing there completely untouched by the fury of emotion that roared and clashed between them.

Pretending that she had no secrets to hide.

He gestured to the armchair before him. 'Come, Arabella, sit. After what has just passed between us there is no room for coyness.' His voice was harsh and his face was set harder, more handsome, more resolute than ever she had seen it. And she knew that he would not change his mind.

'Damn you,' she whispered and the scars throbbed as if they had never healed and his reappearance, after all these years when Arabella had thought never to see him again, sparked fears that she was only just beginning to grasp.

Only once Arabella was seated did Dominic take the chair opposite hers.

'Did you know it was me from the start?'

'Of course I did not!' The fury he felt for both her and himself made his voice harsh. It did not matter what she had done, he would never have taken her out of vengeance.

'Then how did you realise?'

'How did I not realise sooner?' he demanded, but the question was not really for her but, rather, for himself. 'Me, who has known every inch of your body, Arabella.' *One flimsy black-feathered mask alone had been enough to fool him,* he thought bitterly, and knew that was not quite true. It was the fact that this, a bordello, a bawdy house, a brothel, was the last place on earth he would have ever thought of finding her.

The thought of what she had become shocked him to the core. The thought that he had treated her as such shocked him even more. He had dreamt of finding her, both longed for it and dreaded it. But never in all of his imaginings had it been like this. He raked a hand through his hair, trying to control his feelings.

He glanced across at her. Her face was pale, her expression guarded.

Time had only served to ripen her beauty so that she was now a beautiful woman when once she had been a beautiful girl. There was about her a wariness that had not been there before. Then, she had been innocent and carefree and filled with an irrepressible joy. Now what he saw when he looked at Arabella was a cold, angry, determined stranger he did not recognise. And then he remembered the muffled sob he had heard and the sheen of tears in her eyes…and something of his own anger died away.

'You said Marlbrook died.'

She gave a cautious nod. 'Two years since.'

'And left you unprovided for?' He could not keep the accusation from his tone.

'No!' The denial shot from her lips in her desperation to defend the bastard she had married. 'No,' she said again, this time more calmly. 'There was money enough left for a careful existence.' She hesitated as if deliberating how much to tell him.

The questions were crowding upon his lips, angry and demanding, but he spoke none of them, choosing instead to wait with a patience that he did not feel for her explanation.

But Arabella's explanation was not forthcoming. Her expression closed. Her mouth pressed firm and she glanced away.

The seconds ticked by to become minutes.

'Then you are here by choice rather than necessity?' he said eventually and raised an eyebrow.

'Yes.' She tipped her chin up and met his gaze unflinchingly, almost taunting him. 'So now you see the woman I have become, have you not changed your mind about leaving?'

'I am staying, Arabella,' he said, his eyes still holding hers with every inch of the determination he felt.

She bowed her head and glanced away, sullen and angry.

'What does your father make of your chosen profession?' he demanded. 'What does your brother?'

'My father and Tom were taken by the same consumption that claimed Henry.'

'I am sorry for your loss,' he said. The news shocked him, for he had known the family well and liked them. 'And Mrs Tatton? What of her?'

'My mother was brought low by the disease, but she survived.'

'Does she know that you are here, Arabella?'

A whisper of guilt moved across her face. 'She does not.' She tilted her chin, defiant again. 'Not that it is any of your concern.'

In the ensuing silence they could hear the faint rhythmic banging of a bedstead against a wall. Neither of them paid it the slightest attention.

His eyes raked hers. There was another question he needed to ask, even though he already knew the answer by the very fact that she was here in Mrs Silver's House of Rainbow Pleasures.

'There is no other man since Marlbrook? No new husband or protector?'

'No,' she said in a tight voice and eyed him with unmistakable disdain. 'But if there were, it would be no business of yours.'

Their eyes held for a moment and a storm of anger seemed to fire and crackle between them before she rose and moved away to stand over by the long black curtains that covered the window.

Arabella could not just sit there and let the questions continue, not when she feared where they might lead.

Besides, Dominic had no right to question her. He had forfeited the right to know anything of her life when he had made his decision all those years ago. Let him think the worst of her if it prevented his questions and made him leave. Let him think she was the whore he had just made her. Better that than the alternative.

She could not bear for him to see how much she was hurting. And she could not bear for him to know the truth of her situation, of the desperation that had led her to this place. Better his contempt than his pity, and better still that he left knowing nothing at all.

The chink of night sky, between the edge of the curtain and the wall, was very dark. There were no stars, and the street lamps outside remained black and unlit and everything seemed to be waiting and edged with danger. And when she glanced round at Dominic he was sitting staring into the small flames that flickered amongst the glowing coals, the expression upon his face as dark and brooding as the night outside.

'I cannot believe that I have found you here...in a damnable brothel!' Dominic was still reeling from the shock of it. All these years he had imagined that one day he might find her. He had imagined a thousand different scenarios, but not one of them had come close to the reality. She was a lightskirt in an upmarket bordello. Miss Noir, in Mrs Silver's rainbow selection for those men who had enough blunt to pay. He felt sick at the thought.

'Then walk away and pretend that you have not,' she said in a low voice, but she did not look round.

In the silence there was only the crack from the remains of the fire upon the hearth.

'You know that I cannot do that, Arabella.' It did not

matter how aggrieved he was, she did not deserve life in such a place.

He glanced across at her standing there in the flimsy black silk that revealed more of her figure than it covered, and the nakedness of her back where the laces hung loose and, despite everything, he felt desire.

It disgusted him that he could still want her after her faithlessness with Marlbrook and after all he had already taken from her this night in such despicable circumstances. He was not proud of having treated her like a whore, even if that was what she was. And he swore to himself that, had he known that she was Arabella, he never would have touched her. But it was too late for that. He had done a great deal more than touch her.

'Why not? It is what I want. For you to leave…and not come back.'

Dominic felt the stab of her words, but he did not retaliate, nor did he take his eyes from the fire. A section of the molten embers cracked and collapsed and in the space where they had been one small flame remained, burning hotter and more brightly than all the other.

'For the sake of what was once between us, Arabella—'

'I do not want your pity, Dominic!' She swung round to face him, standing there with her hands on hips, her face proud and angry. 'And whatever was between us is long dead.'

'Oh, I am more than well aware of that, Arabella.' Her eyes flashed with a fierceness he had never seen there before. Her lips were flushed and swollen from his kisses, and the creamy swell of her breasts rose and fell with the raggedness of her breath. His gaze dropped to where her rosy nipples were beginning to peep over the black silk.

She saw his gaze and, with a fury, wrenched the bodice higher and held it in place.

'It is a bit late for that, Arabella.'

She might pretend otherwise but, unlike him, Arabella had known with whom she was coupling and Dominic had felt the spark in the response of her lips to his, an echo of what had once been. The love might be dead, but there was still a physical desire that burned strong between them.

His gaze dropped from her back to the fire.

He had not forgiven her, but he could not leave her here.

He could not forgive her, yet he wanted her still.

An idea started to form in his head, one that might finally allow Dominic to purge the demons that drove him.

She was watching him when he got to his feet and moved towards her. He saw the shiver that ran through her body and he found his coat and wrapped it around her shoulders.

Her eyes met his and he saw the surprise and wariness and unspoken question in them.

'You do not have to do this, Arabella.'

'I've already told you that what I do is none of your concern.' Her voice was curt and her eyes cold.

'I could help you.'

'I do not need your help, your Grace,' she countered.

'That may be, but you will hear me out just the same, Arabella.'

She stared at him, her expression closed, yet he could sense her caution and suspicion.

'It would mean that you would not have to sleep with one different man after another, at the mercy of whatever demands they might make of you. You would not fear to be cast out into the streets. Indeed, you would never want for anything again.'

She frowned slightly and shook her head as if she did not yet understand.

'I would give you a house, as much money as you need. You would be safe. Protected.'

'Protected?' She echoed the word and he saw her eyes widen.

'We would come to an arrangement that would be mutually beneficial to us both.'

'You are asking me to be your mistress?' She gaped at him.

'If that is what you wish to call it,' he said.

The silence was tense. From outside the room came the sound of a woman's giggle and a man's booted steps receding along the passageway.

He saw the shock so stark and clear upon her face and knew that whatever Arabella had been expecting it had been nothing of this. And just for a minute he thought he saw such a look of sadness in her eyes, of a pain that mirrored the one he had carried in his heart all of these years past, but it was gone so fast that he was not sure if he had imagined it.

'Arabella,' he said softly and could not help himself from touching a hand to her arm.

He felt the slight tremor that ran through her body before she snatched her arm away.

'You think it to be done so very easily?' she asked.

Her tone was cynical and when she raised her face to his again there was the glitter of some strong emotion in her eyes.

'It can be done easily enough,' he said carefully. 'I would pay off Mrs Silver; she would give us no trouble, I assure you.'

He saw her swallow, saw the way she gripped her hands together as if it was such a difficult decision to make.

'I have come into my father's title, Arabella. I am a very wealthy man. I would rent you a fine town house, furnish it as you wished. Your every want would be satisfied, your every whim met. I am offering you *carte blanche,* Arabella.'

'I understand what you are offering me,' she said and her voice was cool and her expression unmoving.

'Well?' he asked. 'Will you give me your answer?'

'I need time to think,' she said stiffly. 'Time to fully consider your offer.'

'What else can you have to consider?' He smiled a cynical smile. 'Have I not covered it all already?'

Her pause was so slight that he barely noticed. A heartbeat of time in which their eyes met across the divide. And there was something in her gaze that was contrary in every way to the strong cold woman standing before him. A flash of misery and hurt and…fear. But as quickly as it had arrived, the moment was gone.

'Nevertheless, your Grace, I will not give you an answer until I have had some time to think about it.'

Her sullen resolution irked him, as did her whole attitude of contempt. Any other woman in her position would have been eager for such an offer.

'You may play your games, Arabella, but we both

know that whores do as rich men bid, and I am now a very rich man. It is a new day. You have until my return tonight to make your decision. And in the meantime Mrs Silver will be paid so that you are not touched by another. What I have, I hold, Arabella. And what is mine, is mine alone. Be sure you understand that fully.'

Her lips pressed firmer as if she sought to suppress some sharp retort. She slipped his coat from her shoulders and handed it to him.

Dominic donned the rest of his clothing, gave a small bow and left.

And as dawn broke over the city he walked away from Mrs Silver's House of Rainbow Pleasures, leaving behind its black-clad bedchamber with its dark drawn curtains. But his mind was still on the woman that he had left standing there, with the black silk dress clutched to her breasts.

Chapter Three

It was only a few hours later that Arabella made her way up the stairwell of the shabby lodging house in Flower and Dean Street. The early morning spring sunlight was so bright that it filtered through the windows, that the months of winter rain and wind had rendered opaque, and glinted on the newly replaced lock of the door that led from the first landing into her rented room.

The damp chill of the room hit her as soon as she opened the door and stepped over the threshold.

'Mama!' The small dark-haired boy glanced up from where he was sitting next to an elderly woman on the solitary piece of furniture that remained within the room, a mattress in the middle of the floor. He wriggled free of the thin grey woollen blanket that was wrapped around his shoulders and ran to greet her.

'Archie.' She smiled and felt her heart shift at the sight of his face. 'Have you been a good boy for your grandmama?'

'Yes, Mama,' he answered dutifully. But Arabella

could see the toll that hunger and poverty had taken in her son's face. Already there were shadows beneath his eyes and a sharpness about his features that had not been there just a few days ago.

She hugged him to her, the weight of guilt heavy upon her.

'I have brought a little bread and cake.' She emptied the contents of her pocket on to the mattress. Everything was stale as she had pilfered it last night from the trays intended for Mrs Silver's drawing room. 'Wages are not paid until the end of the week.'

Arabella split the food into two piles. One pile she sat upon the window ledge to sate their hunger later, and the other she shared between her mother and son.

It broke her heart the way Archie looked at her for permission to eat those few stale slices, his brown eyes filled with a look which no mother should ever have to see in her child.

There was silence while they ate the first slice of bread as if it were a sumptuous feast.

Arabella slipped off her cloak and wrapped it around her mother's hunched shoulders before sitting down beside her on the edge of the mattress.

'You are not eating, Arabella.' Her mother noticed and paused, her hand frozen en route to her mouth, the small chunk of bread still gripped within her fingers.

Arabella shook her head and smiled. 'I have already breakfasted on the way home.' It was a lie. But there was little enough as it was and she could not bear to see them so hungry.

The sun would not reach to shine in here until later in the day and there was no money for coal or logs. The room was cold and bare save for the mattress upon which they were now sitting. Empty, just as they had arrived home to find it four days ago.

'How was the workshop?' Mrs Tatton carefully picked the crumbs from her lap and ate them. 'They were satisfied with your work?'

'I believe so,' Arabella answered and could not bring herself to meet her mother's eyes in case something of the shame showed in them.

'You look too pale, Arabella, and your eyes are as red as if you have been weeping.' She could feel her mother's gaze upon her.

'I am merely tired and my eyes a little strained from stitching by candlelight.' Arabella lied and wondered what her mother would say if she knew the truth of how her daughter had spent the night. 'A few hours rest and I shall be fine.' She glanced up at Mrs Tatton with a reassuring smile.

Mrs Tatton's expression was worried. 'I wish I could do more to help.' She shook her head, and glanced away in misery. 'I know that I am little more than a burden to you.'

'Such foolish talk, Mama. How on earth would I manage without you to care for Archie?'

Her mother nodded and forced a smile, but her eyes were dull and sad. Arabella's gaze did not miss the tremor in the swollen knuckled hands or the wheeze that rasped in the hollow chest as Mrs Tatton reached to stroke a lock of her grandson's hair away from his eye.

Archie, having finished his bread and cake, wandered over to the other side of the room where there was a small wooden pail borrowed from one of the neighbours. He scooped up some water from the pail using the small wooden cup that sat beside it and gulped it down.

Mrs Tatton lowered her voice so that Archie would not hear. 'He cried himself to sleep through hunger last night, Arabella. Poor little mite. It broke my heart to hear him.'

Arabella pressed a fist to her mouth and glanced away so her mother would not see her struggle against breaking down.

'But this new job you have found is a miracle indeed, the answer to all our prayers. Without it, it would be the workhouse for us all.'

Arabella closed her eyes against that thought. They would be better off dead.

Archie brought the cup of water over and offered it to her. Arabella took a few sips and then gave it to her mother.

And when the food was all eaten and the water drunk, Archie and Mrs Tatton lay down beneath the blanket.

'It was noisy last night,' Mrs Tatton said by way of explanation. And Arabella understood, the men's drunken shouts and women's bawdy laughter echoing up from the street outside would have allowed her son and mother little sleep.

Arabella spread her cloak with her mother's shawl on top of the lone blanket and then climbed beneath the covers. Archie's little body snuggled into hers and she kissed that dark tangled tousle of hair and told him that everything would be well.

Soon the only sounds were of sleep: the wheeze of her mother's lungs and Archie's soft shallow rhythmic breathing. Arabella had not slept for one minute last night, not after all that had happened. And she knew that she would not sleep now. Her mind was a whirl of thoughts, all of them centred round Dominic Furneaux.

When she thought of their coupling of last night she felt like weeping, both from anger and from shame, and from a heart that ached from remembering how, when she had given herself to him before, there had been such love between them. And the anger that she felt was not just for him, but for herself.

For even from the first moment that he had come close and she had smelled that familiar scent of him, bergamot and soap and Dominic Furneaux, she had been unable to quell the reaction of her body. And when he had taken her, not out of love, not even knowing who she was, her traitorous lips and body had, in defiance of everything she knew and everything she felt, welcomed him. They had known his mouth, recognised his kiss and the caress of his hand, and responded to him. And the shame of that burned deeper than the knowledge that she had sold herself to him.

She thought of the offer he had made her. To buy her. To be at his beck and call whenever he wished to satisfy himself upon her. Dominic Furneaux, the man who had broken her heart. Lied to her with such skill that she had believed every one of those honeyed untruths. Could she put herself under the power of such a man? To be completely at his mercy? Could she really surrender herself to him, night after night, and hide the shameful response of her body to him, a man who did not love her, a man who believed her a whore for his use?

She clutched her hands to her face as the sense of despair rolled right through her, for she knew the answer to each of those questions and she knew, too, the ugly truth of the alternative.

Arabella relived the moment that the group of gentlemen had entered Mrs Silver's drawing room, and it did not matter how hard she had tried to deaden her feelings, no matter how much she could rationalise the whole plan in her head, when it had come to the point of facing what must happen she had felt an overwhelming panic that she would not be able go through with it. She closed her eyes against the nightmare, knowing that there was only one decision she could make. Even if there were certain aspects of the negotiations that she would have to handle very carefully.

And as she lay there she could not help but think how differently things might have turned out if Dominic Furneux had been a different sort of man. If he had loved her, as he had sworn that he did, and married her, as he had promised that he would, how different all their lives would have been.

Dominic arrived at Mrs Silver's early and alone. The drawing room was filled with a woman of every colour of Mrs Silver's rainbow, every colour save for black. He knew with one sweep of the room that Arabella was not there and he felt a whisper of foreboding that perhaps everything was not going to go quite how he had planned.

'Variety is the spice of life, your Grace. Perhaps I could tempt you with another colour from my assortment?' Mrs Silver smiled at him and gestured towards the girls who had arrived looking a little breathless and rushed following his early arrival.

'I find I prefer black,' he said. 'Miss Noir...' He

stopped as the thought struck him that perhaps following his discovery of her Arabella had gone, fled elsewhere, to another part of London, another bordello… somewhere he could not find her.

'Will be here presently, your Grace, I am sure,' the woman said with supreme confidence but her eyes told a different story.

He had not contemplated that Arabella would choose this wretched life over the wealth and comfort he had offered. That she would actually run away had not even occurred to him. His mouth hardened at his own naïvety. A man was supposed to learn from his mistakes.

'If you are content to wait for a little.' Mrs Silver smiled again and gestured to one of the sofas.

Dominic gave a curt nod of his head, but he did not sit down. He stood where he was and he waited, ignoring the plate of delicacies and the glass of champagne by his side.

Five minutes passed.

And another ten. The women ceased their attempts to engage him in seductive conversation.

What would he do if she did not come?

By twenty minutes he was close to pacing.

By forty minutes there was only Miss Rouge and himself left in the room and a very awkward silence.

At fifty minutes, Miss Rouge was gone and he felt like he had done that day almost six years ago—angry and disbelieving, a fool and his wounded pride.

He had requested his hat, cane and gloves and was about to leave when Arabella finally arrived.

'Miss Noir, your Grace,' announced Mrs Silver, all

smiles and solicitude as she brought Arabella into the room and left.

The door closed behind Mrs Silver.

The clock on the mantel punctuated the silence.

Dominic's glass sat beside it, the champagne flat and untouched.

She was wearing the same scandalous dress, the same black feathered mask and beneath it her face was powder white. She came to stand before him and he found he was holding his breath and his body was strung tight with tension.

He swallowed and the sound of it seemed too loud in the silence between them.

He waited, not daring to frame the question, any certainty of what her answer would be long forgotten.

'I accept your offer, your Grace,' she said and her voice was low and dead of any emotion. She seemed so pale, so stiff and cold, that he had the absurd urge to pull her into his arms and warm her and tell her everything would be well. But then she moved away to stand behind the cream-coloured armchair and the moment was gone. 'Let us discuss the details.'

He nodded and, like two strangers arranging a business deal, they began to talk.

When Arabella returned to the little room in Flower and Dean Street later that same night it was to find Mrs Tatton and Archie curled again upon the mattress.

'It is only me,' Arabella whispered in the darkness, but Mrs Tatton was already struggling to her feet, armed with the chamber pot as a makeshift weapon.

'Oh, Arabella, you startled me.'

'Forgive me, Mama.' Arabella made her way across

the room by the light of a nearby street lamp that glowed through the little window.

'What are you doing home so early? I had not thought to see you until the morning.' Her mother's hair hung in a heavy long grey braid over one shoulder and she was wearing the same crumpled dress she had worn for the last five days. Then her eyes widened with fear. 'The workshop have turned you off!'

'There has been a change of plan, it is true,' Arabella said and quickly added, 'But you need have no worry. It is for the better.'

'What do you mean, Arabella? What change?'

'It is an arrangement that will ensure we do not end up in the workhouse.' She glanced towards the sleeping form of her son. 'We will live in a warm furnished house in a good respectable area, wear clean clothes and have three square meals a day. I will have enough money that Archie need not go without. And you, Mama, can have the best of medicines in London. We will not be cold. We will not be hungry. And...' She glanced towards the footsteps that passed on the landing outside. She lowered her voice, 'We will be safe from robberies and fear of assault.'

Her mother set the chamber pot down on the floor and came to stand before Arabella, staring into her face.

'What manner of arrangement?'

Arabella felt herself blush and had to force herself to meet her mother's gaze. She had known this moment would come and could not shrink from it. Better they spoke of it while Archie was not awake to hear. They would be moving out of here in a few days and there was no way that Arabella could continue her pretence. She had to tell her mother the truth...just not all of it.

'With a gentleman.'

'Oh, Arabella!' Her mother clasped a hand to her mouth. 'You cannot!'

'I know it is a very great shock to you,' she said in a calm reassuring voice that belied everything she was feeling. 'And I am not proud of it.' She was ashamed to the very core of her being, but she knew in order to make this bearable she must hide her true emotions from her mother. She must stand firm. Be strong. 'But believe me when I tell you it is the best of the choices available. Do not seek to dissuade me from this, Mama, for my mind is quite made up.'

'There was no workshop, was there?' her mother asked in a deadened voice.

'No.' She saw the tremble in the old swollen hand that Mrs Tatton still clutched to her mouth and felt as bad as if she had just reached across and dealt her mother a physical blow.

'And the gentleman?'

Arabella swallowed and averted her gaze. 'It is best that he remains nameless for now.' If her mother knew it was Dominic to whom she was selling herself there would be no force in heaven or on earth that could stop the awful cascade that would ensue.

'Really?' Mrs Tatton said in a hard voice that revealed to Arabella everything of her mother's disillusionment and hurt. 'And have you told him yet of Archie and of me?'

'No,' said Arabella quietly and her heart was racing and all of her fears rushed back as fast and frantic as a spring tide racing up a shore. 'He need know nothing of either of you.'

'It will be his house, Arabella. Do you not think

he will notice an old woman and a child cluttering his path to his fancy piece?' Mrs Tatton's nostrils flared, revealing the extent of her distress.

Oh, indeed, Dominic would more than notice Archie in his path, Arabella thought grimly.

'It will be a large house and he will not visit very often.' She had been very careful in her negotiations with Dominic, forcing herself to think only of Archie's safety and not the baseness of what she was doing, laying out her demands like the most callous of harlots. 'All we need do is keep you both hidden from his sight when he does come.' Words so simply spoken for her mother's sake, but Arabella knew that they would have to be very careful indeed to hide the truth.

'You think you are so clever, Arabella. You think you have it all planned out, do you not?' Mrs Tatton said. 'But what of the servants? It is the gentleman's money that will pay their wages. They will be loyal to him. At the first opportunity they will be running to him behind your back, eager to spill your secrets. And he shall send Archie and me away.'

'Do you think I would stay without you?' she demanded. 'It is true that it is his money that will pay the servants. But it is also true that if I dissolve our agreement, which I would most certainly do were they to tell him of your and Archie's presence, then they shall be out of a job as much as me. I shall put it to them that it is in their interest, as much as mine, that we keep your presence secret from the gentleman.'

'For men like him there are plenty more where you came from. Do not hold yourself so precious to him, Arabella,' her mother warned.

The smile that slipped across Arabella's face was

bitter. 'Oh, Mama, I know that I am not precious to him at all. Do not think that I would ever make that mistake.' The word *again* went unspoken. 'But he will take the house and the servants for me. And were I to leave, he would let them go again just as easily.'

'Then we best pray that you are right, Archie and I.' Mrs Tatton turned her face away but not before Arabella saw the shimmer of wetness upon her cheeks.

Mrs Tatton did not look round again, nor did she return to bed. She just stood there by the empty black fireplace, staring down on to the bare hearth. And when Arabella would have placed an arm of comfort around her mother's shoulders, Mrs Tatton pulled away as if she could not bear the touch of so fallen a woman.

Arabella's hand dropped back down to her side; inside of her the shame ate away a little more of her soul. She wondered what her mother's reaction would be if she knew what the alternative had been. And she wondered how much worse her mother's reaction would be if she ever learned that the man in question was Dominic Furneaux.

Chapter Four

Dominic was supposed to be paying attention as his secretary continued working his way through the great pile of correspondence balanced on the desk between them.

'The Philanthropic Society has invited you to a dinner in June.' Barclay glanced up from checking Dominic's appointments diary. 'You are free on the evening in question.'

'Then I will attend.' Dominic gave a nod and heard Barclay's pen nib scratch upon the paper. But Dominic's attention was barely fixed on the task in hand. He was thinking of Arabella and the discomposure he had felt since seeing her last.

'The Royal Humane Society has written of its need for more boats. As one of the society's patron you are in receipt of a full report of...'

Barclay's words faded into the background as Dominic's mind drifted back to Arabella. While making her his mistress had seemed the perfect solution at the time, in the cold light of day and after a night of fitful sleep, Dominic was not so sure. He had revisited their meeting during the long hours of the night, seeing it again in his mind, hearing every word of their exchange, and he could not remain unaware of a growing uneasiness.

Surviving. The word seemed to niggle in his brain. Her explanation of what she was doing there did not sit well with the later claim that she was in Mrs Silver's House out of choice. *Surviving.* The word pricked at him.

Barclay gave a cough in the silence and cleared his throat loudly.

'Most interesting,' Dominic said, having heard not a word of what the report had been about. 'Organise that they receive a hundred pounds.'

'Very good, your Grace.'

'Is that all for today?' He could barely conceal his impatience. He wanted to be alone. He wanted to think.

'Indeed, your Grace.' Barclay replied, checking the diary again. 'Except to remind you that you are due at Somerset House for a Royal Society lecture this afternoon at two o'clock and that you are sitting in the House of Lords tomorrow to debate Sir John Craddock's replacement in Portugal by Sir Arthur Wellesley.'

Dominic gave a nod. 'Thank you, Barclay. That will be all.'

And when his secretary left, taking with him the great pile of paper, Dominic leaned back in his chair and focused his thoughts fully on Arabella.

Arabella had to endure two days of pleadings. Mrs Tatton begged that Arabella would not cheapen herself

and warned her that once it was done there would be
no going back. She cried and shouted, persuaded and
coerced, but once the shock had lessened and her mother
saw that Arabella would not be moved, then Mrs Tatton's protestations fell by the wayside and, to Arabella's
relief, no more was said about it. She seemed to have
accepted the inevitability and necessity of what would
happen and steeled herself to the task every bit as much
as Arabella.

Which was well, for on the Friday morning of that
week a fine carriage and four arrived outside their lodgings in Flower and Dean Street. Every face in the street
stared at the carriage, for nothing so grand had ever
been seen there before. Archie stared in excitement at
the team of bays and kept asking if he might run down
the stairs to see them more closely. It pained Arabella
to deny him and to force him away from the window for
fear that Dominic himself might be within the carriage.

'Soon,' she whispered, 'but not today.'

'Ohh, Mama!' Archie groaned.

'He must be wealthy indeed,' observed Mrs Tatton
drily with a glance at her daughter that made Arabella
curl up inside. And she was all the more glad that the
carriage was a plain glossy black with no sign of the
Arlesford coat of arms. She worried that her mother
would recognise the smart green livery of the footman,
groom and coach man, but Mrs Tatton showed no sign
of realising the uniform's significance.

'I think he might be awaiting me in the house and I
need time to speak to the servants. Either the carriage
will come back for you, or I will return alone.'

Her mother nodded stoically and Arabella pushed
away the little spasm of fear.

'Either way we should not be parted for too long.'

She hugged Archie. 'I have to go out for a little while, Archie.'

'In the big black carriage?' he asked.

'Yes.'

'Can I come with you?'

Arabella ignored the pain and the guilt and forced herself to smile. 'Not just now, my darling. Be a good boy for your grandmama and I will see you soon.'

'Yes, Mama.'

She kissed his head and took the time to blink away the tears before she rose to embrace her mother. 'Look after him, Mama.'

Mrs Tatton nodded, and her eyes glistened with tears that she was fighting to hold back. 'Have a care, Arabella, please. And…' She took Arabella's face between her worn hands and looked into her eyes. 'For all that I dislike this I know why you are doing it and I thank you. I pray that your plan is successful and that it is the carriage that returns for Archie and for me.'

Those few words from her mother's lips meant so much to Arabella. They strengthened her resolve that was fast crumbling at the prospect of facing Dominic once more.

'Thank you, Mama,' Arabella whispered and she kissed her mother's cheek and, before she could weaken to the tears, she pulled the hood of her cloak over her hair and walked away, closing the door behind her.

The carriage was empty. Of that Arabella could only be glad, for she had no wish for Dominic to see her cry at the sight of her son and her mother peeping from the edge of the dirt-encrusted windows.

Nor was Dominic waiting in the town house that he had rented for her.

It was a fine property in respectable Curzon Street, as different from the hovel in Flower and Dean Street as was possible. The servants were lined up in the hallway for her arrival just as if she were Dominic's duchess rather than his mistress. In some ways their respectful attitude made the whole thing easier, and in other ways, so much harder, for it reminded her of the hopes and expectations she had held for the future all those years ago when she had been a foolish naïve girl in love with a boy who would be duke.

The elderly butler bowed. 'I am Gemmell. Welcome to Curzon Street, Miss Tatton. We are very glad that you are here.'

It was so long since anyone had called her that name. She was Arabella Marlbrook now, even though Henry was dead these two years past. It angered her that Dominic wished to remove any reminder of the man who had saved her. She wanted to correct the butler, to tell him that her name was Marlbrook and not Tatton, but that would only be foolish. It was Dominic's house and Dominic's money; besides, she had no wish to make matters awkward between her and the servants, not when she would be counting on their good favour to keep her secret. So she smiled and walked down the line of servants, smiling and repeating each of their names and telling them how pleased she was to meet them and how she was sure that they would deal very well together.

Gemmell gave her a tour of the house during which she worked hard to breach his wall of formal and very proper servitude. By the time he had served her tea in the drawing room she had managed to coax from him all about his three little granddaughters and ten little grandsons; that his wife Mary, who had been the best housekeeper in all of England, had died three years past; and that he and Mary had previously been employed in the Duke of Hamilton's hunting lodge in Scotland for twenty years before moving south on account of their children and grandchildren because family was what was important.

Arabella knew then that the time was right to raise the subject of her own family, of her son and her mother. And after she had finished explaining, to a limited extent, the matter, Mr Gemmell was just as understanding as Arabella had hoped.

She knew that what she was asking the staff to do was not without risk and so did Gemmell. But she also knew she could do nothing other than ask. And the answer was yes. He promised to instruct the rest of the staff and then he brought her the note that Dominic had left for her.

She recognised the handwriting on the front of the note: determined lettering, bold and flowing from a nib that pressed firmly against the paper. She felt her heart begin to speed and her mouth dry as she broke the seal and unfolded the sheet.

The words were brief, just a couple of lines, saying that he hoped she approved of the house and its contents and that he would call upon her that evening.

Of course he would come in the evening; gentlemen did not visit their mistresses during the day. Not when everyone knew the purpose of their visit. She tried not to think ahead to the evening. She would deal with that when it came. For now she turned her mind to more comfortable thoughts.

She rang the bell for Gemmell, and sent the carriage back to Flower and Dean Street for Archie and her mother.

The sun came out that afternoon. It was a good omen, boding well for their future, Arabella told her mother as they wandered through the rooms of the town house in Curzon Street. Mrs Tatton kept stopping to examine and exclaim over the fineness of the furniture, the rich fabrics of the curtains and the sparkling crystal of the chandeliers.

'Arabella, these chairs are made by Mr Chippendale' and 'Arabella, this damask costs almost thirty shillings a yard,' and 'I have heard that the Prince of Wales himself has a wallpaper similar to this in Carlton House.'

Arabella did not tell her that the gentlemen's clothing hanging in one of the wardrobes within her bedchamber was made by the *ton*'s most expensive tailor, John Weston, nor that it bore the faint scent of Dominic and his cologne.

Having been cooped up for so long in the tiny room in Flower and Dean Street, Archie shouted and ran about in mad excitement at such space and freedom.

'It is all so very grand that he must be very wealthy indeed, this…gentleman,' said Mrs Tatton and she stopped and frowned before her face was filled with worry once more. 'I blame myself that it has come to this,' she said quietly so that her grandson would not hear. She dabbed a small white handkerchief to her eyes.

'Hush now, Mama, you will upset Archie.' Arabella glanced over towards her son and was relieved to see that he was too busy with his imaginary horse games to notice.

'I am sorry, Arabella, but to think that you have become some rich man's mistress.'

'It is not so bad a bargain, Mama. I assure you it is the best I could have made.' A vision of the crowd of drunken gentlemen in Mrs Silver's drawing room appeared in her head and she could not stop the accompanying shiver. She thrust the thought away and forced herself to smile a reassurance at her mother. 'And we will all do very well out of it.'

'You have spoken to the servants?'

Arabella nodded.

'And you are sure that they will keep Archie's and my existence a secret?'

'I do not believe that any of them will be in a hurry to whisper tales in his ear.'

'Then in that, at least, we have been fortunate.'

'Yes.'

Mrs Tatton's gaze met Arabella's. 'What manner of man is he, this protector of yours? Old, bluff, married? I cannot help but worry for you. Some men…' She could not go on.

'He is none of those, Mama,' said Arabella and rubbed her mother's arm. 'He is…' But what could she tell her mother of Dominic? A hundred words sprang to mind, none of which would relieve her mother's anxiety. 'Generous…and not…unkind,' she managed. But what he had done almost six years ago was very unkind. 'Which is what is of importance in arrangements of the purse.'

Mrs Tatton sighed and looked away.

'We will be careful with the money he gives me. We

will save every penny that we can, and soon, very soon, there will be enough for you, me and Archie to leave all this behind. We will go back to the country and rent a small cottage with a garden. And no one need be any the wiser to this whole affair.'

'We will be able to hold our heads up and be respectable once more.' As if Arabella could ever be respectable again. For all that illusions could be presented to the world, she would always know what she had done. Nothing could ever cleanse her of that shame. She linked her arm through her mother's and smiled as if none of this affected her in the slightest. 'It will work out all right, you will see.'

'I would like that, Arabella.' Mrs Tatton nodded and something of the anxiety eased from her face. 'Your papa and I were very happy in the country.' She smiled with the remembrance and the two strolled on together, pretending to each other that the situation was anything but that which it really was. And oblivious to the undercurrent of tension Archie played and ran about around their skirts.

Dominic pretended it was just a day like any other, but it was Friday and there was not a moment when he was not aware that Arabella would be waiting for him at Curzon Street that night.

He spent most of the day closeted with his steward who had come up from Amersham to discuss agricultural matters, namely moving to increased mechanisation with Andrew Meikle's threshing machine. After which Dominic went off to watch a four-in-hand race between young Northcote and Darlington, before going on to White's club for a drink with Hunter, Northcote and Bullford. But for all that day he was distracted and out of sorts. Indeed he had not been *in* sorts since the night of meeting Arabella. His usual easy temperament was gone and with each passing day the unsettled feeling seemed to grow stronger. It should have been desire that he was feeling, an impatience to satisfy his lust upon her, to have her naked, warm and willing beneath him.

But it was not.

Surviving. The word whispered again through his mind and he set the wine glass down hard upon the table before him.

'Arlesford?' Bullford said more loudly.

Dominic glanced round to find Hunter, Bullford and Northcote looking at him expectantly. 'Did not catch what you said.' Dominic's voice was lazy and his fingers moved to toy with the stem of his glass as he pretended a normality he did not feel.

'I was just saying that young Northcote's keen to try out some new gaming hell in the East End,' said Bullford. 'Apparently it is quite an experience and certainly not for the faint of heart. If anyone can wipe their tables it would be you and Hunter. Never known a couple of gamblers with as much luck. Hunter's up for it. Will you come and make a night of it?'

'Not tonight,' he said carefully, 'I have other plans.' The echo of her voice whispered again in his head. *It is my first night here. Forgive me if I am unfamiliar with the usual etiquette.* He tried to ignore it.

Bullford smiled in a leery knowing way. 'Ah, the mysterious Miss Noir. Heard you bought her from Mrs Silver. Got the luscious girl stowed away safe and good from the attentions of the rest of London's most eager males?'

Dominic felt his teeth clench and his body go rigid at the manner in which Bullford had just spoken of Arabella. His response shocked him, for Bullford did not know that Miss Noir was Arabella. And Arabella was indeed a lightskirt. But the rationalisations did little to appease his anger and he had to force himself to slow his breathing and uncurl his tightly balled fists.

But Bullford seemed oblivious to the danger and waded in further. 'Liked the look of her myself in Mrs Silver's. Unfortunate for me that you got to her before I did, or the little lady could have been warming my bed tonight.'

'Rather, I assure you that the turn of events was most fortunate for you.' Dominic's voice was cold and hard. He did not understand why he felt so livid. He only knew that if it had been Bullford that had gone upstairs with Arabella in the brothel... Dominic swallowed hard and felt the fragile thread of his self-control stretch thinner.

'Bullford.' Hunter attracted the viscount's attention and gave a warning shake of the head.

'Oh, I see,' said Bullford smugly. He tapped the side of his nose and winked at Dominic. 'Say no more, old man. Affairs of the breeches and all that. Strictly hush, hush. We will move the plans to another time and let you enjoy Miss Noir tonight.'

It was all that Dominic could do not to grab Bullford by the lapels of his tailcoat and smash a fist into his mouth, even though the man had only said aloud the very thing that Dominic planned to do. It was as if some madness had come upon him.

Hunter adroitly changed the subject.

But Dominic was already out of his seat and walking away, leaving all three men staring behind him.

Archie was fast asleep in bed in a snug little bed-chamber at the top of the house in Curzon Street with his grandmama by the time the carriage rolled to a stop outside.

Arabella had been pacing the drawing room ner-vously, unable to settle to anything through the eve-ning. Dominic's imminent arrival was foremost in her mind. She knew that it was him as soon as she heard the horses. She did not need to wait to hear the footsteps upon the outside steps or the opening of the front door or the gentle murmur of voices to know that she was right. The tempo of her heart began to increase. Her hands grew clammy and she prayed that Gemmell's assertion of the servants' discretion could be trusted.

She grabbed a piece of needlework and sat swiftly down in a chair by the fireplace so it would look as if she was not bothered in the slightest over his visit. She heard the drawing-room door open and close again. And quite deliberately kept her attention focused on the sewing for a moment longer, even though she knew he was standing there.

She steeled her courage. Told herself that this... coupling need mean nothing to her. That she could give him her body while locking away all else. Don so much armour that he would not so much as glimpse her heart, her soul, her feelings, let alone get near enough to hurt them again.

She would not let herself think of him as Dominic. He was just a man. And Arabella was not naïve enough to think that a woman had to love a man before she could give herself to him. After all, she had slept with Henry when what she had felt for him was affection and gratitude, and nothing of love.

The moment could not be delayed for ever so she set the needlework down on the little sewing table with care and rose to her feet, skimming a hand down as if to brush out the wrinkles in her skirt.

Only then did she look at him.

Arabella was a tall woman, but Dominic stood a good head and shoulders above her. Tall with broad shoulders and a build that was well muscled. His tailoring was a deep midnight blue over the pristine white of his shirt, waistcoat and cravat. His tailcoat of superfine looked as if it had been fitted by a master tailor. Long legs clad in dark breeches showed too well the musculature of his thighs, leading down to matching top boots, the gloss of which could be seen even by the candlelight.

His face looked paler than the last time she had seen him, his features as breathtakingly handsome as the man from her nightmares. She knew every plane of that face, had kissed every inch of it. His expression was intense and unreadable. And when her eyes finally met his she knew in that instant that all of her resolve was in vain. For she could not even look at him and remain unaffected.

Her heart skipped a beat and then raced off at a canter.

'Dominic,' she heard herself whisper, and all of the old emotions were back, all of the love, all of the hurt, all of the hate. She felt her eyes begin to well and looked hastily away so that he would not see it, furious with herself for such weakness. She thought of Archie and that gave her the strength that she needed. She might not be able to do this for herself, but she could most definitely do it for her son.

'Arlesford,' she corrected herself and this time she was glad to hear that her voice was strong with just a hint of disdain.

'Arabella.' He made a small bow, but otherwise did not move.

He stood there so quiet and still and yet she could sense the tension that surrounded him. It emanated from every pore of his body. It was betrayed by the slight clenching in his jawline, in his lips, in the way he was looking at her. His eyes were darker than she had ever seen them, so dark as to appear almost black, and he was looking at her with such intensity as if to glean every last thought from her head.

She felt the nervousness ripple right through her body at the thought of all that she sought to hide.

'The house is to your liking?' he asked.

'It is very nice, thank you, your Grace. Beautifully furnished with impeccable taste.' She kept her face impassive and her voice cool.

They looked at each other across the small distance and the silence was awkward and tense. She glanced away, waiting for him to shrug out of his tailcoat and suggest that they go upstairs. But that was not what Dominic said.

'I wish to talk to you, Arabella.'

'Talk?' Her heart gave a stutter. A shiver of warning rippled down Arabella's spine. She did not want to talk. Instinctively Arabella glanced up as if she could see through the floors above to the small bedchamber at the top of the house.

She feared what talking might reveal.

She feared that Dominic would learn of Archie, his son.

Chapter Five

If Dominic knew the truth, then God only knew what would happen to Archie. Her son would be branded a bastard, his life ruined before it had barely begun whether Dominic acknowledged him or not. If he knew he had such a fine son, he might wish to raise Archie himself or send him away to be raised by someone of his own choosing. For what man, especially a duke, as rich and powerful and ruthless as Dominic, would leave his child with a woman he had found in a bordello, no matter the explanations she could offer? Archie would be taken away from her to be with people who did not love him, who did not understand a small boy's tender needs. Arabella trembled from the force of the fear.

She wetted her suddenly dry lips and gave a false laugh to hide the fear. 'But what more is there for us to talk about, your Grace? We have already settled upon all of the relevant details.'

She saw the flash of anger in those dark eyes. 'I would have you call me by my given name. And there is the whole of the last six years that we have barely begun to discuss, Arabella.'

'I thought you already knew.' *Attack is the best form of defence,* she thought and gathered her weapons as best she could. 'I married Henry Marlbrook. He died. I went to Mrs Silver's. That is all you need know, *Dominic.*' She turned away to gain some semblance of control over her emotions once more.

'On the contrary, Arabella. I think I need to know a great deal more than that.'

'What do you want me to tell you?' she demanded bitterly. 'How good a man Henry was?'

'Infinitely better than me. You made that very clear.' His eyes bored into hers.

'He was a thousand times the man you are,' she taunted.

'You forget your position, Arabella.'

'No,' she said and tried to control the raggedness of her voice. She forced a tight smile to her mouth. 'I understand my position exactly.' She glared at him. 'Do you want me in here? Perhaps on the sofa? Or on the rug before the fireplace? Shall I undress for you now?' she demanded.

'Arabella!' he said harshly, but there was a flash of pain in his eyes that matched the pain in her heart.

And she realised that she was doing this all wrong, risking everything.

She closed her eyes, rallied her senses. 'Forgive me,' she said in her normal voice and when she opened her eyes she did not look at him.

'Arabella,' he said more softly.

But his kindness was worse than his contempt. It reminded her too much of the man she had loved.

'What has happened to you?'

'You already know the answer to that question,' she said quietly.

'No, Arabella, I do not.' His eyes studied hers. 'I wish that you would tell me.'

Her heart was knocking so hard against her ribcage that she was surprised he could not hear it.

'All of it that happened across the years,' he said.

She shook her head and forced a smile, trying to fool him.

His gaze did not waver.

'In Mrs Silver's, when you were pretending to be Miss Noir, you said that it was your first night there.'

'A harlot's lie. It is what men want to hear, is it not?' She glanced away and pressed her fingers hard against her lips, hating the words she must say. But say them she would, for she did not want his pity. And she did could not risk his questions.

Dominic stood there still and silent.

'Shall we go upstairs?' She knew her part in all this, knew what he had come for. And once he had it, he would go and the ordeal would be over…at least for now.

He said not one word, but he followed her up the stairs to the large cream-coloured bedchamber on the first floor.

There could be no room for modesty, nor the last remaining shreds of her pride. She knew what was required, knew what she must do.

She turned away from him and forced herself to strip off her clothing, every last stitch. And when she was naked she sat down at the dressing table and took the pins from her hair, uncoiling its long length while her eyes watched his reflection in the looking glass. She watched while he slipped off his tailcoat and abandoned it over a chair. His waistcoat followed.

She sat there, waiting for the inevitable. Gathering her courage for what must come. But Dominic made no move towards her.

The nerves shivered right through her body. She swallowed. Did a mistress wait for her protector to come to her, or did he expect her to go to him? Arabella did not know the answer. But the quicker this was over, the better for herself. So she rose and walked to him. It took every ounce of Arabella's strength not to wrap her arms around herself to cover her nakedness, to make herself stand there before him and let him look at her.

His touch, when it came, was gentle, reverent almost, and she shivered at the sudden flash of unbidden memories from a lifetime ago—of the passion and the love that had been between them.

He ran a hand over her hair, his hand sliding round to the nape of her neck. His fingers rested there light as a butterfly and the tingle beneath them seemed to run through the whole of her body. Slowly, deliberately, he trailed the tips of his fingers down the column of her throat.

Arabella deliberately masked any sign of emotion from her face as she stood there and let him touch her, angling her head to allow him access. He was her protector. This was what he was paying for. It meant nothing. But already she could feel the hard thud of her heart and everywhere his fingers touched, her skin burned, and she felt like weeping.

His hand dipped lower, so that she felt his fingers trace all the way out to the end of her collarbone and all the way back again. She tried to control the unsteadiness of her breathing, the gathering sob, but that only seemed to make it worse.

Not one word did he say. Not once did he meet her eyes, just kept his gaze fixed on the magic that his fingers were working.

He paused.

Arabella held her breath.

And then inch by tiny inch his fingers followed the path down into the valley between her breasts.

Again he halted, but whether it was to torture her, or himself, she did not know. If he continued like this, Arabella did not know if she could bear it. He placed a palm upon her left breast and beneath it she felt her heart jump and race all the harder. Beneath the cover of his hand her nipple was already taut and tender.

Arabella willed herself not to respond. He did not love her. She thought of all he had done six years ago. But when his palm slid away and his fingers teased at her nipple, plucking it, there was nothing she could do to prevent it bead all the harder. Her wantonness appalled her.

She squeezed her eyes closed to prevent the tears, knowing what would follow.

But his hand halted and dropped away, so that he was no longer even touching her.

Each tight line of his body and the bulge in his breeches revealed that he was every bit as aware as she of the tension that hummed between them. Slowly, his gaze raised to meet her own and there was something in his eyes as he stared at her. The strangest expression. Not lust as she had expected. Not victory or even arrogance. Realisation, maybe. And something else that she could not quite define. Something that looked almost haunted.

'Dominic?' she whispered.

But Dominic gave no sign of having heard her. He stood there frozen, staring as if he could see into the very depths of her soul.

And then he backed away, raking a hand through his hair as he did so.

'I cannot…' he said and his face was white. He turned away, gathered up his waistcoat and tailcoat and made for the door.

'Dominic!'

He stopped where he was, hesitated with his hand stilled in its grip of the doorknob, but did not turn round.

And then he left, closing the door quietly behind him.

There was the tread of his boots upon the stairs, the murmur of voices in the hallway and, a short while after that, the sound of a carriage and horses outside.

Arabella watched the dark unmarked carriage drive away into the night. She shivered and pulled the shawl tight around her shoulders, not understanding what had just happened between them.

Dominic did not sleep for what remained of the night. He stood by the window of his library and looked out over the sleeping city and watched the dawn break over a charcoal sky.

He had been a fool to think that he could take Arabella as his mistress and use her as a whore, even if she was exactly that. The past was too strong between them. She might have slashed the ties that had bound them and walked away, but Dominic had only just come to see that what had bound them together could never be completely undone. She was his first and only love. And no matter what she had done, or what she had become, he could not forget that. Every time he looked at her it was flaunted before his eyes. Every time he touched her he felt it in his bones.

If he had thought it would be so easy to treat her just as he had treated all the other women who had come after her, without emotional attachment, he was wrong.

She was engrained upon his mind, engraved upon his heart. He had dreamt of nothing else for nigh on six years. He had longed for her and hated her and needed her all at once. It was Arabella whom he thought of constantly. It was Arabella he thought of even when he was bedding another woman.

He could taste her upon his tongue and smell her own scent, sweet and fresh like roses and summer rain. He could still feel the smooth softness of her pale skin, still feel the firm ripeness of her naked breasts. He wanted to possess every inch of her body with his mouth. He wanted to plunge his aching manhood into her silken flesh and take her in every way imaginable until this endless torment ceased.

But he could not.

The grey dress she wore in the bedchamber in Curzon Street was nothing of the courtesan's guise she had donned before. It was old and shabby and respectable, Arabella's own, rather than something of Mrs Silver's. And when she had stripped it off and stood before him, offering what he had thought he had the right to take, he had willed himself to accept it. He had touched her and tried to coax himself, for God only knew how much his body burned to possess her. But beneath his hand he had felt the flutter of her heart and he had known that he could not do it.

Arabella's words rang through his head. *He was a thousand times the man you are!... A harlot's lie. It is what men want to hear, is it not?* And he realised there had been a part of him that had thought that she would have welcomed him, wanted him. That she would have told him that what happened in the past was all a mistake, that she had loved him all along.

He shook his head with disgust at his own absurdity. Nothing had changed. It never would. She still had the power to hurt him...and was wielding it with deliberation.

He had made this arrangement; he would not break it and see her thrown back down into the gutter. But for Dominic there could be no more visits to Curzon Street.

The decision made, Dominic stood back to watch the new day dawn over London.

In the dining room that morning Arabella was watching Archie eating his breakfast. After seeing him brought almost to the point of starvation she could not help but worry whether that last week in Flower and Dean Street had left its mark upon him. But looking at him now, wolfing down his buttered eggs and sausages and excitedly telling his story, she felt a sense of relief at the resilience of children. She smoothed down his hair and concentrated on listening to how he was going to have a whole stable of horses when he was a grown-up man. But she knew Mrs Tatton's questions would not be deferred for long. Arabella could see from the corner of her eye the way her mother was watching her with concern written all over her face.

She tried to smile and act as if everything was just the same as it had been yesterday, but her heart was filled with humiliation and confusion and embarrassment over what had happened last night. She did not understand what she had done wrong. And she was relieved and angry and ashamed all at once.

Archie helped himself to another two sausages and then climbed down from the table and ran off to play a game of horses.

'Archie, come back. We do not leave the table until we have finished eating,' she called after him.

'Oh, leave him be, Arabella. He will do no harm and has been so well behaved of late despite all of our troubles,' said Mrs Tatton.

'You are right, of course,' Arabella said. 'It has not been easy for him.' The weight of guilt was heavy. She doubted that the memory of those awful last days when he had gone hungry would ever leave her.

'Nor for any of us,' answered her mother. 'Now I know it is not my place to ask and that events of the bedchamber between a man and a woman are best kept that way, but…' Mrs Tatton's brow furrowed with concern. 'I do not think that matters went so well for you last night.'

'Those matters were fine,' Arabella said quickly and felt her cheeks flush at the memory of Dominic's rejection. She was his mistress. She was supposed to bed him, to let him take his pleasure. And she had been prepared to do just that, however much she resented it. What she had not been prepared for was that he would tease a response from her body and then just walk away.

'Do not lie to me, girl. I have eyes to see and ears to hear. And I see your face is powder pale this morning and your eyes swollen and red as if you have spent the night weeping. And I heard him leaving the house before midnight.'

'My eyes are a little irritated this morning, nothing more. And D—' She stopped Dominic's name on her tongue before it could escape. 'And, yes, the gentleman had to leave early. There were others matters to which he had to attend.'

'At midnight?' her mother snorted. 'He was barely here.'

'If his visits are short, does it not suit us all the better?'

'Some men can be inconsiderate in their haste to… to satisfy their own…' Her mother's cheeks blushed scarlet and she could not finish her words.

'No,' Arabella said hastily. 'It was not like that.'

The sight of him. The scent of him. His fingers slowly tracing a line all the way along her collar bone, before meandering down to tease her nipples. The burn of her skin, the rush of her blood…

She winced with the shame of it.

'Tell me the truth, Arabella.' Mrs Tatton reached over and placed her hand on Arabella's.

Her cheeks warmed, and she felt the gall of bitterness in her throat. 'If you knew the truth, Mama, you would not believe it,' she murmured.

'Did he use you ill?' Her mother's face paled, the flash of fear in her eyes making Arabella feel a brute. She was supposed to be reassuring her mother, not worrying her all the more.

'He did nothing, Mama.' Even though she had offered

herself to him like the harlot she had become. She was so angry at herself…and at him.

She was relieved that he had not taken her, so why did she feel so humiliated? It was a confusing hurtful mess.

'Do not lie to me now, Arabella. If he has hurt you… Nothing is worth that. Better that we beg upon the streets than—'

She took her mother's hand in her own and stroked the fragile veined skin. 'Mama, he was gentle and demanded nothing of me. I wept only for what I am become.'

'Oh, Arabella, we should leave this house.' Arabella felt her mother's hands twist within her own.

'And return to Flower and Dean Street?' Arabella raised her brows.

'I could look for work. Between the two of us we could find a way.'

And the work would kill her mother. Arabella knew there was no other way. She shook her head. 'It is too late, Mama.'

What was done, was done. She was a fallen woman. Besides, the past had caught up with Arabella. *I cannot,* his words seemed to whisper through the room and she thought of the haunted expression in his eyes.

'Mama, we are staying here. I was foolish last night, that is all. Tonight will be different.' She hoped. 'You have nothing to worry over except to count the money and the days until we can return to the country.'

'If you are sure about this, Arabella?'

'I am quite certain.'

Her mother did not look happy, but she nodded and went back to eating her breakfast.

* * *

It was barely an hour later when the letter arrived. Again, written in Dominic's familiar bold handwriting. Arabella's heart began to trip as she broke the sealing wax and read the bold penned words within.

'Well?' Her mother glanced up from the chair on which she was sitting. The sunshine bathed the whole of the drawing room in its warm pale golden light.

'He has arranged for a dressmaker to call tomorrow afternoon.' Arabella folded the letter and slipped it into the pocket of her dress so that her mother would not see the crest embossed both upon the paper and impressed within the seal.

'It is only to be expected,' Mrs Tatton said and went back to pouring the tea.

'I suppose you are right,' Arabella murmured, and a vision of the scandalous silk black dress swam in her mind. She glanced down at her own grey gown and knew she would rather wear this every single day, old and shabby as it was, than anything Dominic would buy for her.

'Archie and I will make ourselves scarce.'

Arabella nodded and glanced at her son, feeling a tug of guilt and worry. Hiding them away at night was not so very bad, for both her mother and son slept early. And although the room was near to the attic it was warm and cosy and nicely furnished, and better in every way than the one they had left in Flower and Dean Street. But to force them to stay quiet and hidden during the day while Dominic sat downstairs and chose a wardrobe of fast, provocative clothes in which to dress her sparked an angry resentment in Arabella.

Something of her feelings must have shown in her

face for Mrs Tatton said, 'It is only for one day, Arabella, and it will do us no harm. And as for the rest… well, the clothes are the least of it.'

There was no sign of Dominic by two o'clock the next day when the dressmaker called. Arabella smoothed her skirts for the umpteenth time and forced herself to at least pretend to be attending to her needlework, although she had the sudden thought, just as she heard the knock at the door, that perhaps mistresses did not spend their time in needlework. It was the first time that anyone would be seeing her as Dominic's mistress and Arabella composed her face to conceal her humiliation.

When Gemmell showed the woman into the drawing room, Arabella's heart sank to meet her shoes. *Of all the dressmakers in London that Dominic could have chosen…*

And she remembered those final dark days that had led her to Mrs Silver's House of Rainbow Pleasures. It should not matter that it was Madame Boisseron waiting in the drawing room, for in her desperation Arabella had knocked on the door of every dressmaker, mantua maker and milliner, every corsetry house, tailor and seamstress, seeking work that was not to be found. Any one of London's dressmakers coming here today would have recognised her. But somehow, the fact that it was the woman in whose shop she had met Mrs Silver just seemed to add to the humiliation for Arabella.

But if Madame Boisseron recognised Arabella the dressmaker was wise enough to make no sign of it. Arabella took a deep breath, swallowed down her embarrassment and knew that she had no choice but to deal with the situation as best she could.

Dominic had still not arrived when the little dark-eyed woman, whose accent was soft and French, brought out a book of dress designs. Arabella glanced at the clock, knowing she ought to wait for his arrival before they proceeded, but the thought that Dominic could dictate the clothes she wore, even right down to her underwear, made her feel so angry that she took the book from the *modiste* and began to flip through it.

Some of the designs were positively indecent, barely covering breasts, revealing nipples and leaving little to the imagination when it came to a woman's figure. Not so very different from the black silk dress that she had been forced to wear within the brothel.

'This one but with a higher neckline,' she pointed to one of the sketches, 'and a thicker material.'

Madame Boisseron glanced up at her in surprise. 'You are sure, madam? Gentlemen, they usually prefer a little more...' she paused '...daring in their ladies' dress.'

'I have had quite enough of daring. So if you would be so kind.'

'Certainly, madam,' Madame Boisseron said. 'After all, the Duke, he said that the decision was with you.'

'He did?' Arabella heard the question in her own voice, and then tried to look as if she had known it all along.

'Indeed. There are not many men that would leave their ladies to order the entirety of their new wardrobes alone. I was most surprised when the Duke, he asked me to attend to you without his presence. He will pay only if you are happy—a most unusual nobleman, *non?*'

'Most unusual,' Arabella said and glanced away.

So Dominic would not be arriving this afternoon. She allowed herself to relax a little, and stopped looking at the clock.

By three o'clock, Arabella's measurements had been taken, they had been through the fabric sample book twice and Arabella had ordered a minimal and conservative wardrobe. Madame Boisseron must have been disappointed, given that she knew Arabella had *carte blanche* to order exactly as she wished and as much as she desired. But rather than be tight-mouthed, the dressmaker only smiled and looked at Arabella kindly and told her the clothes would be delivered as each dress became ready.

Immediately the door closed Arabella made her way upstairs to Archie and her mother's bedchamber and turned her mind away from Dominic Furneaux.

But she could not keep him from her thoughts for ever. Too soon the day faded into night and Arabella sat alone in the drawing room, waiting for him to arrive. She knew that he would expect her to thank him for the free rein with the dressmaker and for his generosity of purse, but the words stuck in Arabella's throat and she knew that she would be unable to bring herself to say them.

She waited; the clock ticked loudly and its hands crawled slowly, and the embroidery within her lap remained untouched. She worried over what he might say to her. And she worried over what she might say to him. But most of all she worried over the moment when he would take her to bed.

But Dominic did not come to the house in Curzon Street. Not that night, or the next, or the night after that.

Dominic was trying to check through the accounts for the land that encompassed his estate. It was a tedious task and one that required sustained concentration, which was the very reason he was sitting with the books spread before him this afternoon. Anything to keep his mind off Arabella Tatton.

The tactic was not proving successful and so Hunter's arrival in his study was something of a relief.

Hunter squinted at the pages lying open on the desk and then looked at Dominic with a knowing expression. 'There's enough crossed-out and overwritten ink on that paper to write a novel. Quite unlike your usual precision, Arlesford. Looks to me like you have got something—or some*one*—else on your mind.' Hunter smiled and arched an eyebrow.

Dominic ignored the bait and bent his head to the columns of numbers on the page before him. Hunter was right, he acknowledged dismally. The page had been clear and legible before Dominic had started his checking.

'Came by to drop you a warning.'

Dominic felt his stomach tighten. Hunter would not be here right now if it were not something concerning Dominic.

'You are not going to like it,' warned Hunter.

Dominic thought of Arabella.

Hunter helped himself to Dominic's decanter of brandy and filled two glasses. 'It's Misbourne. Trying a new approach.'

Dominic released the breath he had been holding as

he accepted the brandy from Hunter. He took a sip and watched his friend lounge in the chair on the other side of the desk.

'He is saying that there was some kind of old agreement made between your father and him years ago. An oath to bind the two families by marriage between you and his daughter.'

The news was not anything Dominic wanted to hear, but at least it did not regard Arabella.

'Aye, a pact sworn with the earl when the two of them were young, single and in their cups. My father never meant to hold me to a boy's drunken foolishness. And I'll be damned if I'm pushed to it by a louse like Misbourne.'

'Misbourne is risking much with his tactic; he must be very determined to make a match between you and Lady Marianne Winslow.'

Dominic's gaze met Hunter's and with the mention of marriage the awkwardness of the past—of what Arabella had done—was in the room between them.

Hunter gave a nod. 'Just have a care over him, Dominic. He is not a good man to have as an enemy.'

'I know and I thank you for the warning, my friend.'

There was a silence in which Hunter sipped at his brandy. Then he smiled. 'To change the subject to a lighter note…'

Dominic relaxed and raised the glass to his lips.

'You are creating quite a stir with Miss Noir.'

Dominic stilled, then set the glass down on the desk without having taken a mouthful.

'What do you mean?' He thought of the lengths he had gone to, to keep the transition of Arabella from Mrs

Silver's to his mistress a secret. 'You did not tell them anything of it?'

Hunter raised his brows and there was a genuine wounded look in his eyes. 'I hope you deem me better than that.'

Dominic gave a nod. 'Forgive me.'

'I do not know how, but the whisper is out about you and the mysterious Miss Noir. People are intrigued by the story. And they are asking questions.'

'Then let us hope that they find no answers.' It should not matter if all of London knew that it was Arabella he had taken as his mistress. After what she had done, it was the very least she deserved. But knowing that and doing it were two different things. He knew what the gossips would do to her if they discovered who she was. They would have a field day with the complete and utter destruction of every last aspect of her character.

'She must be something special that you are taking such a care to hide her,' mused Hunter. 'Who is she, Arlesford?'

'None of your damn business,' said Dominic and lifted his glass of brandy to his mouth. He wondered what Hunter would say if he knew the truth.

Hunter laughed. 'Now I really am intrigued, if you are keeping her secret even from me.'

'Especially from you, Hunter,' Dominic said as if in jest, but he had never been more serious.

'I am not such a bastard that I would steal my best friend's woman,' Hunter protested and finished his brandy in a gulp.

Dominic drew a wry smile. 'Knowing your reputation, I am not about to take any chances.' Better to blame it on that than let Hunter know it was Arabella.

Hunter laughed. 'She must be something special.'

All levity vanished from Dominic's face. He tapped the base of the glass against the wooden surface of his desk as he thought of Arabella.

'She is,' he said and glanced away.

'Dominic?' Hunter probed. But Dominic had no mind to discuss the matter even with Hunter, so he just shook his head.

'Do not go further, friend,' he said quietly.

Hunter gave a subtle nod, then smiled, refilled their glasses and raised his in a toast. 'Miss Noir, long may the *ton* fail to unmask her.'

Dominic chinked his glass against Hunter's, but he did not smile. And as he drank the brandy his mind was filled with Arabella Tatton and what it would mean to them both were she to be unmasked.

It was another reason he should not return to Curzon Street. And yet one more reason that did not relieve the compulsion that whispered to him night and day to retrace his steps straight back there.

Chapter Six

'He did not call upon you again last night?' Mrs Tatton enquired over the toast. 'That is the fourth night in a row.'

Four nights during which Arabella's initial relief at Dominic's absence was beginning to turn into something else. A niggle of worry that would not be stilled. She nodded, trying to let nothing of her true thoughts show upon her face, and spread some honey upon another slice of toast for Archie.

'Who did not call?' asked Archie.

Arabella's mother met her eyes over his head. The two women looked at one another.

'Your mama's friend,' said Mrs Tatton. 'Now eat up your toast, Birthday Boy, before it grows cold.'

Archie, mouth filled with toast, started to pretend two of the spoons were horses galloping across the tablecloth.

Arabella felt her cheeks heat from the deception she was weaving, but knew she had no choice. It would all be so much worse if the truth came out.

'Perhaps if his first visit was not entirely to his satisfaction he has changed his mind over the arrangement.' Embarrassment flushed Mrs Tatton's cheeks as she voiced the fear that had been gnawing at Arabella.

'Let us hope not, Mama.' God help them if he had, for Arabella did not think she could go back to Mrs Silver's. But the manner of their parting lent her little confidence.

A knock sounded at the door and Gemmell entered with a letter from Dominic upon a silver salver.

'Delivered first thing, ma'am,' he said and left again.

Arabella felt a stab of dread, wondering if it contained her *congé*.

Mrs Tatton looked on in anxious silence as Arabella opened the letter and scanned its contents.

'He enquires as to my happiness with the dressmaker,' Arabella said with relief.

'Then all is well?'

'It appears so, Mama.' As Arabella read the rest of the bold script she could not keep the surprise from her voice. 'He writes to say that he has given me the use of a carriage and a purse of money to spend so that I will not have to buy on credit using his name.' She glanced up to meet her mother's eyes. 'So no one need know of our...situation.'

Her mother's eyes widened. 'He is either a most thoughtful gentleman, or...' she raised a brow '...one who has much to lose if you are discovered.'

As far as Arabella could see Dominic had nothing to lose by her discovery. Indeed, she would have thought he would have been crowing it from the rooftops. *A most thoughtful gentleman.* Not a description that could ever be applied to Dominic Furneaux. Or so she had thought.

'Much as I detest that he must pay for us...' She glanced across at her mother's shabby dress. 'You and Archie are in dire need of some new clothes.'

'We should be saving the money so that we may leave this situation as quickly as possible. Archie and I can manage just fine as we are, Arabella.'

'Both of you have only the clothes upon your back, Mama, and nothing more. Your shoes have holes in the soles. And your hands have been paining you. His payment is generous.' She pushed away the thought of what it was he was paying for. 'I will ask Gemmell to organise new wardrobes for you. And I will visit the apothecary myself to fetch you something for your joints.'

Mrs Tatton worried at her lip. 'You are sure he will not notice? About the money?'

Arabella glanced again at the letter. 'He makes it clear he does not wish for an account of my spending.'

'Well, I suppose in that case...' Her mother nodded, but the furrow of worry between her brows lifted only a little.

Arabella pushed the thought of Dominic and her situation aside. There were other matters to be considered today, and she intended to apply herself fully to them. 'Let us talk of more pleasant matters. It is a certain boy's birthday.' She raised her voice so that Archie would hear and looked over at her son. 'And as a special treat I thought that we might take a trip to the park. Robert, the groom, has a little mare called Elsie. Would you like to sit up on Elsie's back while Robert walks her around the park?'

'Oh, yes, please!' Archie's eyes were wide with

delight and he slipped down from his chair and started to gallop around in excitement. 'Can we leave right now?'

'We had best get ourselves ready first!' Arabella laughed.

'Are you sure about this, Arabella?' Mrs Tatton asked.

'It is still early, Mama. There should be few enough people about to notice us; even if they do, there is nothing to associate us with this house or its master.'

Archie paused as he galloped past the mantel piece to stroke a hand against the ribbons that Arabella had festooned there. She smiled at the pleasure on his face and knew that the decorations had been worth it, even if she would have to take them down and hide them away just in case Dominic arrived.

'And remember that we are to have a special birthday lunch,' said Mrs Tatton. 'Cook is making a cherry cake and lemonade and some biscuits too.'

'Hurrah!' shouted Archie. 'I love birthdays.'

Gemmell came in to organise the clearing of the breakfast plates. 'And how old are you today, young master Archie?' he asked.

'I am a grown up boy of five years old,' said Archie with pride.

'That is very grown-up indeed,' agreed Gemmell with a smile and gave the little boy the small wooden figure of a horse that he had carved.

And the maid, Alice, chucked Archie under the chin and gave him a packet of barley-sugar twists that she had made herself and knew to be his favourites.

Arabella felt her heart swell at their kindness. 'Thank you,' she said with meaning. 'You are very kind to us.' And today all the shadows of the past and the present seemed very far away. Today they were a proper family—Archie, her mother, Arabella and all of the servants.

Dominic read the card in his hand and knew there was no way he could refuse Prinny's invitation without delivering the prince a monumental insult. How recently a night of drunken revelry and fireworks in Vauxhall Pleasure Gardens would have held appeal for Dominic. Now it did not. He wondered how little time he might need stay there before he could slip away.

He thought of Arabella sitting alone at her needle-work in Curzon Street. And he felt that same surge of desire for her that he had always felt. He burned for her, just as he knew he could not take her. It was an absurd situation of his own creation. An insolvable paradox that tortured him more with each passing day. His brain told him that he should go round to Curzon Street right now and ease the ache in his loins upon her, to ride her as he had done in Mrs Silver's. But even the memory of what had happened in that place soured his stomach. And in his heart he knew that he could not do it. Even if she had been ridden by a thousand men before him.

He glanced again at the card, *Vauxhall and its masked carnival*, and an audacious idea popped into his head. An idea that was both daring and ridiculous. To be with her was a torture, but he craved it all the same. The carnival might be easier than being alone with her in a house he was paying for, with a bed too easily within reach. The thought of having Arabella by his side seemed to make the prospect of Vauxhall much more palatable. He slipped the card into his pocket. It would require another visit to Curzon Street.

Just to tell her of the carnival.

Nothing more.

Tonight.

He anticipated the visit with a combination of dread and impatience.

It was wonderful to escape the house in Curzon Street and it gladdened Arabella's heart to watch her son and her mother enjoy the morning in the fresh air of the park. The trip lifted all of their spirits and so too did the little party they had for themselves and the servants that afternoon.

Normally Gemmell served dinner at four o'clock, which was early for London's society, but it was an hour that gave Arabella and her family time enough to sit down and eat together before preparing for the evening. The preparation involved checking in each room that there was no evidence of either Archie or Mrs Tatton and ensuring that Archie was bathed, changed and tucked up in bed asleep before the master of the house's arrival, should he choose to call. But today, because of the park and the party, and the fact that come four o'clock they were still full of birthday cake and lemonade, everything was running late. And Arabella was loathe to bring a close to the day. Not once had she allowed herself to think of Dominic or her circumstances. She had been determined to make this day as enjoyable as possible for Archie's sake. And it had been. Arabella felt happy for the first time in weeks.

'Have we not had the very best of days?' she asked as they sat down to a light dinner within the dining room.

'Indeed we have, Mama!' His eyes were shining

and his cheeks had the healthy glow of the outdoors about them.

Arabella and her mother laughed.

'And Charlie thinks so, too.' He stroked the little wooden horse that Gemmell had made for him.

They were in the middle of eating when Arabella thought she heard a familiar-sounding carriage outside. *It cannot be,* she thought to herself. *It is barely quarter past six.* But then a very worried-looking Gemmell appeared in the doorway.

'Madam, it is the master!'

'Good Lord!' said Arabella beneath her breath.

'Oh, Arabella!' gasped her mother.

'Show him into the drawing room. I will come through and stall him there while Mama and Archie make their escape.'

Gemmell gave a nod and hurried away.

'What is wrong, Mama?' asked Archie.

'Nothing at all, little lamb. Grandmama wants to tell you a very exciting new story. So you must sneak upstairs to your bedchamber as quickly and quietly as you can. And once you are there you must climb straight into bed and be as quiet as a mouse and listen to Grandmama's new story before you go to sleep.'

'No bathing?' asked Archie, who was looking as if it was something too good to be true.

'Just for tonight,' said Arabella.

'Hurrah!' Archie began to shout.

Mrs Tatton put her fingers to her lips and hushed him. 'Shush now, Archie. Fasten that little button on your lips. Quiet as a mouse, remember?'

Archie nodded and made the button-fastening movement at his lips.

Arabella heard the front door open. She heard the murmur of Dominic's voice and the tread of his shoes on the polished wooden floorboards of the hallway.

Archie was grinning so much a tiny breathy snigger escaped him.

Arabella's and her mother's eyes shot to him, shaking their heads, touching their fingers to their lips in a silencing gesture.

Her heart was thudding as hard as a blacksmith's hammer striking against an anvil. She looked at the door, afraid that Dominic would come striding through it, demanding to know what was going on.

Please God, do not let him discover them.

But his footsteps walked straight on past the dining room door and on along the passageway to the drawing room.

A minute later, and without a single noise, Gemmell appeared at the door. There was a glimmer of sweat upon his brow. The poor man looked every bit as worried as Arabella felt.

She nodded to him. 'Help Mama and Archie. Wait until I am inside the drawing room speaking with him before you make a dash for it.' She thought of the infirmities of both Gemmell and her mother—'dash' was perhaps the wrong word to use.

'Be a good boy for Grandmama.' She kissed Archie on the forehead. And to her mother, 'Take off his shoes that they make no noise upon the floor.'

'I will carry him, ma'am,' said Gemmell.

Archie was quite heavy and she worried that Gemmell could not manage him, but she did not want to insult the old butler by suggesting any such thing. So she gave him a grateful, if nervous, smile. 'Thank you.'

And then, smoothing down her skirts, she made her way through to the drawing room and Dominic.

Arabella was looking a little flustered when she appeared in the drawing room.

'Forgive me,' he said, 'did I interrupt you?'

'Not at all.' She sounded slightly breathless. 'I had almost finished eating when I heard your arrival.'

'I did not mean to interrupt your dinner. It is nothing of importance. I merely wanted to speak with you. Let us go back to the dining room. We can speak just as well there.'

'No. Really.' She thought of the ribbons that still festooned the mantel, and the three settings at the table and their half-eaten meals…and her mother and son still within. 'Besides, I find my appetite has quite deserted me.'

He stiffened at her words, but when his eyes scanned her face there was nothing of disdain or sharpness there.

She caught his expression and only then seemed to realise what she had said. 'I did not mean…that is to say…'

Dominic looked at her in surprise. There was not one sign of her normal cool reserve, nothing of artifice. She was every inch the Arabella he had known and loved. Keeping her here as his mistress had never seemed so wrong, yet he was having trouble tearing his eyes away from her.

'I came to ask if you would accompany me on an evening at Vauxhall Gardens. The Prince of Wales is organising a masquerade and I am obliged to attend. I thought as it was a masked affair…your identity would be quite hidden. And perhaps you would find it preferable to an evening spent with your needlework.'

She opened her mouth to say something, then closed it again. And something of the mask was back upon her face.

They looked at one another across the distance.

'You may think about it, Arabella, and let me know your decision.' He placed the card down upon a nearby table and made to leave.

'Wait.' She stepped towards him, her hand held out in entreaty. 'Please.'

Dominic stopped and looked round at her.

'I would like very much to go to Vauxhall with you.'

Some of the tension he had been feeling eased. He gave a nod of his head. 'Thank you.' His eyes met hers. 'I will leave you to your dinner.' He bowed and turned away.

'Dominic!' There was an urgency in her voice he had not heard before. 'Will you not stay for a little while?'

He peered round at her, hardly believing this sudden change in her.

She gestured to the sofa. 'Let us sit down and…talk.'

There was such earnestness in her face he could not refuse. Besides, if she wanted to talk then he wanted to listen. Maybe she would tell him the answer to the question that had weighed heavy in his mind for every single day of the last six years.

'Tell me about your day.' He could sense the nervousness running through her, see it in the way she wetted her lips and clutched her hands together that bit too tightly.

'You wish to know about my day?'

'Yes. I am interested to hear it. You have not told me

anything of your life.' She perched herself on the edge of the striped green sofa.

'You have not asked,' he said and sat down beside her.

'Then I have been remiss in my duty.' She smiled, but Dominic could not help but notice that the smile did not touch her eyes.

Her fingers were gripping the edge of the sofa. He laid his hand gently over them.

'I do not want you to ask out of duty, Arabella,' he said quietly.

Her gaze met his and the smile dropped away from her face.

A loud clatter sounded from the hallway and Arabella jumped.

'What on earth…?' He got to his feet to go out and see what was going on.

But Arabella was already on hers and standing before him. 'Gemmell is a little clumsy. Do not be harsh with him, Dominic, I beg of you.' Her face had paled and she looked almost frightened.

'I have no intention of chastising anyone, Arabella. I mean only to check that there has been no mishap.'

'Dominic…' She stepped towards him. He saw the intensity of her expression, the uncertainty in her eyes. Slowly she reached her hand out and brushed the tips of her fingers against his face.

And everything in Dominic's world seemed to stop.

She touched her fingers over his cheek as if she were reassuring herself that it really was him.

Dominic held his breath and did not move.

She traced down the line of his nose, omitting his mouth to move over the angles of his chin, first one way and then the other, before coming back to linger within its cleft. Her fingers were chilled as ice against his skin.

Not once did he move his gaze from her, just watched her following the path her finger was drawing.

And then slowly she inched her fingers higher…

Dominic's body tightened.

And higher…

His breath shook.

Until at last, her fingertips touched against his lips and stilled. They were light as a feather and trembling.

Dominic ceased to think. He responded in the only way he knew how with Arabella. He kissed those sweet delicate fingers, kissed each one in turn. And when she came into his arms and her body cleaved to his it seemed the most natural thing in the world to kiss her mouth.

Arabella kissed him and forgot that she was only doing this to prevent the discovery of Archie and her mother. She kissed him and everything else ceased to be. He held her as if he cared for her, kissed her as if he loved her. He was the same man she had known, the same man she had loved. And in this moment as she felt the fast beat of his heart beneath her hand and the warmth and the strength of his body, she felt everything that she had done as a girl of nineteen. He worshipped her with his lips and she believed the illusion his tenderness wove—of love and of protection. She slid her hand up around his neck and gave herself up to the kiss, revelling in it, wanting it all the more. All of these years without him. Her heart clung to his and refused to let go.

Lies, all lies, the little voice in her head whispered.

And she remembered all that he had done. And her son who had no father. And the memories cooled her ardour like a bucket of iced water.

She stumbled back, clutching a hand to her mouth, appalled at what she had just done.

'Arabella?' Dominic's eyes were dark and dazed. His voice sounded low and confused.

'I…' She backed away and shook her head, knowing that there were no words to explain how she was feeling. She did not know what to say to him. She could not even begin to pretend that she was unaffected by what had just happened between them or by anything of this situation.

'I…' she tried again and as her gaze lowered she saw the evidence of his arousal within his close-fitting pantaloons and realised that she had seduced him just like the courtesan she was. What she had done meant he would take her now. And she trembled at the thought of it.

Dominic looked right into her eyes, as if he could see every thought in her head, then walked away without saying a single word.

There was the thud of the front door shutting, and Arabella's eyes closed in anguish.

Chapter Seven

The night of the Vauxhall masquerade came around too quickly.

Arabella slipped the silver-beaded and feathered mask into place and turned to face Dominic. He had barely said a word since entering the drawing room of the Curzon Street town house and there was an atmosphere in the room thick enough to be cut with a knife.

Dominic's gaze perused her face, lingering for seconds that seemed too long, so that it was almost as if she had only just touched her fingers to his lips, only just kissed him with such wanton abandon. The sweat prickled upon her palms and the butterflies were flocking in her stomach.

It was not only the mask she was worrying over. 'My dress…' She had been so very determined to thumb her nose at him during its ordering; now she was aware that its very respectability might reveal more of her identity when she was by Dominic's side. 'It will not attract…'

Suspicion. Speculation '…attention,' she finished, 'will it?'

She watched his gaze drop to the bodice, then sweep down to the skirt and she bit her lip in worry.

It was a dress like none that Arabella had ever owned. Plain yet elegant. Pale silver silk cut to fit her body perfectly. With its small capped sleeves, bodice scattered with small crystal beads that sparkled in the light and décolletage that teased rather than revealed, the dress was beautiful but pure in a way that made it unsuitable for any courtesan. The irony of its styling was not lost on Arabella.

'How could you think it would fail to attract attention, Arabella?' he said in a quiet voice.

Her stomach gave a churn and her gaze shot to his, waiting for his anger.

'It is beautiful. *You* are beautiful.'

She gaped in surprise, and blushed and could think of not one thing to say.

Dominic swept the long black velvet domino around her shoulders. She jumped at the brush of his fingers against her collar bone as he fastened it in place, feeling nervous both at Dominic's proximity and the prospect of the night ahead.

Out there before all those people. At his side. As his mistress.

A wave of uncertainty swept through her. She bit again at her lip.

'No one will know your true identity, Arabella,' he said gently, and carefully pulled up the domino's hood to cover the curls piled high upon her head.

And then he took her hand in his and led her out to where the carriage waited.

* * *

The night was cool, but clear and dry. Tiny stars studded the blackness of the sky as they walked down the grassy bank towards the boats and barges that would carry them across the Thames to the carnival. They crossed the river in silence. Nor did they speak when they arrived at the other bank and the pleasure gardens that were Vauxhall. Dominic was too aware of Arabella by his side, and of the tension that flowed between them.

The gardens were more crowded than usual, with guests who had come to witness the Prince of Wales at the masquerade. Dominic made his meeting with the prince and, when he saw how Prinny was looking at Arabella, steered her away again just as quickly.

She had taken hold of the arm that he offered and they strolled together through the night, in a parody of all the other couples around them. But even in the lightness of her touch he could feel the tension that hummed through her body. He took her to the section of the gardens where there were shows and jugglers and acrobats. And something of the strain between them seemed to lessen as they stood there together and watched. Her grip even tightened a little as she watched with fascination a man who could swallow the blade of a sword. And when that display was done, he moved on, wanting to show her all there was to see.

There were jesters and gypsy women selling lucky white heather and offering to read their fortunes.

Near to the supper booths a group of musicians were playing, filling the surrounding gardens with the sweetness of their music. An area close by was ringed with tables and chairs in the middle of which a wooden dance floor had been laid down upon the grassy surface.

'Shall we dance?' He realised that he wanted to dance with her, to hold her close in his arms, very much.

She touched a hand against her mask, in the same gesture she had used that very first night in Mrs Silver's drawing room.

'No one will recognise you,' he reassured her and slid the dark voluminous hood down to reveal the glory of her hair. 'Even like this. Trust me.'

She looked up at him and nodded, and again Dominic felt something he thought to have long been destroyed stir in his heart.

'It is so long since I danced,' she said and there was uncertainty in her eyes as she glanced at the dance floor where other couples were moving together in each other's arms. 'And I have never waltzed.'

'Just relax and follow my lead.' He offered his hand for hers.

She looked at him and it seemed to Dominic as if she were making some pivotal decision in that moment, not merely deciding whether she would dance with him. Then, without saying a word, she placed her hand in his and let him lead her out on to the dance floor.

Arabella gave herself into Dominic's arms and waltzed with him. There was something soothing about the moonlight and the lilt of the music and the sway of their bodies in the dance. He was holding her scandalously close, so close that the fall of his breeches brushed against her skirts, so close that his heart beat against her breast. But this was Vauxhall and every other couple was dancing just as intimately.

He was looking at her with those dark soulful eyes

just as he had looked at her all those years ago. Whether it was the music or the moonlight or just plain madness, in that moment she let herself forget, and just felt—the music, her heartbeat...and him.

When the music stopped, he led her from the floor towards the buffet of food laid out upon the tables. There were fresh bread rolls and ham sliced fine and thin, and a selection of fruit perfect for the eating.

He fetched them two glasses of punch and filled two plates with a selection of food to tempt her and found them a small table in a spot that was not so crowded. He made a little conversation, polite pleasant words, nothing that touched near anything that was sensitive for them both. Something of her fears for the evening faded.

Afterwards they watched some boats, miniature replicas of the great Lord Nelson's, being sailed down the river, and then there were the fireworks, a burst of rainbow lights that exploded to shower the dark canvas of the sky. And she wished that Archie and her mother could see the spectacle.

Dominic was standing behind her, both of their necks craned back as they stared up at the sky. He bent his head forwards and said something to her, but the explosions all around were so loud that she could not hear. He stepped closer, easing her back against him so that he could whisper in her ear.

But she still could not make out his words, so she turned in his arms and all of a sudden she was looking into his face and he was looking into hers. And she could see the flash of the firework bursts reflected in the darkness of his eyes. But she was no longer thinking of the fireworks, and neither was he. They stared at one another. Alone in the crowd. Silent and serious in the midst of the riotous carnival.

'Arlesford?' The voice smashed the moment apart like a cannon. 'Your Grace, I thought it was you.'

Dominic turned, shifting his stance to manoeuvre Arabella slightly behind him so that he was partly shielding her with his body. 'Misbourne,' he said in his usual emotionless voice and faced the man.

Lord Misbourne was dressed in a domino the like of Arabella's and even wore a mask across his eyes. But there could be no doubt over the owner of the face that was beneath it, with its curled grey moustache and neatly trimmed beard. Misbourne's arm was curled around the waist of a woman young enough to be his daughter and whose large breasts were in danger of imminent escape from her bodice. The girl cast Dominic a libidinous glance and licked her tongue suggestively around her lips before taking a sip of punch from the glass she was carrying.

Misbourne did not notice; he was too busy staring at Arabella. 'Gentlemen must have their little distractions, Arlesford,' he said. 'Nothing wrong with that—as long as they are discreet, of course.' And Dominic understood the message that Misbourne was trying to send him—that his having a mistress would be no barrier to courting Misbourne's daughter.

The earl leered at Arabella and Dominic felt his fists bunch in response. He forced himself to stay calm. Brawling with Misbourne would only draw the wrong kind of attention to her.

'If you will excuse us, sir. We were just leaving.'

'But not before you have introduced me to your lady friend. Could this be the delectable Miss Noir about whom I have heard so many whispers?' He peered around Dominic at Arabella.

Dominic felt the rage flow through his blood. He could smell it in his nose and taste it upon his tongue. Every muscle was primed and ready. Every nerve stretched taut. His loathing of Misbourne flooded him so that he would have knocked the man down had he not felt Arabella's fingers touch his arm in the gentlest of restraints. Only then did he recollect his senses.

'Goodnight, Misbourne,' he said in a tone that brooked no refusal, and when he looked at the man's beady, glittering dark eyes behind his mask he saw that Misbourne understood. The older man took an involuntary step back from the threat.

Dominic took Arabella's arm in his and he was so grateful that she had stopped him.

She did not utter one question, nor throw so much as a glance in Misbourne's direction. She just held her head up and waited.

They walked away together, away from Misbourne and the fireworks. Away from Vauxhall and the wonderful night.

The carriage wheels were rumbling along the road carrying them back to Curzon Street and still Dominic had not spoken.

Arabella could sense the tension emanating from him, the echo of the anger she had seen directed against the man, Misbourne, in Vauxhall. All illusions had vanished the moment Misbourne and the woman had appeared.

'Does everyone know that you bought me from Mrs

Silver?' The words would not be contained for a minute longer.

The carriage rolled past a street lamp and in the brief flicker of light she saw his face through the darkness—handsome, hard edged, dangerous—before the night's darkness hid him again.

'How naïve of me not to have realised.' She shook her head and looked away, feeling sick at the thought. 'What else do they know, Dominic?' *What else have you told them?* she wanted to ask.

'Nothing, I hope. I paid Mrs Silver very well for her silence. And I trust my friends, who were with me that night, enough to make no mention of Miss Noir.'

'You did not tell them?'

'Of course I did not tell them, Arabella! My affairs are my own, not tittle-tattle for the amusement of others.' His voice was hard and angry. 'Do you think I would have gone to such lengths to hide you were it otherwise?'

'You guard your own reputation well.' This was all about protecting himself. How foolish to think it could ever have been about her.

'I am guarding what is left of yours,' he said grimly. Then his tone softened slightly. 'I am not unaware of the…sensitivity of this issue.'

She looked across at the shadowed man through the darkness and was not sure she believed him.

'Of what it would mean to your mother were she to learn the truth.'

'God forbid…' Arabella pressed a hand to her forehead, horrified at the prospect of that revelation, even if it were something rather different to that which Dominic envisaged. But even as she thought it she was wondering why Dominic should have the slightest care over her mother.

'They may know of Miss Noir, but they do not know the identity of the woman behind her mask.'

Yet.

The word hung unspoken between them.

'You may rest assured that I will do all in my power to keep it that way.'

She stared at him, not knowing what to make of his attitude.

'I will make discreet enquiries over—'

'No,' she said too quickly. If he started asking questions, who knew what he would discover. Everything that Arabella had striven so hard to hide. 'No,' she said more gently. 'Words already spoken cannot be unsaid. Asking questions will only make it worse. Besides—' she glanced away '—you are a duke; there will always be an interest in your dealings. And the lure of a coin will mean there are always tongues to be loosened.'

And she could not blame them. She of all people knew what it was like to be poor and in desperate need of money.

'Perhaps, but speed and generosity has always worked in the past to silence them,' he said.

'But not this time.'

'Seemingly not.'

There was a small silence.

'Thank you for trying.' Her words were stilted. Gratitude sat ill with her when it came to Dominic, but for all that she felt she knew how much worse it could be, had he taken her as his mistress as carelessly as he had abandoned her as his betrothed.

The carriage wheels rolled on.

She steered the conversation to safer ground. 'Who was he, the man in Vauxhall? Misbourne.' The man who had stirred in Dominic such barely leashed fury.

There was a small pause before Dominic answered, 'A delusional old fool, Arabella, but not one you need have a worry over.'

Another pause.

'I thank you that you stayed my arm,' he said. 'Brawling with an earl at Vauxhall would not have been conducive to our maintaining a low profile.'

She gave a nod of acknowledgement. And she wondered as to this man who she knew to be a rake and a scoundrel. A man who had made her his whore, yet did not flaunt or humiliate her publically. A man who went to such pains to preserve her privacy and who, it seemed, had a care for her mother's sensibilities.

The carriage came to a stop outside Curzon Street.

The hour was late. She did not know whether he would come in. Whether he would kiss her. Bed her. And she was not sure if she dreaded it or wanted it. Nervous anticipation tingled right through her.

He helped her from the carriage and into the hallway, dismissing James the young footman who was acting as the night porter.

Only two wall sconces were lit and the soft shadowed lighting lent the hallway an unusual intimacy. Or maybe it was the fact that they were standing there alone in the middle of the night facing one another.

Arabella did not know what she should say. She could feel the tension between them, feel the speed of her heart. Her mouth was dry from dread, her thighs hot from desire. She swallowed and it sounded loud in the silence.

'You need not worry, Arabella, I am not staying,' he said in a voice as dark and rich as chocolate. 'I came only to see you safely inside.' As if to reinforce his words she could hear the sound of the waiting carriage from the street outside.

In the flickering of the candlelight she thought he had never looked so dangerous or so handsome. There was a hardness to his face that had not been there all those years ago, but when she looked into his eyes, those dark velvet brown eyes, Arabella saw something of tenderness. And for all that she should have known better, for all of her common sense, she felt the stirrings of old feelings that she had thought never to feel again. There was such an allure of forbidden attraction that the atmosphere sparked with it.

Her breath was shallow and fast, her stomach a mass of fluttering butterflies. 'This arrangement between us. I thought that you would... That it would be different between us...' She met his gaze. 'I do not understand.'

'Neither do I, Arabella,' he said.

Her heart was thudding so hard she thought she could hear it in the silence.

He peeled off his gloves and came to stand before her.

They stared at one another for one beat of her heart and then another. And then he reached out his hand and touched his fingers to her cheek, caressing her face in a mirror of her own actions from an evening not so long ago. His touch was more gentle than she remembered, soft as the stirring of warm breath upon her skin. His movement was unhurried and sensual as he traced the outline of her cheek and up across her eyebrow.

He touched only her face yet every inch of her body

tingled in response. He trailed his forefinger down the slope of her nose, and her breasts felt heavy and sensitive. His thumb brushed against her lower lip and the sensation was as if he had stroked between her legs. She gasped and opened to him so that his thumb probed within the moisture of her mouth. Her lips touched to him, not because she was his mistress but because it felt instinctive and right.

'Arabella,' he whispered and there was something agonised and urgent in his whisper. And then he pulled her into his arms and kissed her.

Arabella kissed him back, their mouths moving in hungry reunion. She felt his hands upon her breasts, upon her hips. Their bodies clinging together, as if nothing of the pain had ever been.

She felt the press of his manhood against her, felt the heat of him, the need in him, and, God help her, but she wanted him too. Her thighs burned. She was moist for him. Her body recognised his and opened as if in invitation. And her heart began to open to him too, just as it had done all those years ago. And suddenly she was afraid, afraid of where this was leading, afraid of what she was feeling.

Dominic seemed to sense the sudden swirl in her emotions. He stopped, raised his head and looked into her eyes and she saw in them a desire and confusion that matched her own.

'No,' he whispered, but did not release her. 'No,' he said again and she knew that it was himself he was denying more than her. His breathing was ragged and she could feel the taut strain in every hard muscle of his body. She could sense his hunger, and yet there was a sudden wariness in his eyes, a restraint almost. She felt his grip loosen. He released her and left; there was only the sound of the front door clicking shut behind him.

Arabella stood there until the sound of his carriage faded into the distance and she touched trembling fingers to her swollen lips, not understanding how she could feel such attraction for a man whom she disliked and did not trust. He had hurt her in the past. He was humiliating her in the present. She knew all of that, yet tonight he had made her forget. He seemed too like the man she had fallen in love with. When she was with him, when he touched her, when he kissed her...

She clutched her hand harder to her mouth and closed her eyes against the memory, feeling confused and ashamed that he could still affect her so and not knowing what was wrong with her. How could she, who was so strong when it came to everything else, be so weak when it came to Dominic Furneaux?

But Arabella knew that she must not give in. Once it had only been her heart and her pride that he had taken. Now there was so much more at stake than that. She glanced upstairs towards the chamber where her mother and son slept and knew she must stay strong.

Chapter Eight

The night was not going well for Dominic in the gaming den.

He looked at the cards in his hands and, despite all his resolutions, thought again of Arabella. Two nights had passed since the night of the masquerade. Only two nights and in that time he had thought of little else.

'Arlesford,' Hunter prompted by his side, and he realised that everyone at the table was waiting for him. He shoved some more guineas into the pile at the centre of the table.

And, contrary to his usual play, promptly lost them. Indeed, he had not won a game since entering the seedy surroundings, much to the delight of the rather rough-and-ready patrons of the establishment. But then Dominic knew he was more than a little distracted.

It was a small tavern in the East End, most of the patrons of which looked like men you would not wish to meet on a dark night. Their clothing was coarse, their language too. The gin and beer flowed freely, in the

hope of addling the wits of those that were fool enough
to come here.

It was, surprisingly enough, the very latest place
to be seen for Gentlemen of the *ton*. Although, Dominic thought wryly, those young fops that ventured in
here would soon realise they had bitten off more than
they could chew. Young Northcote had ignored all of
Dominic's warnings and was now grinning to hide his
nervousness and both drinking and betting more deeply
than was wise. The boy was ill at ease in the surroundings, even if he did not want to admit any such thing; it
had, after all, been his idea to come here.

Did she wonder as to his absence? Did he gnaw in her
thoughts as she gnawed in his? Did she feel this same
craving that plagued him night and day? He doubted it.
To women like Arabella, their arrangement was nothing more than business. To women like Arabella... He
caught the phrase back, and thought bitterly that there
were no other women like Arabella.

He stared across the room, seeing not the overly
warm, smoky den with its scored tables and rickety
chairs and the men with their blackened teeth and their
stubble-roughened faces, but the woman whose image
had haunted him through the years.

The cards had been dealt. Again.

He lost. Again. And saw the way young Northcote's
eyes widened with fear as the youngster realised the
extent of his own loses even at this early hour.

Dominic ached for Arabella, wanted her with a compulsion that bordered on obsession, but each time he
touched her it was both ecstasy and torture. When he
took her in his arms he felt the wound inside him tear
afresh.

She was Arabella Tatton, the woman he had loved, the woman who had so callously trampled the youthful tenderness from his heart. And he could not separate that knowledge from his body's craving for her. There would never be anything of relief. Yet he needed to be with her more with every passing minute. Even knowing that he could not touch her, even knowing the torture would be greater with her than without, he could not fight this growing addiction.

Dominic pushed his chair back, its battered legs scraping tracks through the sawdust that covered the floor.

'I think I will call it a night,' he said to the others and gestured for his hat and gloves to be brought.

Several faces looked up, surprise soon turning to menace.

Even Bullford seemed caught unawares. 'A tad early for you, Arlesford.'

'Certainly is, your Grace,' said a large ruffian employed by the establishment. 'Stay, see if you can win back them golden guineas that you've lost.'

'Perhaps another night, gentlemen,' he said.

The men did not look pleased, but Dominic met their gaze directly, knowing that he could handle himself against them. They looked back but only for a moment, then deliberately moved their attention elsewhere.

Hunter stood by his side.

'Best not leave Northcote here. They will only chew him up all the more and spit him out afterwards,' he said quietly to Hunter.

So the two of them guided Northcote out into the street.

After the haze of cigar and pipe smoke within the

den the clear chilled night air seemed to hit Northcote so hard that the boy staggered.

Dominic hailed a hackney carriage and helped Hunter manoeuvre Northcote into it.

'You are not coming with us?' Hunter asked.

Dominic met his friend's eyes. An unspoken understanding passed between them.

'You do not have your cane with you tonight,' said Hunter.

Dominic said nothing, just looked at his friend resolutely.

Hunter gave a sigh. 'Very well. Just have a care if you are so intent on walking to her,' said Hunter. 'The coves back there were not too keen to let you go. It is only a little after midnight and they had hoped to fleece you for hours yet. Watch your back, Dominic.'

'I will.' Dominic clapped Hunter on the shoulder and watched the carriage depart before he turned and began to walk in the opposite direction.

He had not gone far when he became aware that he was being followed. He scanned the street, seeing that one of the lamp-posts was out a little further along, just at an opening between the buildings. A nice dark spot and a conveniently positioned alleyway. He knew that was where they would attack him.

They struck just where he had expected. Two attackers, one large and burly, the other smaller with no teeth in his head. He recognised them both from the gaming den.

He dodged back into the alley to avoid the first punch.

'Not so fast, your Grace,' a coarse voice said so close to his ear that he could smell the foulness and feel the heat of the fetid breath. A fist swiped close to his face. Dominic ducked and retaliated with a blow hard and low in the belly and had the satisfaction of hearing the man grunt and stumble away clutching at his guts as he bent double and retched against the alley wall. As he turned the second assailant was almost upon him. Dominic twisted to avoid the blow arcing towards him, and managed to avoid the blade—almost. The sting of it sliced across his ribs.

Dominic grabbed the man's wrist and twisted. He heard the soft crack of bone and the yelp of pain as the man fell to his knees cradling his wrist. The knife clattered to land in the wet and filth of the cobblestones below. Dominic picked it up, and then grabbed the kneeling man's hair, jerking his head back and touching the edge of the blade against the exposed throat.

'See that the same does not happen to my friends. Do you understand?'

The man croaked a desperate acquiescence.

Dominic pushed the man away, then walked to face the man cringing against the wall, touching the knife's tip ever so lightly against the fat of the villain's belly.

'You too.'

'They won't be harmed, I'll see to it personally, your Grace,' the rogue promised.

Dominic stared at him for just a moment longer and then he slipped the knife into his pocket and walked away.

The ruffians were kicking at the door, laying siege to it with a hammer. The thuds of the splintering wood reverberated right through Arabella's body. She protected Archie with her body, but the men pulled her aside and wrenched the golden locket from around her neck. And when she looked across the road to the other side of the street where the narrow houses with their boarded windows should have stood, she saw the park and her mother standing waiting there. It was all mixed up and wrong, of course, but Arabella did not notice that in her nightmare.

She woke suddenly, with that same panicked feeling of fear in the pit of her stomach. But the sky was still dark with night, and she remembered that this was Curzon Street and there were no robbers and thieves here. She breathed her relief and relaxed her head back down on to the luxury of a soft feather pillow, and as she did she heard a voice cry out in shock. The cry was cut off as if abruptly hushed. She heard the low murmur of voices in the hallway below, the quiet opening and closing of a door. Hurried footsteps across the marbled floor tiles of the hallway.

Archie!

Arabella scrambled from the bed and, using only the glowing remains of the fire to guide her, was out of the bedchamber door and running down the stairs.

All of the wall sconces in the hallway had been lit. A maid, clad in her nightdress and robe, was coming out of the library with a bottle of brandy in her hand.

'Anne?'

'Oh, ma'am!' The girl jumped and spun round and Arabella could see that her face was wet with tears.

'What is wrong? What are you doing?' The fear was squirming in Arabella's stomach.

'I got such a fright when I saw him.' The maid's face crumpled and she began to sob again.

'What has happened, Anne?'

The drawing door opened and James the footman appeared. 'What on earth is taking you, girl? I would have been quicker fetching it myself.' And then he saw Arabella, and gave a quick bow. 'Begging your pardon, ma'am. I did not see you there.'

'What on earth is going on here?' Arabella demanded.

'It's the master, ma'am.'

'Dominic is here?' The thought had not even entered her head. Even though it was his house. And she was his mistress.

'His Grace has had a bit of an…accident.'

'An accident?' Arabella's stomach dropped to the soles of her feet. Her heart was thumping a fast frenzied tattoo of dread.

The footman lowered his voice even more. 'Not the best of sights for a lady to see, but he won't let me fetch a doctor, ma'am.'

A chill of foreboding shivered right through her. She pushed past James into the drawing room.

Three branches of candles had been lit, yet still their warm flickering glow did not reach to the shadows of the room, nor barely touched the tall dark figure that stood near to the cold fireplace. He had his back to her, but he appeared to be as he ever was, smartly dressed in dark tailcoat and pantaloons, with the air of authority and arrogance that he carried with him. He seemed well enough. She could smell the damp night air that emanated from his still figure. One hand hung loose by his side, the other looked to be tucked into the inner breast pocket of his tailcoat.

'I should not have come,' he said without looking round. 'I had not realised that the hour was so late.'

'James said you met with an accident.'

'James exaggerates. I did not mean to wake you. You should go back to bed.' Still he did not move. And the apprehension that had faded on her first sight of him was back as if it had never left.

'What has happened, Dominic?' she asked carefully.

He turned then, and still nothing appeared out of place, except that his right hand remained tucked beneath the left breast of his tailcoat.

'A minor altercation. Nothing of concern. As I said, go back to bed.'

And then she caught sight of the dark ominous stains upon the white cuff that protruded beneath the dark woollen sleeve of his coat and, lifting the closest candelabrum, she walked towards him.

'Arabella,' he said, holding out his exposed hand as if to stay her. But she kept on closing the distance between them, for she had a horrible fear of just what those stains were.

'This is not for your eyes.'

She felt sick to the pit of her stomach. Her body felt stiff and heavy with dread. 'Take off your coat.'

'Arabella…' One last warning.

She ignored him and took hold of his lapel, pulling back the left breast of his tailcoat.

She gasped at the sight that met her eyes. His white shirt and waistcoat were sodden with blood. She froze, and in that single moment everything changed in her world.

'Dominic!' she whispered.

His hand took hers, his grip strong and reassuring. But she felt that it was wet and when she looked she could see the blood that stained it glisten in the candle-light.

'Oh, my God!'

'It is but a scratch that bleeds too much.'

But there was blood everywhere, and all of it was his.

'Go. James will help me.'

She took a deep breath and raised her gaze to his. Their eyes held for a fraction of a second, a heartbeat in which everything she had told herself she felt about him these years past was revealed as a lie.

'No,' she said. '*I* will help you.' And then she glanced round at the footman and prepared to do what she knew must be done.

Dominic watched as Arabella shifted from shock to take charge of the situation. She sent the maid for clean linen and a glass, and instructed the footman with equal calm proficiency, directing James to help divest him of his upper clothing while she half-filled the glass with brandy.

Only once he sat on the sofa wearing only his panta-loons did she pass him the glass. 'Drink it.' Her voice was calm, but brooked no refusal.

He did not argue, just did as she directed, downing the contents in one go.

As he drank she rolled up the sleeves of her night-gown, tore a strip off the linen and dowsed both it and her hands in brandy.

Then she sat down by his side, eased him back a little against the sofa.

Her gaze met his. 'This is going to sting,' she warned. And her eyes held a concern that Dominic had never

thought to see there again. It touched his heart much
more than he could ever have imagined.

'Do your worst,' he murmured.

He could not prevent himself flinching from the initial touch of the brandy to the wound and saw the pain
mirrored in Arabella's eyes. Yet she did not hesitate, or
weaken from her purpose.

Her touch was gentle, her movements reassuring. She
worked methodically and with a calmness that seemed
to stroke away his tension despite the pain. With strip
by patient strip of brandy-soaked linen she cleansed the
blood away until all that remained was a thin red line
against the paleness of his skin.

'We should send for the doctor. He may wish to stitch
the wound.' She had not looked at him, not once, since
she had taken control of the situation.

'No doctor,' he said. 'The cut is shallow. A week of
binding and the skin will knit together well enough.'

'Dominic—'

'No doctor,' he said again.

'Very well.' She laid a pad of linen against the
wound, then bound it in place. And then she got to her
feet, passed the tray of bloodied rags to James.

'Thank you, James, Anne. You may leave us now.'

She waited until the door closed behind the servants
before she sat back down. Side by side they sat on the
sofa. Not looking at one another. Not speaking a word.
The tension was still between them. But it was different
somehow, as if some barrier that had been there before
had given way.

The silence seemed to stretch between them.

He slipped his hand to cover hers.

'Are you going to tell me what happened tonight?' she asked.

'A small disagreement with two gentlemen from a gaming den.'

'I did not know you frequented such places.'

'There is a lot you do not know about me, Arabella.'

'And too much that I do know,' she said quietly. 'I cannot forget…'

'Nor can I.'

The clock's ticking seemed too loud. It seemed to match the beat of his heart.

'It was not supposed to be like this, Arabella.'

'None of it was supposed to be like this,' she said and he heard the huskiness in her voice.

'Arabella.' He looked at her, willing her to look round at him.

She shook her head at first, but he could hear the slight sob in her breath. He stroked his thumb against her fingers where his hand covered hers.

She turned her face to his, then met his gaze, and the emotions he saw there were as raw and aching as those that beat in his own heart.

'Dominic,' she whispered and the tears spilled from her eyes. He took her in his arms and he kissed each one away and then he held her.

He held her and the minutes passed.

He held her. And then as if by some silent communion they both rose. He blew out all save one branch of candles, then he took her hand in his and together they walked out of the drawing room.

Chapter Nine

Within her bedchamber they spoke not one word.
Dominic stripped off his pantaloons, while Arabella
unfastened the ties of her nightdress and loosened it so
that it slid down her body to lie in a white pool around
her feet.

The candles flickered upon the nightstand, so that
she could see him standing there naked. His body as
tall and strong and well muscled as she remembered. A
sprinkling of dark hair covered his chest and narrowed
to a line that led down to his manhood. His skin glowed
a honey gold in the candles' light, the whiteness of the
linen bandage stark against the rest of him.

There was no need for words. She sensed his feelings
as keenly as her own. She wanted him. And needed him.
Not out of lust. Not even out of desire. The need ran at
a much deeper level than that, in a place that touched
both her heart and her soul. She did not analyse the
feeling. Nor did she think about the past.

Arabella knew only this moment. Dominic was alive.

And that, had a blade pressed a little harder this night, he would not be.

She placed her palm upon his chest over his heart and felt its strong steady beat. Beneath her fingers she could feel the roughness of his chest hair and in her nose was the scent of brandy and cigar smoke mingled with Dominic's cologne.

He threaded a hand through her hair at the scalp, angling her head so that he could look into her eyes.

She did not look away. She did not try to hide anything. They looked at each other with an honesty that belonged only to that moment. His eyes were deep and dark and sensuous and in them was a vulnerability that she had never ever thought to see.

Slowly he lowered his mouth to hers. Their lips touched, the kiss small and gentle. And touched again, before stilling so that their lips rested together, not kissing, but sharing their breath. She slid her hands up from his chest, to dip her fingers into the hollow between his collar bones, before spreading out to slide across the tense hard muscle of his shoulders. Their faces were so close she could feel the brush of his eyelashes every time he blinked.

His free hand followed down the line of her arm to capture her hand in his, hooking both their hands against the small of her back to arch her body all the closer into his. His chest was hard as a rock, the hair that covered it rough against her nipples. Her breasts felt heavy and sensitive, and deep in her belly was a heat that had never expired. She could feel the call of his body and the answer of her own. Just as it ever was, except this time it was different. She could feel the difference. And she knew that he could feel it too.

He bit gently at her lower lip, then salved the nip with his tongue. She tasted him, opened to him, felt his tongue accept the invitation as his lips slid against her own. They kissed. A deep sensual coupling of their mouths. A sharing of such intimacy and tenderness. They kissed and his every breath, every stroke of his tongue, every touch of his lips was a caress of her soul.

He sat down on the edge of the bed, drawing her in so that she was standing straddling his thigh. He kissed her again, then trailed his mouth down over her neck, his breath hot, his tongue tasting her. His hands caressed her breasts, weighing them, stroking skin that was sensitive to his touch, teasing at peaks that were already beaded hard. His hands stilled, his thumbs resting lightly on her nipples, as his gaze slid up to hers. And then, keeping his eyes locked on hers, he shifted one thumb aside and leaned his mouth down to take her nipple into his mouth.

He did not suckle. He did not even move his lips, but his breath was hot and moist against her. He was still watching her when his tongue began to flick against the tender swollen bud. A low soft moan escaped Arabella. She arched her back, driving her breast harder against his mouth. He began to kiss her nipple, to suck it, while his thumb and fingers worked upon the other. When she felt the gentle scrape of his teeth, she clutched that dark head to her, watching his mouth work thoroughly against first one breast and then the other.

His hands found her hips and drew them lower so that she felt the tease of the hairs on his broad muscular thigh against the hot wet centre of her womanhood. Her grip shifted to his shoulders and tightened as he rubbed his thigh gently against her. Arabella moaned again and slid higher up his thigh, until she could feel the probe of his manhood against her hip.

They stilled, his mouth coming back to find hers. And when he rolled her on to the bed their bodies clung together. He lay on his uninjured side, clutching her to him. And she could feel the raggedness of his breathing and the race of his heart as they positioned their legs to minimise the strain on his wound. And when at last she welcomed him into her body it had never felt so right. There was no dominant, no submissive. Nothing of taking, only of sharing. They moved together in a partnership, both rejoicing in their union and striving to the same end.

They loved, for there could be no other word for it. And Arabella was only aware of the moment and the man. Dominic filled her senses. Dominic filled her body.

'Dominic,' she gasped as she exploded into a thousand shards of shimmering pleasure.

'Arabella,' he groaned and she felt the warmth of his seed spill within her.

They lay in each other's arms, feeling the pulse of their bodies and the beat of their hearts.

And eventually they slept.

Dominic came every night to Curzon Street after that. And every night they made love. Arabella was no longer fool enough to believe that she could fight against the mire of complex emotions that she felt for Dominic. Since the night he had come to the house covered in blood she had known that much as she hated what he had done to her, she did not hate *him*. Indeed, there was a part of her that knew they would always be bound together, and not just through Archie. If Arabella had allowed herself to think too much of her situation it would have been unbearable.

She knew what she was—his mistress, a woman he had bought from a brothel.

And she knew what he was—a man who had betrayed her and ruined her life.

And she knew, too, that contrary to everything that she should feel she still cared for him.

Arabella did not want to think what that said about her. Or what it implied about Dominic.

Dominic watched Hunter as the other man pulled up the tails of his coat and stood with his back before the warm flame of the fire. There was only the slow steady tick of the clock on the mantelpiece and the soft sounds of the flames upon the coals.

'I am sure I saw Arabella Tatton coming out of an apothecary shop in Bond Street the other day.' Hunter's voice was steady and he was watching Dominic.

'Did you?' Dominic's heart picked up some speed but he feigned indifference.

'She was carrying her gloves…and she was not wearing a wedding ring.'

'Really?' Dominic pretended to examine his nails.

'And she asked her coachman to take her home to Curzon Street.' Hunter shifted his stance and Dominic could smell hot wool.

Silence.

'It all begins to make sense. Why you are so very protective of Miss Noir's identity. Why you have been so intent on keeping her hidden from view. Not one party. Not one ball, save Prinny's *masked* carnival at

Vauxhall, so I hear. Hardly your normal treatment of a woman...unless there is something of her identity that you wish to conceal.'

Still Dominic said nothing, but he felt his body tense as if in preparation for a fight. He thought of the tenderness of their lovemaking. And he wanted to protect her, even from Hunter.

'It is her, is it not?'

'You are mistaken, Hunter,' he said and the look in his eyes bellowed the warning that his words only whispered at.

'Hell's teeth, Dominic! I am not a fool. I know that Arabella is Miss Noir.'

Dominic did not remember moving, but the next he knew he was two inches in front of Hunter's face, staring down at him as if he would like to rip him limb from limb.

Hunter shook his head and met his gaze. 'Do you honestly think I would breathe one word of this outside of this room? Your secret is safe with me.'

Dominic knew that it was, but it did not make him feel any better.

'I think I am in need of a drink,' said Hunter weakly and ducked under Dominic's arm to stroll across the library and pour them both a large brandy. He passed one glass to Dominic and took several swigs from the other himself. 'I hope you know what you are doing.'

Dominic took a sip of brandy. 'Everything is under control.'

'Is it?' asked Hunter and the look on his face said that he did not believe it. 'Have you forgotten what she did to you?'

'I have not forgotten.' Nothing of the pain.

'Then this is some kind of revenge?'

Dominic set his glass down upon the mantelpiece with a thud that threatened to fracture the crystal stem. 'Hell, Sebastian, what kind of man do you take me for? I found her in Mrs Silver's that night! What did you expect me to do? Walk away and leave her there?' he shouted.

'After breaking your betrothal to run off and marry some other man? Yes. That is exactly what I would have done.' Hunter shook his head again. 'I thought you were over her. I thought you had learned your lesson from her. Lord, but she made a damn fool of you!' Hunter peered closer at Dominic's face. 'But you still want her,' he said slowly as if the pieces of the puzzle were falling into place to reveal the answer.

'Yes, I want her,' admitted Dominic. 'I have never stopped wanting her. Any sane man would. I do not have to like her to bed her.'

Hunter was still looking at him. 'Were that true you would not give a damn who knew she is your mistress. The shame would be on her, Dominic, not on you. No, there is more to it than that.' His eyes narrowed with speculation.

'Leave it alone, Sebastian,' Dominic warned.

But Hunter never could take a warning. 'You still care for her,' he said quietly.

The glass within Dominic's hand shattered, sending the splinters of glass flying across the mantelpiece and spilling the brandy to pool with the blood, but Dominic felt nothing of the pain.

Hunter pulled a clean white handkerchief from his pocket and appeared by his side. First he checked there were no glass fragments in Dominic's hand, then used the handkerchief as a bandage to staunch the bleeding. He eyed Dominic with concern. 'This is worse than I thought,' he said, and Dominic knew Hunter was not referring to the cut upon his hand. 'You do not want me to, but I will say it anyway. You are making a mistake with her, Dominic.'

'Be that as it may, I will not give her up,' said Dominic; he knew he sounded stubborn and bad tempered and that he should relax and pretend that she did not matter to him in the slightest.

'I did not think that you would,' replied Hunter quietly. 'You do care for her, Dominic.'

'I care only that she warms my bed,' said Dominic and knew that he was not fooling Hunter for a minute, yet his pride would not let him admit the truth. He did not think he even understood himself what the truth was any more.

He tensed against any more of Hunter's questions, but his friend let the matter drop, clapping a hand of support against Dominic's shoulder. 'I think you are in need of another brandy.'

'It is just an arrangement for sex,' he insisted. Except Dominic knew that he was lying. Even Hunter knew he was lying. There were other aspects to what was between Arabella and him that he did not wish to think about. Depths he had not yet come to terms with. 'I know what I am doing, Sebastian.'

'I hope so, Dominic.' But Hunter did not look convinced.

A fortnight had passed when Arabella awoke with the sunlight streaming in through a crack in the curtains. The bed was still warm from Dominic's presence although he had left before dawn, as he did every morning. Whatever else Dominic was, at least he was discreet.

From the chamber above she heard the scurry of little footsteps. Archie. She smiled as she pulled on her dressing gown and went to find her son and her mother.

'You two slugabeds had best get yourselves up and readied, for today we are going out.'

'Is that such a good idea?' Mrs Tatton glanced round at her in surprise.

'I have heard tell of a wonderful new apothecary in Oxford Street who can mix the best of liniments for the joints. Besides, we have not been out of the house since our outing to the park and such confinement is not good for Archie, or for you. The weather is fine and an outing will do us all good.'

'What if we are seen by your gentleman while we are out?' said Mrs Tatton.

'We will be very careful. And he hates shopping.' She doubted Dominic had changed in that respect. 'I cannot think that we would meet him in the apothecary.'

'But after that last time, when he almost caught us... My stomach has been sick with nerves.'

'We will make sure we return here in plenty of time.' Arabella placed a reassuring hand on her mother's shoulder. 'Please come, Mama. I think it would do you good. And I promise you, nothing will go wrong.' Arabella felt a shiver of foreboding as soon as the words had left her mouth. She turned to her son, and lifted him on to her knee. 'What say you, Archie? I thought we might visit Gunter's for some ices before the apothecary.'

'Oh, can we, Mama?' His eyes shone with excitement.

She kissed Archie's cheek and then her mother's. 'Chop chop, then,' she said with a smile.

There really was very little chance of something going wrong, she told herself again and again, but that stubborn feeling of unease sat right there in her stomach and refused to shift.

She would only later learn that the feeling was called instinct and that she should have listened to it.

Chapter Ten

'I am so glad that you persuaded me to come. It is a lovely day and Archie is having such a fine time.' Her mother smiled as she and Arabella strolled along arm in arm, with Archie running before them breathless with excitement.

'Ooh, do look at that display, Arabella!' Mrs Tatton pulled Arabella over to admire the array of perfume bottles in the shop window. 'All the way from Paris and with matching scented soaps. How lovely.'

'This is the place of which I was speaking to you of—the apothecary who is highly recommended. Gemmell was telling me that he bought some liniment for the stiffness in his joints and it has worked wonders for him. And Cook swore that a tonic brought her sister back to health when she was dreadfully weakened following a fever. I was thinking we could buy some remedy for you, Mama.'

'If you think it would help.'

'There will be no hurt in trying.' Arabella raised

her eyebrows. 'And perhaps we might treat ourselves to some of that fine French soap while we are on the premises.'

Mrs Tatton laughed. And when Archie copied her, even though he did not understand what his grandmother was laughing about, Arabella could not help but join in.

The bell rang as they entered through the door, making the women who were standing in the middle of the shop floor beside a display of glass bottles glance round and notice Arabella and her family. The bottles which the women were inspecting were the same expensive Parisian perfumes as displayed in the shop's window. On seeing that Arabella was no one that they knew, the ladies ignored her and went back to choosing their perfume. Arabella watched them taking great pains over sniffing the scents that the shop assistant had touched to their hands using a variety of thin glass wands.

Two of the women were older; Arabella would guess of an age similar to her own mother's. But they were as haughty as Mrs Tatton was not. One look at their faces and Arabella could not help but draw a less-than-flattering conclusion as to their characters. The third woman was much younger, barely more than a girl. In contrast to the older women, one of whom Arabella was sure was the girl's mother due to a faint family resemblance, the girl seemed very quiet and eager to please.

'What do you mean, you like the sandalwood, Marianne?' demanded one of the formidable matrons. 'It is quite unsuitable for a young lady. Whatever would Sarah say were she to receive that as her birthday gift?'

The matron looked quickly to her companion. 'Forgive Marianne, Lady Fothergill, she can be such a silly goose at times. I am quite certain that she will admit that the rose fragrance is quite the most appropriate scent for her friend, albeit one of the most expensive choices.'

Arabella felt a pang of compassion for the girl. *Life with a mother like that could not be easy,* she thought as she turned her attention back to the apothecary who had arrived at the counter to serve them.

In the background she could hear the drone of the women's conversation, but Arabella was not listening. Rather she was concentrating on showing the apothecary her mother's hands and explaining about her mother's lungs. He suggested a warming liniment for Mrs Tatton's joints and a restorative tonic for her lungs, and disappeared off into the back of the shop to prepare them.

Mrs Tatton fitted her gloves back on while they waited and Arabella looked down at Archie. He was crouched by her side making his little wooden horse, Charlie, gallop around his feet and clicking quiet horsy noises to himself. Arabella smiled at the look of absorption upon his face. It was then that she heard the name 'Arlesford' spoken as clear as a bell. She tensed and could not help but listen in to the women's conversation.

'Close your ears, Lady Marianne, this is not talk for you,' one of the women was saying.

'Yes, Lady Fothergill,' said the girl, and Arabella resisted the urge to turn around and see if Lady Marianne had actually put her hands over her own ears. Then in lower quieter tones as if it were the greatest secret, Lady Fothergill continued, 'I am afraid I have to tell you the latest word, my poor dear, but they say that he has a mistress, and not just any mistress, one he bought from a bordello. Can you imagine?'

Arabella felt her blood run cold. She tried to keep her face clear and unaffected. The apothecary returned carrying a dark blue bottle and a small brown jar and placed them both down upon the counter.

'Might we also view your perfumed soaps, the ones that you have displayed in the front window?' she managed, and the smile fixed upon her face was broad and false.

'This is such a treat, Arabella,' said her mother.

'Yes.' Arabella nodded, still smiling, but almost the whole of her attention was focused on the conversation taking place behind her.

The other woman's voice stiffened with a defensive tone. 'Lady Fothergill, gentlemen will have their little foibles, but Arlesford is a duke and he knows his duty. I am sure that he will make a good husband.'

Arabella saw her mother's ears prick up at the mention again of Dominic's name and her stomach clenched all the tighter. She felt Mrs Tatton nudge her arm in a not altogether subtle way, and then her mother gestured with her eyes in the direction of the women behind them.

Arabella gave a tiny nod of acknowledgement to show that she understood the message.

'So is he still interested in Lady Marianne, Lady Misbourne?'

Arabella felt her blood run cold. Misbourne? An image of the masked bearded man from Vauxhall garden flashed in her mind, and she remembered the anger that had simmered within Dominic at their meeting, and his glib reply when she had asked who Misbourne was. No wonder he was so put out; meeting one's prospective father-in-law with your mistress on your arm was hardly the done thing.

The apothecary returned with the soaps, but Arabella and her mother were still listening intently. Arabella heard Mrs Tatton ask him to unwrap each soap that they might compare the smells, but Arabella could not move. She was frozen, holding her breath while she strained to hear Lady Misbourne's answer.

'Let us just say,' said Lady Misbourne, her voice less friendly than it had been at the start of her conversation with Lady Fothergill, 'that we are expecting an offer in the not-too-distant future. But that little piece of news is for your ears only, Lady Fothergill,'

'Of course,' said Lady Fothergill and there was something in the silky way that she said it that Arabella knew Lady Misbourne's news concerning Dominic and her daughter would be all around London by tomorrow. 'I think I shall choose the jasmine, Lady Misbourne. It is so exotic and so very expensive.'

The apothecary was clearing his throat and she felt her mother give her arm a little shake.

'Arabella, you are wool-gathering.' Mrs Tatton gave a false little laugh and slipped a hand to cover the white shining knuckles of Arabella's hands where she was gripping so tightly to the counter. 'I have come over a little unwell, my dear. Would you mind terribly if we were to come back for the soaps another day?'

Bless you, Mama. Bless your kindness, when her mother did not even know the full extent of the shock.

'Not at all,' Arabella said and then searched in her reticule for her purse to pay the apothecary. Her hands were trembling slightly in her haste to be gone and she set the money quickly down upon the counter, hoping that the apothecary would not notice. With the jar and bottle wrapped up in paper and tied with a handle of string, she took hold of Archie's hand and followed her mother out of the shop.

'Arabella, do not even think about that man. He is not worthy of it. From what I saw in there Dominic Furneaux is moving in all the right circles and most deservedly so I say. I wish him unhappy,' Mrs Tatton said, pure venom in her voice. She tucked Arabella's free hand into the crook of her arm. 'Now, we will not let their words bother us.'

'Indeed we will not,' said Arabella resolutely but she felt numb and chilled to the marrow and her mind was still reeling from what she had heard. Dominic was to marry. It should not have been such a very great shock. He was a duke. It was his duty to beget an heir, but she felt sick at the thought. Sick to the pit of her stomach at the memories those words stirred.

Her mother hurried her along the street and she just wanted to get away from this place and those women.

She heard the shop door-bell ring behind them.

'Excuse me, ma'am.' The girl's voice was tentative and as gentle and unassuming as her mother's was harsh and arrogant. Arabella did not need to turn round to know that it was Lady Marianne who had come out behind them. Lady Misbourne's daughter. The girl that Dominic was to marry.

Arabella did not want to look round. She wanted to keep on walking, to run away from this nightmare. But her mother had already stopped and turned.

Arabella had no choice.

'Your little boy, he left this behind.' There in the

girl's outstretched pink gloved hand was little wooden Charlie.

Lady Marianne was short and slender. A few fair curls that had escaped her pins peeped from the straw of her bonnet. She was dressed in an expensive pink walking dress and pelisse overloaded with lace and ribbon, chosen by Lady Misbourne Arabella guessed. But the outfit did little to detract from the girl's beauty; her sweet face was stunning. Her skin had the smooth creamy opalescence of youth, her features were fine and neat, and her eyes were large and a deep dark brown.

'Thank you,' Arabella said with a smile that would not touch her eyes no matter how hard she tried to make it, and she took the little wooden horse from the girl's hand.

'Thank very much, miss,' said Archie politely so that even given the strain of the situation, she was proud of him and his manners.

Lady Misbourne's daughter smiled at Archie. 'You are very welcome,' she said to him kindly. 'He looks as if he is a very special horse.'

'Oh, he is,' said Archie. 'Gemmell made him for my birthday, and my mama took me to the park and let me and Charlie ride upon a real horse.'

'That is quite enough, Archie. I am sure that the lady is too busy for your stories.'

'Oh, not at all,' said Lady Marianne shyly. 'He is such a sweet boy.'

'Marianne!' Lady Misbourne appeared in the doorway and cast Arabella and her mother a haughty look of dislike.

'Please excuse me,' said Lady Marianne to Arabella and Mrs Tatton, 'but I must not keep my mama waiting.'

She gave Archie a big grin and then she hurried back to where her mother's face was growing sourer by the minute.

Arabella, her mother and Archie walked on along the street.

'I liked that lady,' said Archie and gave a little skip. 'And so did Charlie. I think when I am a grown-up man I shall marry her.' His innocent words drove the blade deeper, right up to the hilt.

'Archie, stop talking such nonsense and walk smartly,' she heard her mother say brusquely.

Arabella's heart was throbbing. And this time she could not force herself to smile. She felt bitter and angry and unbelievably hurt. He had lied to her and betrayed her. He had bought her to keep as another one of his possessions. All of that and yet she was overwhelmed with such a terrible sense of grief, a raw keening agony that gouged at her heart.

The journey home seemed never ending. But, at last, she was able to climb from the coach outside the town house in Curzon Street and make her way in through the opened front door to the welcome of Gemmell, while her mother and Archie stayed hidden in the coach until it drove round to the stables.

Dominic sent a note to say that he could not visit that evening, and Arabella lay alone in bed that night, mulling over the dismal mess of the situation. Everything she had done had been for Archie, everything she was still doing was for her son. She had sold herself, swallowed the humiliation of becoming Dominic's mistress. Worse than that, she had given herself to him in love, because even after everything she could not pretend that her heart was so divorced from him. But now she had to consider the implication of his impending marriage.

He was a duke. Of course he was required to marry. How naïve she had been not to think of it. Once upon a time it was Arabella who would have been his wife. Now she was his whore. The knowledge hurt, as did the thought of him making another woman his wife. And what would it mean for her when he married? Would he still expect their arrangement to continue? Would he come seeking her bed at night before going home to that of Lady Marianne? The thought was anathema to Arabella. She could not bear to think of it.

She climbed from the bed and went to stand by the window, to look out upon the moonlit street. The hour was late and the street was empty except for the night-soil cart that was travelling slowly past and the squat man that walked by its side. She stood and watched, knowing that she was not going to find sleep that night. And in the dark shadowed corners of her mind was the image of the Whitechapel workhouse not so very far from Flower and Dean Street.

Chapter Eleven

Within the drawing room the next evening, after they had eaten and put Archie to bed, Arabella and her mother were darning a pile of Archie's stockings, during which Mrs Tatton was making every effort to cheer Arabella just as she had been doing since they had heard about Dominic Furneaux during their shopping trip. But rather than making her feel better, Mrs Tatton's diatribe on Dominic Furneaux and his failings was making Arabella feel worse.

'If that wretched man had done his duty, it never would have come to this. Why, if I were ever to clap eyes on him again I would tell him exactly what—'

There was an urgent knock at the drawing-room door and then Gemmell hurried in without waiting to be told to enter. One look at the butler's face and Arabella realised that something was wrong. Even Mrs Tatton's heated harangue ceased when she saw him.

'It is the d—' He glanced at her mother and then

amended what he had been about to say. 'The master,' he finished. 'Just drawn up outside this very minute.'

'I did not hear his carriage,' said Arabella.

Her mother paled with fright.

'Come quickly, Mrs Tatton, James here will help you upstairs.' Gemmell gestured to her mother.

Her mother jumped to her feet, forgetting all about Archie's stockings that she was darning so that they tumbled on to the floor. 'Oh, my word! Oh, my word! He will catch me for sure.' Her arms were flapping about in a panic.

'Stay calm, Mama, there is time enough yet. No, leave that,' Arabella said as her mother stooped to pick up the scattered stockings. 'I will see to them. You go with James, quickly now.'

Mrs Tatton half-ran, half-hobbled from the room to take hold of the footman's arm and the last Arabella saw, her mother was being propelled along the passageway on the arm of the footman.

She wasted no further time, for Gemmell was already hurrying to the front door to have it open in time for Dominic to reach the top of the stone stairs that led up to it. Arabella trusted him and knew that the old butler would not open the door until her mother had disappeared from sight, even if it meant he had to do the unthinkable and keep a duke waiting outside his own front door.

She crouched on the drawing-room floor and began gathering up Archie's stockings. The front door opened.

Gemmell's voice.

Then Dominic's sounded. And there was the steady tread of booted footsteps coming along the passageway. She had grabbed the last stockings and was hiding them behind the cushion of the armchair just as Dominic entered the drawing room.

Arabella jumped and looked flustered. There was a hint of colour in her cheeks, some of her hair had escaped its pins to fluff around her neck and face and she seemed a little out of breath.

'I was just darning some stockings,' she said and stuffed the stockings out of sight.

'What need have you to darn anything? Am I not paying you enough to buy new?'

He saw the way she stiffened and the heightened colour on her cheeks and regretted his words immediately.

'I do not like waste,' she said. 'A few stitches with a needle and the stockings are repaired almost as new.'

Make do and mend. And that same unease whispered about him as to the circumstances of Arabella's life that had led her to a brothel.

There was an awkward silence between them and then she said, 'You should have told me about Lord Misbourne's daughter, Dominic.'

So, Misbourne's lies had permeated even this far. 'There is nothing to tell, Arabella.'

'Nothing?' She stared at him and he saw the anger flash in her eyes. 'I know better. Little wonder that you were so displeased to meet him with me upon your arm! I *know*, so you need not pretend otherwise.' She was angry and reckless with it. Her face was pale, her eyes troubled.

'You know nothing other than a false rumour, Arabella.'

'Stop it, Dominic! I heard it from Lady Misbourne's mouth with my own ears.'

He stilled, his pulse suddenly beating fast. 'You have spoken to Lady Misbourne?'

'Not directly. I overheard her conversation with another.'

'And what exactly did you overhear?'

'That you are interested in her daughter as your duchess. That they are expecting you to offer for her shortly.'

He gave a cold hard laugh, although there was nothing of mirth in what he was feeling. 'They may expect, Arabella, but they shall receive nothing.'

'But she is wealthy and an earl's daughter,' and he heard the slight bitterness in Arabella's voice. 'Surely you cannot fault that *she* is a suitable match for you?'

'I have no intention of marrying Lady Marianne Winslow.'

Something changed in her face as if a new thought had only just made itself known to her, and all of the bitterness dropped away to be replaced with concern. 'You have not ruined her, have you, Dominic?'

He gave a cynical laugh that she could believe such a thing of him. Even though he was a rake. And even though everyone knew that fact. 'You need have no fear for the girl's virtue on my score, I assure you, Arabella,' he said coldly.

'At least have the decency to tell me the truth!'

'I *am* telling you the truth,' he said.

'I heard Lady Misbourne's words.'

'She is misinformed, I tell you.'

'No.'

'Yes, Arabella!'

They looked at one another, with only the sound of their breath in the silence.

'I will not marry Lady Marianne for the same reason I will not marry any other.'

He saw the shock, the confusion, the suspicion in her eyes. He should stop now, but he could not. He moved forwards.

'Shall I tell you why there will be no Duchess of Arlesford? Do you want the whole ugly truth of it?'

She backed away a little.

'Of how I have longed for you through the years?' He stepped closer.

She edged back.

'Of how I have relived those last moments a thousand times in my head?' Another step. 'God dammit, Arabella, I loved you!'

'No!' she cried. 'Do not say it. I do not want to hear more of your lies. You never loved me! You only wanted me in your bed and once you had had that—'

Dominic backed her against the wall and placed a hand around the nape of her neck, forcing her to look at him that she might see the truth from which she was so intent on hiding.

'*I loved you,* Arabella,' he said savagely and stared down into her eyes.

'Stop it!' She tried to turn away, but he would not let her. 'Why are you doing this?'

'Because I loved you,' he said again, more gently this time and he could no longer hide the hurt of what she had done to him. 'Arabella,' he said softly, and her gaze moved unwilling to his. 'Arabella,' he said again and looked into her eyes and let her see the truth.

She stopped struggling. Stilled. Stared at him. And the pain that he saw in her eyes was as raw and aching as that in his heart. They stared at one another and everything else in the world ceased to be.

'I loved you too, Dominic,' she said and her voice was thick with emotion.

In the silence he could hear the soft sound of her breath and beneath his fingers he could feel the throb of her pulse.

'Then why did you marry Marlbrook?' It was the question he had waited almost six years to ask.

She opened her mouth to reply, then closed it again and shook her head. But there could be no mistaking the look of anguish upon her face. She looked as tortured as he felt.

His hand moved from the nape of her neck to thread through her hair. He angled her face all the closer to his so close that her lips were within an inch of capture.

'Tell me,' he insisted.

She shook her head again in an infinitesimal motion of denial, but in her eyes he saw something of her resolve crumble and beneath it the flicker of fear.

'You know that I would never hurt you, no matter what,' he said softly.

'You already did, Dominic,' she whispered.

He felt something break apart inside of him at her answer. 'I do not understand. Tell me,' he said again.

She looked deep into his eyes. 'How can you really not know?'

'You married Marlbrook,' he said and knew that he was missing something of monumental importance.

'Yes.'

'Then you did not love me.'

'I loved you more than anything.'

'Then why?' he demanded.

'God, please help me,' she whispered and her voice was trembling. Then she raised her mouth to his and kissed him. Something of that kiss seemed to reach in and stroke against Dominic's soul so that when she withdrew her lips he felt almost bereft. They stared into each other's eyes, and the intensity of the moment was taut between them.

He knew that she was hiding something of the truth from him. And standing here right now looking into her eyes it did not make any difference. He still needed her at every level that was possible. And he knew that whatever else she said, Arabella needed him too. With all of the emotion that was roaring between them it was only a matter of time before she told him what he wanted to know.

His heart was beating in hard steady strokes as he kissed her. His hand slipped around hers and then he took her to bed and made love to her.

Arabella awoke with the early morning light stealing through the curtains to find Dominic still in her bed. He was snuggled against her back, his hand draped against the nakedness of her stomach and her bottom nestled into his crotch.

She lay there for a moment, letting herself revel in the warm strong feel of him before letting reality and all of its worries back in again.

I loved you, Arabella. She heard the whisper of his words running through her head again and knew she should not believe him. If he had loved her so much then he would not have treated her so badly. Words were cheap and so easily woven into a pretty pattern of lies. Actions were what counted. A man's deeds. What he did rather than what he said. And yet even knowing all that, lying here naked in Dominic's arms, her body bearing the scent of his loving, she knew that she wanted to believe him. Her head might know he was lying, yet her heart was a different matter all together.

She craned her neck up to see the clock on the mantel. Five o'clock. Too early, but she knew from the hum in her body that she would not go back to sleep. She was too aware of Dominic and all that was happening between them, the tumultuous peaks of physical ecstasy and troughs of emotional misery. She tried to ease his fingers from her stomach, but the large hand with its long fingers tightened against her.

'Arabella?' His voice was husky from sleep. She felt the stirring of his arousal against her buttocks.

'You are awake.' She rolled round to face him, carefully opening up a small distance between them, not knowing how things would be between them this morning, whether he would probe again into the past, asking questions that were too dangerous to answer.

He smiled and there was about him this morning none of the tension that had been so evident between them last night.

The growth of dark stubble peppered his cheeks and chin. He looked piratical and dangerous and wicked and yet the look in his eyes was loving and velvet and molten. He glanced towards the clock, then smiled again in that way that made her heart somersault.

With an easy, unhurried air he rose from the bed and, without the slightest self-consciousness over his nakedness, made his way over to the pitcher and basin to wash. Arabella sat up, pulling the sheets up high to cover her own nudity, and watched him. His shoulders were broad, tapering down to slim hips. His every movement created ripples in the muscles that defined it. She watched the droplets of water roll down the pale golden skin of his back.

He glanced round and saw her sitting there watching him. She felt her cheeks heat and looked quickly away.

'I will call one of the footman to help you dress.' She slipped from the bed, grabbed up her shift and held it against her to preserve some measure of modesty, then hurried over to the wardrobe to fetch her dressing gown. She opened the wardrobe door using it as a screen between herself and Dominic. The shift dropped to the floor and she slipped on the thin cotton dressing gown, tying its belt around her waist. But when she closed the cupboard door Dominic was standing right there looking at her.

'I do not need a footman.' His voice was husky and his eyes seemed to darken with hunger as he looked at her. She saw his gaze drop lower and watched while he reached a hand across to rub the back of his wet knuckles gently against her breast, wetting the thin white cotton to render it transparent. Her nipple hardened and strained rosy and peaked through the material. He rubbed against it a little longer and she felt desire shimmer right through her. His hand dropped lower to tug one end of her belt so that the loose knot parted and the gown fell open.

'I am not washed,' she said, feeling embarrassed at how wantonly her body was responding to him even in daylight.

He leaned in closer and took her mouth with his, kissing her to make her forget all of her protestations. He smiled again. 'Then let me wash you.' And he lifted the soap.

'Open your legs.'

Arabella stared at him. Her heart was beating very fast. 'You cannot,' she whispered.

'Don't you want me to?' he replied against her lips, then nuzzled kisses against her neck.

She knew that it was wrong, that she should not want any of this. But when he peeled the dressing gown off her shoulders, sliding it down her body to land upon the floor, and kissed her, she wrapped her arms around him and returned his kiss with passion.

Dominic deepened the kiss and ran his hand over her body, stroking her, and caressing her with a touch that was both gentle yet possessive. And then he moved away and she saw him lather up his hands in the water. And her mouth went dry.

He turned to her; there was such a hunger in his eyes that she felt herself tremble. One arm snaked around her waist, pulling him to her.

His mouth was hot against her ear. 'Open your legs,' he whispered.

'Dominic…' she protested.

He kissed her mouth, a long stroking sensual kiss that ended in him biting softly against her lower lip.

Her body reacted independently of her mind; her legs opened for him and she felt him touch her. The water was cold against her heat and she gasped both from the shock of that and the audacity of what he was doing. He massaged her gently, washing her with a thoroughness that made her legs tremble. And then he rinsed her, cupping handfuls of water over her so that it ran it rivulets down her thighs while she gasped with the wanton pleasure of it. Her legs were shaking so much that she collapsed against him. Dominic gathered her up in his arms and carried her to the bed.

She pulled him to her, knowing where this was leading and wanting it all the same, wanting him as if she still loved him. Because when he touched her something inside opened up to him and she could not stop herself from this any more than she could stop her heart from beating or her lungs from breathing. It was more than desire, more than just a physical intimacy. She needed his warmth, his strength, his tenderness. She needed to be able to forget the worry and the pain. She needed to feel this sharing of a heart. Love, even pretended, after all the years of unhappiness, was a balm to Arabella's soul.

'Dominic,' she breathed and felt him move over her and kiss her all the more. She opened to him, wanting him to take her, needing to feel him inside her. And in response the probe of his manhood pressed between her legs. She wriggled her hips, her hands sliding to his firm flank to pull him against her.

'Arabella,' he groaned her name, and she could hear his need in his voice and feel it in the tension that vibrated throughout his body. For all that his movements were controlled she could sense the urgency beneath. His mouth left hers and he adjusted his position to slide lower down her body so that she thought he meant to kiss her breasts, to taste her, to suckle from her. Her nipples hardened with unbearable sensitivity just at the thought of it and between her legs grew even slicker.

But Dominic did not stop at her breasts. When he kept on moving she threaded her fingers through his hair and tried to guide him back to where her nipples ached for his touch. His gaze held hers, all dark and blazing with desire, and as she watched he placed a single kiss just below her ribcage. And then, keeping his gaze locked with hers, he kissed her again, this time lower, in the centre of her stomach…and then a third time, just at the line of her pelvis.

'Dominic!' She tried to close her legs. 'You surely do not mean to—'

But he did.

His warm breath stirred the small patch of golden hair as his mouth touched to her secret woman's place.

She gasped at that first kiss, at the wonder of the sensation that shot through her body. And by the time he was working a magic with his tongue she forgot to bite her lip and groaned her pleasure aloud.

'Dominic,' she whispered, but he did not stop and she was arching her back and driving herself harder into his mouth, reaching for him, needing him with an urgency that obliterated all else. And when his hands closed over her breasts and she felt his fingers pluck at her taut straining nipples she reached her climax, exploding in the sensation, her body soft and pulsing her pleasure against him.

He kissed her thighs, kissed the curve of each hip, kissed his way up to take her in his arms. And then he gently stroked the long wanton curls from where they spilled over her face and looked at her with such love that her heart welled with joy to see it.

'Arabella,' he whispered and she loved him in that moment despite everything, she loved him against all rhyme and reason.

She pulled him closer and felt his hardness press against her leg. She wanted to pleasure him as he had pleasured her. She reached down and touched him.

She stroked the long hard length of his manhood and heard the breath catch in his throat and felt the tremble that racked his body. He lay still and let her take him, giving her the power to do whatever she willed.

She moved back, wanting to see him, wanting to see her fingers as they caressed his member, stroking that silken skin from its tip all the way down to the base amidst the nest of dark hair.

The groan escaped him. She held his gaze and bent her head to taste him...just as a door slammed shut upstairs.

The noise brought Dominic crashing back to reality. He could feel that Arabella had frozen at the sound.

'It is nothing, Dominic.' Her voice was too loud, too desperate, and he saw the flash of fear from her eyes. 'Let it not interrupt us.'

But then the thud of running footsteps sounded through the ceiling above.

Arabella's eyes widened. Her hand gripped tighter to his shaft.

She tried to stop him as he pulled away from her and tugged on his breeches. 'No, Dominic, please!' She jumped up, pulling on her dressing gown and tying its belt quickly around her waist.

They could both hear the tumble of feet on the main staircase.

'No!' She ran in front of him, blocking his path to the door. Her hair was long and wild, her face devoid of all colour and in her eyes was desperation. 'Dominic!' she cried and tried to push him back. 'Do not!' She threw her full weight against him, trying to prevent his continued progress.

The footsteps grew louder as they headed along the passageway towards them.

He grabbed her wrists, secured her hands behind her, resting them lightly against the small of her back so that her breasts were thrust against his chest.

'Who have you hidden in this house, Arabella?' he asked, and even to his own ears his voice sounded harsh. He thought of Marlbrook and a wave of jealousy swept right through him.

'No one!' She struggled against him. 'Please, Dominic, I beg of you!'

'Mama!' a child's voice called and little fists pounded at the door.

The shock stole the words he would have spoken. He released his hold of her wrists. Her eyes were wide with anguish as she stared up at him.

'Where are you, Mama?' the child cried. 'I dreamt that you and Grandmama had gone away and when I woke I was all alone.'

She turned and, opening the door, scooped the child, clad in a long white nightshirt, up into her arms. 'Here I am, little lamb. It was just a silly old dream. I have been here all along, in my bedchamber, as I always am. Now hush, Archie, there is no need for tears.' And she kissed the child and hugged him to her, and soothed a hand against his hair.

Dominic stared and his heart contracted as hard as if a fist had squeezed it, for the little boy in Arabella's arms was the very image of himself.

Chapter Twelve

He watched as Arabella glanced around at the woman puffing breathlessly along the corridor.

'Forgive me, Arabella.' She hurried right up to Arabella and he saw at once who she was. 'He was asleep and I was only gone for a minute to take care of my needs. I am so very sorry.' And then Mrs Tatton glanced anxiously towards him standing there in the bedchamber. Her mouth fell open and she stared with an expression of horror at her daughter. 'Dominic Furneaux! You did not tell me it was him! He is your protector? The one who has paid for all of this?'

Arabella nodded as she rocked the child gently in her arms.

'How could you, Arabella,' Mrs Tatton burst out, 'after what he did to you?'

Arabella made no sign of having heard her mother's words. She spoke to the child again. 'Now, Archie, you must let Grandmama take you back to bed, for it is too early to be up and about.' She kissed the little boy's forehead and smoothed the tangle of his dark locks. 'Be a good boy—I will be up to see you soon.'

'Yes, Mama,' the child said and when she set him back down upon the ground he dutifully took hold of Mrs Tatton's hand, and glanced with curiosity at Dominic as she led him from the room. Mrs Tatton followed the boy's gaze and if looks could have killed the one that the older woman shot him would have had him dead upon the floor. The door closed with a brisk click behind them.

Arabella had not moved. She stood where she was, her eyes hooded and cautious, her face pale.

'He is my son, isn't he?'

She did not answer, just stood there so still yet he could see the rapid rise and fall of her chest beneath the dressing gown and feel the strain in her silence.

'Isn't he, Arabella?' he demanded and he knew his voice was harsh with the shock that was coursing through him.

'Of course he is your son! Why else would I have married Henry Marlbrook in such haste after you left me?' The words exploded from her. 'But do not think, for one minute, that I shall let you take him from me, Dominic!' There was something of the tigress in her eyes, a ruthlessness, a strength, an absolute determination, and he knew that she would fight to her last breath to defend their child.

'I have no intention of taking him from you.' Mrs Tatton's words echoed in his head: *...after what he did to you...* The hostility of the woman's attitude, and of Arabella's own words—*after you left me*—prickled a warning at the nape of his neck. And foreboding was heavy upon him.

'You speak as if it was I responsible for our breaking apart,' he said slowly.

'How can you deny it?' she retorted with eyes that flashed their fury. 'You just upped and offed without so much as a word. Not one consideration for my feelings, not one for what you might be leaving behind. I was nineteen, Dominic. Nineteen!'

His blood flowed like ice. His stomach was brimful with dread. 'What do you mean, Arabella?'

'You know very well what I mean!' she shouted.

'I do not.' He forced himself to remain calm, to carry on despite the dread deep in the marrow of his bones. 'Tell me.'

'John Smith saw us coming out of Fisher's barn that last day. He told my father and my father had the truth from me. He already knew, Dominic, and I could not lie to him. He was angry and disappointed. He went to your father, the duke, and told him that our betrothal must be made formal and the wedding arranged as soon as possible.'

That Mr Tatton had ever visited on such a mission was news to Dominic. He had a terrible premonition of what his father had done.

'Why are you even making me tell you all this?' she cried. 'Was it not cruel enough the first time round?'

'Tell me, Arabella.'

She pushed at him and tried to turn away, but he grabbed hold of her and pulled her back round to face him, knowing he needed to hear every word of the nightmare. 'For God's sake, tell me,' he insisted. 'What did my father say?'

'That the matter would rest with you and you alone.

And like a fool I thought everything would be all right.' The tears spilled from her eyes to roll down her cheeks.

'Arabella,' he whispered and tried to wipe them away, but she struck his hand away as if she could not bear to have him touch her. And then she hit out at his chest, pushing him, trying to free herself, again and again until he captured her wrists and held her still.

'You coward!' she yelled through the tears. 'To send your father in your stead because you had not the courage to tell me yourself!'

The ice spread through his veins. 'You are saying that my father visited you.' It was no question for he could already see the whole horrid story beginning to unfold before his very eyes.

'You know that he did, for you sent him, Dominic!' She ceased struggling, but she was crying in earnest now, the tears streaming all the harder.

'No, Arabella, I did not,' he said, 'I did not send him, Arabella. I did not even know that your father had come to the house.' He felt numb and sick and furious all at once.

'Why are you lying?' she cried. 'Have you not humiliated me enough? Is it not enough that I am your mistress? That you own me? Must you seek to hurt me more with these lies?' She bowed her head that he would not see her crying.

'Arabella, look at me!' And when she would not he took her face between his hands and made her. 'I am not lying.'

She fought against him.

'I am not lying, Arabella.'

And something of his sincerity must have reached her for she seemed to still and hear what he was saying properly for the first time. She looked up into his eyes. And there was such vulnerability there, such hurt that it made everything he had felt across the years pale in comparison.

'I am not lying,' he said for a third time, soft as a breath against her face. 'I swear it on all that is holy.' His hands slid down to her upper arms, holding her in place, supporting her. He could hear the small shudder in her breathing and feel the tremor that ran through her body.

'I do not understand.' Her words were a cracked whisper.

'I think I am beginning to,' he said grimly. 'Tell me what my father said to you, Arabella?'

'He explained it all very carefully. That you did not want me. That young men will be young men and sow their wild oats. And when my own father pointed out that young men must be held responsible for their actions and demanded that you be forced to wed me, he said that he would do no such thing—for surely we could all see that, despite my gentle birth, I was too poor and lowly to be a future duke's wife. He said that such a marriage would be a *mésalliance* and that we had never really been betrothed.'

'That bastard!' The curse could not be bitten back. 'He knew that I loved you and meant to marry you. Hell, he even knew about the locket!'

'My father showed him the locket, and the duke laughed and said that it was no proof of a betrothal and that we could hardly sue for breach of promise. He gave my father money and told us it would go better for us if we kept quiet.' Every word that she spoke was like a cut to his heart. Every word revealing the terrible enormity of what his father had done.

He shook his head, even now hardly able to believe it. 'My own father did this,' he whispered, more to himself than Arabella. The man he had loved and respected and admired. The very foundation on which he had built his life shifted, making a mockery of everything in which he had believed for the last years.

'My God!' There was a sickness in his stomach and he felt chilled to the very core of his being. It took every last drop of his determination to hang on to his self-control.

Arabella could see the strain in Dominic's face, his pallor, the tight press of his lips as he struggled with the magnitude of emotion. In his eyes was such a deadly rage that she almost felt afraid. And she knew from the terribleness of his reaction that he was telling the truth. And if he was telling the truth, then that meant...

The floor beneath her feet felt as unsteady as everything else in her world. She was reeling, floundering with a realisation beyond anything she could ever have imagined. She swayed and felt him clutch her hard against him.

There were a thousand thoughts milling in her head, all of them tearing at the beliefs she had constructed for herself over the years. She felt chilled all the way through, so cold that she could never imagine being warm again. And she knew that she was trembling, but she just could not stop no matter how hard she willed it.

Dominic swept her up into his arms and carried her to the bed where he sat her down on its edge and swathed the covers around her.

'Why would he do such a thing, Dominic?'

Dominic's face was hard and cynical. *'My father,'* and his lip curled with disgust as he spoke the words, 'did not think you a suitable match, Arabella. He said that you were a young man's infatuation. That I would tire of you eventually. That I had a duty to the dukedom to marry either money or status.'

She had known her own unsuitability even then, but Dominic had told her that he would make his own choice and that his choice was her. 'But the old duke was only ever affable to my face. He never so much as suggested a murmur of these thoughts. I believed him understanding of our betrothal.' She shook her head at her own naïvety.

'It was my father who persuaded me to keep the betrothal quiet and informal. He said that if it lasted then he would give it his blessing and make a formal announcement. I never imagined for one minute that he would stoop to such a level.'

'I cannot quite comprehend what you are telling me, Dominic,' she whispered; she felt frozen and numb inside.

'I can barely credit it myself.' His voice was soft, but she shuddered to hear the intensity within it.

He sat down on the bed by her side. And they just sat there in silence.

'Tell me what happened to you,' she said. Every word was torture, but she needed to know. And she knew he needed to tell her. 'You went away.'

'He sent me to my uncle in Scotland. Told me some story of a sudden illness and that he did not feel up to making such a long journey. Could I go in his stead?' His voice was low, his words deadened almost, with a something of a terrible unnatural quiet to them. 'I was forced to leave that very night, but I wrote you a note of explanation and left instructions for its delivery to you. And then I wrote to you every day from Scotland.' He gave a laugh so hard and cynical that it made her blood run cold. 'Little wonder that there was never a reply. You did not receive my letters, did you, Arabella? My father saw to that.'

She shook her head. 'There was no note of explanation. There were never any letters.'

'Was my uncle a part of this ruse? Was he even really ill at all?' He stared into the distance as if he could see the past there. 'Will we ever really know the level of treachery, Arabella?'

She could not answer. She did not know.

He shook his head as if he had his own answer.

'I stayed with him during what I thought was his convalescence and when I returned home you were gone. Married to Marlbrook, they said. A man old enough to be your father.' He looked round at her. 'I thought you had forsaken me for him, Arabella.'

'Never.' Her voice was thick with strain. 'What choice did I have once I realised our child was growing in my belly? Henry was kind. He knew of my situation and was prepared to overlook it.'

'That is why you married him. At last I understand. You thought I had abandoned you.'

'For all these years,' she whispered.

'You were my love, Arabella. My heart. My life.' His voice cracked and she saw the restraint within him shatter and the great storm of emotion unleash. He sprang to his feet. 'Damn my father to hell! Damn him, Arabella. I would kill him myself were he not already dead! He has ruined my life, and your life, and that of an innocent child!' His voice shook with passion. 'I have a son, Arabella, and I did not know! A son!' The words tore from his throat as he turned away and punched his fist hard into the door. His head drooped and in the resounding silence that followed she could hear only the raggedness of his breathing. He turned to her then, and looked at her and the agony on his face was terrible to see.

'Tell me, Arabella,' he said quietly, 'did my father know the truth of that too?'

'No.' She could spare him that at least. 'My own father was a proud man. He said that the duke had already made his feelings clear and he would not go back on his knees and beg. He thought it bad enough that we had taken his money and that it was as if you had enforced the *droit de seignuir* from the old feudal days when the lord thought he had the right to take the maidenhead of his serfs.'

He flinched at the word. He walked to stand before her. 'You moved away so that I would not know.'

'It was one of the duke's requirements. Henry raised Archie as his own even though the truth was so plain to see.'

Dominic looked like he was breaking apart as he stood there. She watched him close his eyes. Heard him murmur, 'My God, Arabella.'

On the door behind him she could see the smear of his blood. Nothing seemed real. Dominic had not left her. He had not abandoned her. And truth revealed only a worse tragedy than any of them could have imagined. For Dominic, and for her, and for their son upstairs.

'You are bleeding,' she said.

He did not even glance down at his hand with his

grazed and bruised knuckles. 'I should have been there to protect you, Arabella.'

'Please, Dominic…' Her voice broke. There were no words that could make any of it better.

'I should have been your husband, Arabella. I should have been a father to my son.'

She began to weep for all that they had lost.

He came to her and sat beside her, scooping her on to his lap as if she were a small child. And then he held her close and rocked her, and she heard his voice against her hair.

'God help us, Arabella. I will do my best for you and for Archie. I swear it.'

And Arabella laid her head against his chest.

Chapter Thirteen

The clock on the mantel was striking two as Arabella watched Archie pretend to groom the little wooden horse that Gemmell had given him.

'You must go to sleep in your stable, Charlie.' She could hear the softness of his voice as he spoke to the toy before hiding it behind the cushion of the sofa and galloping off across the drawing room making neighing noises.

Sitting on the sofa beside her, Mrs Tatton leaned closer and lowered her voice.

'I cannot believe that Dominic Furneaux is behind all of this.' She peered angrily at Arabella. 'You should have told me, Arabella.'

'Mama,' Arabella sighed. 'You must realise why I did not. It was a difficult situation and I knew how you felt about him.'

'I thought you felt the same,' said her mother. 'Lord, but that man ruined your life. He ruined all our lives!'

'Mama, I have already explained that none of it

was Dominic's fault. He suffered as much from this as we did.'

'Nowhere near, Arabella,' said Mrs Tatton. 'He did not have to work his fingers to the bone, or live in a rookery, or go hungry.'

'No, Mama. But he suffered all the same.' When she thought of how much of his son's life he had missed out on she felt terrible.

Her mother gave a snort of disbelief and moved on. 'What are his intentions now that he is aware of Archie and me?'

'He means to do his best for us.'

'And precisely how does he plan to do that?' Mrs Tatton demanded.

'There are no easy answers to any of this. The past cannot be so easily undone.' Lost years could not be recaptured. A little boy's childhood could not be relived. The knowledge broke her heart.

'Nor undone at all, Arabella. How can what happened ever be made right?'

'I do not know, Mama. I need time to think. Dominic needs time to think. There is much to be considered.'

'Much indeed,' muttered her mother. She glanced up to the ceiling and lowered her voice again. 'Why is he still up there? Why does he not leave?'

'He is giving us some time together, and when I feel that we are ready I will ask him to come down. He wishes to meet Archie.'

'I'm sure he does.' Her mother's mouth pressed into a thin line of disapproval. 'Abominable rake! Do you think he will marry you?' Mrs Tatton made it sound ridiculous.

'I know he cannot marry me, Mama. Not now.' The words were bitter in her mouth.

'He is the Duke of Arlesford, Arabella. It would be unimaginable if he were to marry you. Think of the scandal.'

'I know, Mama.' He would keep her here as his mistress and make love to her at night, and pay for everything that she and his son wanted. There would be no more skulking and hiding for her mother and Archie. She should have been glad of it but her heart was heavier and more aching than it had ever been. She sat the teacup and saucer back down upon the table lest its tremor betray her distress.

'Dominic has a duty to the Arlesford seat. No, Arabella, believe me when I tell you that he must marry some rich, well-connected girl, a girl with an untarnished reputation and a father that moves in the right circles.'

A girl like Lady Marianne Winslow.

It was Arabella's unsuitability to be his bride that had caused this whole mess in the first place.

'And when he weds her, what then of you, Arabella? Will he keep you here as his mistress while he begets children on his duchess?' Mrs Tatton shook her head and stared at Arabella with concern. 'And what of Archie? What will become of him when Dominic begins to fill the nursery at Shardeloes with sons who are not born out of wedlock?'

She stared at her mother, appalled at the images she was conjuring.

'He will not be so keen to visit his bastard son then.'

'Archie was not born out of wedlock. I was married to Henry,' she whispered furiously.

'If you think that there is anyone who will believe Archie to be anything other than Dominic's you are fooling yourself, girl! One look at the boy and it is clear. Arabella...' Mrs Tatton sighed again and she took Arabella's hand in her own. 'You must handle this negotiation very carefully indeed both for your own sake and for Archie's.'

'Negotiation? You make it sound like some new arrangement with a protector!'

'Is that not precisely what this is, Arabella? A renegotiation?'

'No! It is not like that.'

'Then what is it like, Arabella?'

Arabella turned her face away, and could give no reply. She did not know herself what it was like, this situation into which they had all been thrust. There were no words to describe what she felt. Confusion and hope and bruising. Love and anger and resentment. And disbelief, an overwhelming sense that this was all some awful nightmare from which she would awaken. She loved Dominic, but her heart was still aching. And there seemed no way to make it better. She loved him, but it was all too late. Because her mother was right. No matter how she dressed it up otherwise, he had bought her from a brothel and made her his mistress. And nothing could change that.

'Mrs Tatton,' Dominic bowed to Arabella's mother.

'Your Grace,' said Mrs Tatton grudgingly and looked at him with daggers in her eyes.

Dominic turned and stared at the little boy; he felt his heart contract and a feeling of tenderness expand through him. Archie was a miniature youthful version of himself. The same dark brown eyes, the same purposeful chin, his hair only a slightly lighter shade of brown than Dominic's own.

'Dominic, this is Archie.' Arabella had a hand upon the boy's shoulder in a gesture to reassure the child.

'Are you my mama's friend?' He saw the innocent curiosity in Archie's eyes.

Dominic's gaze fleetingly met Arabella's before coming back to the child's. He crouched down, so that Archie did not have to tilt his head right back to look at him. 'I am your friend too, Archie.' He was aware of Mrs Tatton sitting in one of the armchairs in the background and the blatant look of dislike upon her face, but he paid her no attention.

'This is Dominic,' Arabella told the child.

Your father, he wanted to say, but knew that he must not. Arabella was right, they must handle this very slowly and gently.

Archie gave a polite little bow. 'I am very pleased to meet you, sir.'

'And I am very pleased to meet you too, Archie.' This was his son, flesh of his flesh, blood of his blood. 'Your mama tells me that you are very fond of horses.'

Archie nodded.

'That makes two of us.' He smiled. And Archie smiled back at him, and at the sight of it Dominic felt a huge wave of emotion hit him and his heart seemed to melt into a pool of overwhelming love. He gave a gruff nod and, suddenly frightened that he was going to start weeping, rose to his full height and cleared his throat.

'I will return tomorrow, Arabella,' he said.

She nodded; there was a look of such tenderness in her eyes when she looked at their son that it made him want to weep all the more. He made his bow to her and to her mother, and he left, while he still could.

Dominic waved his secretary away with his diary of missed appointments. He shut the door of his study within Arlesford House in Berkley Square and leaned his back upon it. His gaze wandered around the room, seeing the papers on his desk, his books, everything, just as he had left them. And now, less than twenty-four hours later, everything had changed. Nothing would ever be the same again. He thought of what his father had done. He thought of what Arabella had become. And he thought of the little boy who did not know he was his son. And he wept.

Dominic did not sleep that night. There were too many thoughts in his head. Too many conflicting emotions. Rage and bitterness. Betrayal and hurt. Disbelief and regret. Possessiveness and protectiveness. And love.

By the time the next morning arrived the thoughts were all still there. He pushed the breakfast plate away with the kippers and scrambled eggs upon it barely touched and called for some paper, pen and ink.

Dominic did not go to Carlton House that day to meet with the Prince of Wales. Instead he went to Curzon Street—to Arabella and his son.

Arabella watched Dominic with Archie, father and son, the two dark heads bent together, their faces so alike, and she felt her chest tighten with emotion and heard that same whisper of guilt that had been there before.

Archie's initial shyness had disappeared. He was

laughing and running around the chair on which Dominic was sitting, jumping over Dominic's long legs that were stretched out before him. As she watched, Archie clambered up on to Dominic's knee and with his little hand took hold of Dominic's large one. She saw the depth of emotion that swept across Dominic's face before he hid it. Archie was giggling and Dominic laughed too as he tweaked Archie's nose and pretended that he had captured it from the little boy's face. Arabella had to turn away to stop the tears welling in her eyes.

Father and son played together until Arabella knew that Archie was getting tired and overexcited.

'It will soon be time for dinner, Archie. You must say farewell to Dominic for now and go and get washed and changed.'

'But, Mama,' groaned Archie, 'we are not finished playing the horses game.'

'Dominic will come back another day to play with you.'

'Please, Mama,' Archie pleaded.

'You must do as your mama says,' said Dominic and, lifting Archie to his feet, rose to stand by his son's side. 'I will see you again soon.'

'Tomorrow?' Archie took hold of Dominic's hand and looked up at him.

'Yes, tomorrow,' said Dominic and ruffled Archie's hair.

Archie smiled. 'And we will play the horses game?'

Dominic smiled too, in exactly the same way. 'We will play the horses game.'

'I like you, Dominic.'

'I like you too, Archie.'

Arabella's lips pressed tight to control the swamp of emotion.

She took Archie away to the large bedroom next to her own that had, at Dominic's instruction, been transformed overnight into a nursery. Mrs Tatton sat in there reading, having resisted all persuasions to even be in the same room as Dominic. Her face was sullen as she set the book down and took Archie from her daughter. And when Arabella tried to speak, her mother turned away and would not listen.

By the time Arabella returned to the drawing room Dominic was staring down into the empty fireplace deep in thought. He did not look round until she had closed the door.

There was a poignancy about him, and both an anger and something that looked like disappointment that shadowed his eyes. The very air seemed thick with the tragedy of what might have been.

The question, when it came, hit her harder than she had expected.

'Why did you hide Archie from me, Arabella?'

'You know why, Dominic. I believed the worst of you.'

'Even so, what man, even a scoundrel as you believed me, does not have a care for his own son? You should have told me.' He raked a hand through his hair. 'Hell, Arabella, he is my son! Did you not think I had a right to know?'

Deep in the pit of her stomach was guilt and regret. 'I did not think your right important beside that of protecting Archie.'

'Protecting him from *me?* Damnation, Arabella what did you think I would have done to him?' He looked tortured.

'All of London names you a rake, Dominic, a man who takes what he wants without a care. You are rich and powerful, a duke. I am poor, without connection. You found me in a bordello. I feared you would take him from me.' She squeezed her eyes shut, unable to bear even the thought. 'He is only just five years old, Dominic, a little boy. He needs love, not to be raised by strangers who do not care for him any further than the wage they are paid.'

'I would never have taken him from you.'

'I did not know that.'

'All those times I came here, all those times we made love, and all the while you had our son hidden up in the attic!'

She gasped. 'You make it sound something it was not! I love Archie. I would lay down my life to protect him. Yes, I sold myself for his sake, but you, Dominic Furneaux, are the man who bought me. So do not dare to stand there in judgement of me!'

'If you had told me of Archie it would have changed everything.'

'What would it have changed, Dominic?' she cried. 'That you paid Mrs Silver to have sex with me? That you bought me from her? That you made me your mistress?'

He winced at her words as if it pained him to hear them. But she could not stop; she wanted him to understand.

'I believed you a man who had taken my virginity and my trust and broken my heart. I believed you a man that left me at nineteen, ruined, unmarried and disgraced. A man who was willing to buy me—to use me for his own selfish pleasure.'

Her eyes raked his. 'Would you have me hand Archie over to such a man? Someone I did not trust? Someone with whom I was so angry and did not even like? A man I thought to be ruthless and selfish and arrogant and capable of inflicting such hurt. What kind of mother would that have made me to our son, Dominic?'

'I understand your reasons, Arabella, but—'

'There are no "buts", Dominic.' She needed him to know. 'I did what I had to for Archie's sake. I will always do what I have to, to protect him, no matter what you say.'

They looked at one another.

'Would you ever have told me had not the truth come out?'

Would she?

'I do not know,' she said honestly. 'I felt matters were changing between us. I found that in spite of everything I believed of you that I still had…feelings for you. That perhaps it might have been the same for you.' The words hung awkwardly in the air between them and she wished that she had not said them. Her pride was still too delicate and she did not want it crushed. She turned away, but Dominic took hold of her and pulled her round to face him.

'I never stopped having feelings for you, Arabella,' he said and there was such a strength and determination in his words that she could feel it in the grip of his hands. 'For all that I said in my bitterness, never think it was otherwise.' He brushed his lips against her forehead.

'What are we going to do, Dominic?' It was the question that preyed on her mind constantly.

'I do not know, Arabella. I only know that I will not lose you again, and I will not lose Archie.'

Archie was in a frenzy of excitement the next morning. All he spoke of from the moment that his eyes opened was Dominic's visit.

'We are to play at horses,' he told Arabella and she had not seen him smile so much before.

Mrs Tatton, by contrast, looked pale and tired. She seemed to have aged in the past few days. There were deep lines of worry etched upon her face and shadows beneath her eyes.

'Are you feeling unwell, Mama?' Arabella looked at her anxiously, worried at the strain events were exerting upon her.

'I am tired, Arabella, nothing more. I have barely slept a wink since that terrible night.'

'Mama…' Arabella came to her and rubbed a hand against her arm '…maybe you should go back to bed.'

'What good would it do when I cannot sleep?' Her mother shook her head. 'Oh, Arabella, I wish you would see Dominic Furneaux for what he really is. It pains me that you can so easily believe his lies.'

'What reason would he have to lie about this, Mama?'

'Because he wants the boy without losing you from his bed.'

'Trust me, Mama…' Arabella shook her head '…he is not lying.'

'Forgive me if I find that hard to believe. For all his pretty words, Arabella, his loyalty lies with himself and his title. Once he has found himself a bride he will leave you behind as he did before, taking the child with him when he goes.'

'No, Mama, you have this all wrong.'

'No, Arabella, you are the one whose judgement had gone a-begging. I cannot bear to stand by and watch him destroy you all over again. What will it take to make you realise? Will you wait until he plants another babe in your belly and walks away before you see?'

Arabella stared at her mother, stunned.

'Grandmama, look at me!' shouted Archie. 'I am a horse all ready for Dominic!' He was jumping all around her mother, pulling at her skirt.

'Stop this nonsense, Archie, and go and sit down quietly!' Mrs Tatton snapped, shooing him away. 'I do not want to hear another word about Dominic Furneaux!' Archie's bottom lip trembled and Arabella bit her own to capture the sharp retort she would have uttered to her mother. Instead she turned to her son and spoke calmly.

'Grandmama is tired, Archie. She needs some peace and quiet. Go and find Charlie and we will take him to the park.' And then to her mother, 'We will leave you to your rest, Mama.'

'I am sorry, Arabella,' her mother said softly. 'I did not mean to snap at him. I am just so worried for us all.'

'I know, Mama.' Arabella kissed her mother's cheek. 'Try to rest; it will make you feel a little better. We will not be gone for long.'

Mrs Tatton nodded and watched them leave.

Dominic had not slept again. He had cancelled all of his appointments for the coming week, refused to see Hunter when his friend had called upon him last night, and thought endlessly over Arabella and Archie and the nightmare in which they were all imprisoned. He knew it was too early to call upon them, but he called for his horse to be saddled anyway. Dominic made his way to Curzon Street and in his pocket was a neatly rolled little scroll tied with a red ribbon.

Gemmell showed him in and as he waited in the drawing room he looked behind the curtain where Archie liked to play his games. A little boy's den. He moved away when he heard her footsteps coming down the stairs. Followed them along the corridor. But it was not Arabella who entered the room.

'Mrs Tatton.' He bowed.

'Your Grace.' Mrs Tatton's voice dripped with contempt. 'Arabella and Archie have gone out, but I wish to speak to you.'

He gave a nod and gestured for her to sit down, but she ignored him and stood facing him with undisguised hostility.

'Arabella tells me you have been unwell. I hope you are feeling better.'

'How could I feel better, sir, with what you have done to my daughter and grandson, and with what you are doing to them still?'

'It is a very difficult situation. My father—'

'Oh, do not waste your lies on me. You may fool Arabella, but you do not fool me for a minute. Have you not already hurt her enough? Are you not yet satisfied that you must do it all over again?'

'I would never knowingly have hurt Arabella. I loved her. I love her still.' It was the first time he had admitted the truth even to himself.

'Love? You, who, in her greatest hour of need, bought her as if she was some piece of cheap Haymarketware!

She needed help. Any decent man would have given her just that.'

Mrs Tatton's words confirmed every thought that had taunted him since he had found Arabella in Mrs Silver's. 'You are right and I have regretted my action most sincerely, ma'am. There is no excuse. I should not have allowed myself to be influenced by her circumstance.'

'Which circumstance was that, sir? That of her poverty?'

'I found her in a bordello, Mrs Tatton.'

Mrs Tatton hit out at him, her swollen old hands thumping ineffectually against his chest.

'Do not dare condemn her!' she cried and her breath was heavy and wheezing.

'Mrs Tatton, please calm yourself. I make no condemnation of Arabella. I know she would not have gone there lightly.'

He caught hold of her, worried for her health, and steered her to the armchair.

She sat down heavily, sobbing and clutching her hands to her face. 'I should have known it was such a place. But she told me it was a workshop where women sewed night and day to ready garments faster than anywhere else.'

He remembered Arabella facing him so defiantly that night in Mrs Silver's, and the expression upon her face when she admitted that her mother did not know she was there.

'She wished to spare your feelings, ma'am.'

Mrs Tatton nodded and, wrapping her arms around herself, began to rock. 'She only went there to save me and the boy. After the robbery we had nothing. God knows we had little enough before, but after...' She shook her head. 'Arabella trailed the streets of London from dawn to dusk, looking for honest work. Day after day she walked those streets, walked until her feet were rubbed raw and bleeding, and her shoulders bowed with weariness, and the last of the doors had been shut in her face. She pawned the wedding ring from her finger, the cloak from her back, the shoes from her feet, to keep us from starving. And then there was nothing else left to sell.'

Except herself.

Dominic felt sick to the pit of his stomach. The thought of what she had suffered made him want to cry out against the injustice of it and drive his fist into the wall again and again and again, but he knew that he must control himself. Mrs Tatton was already distressed enough. He passed her his handkerchief and she took it with a murmur of gratitude.

'You spoke of a robbery.'

He saw Mrs Tatton raise her head and look at him in surprise. 'She did not tell you?'

'She told me nothing.'

'I do not understand...'

And neither did Dominic, but he was beginning to. 'Arabella believed the worst of me. It must have been beyond humiliating for her to see me there that night.' He did not tell the old woman sitting before him the full extent of how he had humiliated her daughter, taking her, unknown, masked, to slake his lust upon. The knowledge raked him with agony; he knew it would hurt Mrs Tatton all the more. 'All she had left was her pride.' He took her hands in his. 'Tell me of the robbery, ma'am.'

She looked into his eyes, as if she were seeing him for the first time and was trying to take his measure. She looked and the minutes seemed to stretch, until at last she began to speak.

'Villains broke down the door of our lodgings with a hammer and stripped the place bare. They took every last thing save our mattress from which they had already prised the little money we had hidden there, and that damnable gold locket you gave her. We had already sold most items of value through the years, to make ends meet. But she would not sell the locket for all that it pained her to look upon it.' She looked at him steadily; the fury was gone and in its place was a terrible sadness and exhaustion.

'You have made my daughter your mistress and my grandson your bastard, to be looked down upon and shunned by all society. Set Arabella and Archie and me free, Dominic. Give us enough money to set up elsewhere, to start afresh and at least pretend we are respectable. Please. I am begging you.'

'I cannot do that, Mrs Tatton. I will not lose them again.'

'Then damn you to perdition, Dominic Furneaux.' Her complexion was puffy and grey, and her eyes swollen and red as she looked at him, yet there was about her the same dignity that he had seen in Arabella. 'I have nothing more to say to you, your Grace. If you will be so kind as to leave this house…' The hand with which she gestured to the door was shaking. 'Please leave at once.' She looked ill and trembling with passion. He dared not risk her health further.

Dominic rose from where he sat beside her on the sofa and did as she bid.

* * *

It was later than Arabella anticipated by the time that she and Archie returned to Curzon Street. Mrs Tatton had retired to bed and Dominic had not arrived.

The day wore on and when there continued to be no sign of Dominic Archie's excitement gradually changed to something else.

'Where is Dominic? Why does he not come, Mama?' Archie looked up at her with disappointment in his eyes.

Arabella smoothed his hair into some semblance of tidiness. 'Dominic is a very busy gentleman. I am sure that he will call upon us when he is able.'

'But he said that he would call today.'

'I know he did, little lamb. A very important matter must have arisen to prevent him.' But she was angry at Dominic for dashing a small boy's hopes, and angry at herself for trusting in him.

Archie climbed down from her knee and went off to play behind the curtain.

'Mama, Mama!' He came running up to her a minute later. 'Look what I have found.' In his hand he held a small scroll of paper tied with a red ribbon.

Arabella unfastened the ribbon and looked at the pen-and-ink coloured drawing on the paper before her. And she felt a wave of affection wash through her.

'This is your own little horse drawn by Dominic.' She smiled at Archie.

Archie's eyes widened. 'It is Charlie, Mama!'

'Yes, I think it is.' Arabella smiled, thinking that Dominic must have sent the drawing for Archie because he could not call.

'I cannot wait till I see Dominic!'

* * *

It was only later when Archie had been put to bed and her mother had risen from hers that Arabella learned something of what had really transpired that day.

'You sent Dominic away? But this is his house, Mama.'

'I sent him away, like the rogue he is.'

'Did you speak to him?'

'Oh, yes, Arabella. I told him what you should have.' Her mother looked even more pale and exhausted than when Arabella had seen her last, despite the hours of rest.

A shiver of foreboding moved down Arabella's spine.

Her mother looked at her with the strangest expression. 'Sweet Arabella, with your dignity and your pride,' she said softly. 'Why did you not tell him? And why did you not tell me?'

'What do you mean, Mama?' She had a very bad feeling. 'What was said?'

'I damned him to hell and told him to leave.' Mrs Tatton smiled, but it was the saddest smile that Arabella had ever seen.

'Oh, Mama,' she said softly. And she handed her mother the drawing he had penned for Archie.

Her mother unrolled the scroll and in the silence there was only the ticking of the clock.

And her mother looked at her and knew what she was thinking. 'Do not go to him, Arabella.'

'You know that I have to.' Arabella pecked a kiss on her mother's cheek. 'Archie is asleep. Listen out in case he wakens before I am returned. I should not be gone for long.' And she rang for her carriage and her cloak.

* * *

Dominic glanced round at the commotion that was sounding from his hallway. He raised an eyebrow at the man seated opposite him within his study.

'Please excuse me for a minute.' He set down his brandy and the pile of political papers that had just been handed to him and went to investigate, pulling the door closed behind him.

Out in the black-and-white chequered floor hallway Bentley's frame partially obscured a dark figure with which he was engaged in an altercation.

'I tell you that he will see me!' the voice insisted. Dominic's stomach tightened as he recognised it as Arabella's.

'And I tell you, madam, that he is not at home. Now if you do not leave the premises I will be forced to—'

Dominic stepped quickly forwards. 'It is all right, Bentley. Let her in.'

'Dominic,' she said and slipped the voluminous black velvet hood down to reveal herself, and he smelled the waft of cool night air mixed with the rose scent of her perfume. Her hair had been scraped back into a chignon, but the hood of the cloak had displaced some of the pins enough to let some golden curls escape. She looked beautiful and worried.

'What are you doing here, Arabella?' His voice was hushed as he hurried her into the shadows. His first thought was of the risk she was taking coming here, much more than she realised. And his second was that Arabella would not have come were there not a very good reason. A horrible fear suddenly struck him. His hands tightened around her arms.

'Has something happened to Archie?' he asked and his eyes searched hers.

She shook her head. 'Archie is fine.'

'Your mother?'

'She is well enough, Dominic.'

'Then why are you here?'

'What did you say to my mother today? I have to know.'

'Much as I wish it otherwise, now is not the time to be having this discussion, Arabella. You must leave here at once.'

He saw the hurt flicker in her eyes before cynical realisation showed on her face.

'You are angry that I have come.'

'Very.' He could not lie.

'I see.' Her lips tightened slightly.

'No, you do not.' He hauled her to him, until their faces were only inches apart. He stared down into her eyes, his heart thudding too hard at the danger she was in. 'Arabella, I am not alone this evening. I have visitors, albeit unwelcome ones, in the library—the Earl of Misbourne and his son Viscount Linwood.'

'Misbourne?' Everything about her stilled. 'Lady Marianne's father.' He could see the sudden doubt that flashed in her mind as clear as if she had voiced it aloud.

'Their visit is on a political matter and has nothing to do with Lady Marianne.'

Her gaze was fierce and strong and determined. 'If you mean to marry her, Dominic, please be honest enough to tell me. I understand your position and your obligations mean that you are required to marry and beget an heir—'

But he cut her off, his voice harsh and urgent. 'We

have been through all of this before, Arabella. There has only ever been one woman I wanted to marry and that is you.'

'We both know that is an impossibility now,' she whispered.

'Is it?' His grip was too tight around her arms, but he could not loosen it. 'Do I not already have my heir?'

They stared into one another's eyes and he could feel that she was trembling.

'Return to Curzon Street, Arabella. I am bound into this meeting, but I will come to you tomorrow and we will talk then.' He pressed a short hard kiss to her lips before pulling the hood up over her head and releasing her.

Bentley and a footman appeared and Dominic spoke softly and quickly. 'Help the lady to her coach. Discretion is paramount.'

'Very good, your Grace.' Bentley gave a bow. Arabella was already gone by the time the butler's gaze flitted towards the library door in a warning.

Dominic glanced round to see Misbourne and Linwood standing there.

'Everything all right, Arlesford? No trouble, I hope.'

'No trouble.' Dominic's expression was cold and hard as he made his way back into the library and topped up his guests' glasses. And he wondered just how long the men had been standing there and how much Misbourne had seen. For all their sakes, he hoped that the answer was not very much at all.

Chapter Fourteen

From the minute that Dominic arrived at Curzon Street the next day Arabella could see the determination in his gaze. She thought of what it was he had come to discuss and her heart missed a beat. She was frightened and hopeful and confused all at once.

'Dominic!' Archie ran up, so happy and joyful to see his father that Arabella's guilt at keeping the two of them apart weighed heavier than ever upon her. 'Are we playing the horses game today?'

'Archie, let Dominic come in and at least remove his hat and gloves before you pester him. I told you that he is busy and might not have time to play today,' said Arabella, but Archie was already by Dominic's side looking up at him hopefully.

Dominic smiled and ruffled Archie's hair. 'Of course I have time for the horses game…that is, if your mama and grandmama give us their permission.'

Archie peered across at her and Mrs Tatton.

Arabella glanced at her mother, who was watching

Archie and Dominic together. 'Mama?' she said softly, wanting her mother to be a part of this.

Mrs Tatton nodded. 'Let them spend time together.'

'Thank you,' said Dominic. Arabella knew that he had no need to ask for permission—it was his house and his son. But the fact that he had understood how important this was to her and that he had consideration for her mother's feelings gladdened her more than any fancy words or gifts could have done.

'Hurrah!' Archie shouted and produced a rather crushed and tatty-looking scroll of paper from his pocket. 'I have my picture all ready.'

And when they went through to the drawing room, Mrs Tatton did not make her excuses, but came and sat with them too.

Dominic did not cease to marvel at Archie. The more he came to know him the more he realised that, although the boy had his looks, he had many of Arabella's mannerisms. The way he tilted his head to the side when he was listening, and the way he chewed his lip when he was unsure of himself. Dominic never tired of the wonder of his and Arabella's child.

His tailcoat had long been abandoned, his waistcoat was unbuttoned and the knot in his cravat loosened. Archie insisted on removing his shoes and demonstrating with pride to Dominic how well he could run and slide in his stocking soles across the polished floor. Dominic remembered doing the very same thing at home in Shardeloes Hall when he was a boy.

Dominic took a seat on the sofa and felt something hard jab into his back. He glanced round and found a small carved wooden horse half-hidden by the cushion.

'Oh, you found Charlie sleeping in his stable.' Archie smiled.

'So his name is Charlie,' said Dominic.

'Gemmell made him for me. For my birthday.' Archie smiled even more widely. 'And my mama took us to the park and allowed me and Charlie to ride upon a real horse.' Archie was beaming fit to burst.

'I am sure you enjoyed that.' He slid a gaze to meet Arabella and wondered how all this could have gone on beneath his very nose without him having an inkling of it. Her cheeks flushed and she bit her lip.

'Oh, indeed, yes! It was the best treat ever.'

'So now you know, Dominic,' piped up Mrs Tatton. 'She should have told you of the boy and the rest of it at the very beginning.'

'Mama!' whispered Arabella, scandalised.

'Well, you should have,' said Mrs Tatton to Arabella before turning back to him. 'And you, for all that you can plead your excuses, should have treated my daughter a deal better than you have.'

'You are right, ma'am,' he conceded. 'But I am here today to resolve that matter.'

Mrs Tatton's eyes widened slightly. Her gaze shifted momentarily to Arabella and he saw in it both the question and anxiety before it came back to rest upon him.

No more was said of it, but Dominic stayed for dinner and was still there to kiss his son goodnight when he went to bed.

By the time Arabella and Dominic were alone in the drawing room Arabella was feeling distinctly nervous. She smoothed her skirts and perched on the edge of the sofa.

'Your meeting with Lord Misbourne went well last night?' she asked.

'Well enough.' He was standing over by the fireplace, which was still unlit on account of the warmth of the evening.

There was a silence that she quickly filled.

'Would you like some more tea?'

'No more tea, thank you, Arabella.' His dark pensive gaze came to rest upon hers. 'I meant what I said last night—about marriage—to you.'

'Dominic.' She sighed. It was such a sensitive subject for them both. 'How can we possibly marry after all that has happened?'

'How can we not?' There seemed to be a still calmness about him, yet the flicker of the muscle in his jaw betrayed the tension that ran beneath that stillness.

'I am your mistress, for pity's sake!'

'And have not other men married their mistresses? What of Mountjoy? Besides. I shall hardly be introducing you as such.'

'Too many people know of Miss Noir and Mrs Silver.'

'Maybe, but there is nothing to connect them to Mrs Marlbrook. Rest assured I will take every step to ensure that any such links be taken care of and that your background is nothing but respectable. Are you not the respectable and widowed Mrs Marlbrook recently come to London? They shall think it is a love match.'

Once it really had been a love match. And now... She looked into Dominic's eyes.

'We have to do this, Arabella, for Archie's sake. I have a duty both to my son, Arabella, and to right the wrongs I have dealt you.'

Duty? Her hope, still so new and tender and rising, was crushed. There was no talk of affection, no mention of love.

'This is about duty and appeasing your own guilt,' she said. *How foolish to have thought it could be anything other.*

'My guilt? It was you that hid Archie from me, Arabella.' Her eyes widened as his words found their target.

'What choice did I have? I did what I thought was best for Archie. He is my son.'

'He is my son, too. Do I not also have the right to do my very best for him, or do you continue to deny me that right?'

She turned away to hide her hurt. 'Archie looks so like you that everyone will know he is your son. He will be subjected to their gossip.'

'I care not what they think, Arabella. They may whisper their suppositions, but I am not without power and influence. Besides, unless you mean to keep him hidden for ever they will find out soon enough and I can protect him all the better once we are married—just as I can protect you.'

She knew what he was saying was right, yet she was overwhelmed with a feeling of disappointment and sadness. She should be glad that he had such a care for his son, that he had a sense of honour. And she was. Truly. But she could not help thinking of the first time he had asked her to be his wife, when they had been young and naïve and in love. Everything was different now. Too much had happened. There could never be any going back. And she hurt to know it.

'I am unsure, Dominic.'

'What is the alternative, Arabella? That I keep you here as my mistress with Archie as my bastard? Is that your preference?'

'No!'

'Then there is nothing else other than that we wed.'

She could feel the fast hard thump of her heart against her chest. He was asking her to marry him. The man she had loved; the man she loved still. Yet her chest was tight and she felt like weeping.

'There is another alternative that you have not considered,' she said slowly and it seemed as if the words did not even come from her own mouth. She felt chilled in even saying them, but they needed to be spoken. 'I need not be your mistress. My mother and Archie and I could go to the country. If we had a little money, enough for a small cottage, we could live in quiet respectability and you could—'

He grabbed hold of her upper arms and pulled her close to stare down into her face, eyes filled with fury. 'Is that what you want, Arabella?'

And behind his anger she saw the hurt of the wound she had just inflicted and she could not lie. 'You know it is not.' She shook her head and felt the tears prick in her eyes. 'But this is not about *want,* is it? As you have already said, this is about *duty* and what is best for Archie.'

'And you think it is best to take him away from his father?'

'You could still visit him and—'

But he did not let her finish. 'You may choose to marry me, Arabella, or to remain as my mistress. There is no other choice, for I will let neither you nor the boy go. So what is it to be, Arabella? Will you marry me?'

She felt angry and hurt and saddened. Her head knew his proposal made sense. He was offering what was best for Archie. He was offering what any woman in her situation should have jumped at. But her heart... Her heart was saying something else all together.

'You set it all out so clearly,' she said. And she remembered what he had said that very first night in the brothel: *Whores do as rich men bid.* And part of her revolted against both it and his possession of her.

His gaze held hers, waiting for her answer.

'Yes, Dominic, I will marry you.' *For Archie. Only for Archie.*

He gave a nod, and she felt something of the tension in his grip relax.

They looked at one another and there seemed so much anger and tension and sadness between them.

Then he took a small red-leather ring box from his pocket, inside of which was a ring of sparkling diamonds that surrounded a large square sapphire of the clearest, bluest blue.

'The Arlesford betrothal ring,' he said and slid the ring on to the third finger of her left hand.

She could not say a word, for she feared that all of what she felt would come tumbling out.

'I will make the necessary arrangements.'

She nodded.

Dominic bowed, then he left.

It should have been one of the happiest days of her life, but for Arabella it was one of the saddest. Dominic was marrying her not out of love, but for Archie. They were both doing this for Archie. It was the way it had to be. And she should be used to giving herself to a man who did not love her.

'But what if they discover the truth of us—that we have not lived so quietly since Mr Marlbrook's death?'

'They shall not discover any such thing; Dominic has taken care of everything. Now take a deep breath, Mama, and let us have one last look at your outfit.'

Mrs Tatton turned back to the looking glass.

Arabella's gaze roved over the purple silk which her mother was wearing. The colour suited her mother's skin and brought a healthy glow to her complexion. It was high necked, the bodice closed over by a line of amethyst buttons that sparkled in the candlelight. On Mrs Tatton's head was fitted a small turban in matching purple silk; the hair beneath had been curled and coiffured to soften the turban's edges. The shimmer of purple silk picked out silver highlights in the grey curls. Arabella had not seen her mother look so well in years.

'You are quite lovely, Mama.'

'Thank you, Arabella.' Her mother smiled, her nerves forgotten for the moment. 'You look lovely yourself. Every bit a duchess-in-waiting.'

Arabella glanced down at the deep blue silk gown. It was plainly, but expertly, cut in the latest fashion to do justice to her figure. In the candlelight her skin looked pale and creamy beside the dark intense colour of the dress. The sleeves were short and sitting off her shoulders and the long evening gloves and reticule were of a shade that exactly matched the dress. Her décolletage was bare and Arabella touched her fingers against the skin and thought fleetingly of the golden locket that had meant so much more to her than the diamond-and-sapphire ring that was now upon her finger. She pushed the thought aside, knowing that she must show nothing of her true feelings, that tonight was all about playing the role of a respectable widow who had captured a duke's heart.

'Thank you, Mama. I shall just have a quick peep at Archie before we leave.'

'He will be sleeping, Arabella.'

'I hope so.' Arabella smiled, but it was all for her mother and there was nothing of happiness inside. 'But I will check so that I am certain. And ensure that Anne knows what to do if he should wake before we have returned.'

Dominic had always thought Arabella a beautiful woman, but the sight of her with Mrs Tatton coming in through the hallway of Arlesford House quite took his breath away. She was lovelier than he could have imagined. Wearing a shimmering silver shawl, under which he could see a plain dark blue dress that was expensive, respectable, and perfectly in keeping with her role as a widow of two years. And yet the dress showed off the curves of Arabella's figure in just the right way. Her hair was an elaborate arrangement of golden curls piled upon her head. Several loose tendrils framed her face and wisped softly around her neck. Even Mrs Tatton appeared to have more colour in her face and was wearing a purple outfit complete with turban, and a purple-and-blue fringed shawl.

He bowed to them both, although it was hard for him to drag his gaze from Arabella for long.

'Your Grace,' she said and curtsied, all formality, just as it had been between them in private these past two weeks.

He could hear the murmur of curiosity amongst the guests that already packed the ballroom.

'And Mrs Tatton,' he said and bowed to her mother.

The hundreds of candles in the three chandeliers in the ballroom sparkled on the sapphire-and-diamond betrothal ring on Arabella's finger as he raised her hand to his lips. The surrounding murmur grew louder.

He spoke to Arabella and her mother in the politest of terms, knowing that their every word was being listened to even above the singing of the violins that sounded so clear and sweet from the musicians up on the balcony.

'You are well, Mrs Marlbrook?' he enquired and his gaze was intent upon hers. He gave her hand that was tucked within his arm a little squeeze as he led her and Mrs Tatton to a small collection of chairs that he had been keeping just for them. He wanted to know how she was bearing up to such pressure, for he knew that beneath that mask of cool tranquillity she would be worried.

He felt the return of the slight transient pressure of her fingers against the muscle of his arm. He gestured to a passing footman carrying a silver salver of filled champagne glasses and passed Arabella and her mother each a glass of champagne. They chatted for a little while, about the weather, about how she and her mother were enjoying London, about horse riding. And then he took Arabella and Mrs Tatton over to where the Prince of Wales was holding court and presented them.

The wave of whisperings and staring was passing right through the room. Dominic was looking forward to making the announcement. He watched Arabella and the prince together and knew that Prinny was giving her his royal approval. No one would dare question her respectability now. He gave a small nod of acknowledgement at the prince and saw Prinny give a nod back.

A royal prince needed his allies every bit as much as a duke. And then Dominic signalled to the musicians to cease playing. It was time.

Arabella was so busy keeping an eye on her mother and guarding her conversation with the prince that she did not notice what was happening until the music stopped. A hushed chatter filled the silence.

Dominic's ballroom was large and there must have been at least a hundred people packed within its glittering splendour. Arabella could see what seemed like the flicker of a thousand candles sparkling against the myriad of faceted crystal drops on the massive chandeliers. The ceiling, the top of the walls and the front of the balcony were decorated with the most pure and beautiful plasterwork. The walls themselves were painted a cool pale green, which lent the room an airy spacious feel. Above the massive fireplace, which thankfully had not been lit, was a huge looking glass that reflected the light from the chandeliers and made the room even brighter. The oak floorboards had been scraped and polished until they gleamed like a rich dark chocolate. Around the room were tables and chairs, and wall sconces that dripped with crystal in a fashion that mirrored their parent chandeliers. It was beautiful and elegant and most luxurious.

And then Dominic's butler was ringing a small bell. 'Pray silence your majesty, my lords, ladies and gentlemen. The Duke of Arlesford wishes to make an announcement.'

She heard the buzz of whispers go around the room. Arabella was standing with the Prince of Wales on one side and her mother on the other. Dominic was on the other side of the prince. Although most of the attention in the room was fixed on Dominic, she could see a few of the gazes upon herself. Every pair of eyes in the room was filled with question. Everyone wanted to know what was so important that the Duke of Arlesford intended making an announcementr.

And then Dominic took her hand and drew her over to stand by his side. And she saw the shock and surprise on some faces and the confirmation of guesses on others. His fingers closed around hers and she felt all of his support flowing through that warm touch.

Dominic began to talk, and her heart gave a little jump, her stomach a little jitter and she realised that this was it.

'I would like to present to you all, Mrs Arabella Marlbrook.'

She could hear him talking and she stood there so still, so calm, facing that sea of faces as if she were the very proper, very respectable widowed Mrs Marlbrook whom Dominic was describing. He was still talking.

'I am very happy to be able to tell you that Mrs Marlbrook has accepted my proposal of marriage. We are to be married as soon as matters can be arranged.'

Which would be in two months' time, at the height of the summer, in Westminster Abbey, if all went according to plan. She would be a duchess, and Archie, his father's son and heir to a dukedom. Her mother would never again go cold. Her son, never go hungry. There would always be enough money for food and medicines and coal. He had made her respectable again. He would make her his wife. But Arabella could not smile.

Dominic raised her hand to his mouth and placed a kiss against it. Every person in the ballroom began to applaud and she could see her mother smiling by her side, and she could see, too, the look in Dominic's eyes when he looked at her—dark and possessive and filled with all they had not said to one another in the past two weeks. She forced herself to smile because it was what everyone was expecting. She smiled as she met the gazes of Dominic's guests. Smiled sadly at the good will she saw in those faces because she knew, if they knew the truth, there would be nothing of good will there. And then her gaze passed over two faces that were not smiling.

One was the grey bearded man whom she had seen in Vauxhall on the night of the carnival—Lord Misbourne—and the other was a taller, younger, dark-haired man by his side. The younger man's expression was filled with such coldness that it shocked her and sent a shiver down her spine. Arabella's feigned smile was all the broader to hide her sudden unease.

Beside her she heard the prince raise a toast to Dominic's and her future happiness. She was obliged to curtsy her acknowledgement to him and take the glass of champagne from the footman who appeared by her side, so that she might raise it in response. And when she looked again to find the face that had so distressed her, it had gone and so had Misbourne's. Her eyes scanned the crowd, searching for the men, but there was not one sign of them.

And then the cheering began, and although Dominic was smiling she could see the darkness in his eyes, and she was smiling even more to hide her unhappiness and discomfort. The band began to play again and people pressed forwards to offer their congratulations. But Arabella's eyes were still searching for the man and, although she took every step to mask it, the unease that he elicited remained. And it seemed that in the background of all the laughter and music that surrounded her she could hear a whisper of foreboding.

Chapter Sixteen

Hunter made no mention of his and Dominic's disagreement over the marriage as the two men rode together in St James's Park a few mornings later.

'How goes the word amongst the *ton?*' Dominic asked. 'Any suspicions?'

'Not a one,' said Hunter. 'There are a few queries as to whether you have rid yourself of Miss Noir or are just being discreet because of your forthcoming marriage. The consensus of opinion seems to be in favour of the latter.'

'I am glad that they think so highly of me,' said Dominic sarcastically.

'You can hardly complain, Dominic, when you have spent the last few years in our dissolute company proving yourself a rake.'

'I suppose not,' he said drily.

'Are you sure that you wish me as your best man? I mean, now that you are trying to clean up your image.' Hunter was not joking, he realised, judging from the serious expression on his friend's face.

'Of course I want you. Who else would I ask?'

'True.' Hunter gave a sniff and a shrug of his shoulders. 'Not much choice when all your friends are rakes. I suppose if you really wanted to be a bastard about it you might ask Misbourne or Linwood. They would certainly get the message that you did not wish to marry their precious Lady Marianne then.'

'I think they already have that message, Sebastian. Why else do you think I invited them to the ball?'

'You should have told Misbourne in no uncertain terms at the very start that you had no intention of marrying the chit.'

'I did, on several occasions.'

Hunter arched an eyebrow.

'But Misbourne is persistent to say the least. He feels his claim is justified and I have no wish to injure his pride any more than I already have. He owns most of the newspapers in London and he is as sly as a snake in the grass.'

'Why you do not cut him dead mystifies me,' said Hunter.

'We are obliged to work together on political matters; besides, you have heard the saying, keep your friends close and your enemies closer still.'

'All the more reason to have called him out and put a ball in the rogue's shoulder,' said Hunter.

'With Misbourne it would have to be a ball in the heart. Otherwise he would just keep coming back. Remember what he did to Blandford?'

Hunter gave a murmur of disapproval. 'Poor old Blandford.'

'And I would not just be able to walk away having murdered a fellow peer.'

'Trip to the Continent called for,' said Hunter.

'A bit more than that. And I will not have Misbourne dictate the course of my life. Besides, the matter is settled now. He might not like the fact that I am about to marry Arabella, rather than his daughter, but there is not a damnable thing he can do about it.'

For Arabella the week that followed Dominic's ball was a whirl of activity and she was glad of it, for it gave her little time to think about the way things lay between them and their marriage that lay ahead. She played a role, went through the motions and was careful to concentrate at all times lest she allow something of their secret to slip.

Arabella, Dominic and her mother attended a musical evening at Lady Carruthers's on Monday, a rout at Lady Filchingham's on Tuesday evening, a showing of Shakespeare's *Hamlet* at the King's Theatre on Wednesday, a ball at Lord Royston's on Thursday, and a visit to the opera on Friday. On top of that she had received three sets of afternoon visitors in Curzon Street. It was now Saturday morning and they were due to attend yet another ball that evening.

Mrs Tatton was yawning and half-dozing in the armchair by the fire, while Arabella was teaching Archie a card game at the little green baize covered table.

'I win!' Archie shouted triumphantly and spread his cards for Arabella to see.

'Hush, you rascally boy,' she whispered with a laugh. 'You will wake your grandmama.'

'I am not sleeping,' Mrs Tatton muttered, 'just resting my eyes for five minutes while I have the chance.' Her voice trailed off and her breathing reverted to the regular heavy breaths of sleep with the slight snore that her mother always made.

Archie giggled. 'She *is* sleeping. Listen, Mama.' And then he laughed again as Mrs Tatton made a soft snoring sound right on cue.

The rat-a-tat-tat of the brass knocker on the front door sounded loudly, making both Arabella and Archie start and wakening Mrs Tatton.

'Is it Dominic come to see me again?' Archie asked. 'I hope so for I do like him, Mama.'

'I am glad of that,' said Arabella and she truly was, no matter how matters lay between her and Dominic, for as the days passed she was coming to see that even if Dominic did not love her, he loved his son.

'Is it Dominic? Are we expecting him at this time of the morning?' Mrs Tatton rubbed at her eyes and sat up straight. 'Dear Lord, I do not know why I am so very tired these days.'

'Too many late nights, Mama,' said Arabella with a smile. 'And, no, we are not expecting Dominic or any other visitors at this hour. Gemmell will deal with it.'

But less than five minutes later Gemmell appeared in the drawing room. 'Excuse me, madam, but there is a gentleman at the door who is most insistent that he speak with you, a Mr Smith.' Quite what Gemmell thought of a gentleman caller bothering his mistress, particularly at this time of the morning, was written all over his face, as if she were the respectable Mrs Marlbrook she was pretending to be. Arabella felt a rush of affection for the elderly butler.

'I tried to send him away but he is refusing to leave until I pass you a message. I could have him thrown down the steps on to the street, but I thought that such a drastic action would attract attention of an undesirable nature.'

'You are quite right to come to me, Gemmell.' Arabella did not know any gentleman by the name of Smith, and, moreover, she was anxious not to receive any gentleman callers other than Dominic, but neither did she wish to be creating gossip and scandal by having the caller manhandled from her front door. 'And the message is?' she asked Gemmell.

'The message is...' She saw Gemmell's cheeks colour in embarrassment. He cleared his throat. 'Miss Noir.'

The name seemed to echo in the silence that followed his words. Arabella could not prevent her eyes widening in horror. Her heart's steady rhythm seemed to stumble and stop and she felt a chill of dread spread right through her.

Miss Noir. An image of herself as she had stood before the looking glass in Mrs Silver's house flashed in her head. Of the black translucent dress that showed hints of what lay beneath, of the indecent way it clung to her every curve. Of the black-feathered mask that hid the top of her face.

Someone had seen her.

Someone knew.

'Miss *Noir?*' Mama repeated and looked confused. Fortunately Archie was playing with the cards, oblivious to what else was going on in the drawing room.

Arabella's heart began to beat again, each beat resounding after the other in a series of rapid thuds so heavy that she could feel them reverberate in the base of her throat.

'I will deal with this, Mama, then the gentleman will

leave us in peace.' Then to Gemmell, 'Show him into the library.'

Gemmell cleared his throat awkwardly as if even he had heard of the infamous Miss Noir.

Arabella rose, smoothed out her skirts, checked her appearance briefly in the peering glass to ensure that she did not look as frightened as she felt, and then, taking a deep breath, she walked out to face the gentleman caller.

She closed the library door quietly behind her.

The man was standing by the bookshelves, with his hat and gloves dangling from one hand, browsing the titles of the leather-bound books arranged upon it, and when he looked up at the sound of the door she saw at once who he was.

He was of medium height with a lithe lean build, and the lazy loose way he was holding his hat and gloves belied the tension that seemed to ripple through the rest of his body. His hair was a raven black against a face that was of pale olive complexion. But it was his eyes that she noticed the most, for they were black and dangerous and filled with fury. And he was looking at her with cold dislike, just as he had looked at her from his place upon the crowded floor beside the Earl of Misbourne on the night of Dominic's ball.

'Mrs Marlbrook,' he said in a smooth voice. 'I thought that you would see the sensible course and respond to my message.'

'Mr Smith.' She gave the smallest inclination of her head and attacked first, hoping to call his bluff with a confident assault. 'I will speak bluntly and with the same lack of consideration that you have shown in coming to my door bandying such a name. I do not know who you are, or why you have come here on such a malicious mission, but I will tell you, sir, that if you are seeking to make mischief between the Duke and myself, then you are wasting your time. I am a widow, sir, and not completely ignorant of the workings of the world. What his Grace has done in the past and with whom is no consideration of mine. You have had a wasted journey, Mr Smith. So, if you will be so good as to leave now.' She kept her head high and her gaze level with his.

Mr Smith clapped his hands together in a slow mockery of applause. 'A performance worthy of Drury Lane, Mrs Marlbrook,' he said.

'How dare you?' Her cheeks warmed from his insolence. 'I shall have my butler escort you out.'

'Not so fast, madam. Unless you want it known that the respectable widow to whom Arlesford is betrothed is the same woman who visited his house alone at night a matter of weeks ago. And the same woman who bears a startling resemblance to the whore that he bought from Mrs Silver's bawdy house and took with him to the masquerade at Vauxhall. I guarantee you that I can have the story published in more than one of London's newspapers. People will draw their own conclusions, but I would warrant that you will not be so warmly received then, for all of Arlesford's connections.'

'I have never been so insulted in all my life!' Truly the performance of an actress, just as he had said. 'I will not even deign to reply to such scurrilous and ridiculous accusations.'

'You may protest all you like, madam, and indeed I would expect nothing less from a woman like you. I might even believe you had I not seen you with my own eyes,' he said. 'From doxy to duchess in a few weeks. That is quite an achievement.'

'Get out!' She pointed to the door, showing all of her anger and none of her fear. 'You can be very sure that I will inform the duke of your interest in the matter, Mr Smith.'

'Please do, Mrs Marlbrook. And tell him also that although he was very careful in fabricating a cover for you, with Mrs Silver, Madame Boisseron and your landlord at Flower and Dean Street, there are always those in the background who are missed. He cannot catch every faceless soul upon the street, every witness to the truth. And you would be surprised at what some people are willing to do for money, Mrs Marlbrook. But then again, madam, perhaps not that surprised after all. I know quite conclusively that you are Miss Noir.'

'You have a villain's tongue in your head, sir! Be gone from here. I will not tolerate your presence for a moment longer.'

He cocked his head to the side. 'Not even to hear what it is that I want in order to keep your secret from the newspapers?'

The fear was pumping through her veins, the scent of it filling her nose, the taste of it churning her stomach. Yet still she faced him defiantly, keeping up the pretence to the end. 'Publish your lies if you will, Mr Smith. Now, leave my house, sir.' She strode towards the door and, opening it, stepped out into the hallway, intending to have Mr Smith escorted out. And the sight of what greeted her eyes made her stop dead in her tracks and snatched all of the wind from her sails.

There was a light drumming in her head and she felt sick.

'Mama?' the little voice uttered quietly. For there, sitting on the floor at the side of the library door, his back leaning against the wall, playing cards spread out on the floorboards around him, was Archie. 'Grandmama fell asleep again and I was bored waiting for you to return.'

'Well, how very interesting,' said the gentleman's voice from directly behind her, although he had not yet crossed the threshold from the library. 'You might not have a care how your own name is discredited within the newspapers, Mrs Marlbrook, but your son—and Arlesford's, if I am not mistaken—well, I fancy that might be a different matter all together. Only think of the interest that the duke and his bastard will arouse. Even with Arlesford to smooth the way for him the boy would never completely escape the scandal. He, as well as you, would be the talk of the *ton*.'

Gemmell appeared just at that moment, barely concealing the scowl he directed at Mr Smith. 'Madam?' he enquired.

Somehow Arabella found the strength. She looked at Gemmell quite calmly. 'If you would be kind enough to take Archie through to my mother, and see that he is entertained with a game of cards.'

'Very good, madam. And shall I then return to escort Mr Smith out?' He eyed the gentleman with disdain.

'No, that will not be necessary, thank you, Gemmell. Mr Smith and I have not yet concluded our discussion.' And, walking back into the library, she closed the door behind her.

'What do you want?' She faced him squarely, keeping her face as impassive as she could, although she knew full well that her disgust of him must have been blazing from her eyes. They stood as if they were two opponents in a fight, sizing one another up for strengths and for weaknesses.

'For you to leave Arlesford. Break off your betrothal and go, I do not care where, as long as it is not London.'

'Why should it matter to you whether I marry him?'

'That is my business. You will not marry him, nor will you remain here as his mistress.' He slipped a hand into his pocket and produced a cloth-wrapped package. 'There is five thousand pounds here. Admittedly a good sum short of what Arlesford could give you, but enough to pay for your expenses to set up elsewhere and find yourself a new protector.' He held out the package to her.

It was all she could do not to dash the package to the floor, such was her contempt for his offer. But she restrained herself and just turned away. 'You are under a gross misapprehension as to my character, sir.'

'I do not think so.' He held the money out for just a moment longer, then, when he realised she had no intention of taking it, he sat it down on the closest table.

'No one would print your lies. It is all of it an idle threat,' she taunted, but even as she said it she knew that it was not. Just one whisper of his accusations would be enough. Once word of Archie was out, the press men would be peeping in their windows, stalking their every move. She could run their gauntlet, but she could not risk subjecting her son to any such torture.

'I assure you most solemnly that I can have the story in print and on the front pages by Monday morning.' He looked at her with an expression upon his face that told her what type of woman he thought her.

'And do not think to go running to Arlesford with a tale of this meeting or of me. If he hears one word

I will know and not only will I publish, but…well, let us just say that London can be a dangerous place, Mrs Marlbrook, even for a man such as Arlesford.'

'You are threatening his safety?' She stared into those black eyes, reeling at the ruthlessness she saw there.

'Take my words in whatever way you will.' He smiled the coldest smile of promise she had ever seen and she knew with an absolute certainty that this man would have no qualms about executing all that he threatened. Arabella shivered and felt goose pimples break out over her skin.

'If you have not left Arlesford by tomorrow I will go ahead and make good on my promise to publish. Do you understand, Mrs Marlbrook?'

'I understand, sir, and I will do as you ask.' The gall was rising in her throat. 'Take your money. I do not want it.' She lifted the packet of money from the table and handed it to him.

'If you insist.' He smiled and slipped it back into his pocket. 'Do not bother calling your butler. I will show myself out.'

When the front door shut after him she went to the window and saw him walking along the street. There was no horse; there was no carriage. Mr Smith vanished as quickly as he had appeared.

She leaned heavily against the table, trying to smooth the unevenness of her breathing, trying to calm the anger and the fear that had set her whole her body trembling.

What choice did she have? He had threatened to expose Archie and end Dominic's life. Arabella dared not risk either. There was no one she could tell. No one who would help her. She did not want to panic and frighten her mother. She knew this was a decision she would have to make on her own. Except that there was no decision to make. How could there be when it came to those whom she loved?

One more deep breath and then she stood up straight and walked through to tell her mother to start packing.

Arabella heard Dominic's carriage come to a halt outside Curzon Street at nine o'clock that evening. He had come to collect her for the ball. Arabella was sitting alone in the drawing room, dressed not for the ball but in a plain day dress with a shawl wrapped around her shoulders. The curtains were drawn; there was no fire upon the hearth, and only a single candle had been lit. The room was in semi-darkness, just as she wanted it, for she did not want him to be able to see the truth upon her face when she told him.

She heard the closing of the front door and the steady sound of his footsteps as he approached the drawing room. Her stomach clenched with the dread of what she must do.

'Arabella?' She could see the surprise upon his face. 'What is wrong? You are not ready for the ball.'

'I am not going to the ball.' She rose from the chair and stood very still facing him. She felt chilled, so chilled that her legs were trembling. 'Dominic, I have to speak to you.' It did not matter how many hours she had spent rehearsing the words, now it came to speaking them they would not come to her lips. She felt sick to the pit of her stomach, so sick that she wondered if she was going to be able to go through with this.

'What has happened, Arabella?' The growing concern in his eyes made it impossible for her to look at him. And she wanted to tell him the truth so much, all about Smith and his horrible threats. But the promise of what that villain would do was too clear in her head. Smith would ruin Archie and God only knew what he intended for Dominic. She thought of the night Dominic had come here with the mark of a blade across his ribs, and she wondered if that, too, had been Smith's handiwork. She was shaking so much at the thought she feared Dominic would see it. She thought of how much she loved both Archie and the man who was his father, and knew she had to do this, for both their sakes. She forced herself on.

'Matters have changed. I...I have reconsidered my situation...' She gripped her hands tightly together.

He came towards her and she knew he meant to take her in his arms and she knew absolutely that she could not let that happen. 'No!' She put out a hand to stay him and backed away. 'Please come no closer.'

He stopped where he was. 'Arabella, are you going to tell me what this is about?'

She took a breath. And then another. There was no excuse she could give.

'I...' There was nothing that would make it any easier for either of them.

'I cannot...' She must say the words.

'Dominic...' She must say them no matter how like poison they were on her tongue.

'I cannot marry you. I am breaking our betrothal.'

He gave a half-gasp half-laugh, but his eyes were serious and tense. 'Is this some sort of jest?'

'It is no jest.' She could not bring herself to meet his

gaze. She willed herself to think of Archie, not of what she was doing to them all.

There was a moment's silence as he absorbed what she had said.

'Why?' It was the question she had known he would ask and the one she could not bear to answer. She shook her head.

'Have I pushed you too much into the public eye? If all these outings are too much we can reduce them. Spend some evenings more—'

'No,' she interrupted him. 'No,' she said again.

'Is it the wedding? We can make it a small quiet affair if that is what you prefer.'

'No, Dominic.' It was harder even than the worst of her imaginings. 'It is none of that, nor anything that you have done. Please believe me.'

'Then what?'

She shook her head again.

'I love you, Arabella.'

The words hung in the air between them. Words that, had he uttered them yesterday, would have filled her with such joy. Now they broke her heart.

She gave a strangled breathy laugh at the irony of it and squeezed her eyes shut to stop the tears. '*Now* you tell me.' She felt a tear escape to trickle down her cheek and wiped it away with the heel of her hand.

'I've never stopped loving you,' he said.

'You never told me. You never said it.' Her self-control was stretched so thin she could not think ahead, could only handle the awfulness of the situation one second at a time.

'I am sorry that I made such a hash of the proposal.'

He raked a hand through his hair. 'But why else did you think that I asked you to marry me?'

'For Archie. Out of duty.'

'That is only a part of it. I am marrying you because I love you, Arabella. I should have told you.'

'Oh, God,' she whispered. 'Please do not make this any harder than it already is. I cannot marry you, Dominic.' The tears were running down her cheeks now and she could not stop them. 'I cannot.'

He moved to her.

She backed away, stumbling, as she bumped against an armchair. Dominic caught her and pulled her to him, his hands gripping her upper arms tight as he stared down into her face.

'I know that you love me too, Arabella.'

She shook her head, but could not say the words to deny it. 'I cannot marry you,' She clung to the mantra, knowing that she dare not trust herself to say much else.

'You are out before all of society. Fading into the background to be my mistress once more is not an option.'

'I cannot marry you and I cannot be your mistress. I have to go away, Dominic, away from you and away from London. Tonight.'

He gave a hard-edged laugh that rang with incredulity. 'And you think I will let you go, just like that?' He shook his head and she could see the determination in his eye. 'I do not know what this is about, Arabella, but I told you before and I meant it, I have no intention of losing you again. And I have no intention of losing the son that I have only just found.'

And she was more afraid than ever because she

recognised that implacable look on his face. 'You have to release me and Archie, Dominic.'

'No, Arabella, I do not.' His jaw was set firm.

'Please.' She looked directly into his eyes for the first time. His life and that of their child hung in the balance. 'I am begging you, Dominic. Believe me when I tell you that it is better this way.'

'Better?' His eyes held hers with possession and fierce protectiveness and suspicion. 'You know that I love you. I would make you my wife, my duchess. I would give you and Archie everything you desire. And I know that you love me. So what are you running from, Arabella?'

He was coming too near the truth without even knowing what it was he was risking. She looked at him, this man that she loved so much, and she knew what she had to say to make him release her. To say it would kill a part of her for ever. But it would save him. And it would save Archie.

She looked into his eyes, so like those of their son. Inside her chest she felt the slowing of her heart. And inside her mind she felt a shutter close.

'You are mistaken, Dominic. I do not love you.' The words slipped from her mouth, slowly, quietly, to lie in the room between them. She felt as if she had screamed them at the top of her voice. She saw the shock in his eyes, the hurt, the pain, the disbelief. And it was as if she had taken a knife and plunged it into her own heart, and twisted that blade as cruelly as she could.

The clock on the mantel marked the seconds.

Tick.

Tick.

Tick.

'I do not believe you,' he whispered.

'I do not love you,' she said again, and her heart beat once…and twice…and a third time. There was nothing of warmth left in her. Where once blood had flowed in her veins there was only ice.

He stared down into her face and she saw the depth of the wound she had dealt him. She realised that in hurting him so badly she was destroying herself.

And still she stood there, so still, so immobile, and she did not allow herself to think, only to speak the lies.

'And you have only just decided this?' She saw the dangerous darkening of his eyes and the slight raising of one of his eyebrows. The hurt was still there, but there was anger before it, vying with incredulity. If she weakened in the slightest, if she gave him one sign of the truth… She grasped the handle of the knife that was already within her heart and stabbed it even deeper.

'I should not have pretended otherwise.' Her heart broke apart. She looked away because she could not bear to see the raw pain in his eyes.

'You *pretended?*' She could hear his anger. But she could bear his anger better than his hurt.

'Yes,' she said and forced herself to meet his eyes.

'When we were making love? When you cried out your pleasure as I spilled my seed within you? When I lay with you all the night through?' he demanded savagely.

'Yes,' she said again. And it was easier now that she could see his fury was taking over. She had to make him believe her.

The silence hissed between them. The seconds seemed too long. She stood there and waited, waited and waited, beneath the blast of his scrutiny, until at last he said,

'Then I will not bind you against your will.'

'Thank you.' The words sounded distant as if it was not Arabella who had spoken them, but someone else far away. She did not even feel like she was really there in the room, but was standing outside of her body watching a tragedy unfold before her.

His eyes were glacial, but she knew they only masked a hurt deeper than her own. 'Then let us sort the practicalities of this separation.'

'There is nothing to sort. We will leave tonight and go to the village of Woodside; we lived there for a while when Henry was still alive."

'Oh, no, Arabella. You will wait until morning and then you will go to Amersham, to the cottage you once shared with your family.'

'I—' she started but Dominic cut her off.

'The deeds of the cottage are already in your name, Arabella. It was to have been one of my wedding gifts to you. And do not refuse me, for I tell you that this is one of the stipulations by which I will release you.'

He had bought her the cottage. She batted the thought away, knowing she could not afford to let it in, not yet. Her mind felt frozen, but she could feel the great cracks that were spreading across the ice and she knew the barrier would not hold for much longer.

'And your other stipulations?' Second by second. It was nearly done.

'Archie is my son and I mean to provide for him and keep both him and his mother safe. You will never go near a bordello again. Do you understand, Arabella?'

'Yes.' She understood what he still thought. She had

never told him the truth. That there had only been that one night. That there had only ever been him.

'I will provide you with an allowance and I will visit Archie regularly. A boy needs a father, Arabella.'

'But—' *What would Mr Smith say to that?*

'But nothing. These are my conditions. I will agree to nothing less.'

His eyes were hard as flint. His jaw was clamped and resolute. She knew he meant exactly what he said. Smith had specified that she must not marry Dominic nor be his mistress, and that she must leave London. There had been no mention of anything else, although she did not trust what the villain would do if he came to hear of it.

'It will be as you say.' She could not hurt him or Archie any more than she had to. Hurting them to save them. Breaking Dominic's heart to save his life. Such cruel irony.

'Take the coach and what servants you will. I will close up this house when you are gone.'

She lifted the little red-leather box from beside the candlestick on the table and opened the lid to reveal the Arlesford betrothal ring nestled inside upon the cream velvet. In the dim light of the drawing room the sapphire had turned from a clear sky blue to a deep inky black as if it was in mourning. The diamonds glittered and winked in the flickering light of the solitary candle. She held the box out to him.

He hesitated for just a moment before taking it from her. The lid shut with a snap and he slipped it into his coat pocket.

'Goodbye, Arabella.' His eyes met hers and what she saw in them broke her heart into a thousand pieces. She did not trust herself to speak as she stood there barely hanging on to the shreds of her self-control.

He turned and walked away. And she just stood there, facing straight ahead at the paintings on the wall. She heard the click of the door shutting. Heard him speak to Gemmell and then his footsteps receding along the passageway. The front door closed with a slam that reverberated throughout the whole house. Only then did the ice barrier shatter as the great tide of raw emotion swept right through her, ravaging her with its ferocity. And she felt, absolutely felt, every last bit of what she had just done.

Arabella fell down to her knees and began to sob. She had saved the man she loved and their son, but at a cost so great she did not know if she could bear it. Arabella put her head in her hands and wept all the harder.

Chapter Seventeen

Dominic was in his study in Arlesford House sitting at his desk with all of the paperwork pertaining to Curzon Street open before him. He knew he should be checking through the details. But he barely noticed the letters. He was thinking of Arabella and that terrible last scene between them.

Over the subsequent days the shock and initial flare of reaction had diminished enough for him to at least begin to think straight. He was still hurt and angry beyond words, but he was also aware of an underlying feeling that something was not right. Not that anything could be right about her jilting him, again, or looking him in the eye to tell him that she did not love him. But he could not rid himself of the notion that there was something else, something that held the key to why Arabella had suddenly changed her mind. He revisited the scene in his head for the thousandth time, hearing her words again.

I cannot marry you. That same expression repeated

again and again, so stilted, and with nothing of an explanation even though he had pushed for it. She refused to be either his wife or his mistress.

I have to go away, Dominic, away from you and away from London. Tonight.

The words had made his blood run cold, but now that he analysed them stripped of all emotion, he could see that they were all wrong.

He thought of her response to his baring his heart. She had wept as if her heart was breaking, yet she had not backed down.

And when he had told her he would not let her go she had begged. Arabella, who had led him to believe she was in a brothel out of choice, rather than reveal her dire circumstances. Arabella, who had suffered so much for the sake of her pride. Arabella, who had not begged even in the worst of her situations.

And as he listened again to that conversation, without letting the hurt and the anger cloud his mind, it dawned on him that only when she had realised he was serious about not releasing her had she said that she did not love him. It smacked of a woman lying out of desperation.

What are you running from? He heard the echo of his own question and remembered the sudden flicker of fear and panic in her eyes.

And he shivered at the realisation.

A knock sounded on the door and Bentley showed in Gemmell.

Dominic was barely listening as the elderly butler detailed how all that Dominic had bought had been packed away and removed from the Curzon Street house. He was aware that he had been so selfishly

caught up in his hurt and his anger and his righteous-
ness that he had missed what was before his very eyes.

Gemmell stood on the opposite side of the desk.
'Everything is recorded in the list drawn up in the
housekeeping book.' The butler gestured towards the
open book on the desk before Dominic. 'The furnishings with which the town house was rented are all back
in place. All is in order, your Grace, and the servants
that did not accompany Mrs Marlbrook have been paid
off. Several are asking if your Grace would be so kind
as to furnish them with a character.'

'Of course.' Dominic gave a nod. 'Who did Mrs
Marlbrook take with her?' He looked at Gemmell and
it occurred to him that that the old butler, and indeed all
of the staff of Curzon Street, had always behaved as if
Arabella was their employer rather than Dominic. Not
a single servant had told him of the presence of Archie
or Mrs Tatton in the house for all of those weeks. In a
matter of loyalty Gemmell would do what he thought to
be best for Arabella. He wondered what else Gemmell
might not have told him.

'A manservant and two maids.' As if to prove the
path Dominic's thoughts were taking, Gemmell added,
'Madam asked me to move to Amersham with her, but
unfortunately I had to decline. I have family commit-
ments in London. Thirteen grandchildren to be precise,'
he said with a note of pride. Gemmell handed him the
keys. 'The house is locked up secure, your Grace.'

Dominic took the keys. 'Thank you.'

Gemmell gave a nod. 'Will that be all, your Grace?'

'Not quite.' Dominic met the old man's eyes. 'Did
anything unusual happen between Mrs Marlbrook's

return from the opera on Friday night and my visit on Saturday?'

Gemmell's gaze shifted away and there was about him a slight uneasiness. He gripped the hat and gloves in his hands a little too tightly.

'Any messages delivered? An unusual letter, perhaps? A visitor?'

He saw Gemmell's mouth tighten slightly, and felt his own expression sharpen at the small betraying gesture. Yet still Gemmell hesitated as if, even now, he thought that to tell Dominic would be to compromise his loyalty to Arabella.

'Gemmell,' said Dominic quietly, 'I have only Mrs Marlbrook's welfare at heart.'

Gemmell looked at him and Dominic saw the old man wrestle internally with the dilemma before he gave a nod.

'There was something, your Grace. A visitor called on Saturday morning. A...' the slightest of hesitations '...gentleman by the name of Mr Smith.' Dominic could sense his discomfort and understood that Gemmell had been trying to protect Arabella.

'Go on,' he encouraged.

'They spoke in the library for some twenty minutes and then I heard the door open and I thought that the gentleman meant to leave, but when I arrived there, Master Archie had escaped Mrs Tatton and was playing outside the library. Mrs Marlbrook told me to take Archie to her mother and she went back into the library with Mr Smith.' Gemmell must have been aware of how bad it sounded, for he looked as if he wished the ground would open up and swallow him.

Dominic was thinking fast. 'Did Smith see Archie?'

'He did, your Grace.'

'And when he departed, did Mrs Marlbrook ring for anything?'

'Indeed, sir. Immediately that the gentleman was gone Mrs Marlbrook and Mrs Tatton started packing for a journey.'

There was a silence after the butler's words during which Dominic digested what Gemmell had just told him.

There was some measure of foul play at work; Dominic knew it.

Words that Arabella had once uttered played again in his mind: *I did what I had to for Archie's sake. I will always do what I have to, to protect him, no matter what you say.*

And Dominic knew that whoever Smith was and whatever hold he had over Arabella, this was somehow about Archie. The significance of the man seeing his son made Dominic's blood run cold.

'Mrs Marlbrook received Smith's visit without question?'

'No, your Grace. He gained admittance by means of a message.'

'What was the message?'

The hint of a blush crept into the butler's cheeks. 'It was the name, your Grace...of a lady.' Gemmell cleared his throat and shifted his feet and did not meet Dominic's gaze.

'And the lady's name?'

'Miss Noir.'

The words fell into the silence and the study seemed to echo with their significance. Dominic felt everything in him focus and define. Arabella had done none of this of her own accord. He felt sure that the man calling himself Smith had threatened her. What he did not understand was why she had not just come to him and told him.

He rose abruptly and walked away to look out of the window until he was sure the emotions were schooled from his face. He felt his resolve harden and he knew he would find who this man was and just what dangerous game he was playing.

'Smith—what did he look like?' Dominic glanced round at Gemmell.

'He had dark hair and was well dressed. He carried a cane and was well spoken.'

Just like a hundred other gentlemen in London, thought Dominic.

'Tall, short? What of his build?'

'I am afraid I did not notice.'

'There was nothing else to distinguish him?' Dominic needed every scrap of information Gemmell could give.

'Nothing, your Grace.'

'And what of his carriage?'

'He travelled on foot. I am sorry I cannot be of more help.' Gemmell looked worried.

'Thank you for telling me, Gemmell.' Dominic sought to reassure the old man.

When the door closed quietly behind Gemmell Dominic rang the bell for his horse to be readied.

If 'Smith' had known that Arabella was Miss Noir, there was only one place he could have learned that information.

Mrs Tatton was settling back into life in Amersham just as if she had never been away. Arabella was not.

Dominic had had the cottage refurbished but, aside from that, the little house and its long garden were as Arabella remembered, except that now there was no need to scrimp over coal or count the pennies for food. The generosity of the allowance that Dominic had settled upon her made the misery weigh all the more heavily in her heart.

Dominic. She tried to turn her mind away from consciously thinking of him. She had to survive for Archie's sake, but if she allowed herself to think of Dominic and of the extent of the hurt she had been forced to deal him, she was not sure she could make it through the rest of this day, never mind the next.

He would come to visit Archie, and Arabella dreaded to see him. But she longed for it too.

She toyed with the food on the dinner plate before her.

'Eliza Breckenbridge invited all three of us for dinner next week,' her mother was saying with an excited air. 'And Meg Brown could scarce believe what a fine boy Archie was.'

The country air had been good for her mother's lungs, Arabella thought as she glanced across the kitchen table at her. Mrs Tatton's appetite had improved and Arabella had not seen such a healthy colour in her cheeks in years.

'Are you even listening to me, Arabella?'

'Of course, Mama. You were telling me of your friends.'

'And not one bad word have they said, not one slight, though they must have guessed by now the truth of Archie's parentage.' Mrs Tatton added a little more butter to her potatoes before finishing them off. 'It is good to be back here, Arabella; I had not realised how much I missed the village.'

'I am glad that you are happy, Mama.' Arabella forced her lips to curve in the semblance of a smile. But it felt as dead and wooden as the rest of her.

'Dear Arabella.' Her mother sighed and reached across the table, taking Arabella's hand in her own. 'You are so brave in light of what that man did to you.'

'Please, Mama. Let us speak of it no more.' She was not proud of the lie she had told her mother, but she knew Mrs Tatton understood her too well to believe that Arabella had just changed her mind over the marriage. And she did not trust that if she had explained about Mr Smith and his threats her mother would not have gone straight to Dominic and told him of it. And she could not risk that. Not when Dominic's life and her son's welfare hung in the balance. Any thaw in relations between Mrs Tatton and Dominic had ceased with Arabella's lies. In her mother's book Dominic Furneaux was akin to the very devil himself.

'Abandoning you for a second time. I knew I should not have trusted him for a minute. Such untruths, and about his own father!'

'Mama,' she said firmly, 'I have asked you not to discuss these matters in front of Archie.'

'You are right, Arabella.' Mrs Tatton had the grace to blush. 'I beg your pardon.'

Arabella turned her attention to Archie, who was sitting listening with a worried expression upon his face. She reached across to Archie's plate and cut the chicken breast that lay there untouched into small tempting pieces. 'Now come along, slowcoach. You have not eaten your chicken. And you have not told me how school was today.' Archie was a new attendee at the village school.

He seemed unusually quiet this evening, and he had eaten little of his dinner.

'I am not hungry, Mama.' He kept his face downcast and did not meet her gaze.

'Archie?' Arabella looked more closely at her son's face, placing her fingers on his chin and angling his face in the light to peer at the faint beginnings of a bruise around his eye and a slight swelling upon his lip. 'Is there something that you wish to tell me?'

'No, Mama.'

'Have you been scrapping with the other boys?'

'The bigger boys said bad things about you, Mama, so I hit them and they hit me back.'

She felt her heart turn over. 'Well, I thank you for your defence of my good name, Archie.' Arabella stroked a hand to his hair. 'But they are just silly boys and they do not know what they are saying. Stay away from the big boys and play with the little boys who are more your age.'

'What is a bastard, Mama?'

Mrs Tatton gasped with the shock of it, inhaled the mouthful of food she was chewing and started to choke and cough. By the time Arabella had dealt with her mother and the coughing fit was over, Archie had run off to play in the garden, and there was no need to answer his question. But Arabella knew she could not avoid it for ever, even if Archie was not illegitimate in the strict sense of the word.

Arabella stood that night at the window of the little room she shared with her son. Archie's soft breathing sounded from the truckle bed behind her, regular and reassuring. She stared out at the darkening blue of the sky and the tiny pinpricks of stars that twinkled there. A crescent moon curved its sickle amongst the stars and she knew that soon the sky would wash with inky blackness. Her heart was heavy and aching as she stood there and watched the night progress. No matter how bad she had thought it when she believed Dominic to have left her all those years ago, nothing compared to how she felt now. A part of her had died. She wondered if she would ever feel alive again.

It did not matter what she did, she could not protect Archie from every hurt. She was all that stood between him and the world, and she thought of how she had deprived Archie of his father and Dominic of his son. And for the first time she wondered if she had done the right thing over Mr Smith's blackmail. Maybe she should have gone to Dominic and told him of the man and his threats. Maybe Dominic would have dealt with Smith…and maybe Dominic would have been found dead in an alleyway with a knife between his ribs.

She could not risk his life because of her own weakness. She stood and watched the night and she knew that, were the choice laid before her again, she would make the very same decision. The knowledge did not make her feel any better. She dropped a kiss to Archie's forehead and silently slipped from the room.

'I paid you most handsomely, madam, and now I find that you have been less than discreet.'

Within the drawing room of her House of Rainbow Pleasures, in which they both were standing, Mrs Silver paled beneath the cold raze of Dominic's gaze. 'My girls and I took your money, your Grace, and we kept our side of the bargain. We have spoken not one word of Miss Noir to anyone else. Of that I give you my most solemn word.'

'You cannot be so certain of your girls.'

'I am certain enough, your grace.' The dark coiffure of her hair made her skin look almost bloodless. 'I trust them.'

He was thinking fast. Smith had to have recognised Arabella somehow. There were possibilities about which he did not want to think, and yet he knew that he had to.

'Was there ever any trouble between Miss Noir and any of her...' he forced himself to say the words, '...gentlemen customers?'

Mrs Silver looked at him with a strange expression. 'There was no one else, your Grace.'

'Think back very carefully. It is important. Maybe there was someone she made mention of as—'

'No, your Grace,' Mrs Silver interrupted him. 'When I say that there was no one else, I mean exactly that. Arabella only came to me on the day of your visit. She had sold herself to no one before you. I thought you knew.'

Dominic was reeling. Arabella had not been a whore, until he had made her one. He felt the chill ripple right through him and with it the magnitude of the guilt of what he had done to her. No wonder Mrs Tatton had thought him a scoundrel. No wonder Arabella had balked at him making her his mistress. He had spent the last few weeks blaming it all on his father. But he knew now that he was as much to blame as the late duke.

It was even worse than he had thought. Mrs Tatton had been right; had he been a better man he would have helped Arabella without making his own selfish demands. He would have given her the money to leave the brothel and set her up without making her his mistress. And it should not have mattered if she was already a whore or not. But Dominic knew he was not a good man. He had wanted her...and he had taken her. And now he must live with the knowledge of the terrible thing he had done to her for the rest of his life.

And he had wondered why she had not told him of Archie!

Mrs Silver was staring at him and he knew he had to pull himself together. He composed his thoughts.

'How did she come to be here?'

'I saw her in a dressmaker's shop when she was seeking employment. Times are lean; there is not much work to be had. She looked tired and down on her luck.'

She had been desperate.

Dominic remembered what Mrs Tatton had said of her selling her shoes. She had sold herself to him to save their son. And he, like the bastard he was, had bought her.

'But, even so, she was a beautiful woman, and I knew she would be an asset to my rainbow. So I told her of the money she could earn and gave her my card. And she came here the very same evening as you.'

Hell! He clenched his teeth to stop the curse escaping. 'And the dressmaker in whose shop you found her?'

'Madame Boisseron.'

Dominic closed his eyes and bit down even harder. He wondered if he had done anything right by Arabella in all of this time.

'She has a shop in—'

But Dominic was already on his way out to find the woman he had employed to dress Arabella as his mistress.

In Amersham Archie was suffering from another sore stomach.

'This is the third time this week that the boy has been in this state, Arabella.' Mrs Tatton's face was creased with worry.

Archie was moaning and tossing and turning within the bed. A faint sheen of sweat was moist upon his brow and his face was pale. Arabella placed a hand over his forehead to feel how hot he was, and found the skin beneath to be surprisingly cool. She peered anxiously into his face.

'My tummy is sore, Mama,' Archie moaned.

'We have sent for the doctor to come and examine you.'

Archie began to cry. 'I do not want the doctor.'

'What nonsense is this?' said Arabella gently. 'He is a kind old man who will make you better.'

Archie said nothing, just closed his eyes.

There was a knocking at the front door of the cottage and Arabella hurried down to let in the elderly Dr Phipps whom she had known all her life, and indeed who had delivered her into this world as a baby. But when she opened the front door it was not Dr Phipps standing on the step.

'Mrs Marlbrook?' The man was as young as Arabella, and had striking blue eyes that held a tinge of green. His hair was muddy blond and he was smiling a very pleasant smile. 'I am Doctor Roxby, Doctor Phipps retired last year, I am afraid. You sent a message that your son is unwell.'

Arabella invited the young doctor inside. 'Archie has been complaining of a sore stomach, twice last week and three times this week. The pains are severe enough to keep him bedridden and they seem to be getting worse.'

Arabella and the doctor climbed the narrow spiral staircase of the cottage to reach the bedchambers upstairs.

Doctor Roxby ducked his head to enter the bedchamber that Arabella and Archie shared. 'Rest assured, ma'am, I will do everything that I can for him.'

The doctor examined Archie carefully while Arabella and her mother looked on. His manner was kind and reassuring. And while he worked he spoke to Archie telling the boy what he was doing and asking Archie questions. Did it hurt when he pressed here? Was this worse? Or better?

'Is he using the chamber pot regularly, Mrs Marlbrook?'

'He is.'

'And eating as normal?'

'His appetite has been impaired of late.'

'Nothing that we cannot sort, young man,' said the doctor, smiling down at Archie.

Arabella and her mother went downstairs with the doctor, leaving Archie to rest.

'I can find nothing wrong with him, ma'am. Perhaps it is more a problem of his sensibilities. Archie tells me that he has recently started at the village school. Might there have been any associated problems?'

Arabella saw her mother throw her a meaningful

look, and thought of the fight that Archie had got into during his first week there.

'I will look into it, Doctor,' she said, not wishing to reveal the details of the affair.

Mrs Tatton, who had been standing quietly listening to all that the doctor had to say, stepped forwards. 'My daughter has been a widow these years past, Doctor, and the boy suffers for the lack of a man's influence.' She looked pointedly at Arabella as if to remind her that it was all Dominic's fault.

Arabella looked away, feeling the sting of guilt at blaming Dominic for a crime of which he was innocent.

'I will call again in a few days to check upon Archie.' Doctor Roxby accepted his payment and took his leave of them.

As soon as the door shut Arabella leaned her back upon it.

'Well, I have never heard of such a thing in all my life,' said Mrs Tatton.

'Now that he has said it, I begin to see the signs,' said Arabella. 'Archie is better on the days he does not have to go to school. After only one day back there he is ill again. He speaks so very little of it. And never makes mention of the other boys.' She felt quite sick at the thought that the bullying had continued. 'Why did he not tell me, Mama?'

'Maybe he did not wish to cause you worry or perhaps he has been threatened into silence by the bullies.'

How could she not have realised?

'We can guess the cause of the bullying. You heard what he asked at the dinner table the other week.' Her mother lowered her voice. '*Bastard,* indeed! You see what *he* has done to the boy, Arabella? Why could he not have just married you, and been done with it? And then none of this would have happened. But, no, he decides that you are not good enough for him— again—and now we are come to this, with your son lying upstairs afraid to go to school for fear of what the other boys are saying about his parentage.' Mrs Tatton sat down heavily and placed her trembling hands upon the parlour table.

'There is no good to be had going down that route, Mama. Let us just deal with this the best we can. Please be kind enough to check upon Archie while I visit the schoolhouse.' And Arabella left before she could no longer stopper her tongue and the terribleness of the truth burst out, revealing to her mother the whole mess of it.

Dominic's visit to Madame Boisseron's shop had convinced him of her innocence. The woman was honest and he believed her assertion that, such was the delicacy and secrets involved in the affairs of her clientele, for her to talk of any of her customers would be to lose her business.

That evening he was sitting alone in his study trying to think of how on earth he was going to trace the man calling himself Smith, when Bentley showed Hunter in.

Hunter sat down in the wing chair on the other side of the desk from Dominic.

Dominic poured his friend a large brandy using the crystal-cut decanter and glasses on the silver tray by the window.

'Not having one yourself?' Hunter took the glass with thanks and lounged back in his armchair.

Dominic shook his head.

'Misbourne has been asking around about you at White's.'

'Just what I want to hear,' said Dominic. 'Did you come over to tell me that?'

'No. I came to see how you are.' Dominic could feel Hunter's watchful gaze.

'I take it you know?' Dominic could tell from the compassion on his friend's face that he did.

'All of London knows. It makes no sense, Dominic. Arabella has even more reasons than you to want this marriage. Why would she break the betrothal?'

'I believe she was acting under duress. Someone got to her, Sebastian. Someone who knew that she was Miss Noir.'

Hunter's face sharpened. He sat up straighter in his chair. 'I think there is something you should hear, concerning Miss Noir, Dominic. I paid another little visit to Mrs Silver's house the other night, to see Tilly, Miss Rose. In the course of things she mentioned that there have been quite a few enquiries about Miss Noir.' Hunter met Dominic's gaze.

'It is not unexpected. They were well paid to stay quiet. And Mrs Silver is adamant they have not talked.'

'And I think she is correct for Tilly would not speak of Miss Noir to me. But she did let slip that there was one gentleman who offered serious gelt—I mean hundreds of pounds—for the smallest scrap of information concerning Miss Noir. Tilly thinks that one of the footmen may have been tempted to break his silence. Apparently the servant has recently disappeared. And there were whispers that he was experiencing financial difficulties of a nature similar to my own.'

'Gambling debts?'

Hunter gave a nod.

'And what of the gentleman asking the questions?'

'A Mr Smith, apparently, although I doubt he would have been fool enough to use his real name.' Hunter gave a grim smile, which soon faded as his eyes met Dominic's.

Dominic's gaze narrowed. 'Smith?'

'Indeed. I see it has some significance for you.'

'Did the girl tell you anything else other than his name?'

Hunter smiled again. 'Oh, yes. Very observant is Tilly. She described him right down to his "dark dangerous eyes", and his walking cane with a "monstrous silver wolf's head" as its handle. She noticed it because it had tiny emerald chips for eyes.'

A wolf's head on a walking cane? There was something familiar about that. Dominic had seen such an item before, but he could not remember where. 'Cannot be too many of those around.'

'No,' said Hunter with a meaningful smile. 'I see your mind follows the same path as mine. I suppose now you will be off hunting down this Smith character tonight rather than hitting the town with young Northcote and Bullford and a few of the others?'

The two men exchanged a look.

'Damned shame. Thought you might have changed our present run of bad luck on the tables.'

'Another night, my friend,' Dominic said and gave Hunter a light thump on the shoulder. 'After I have found Smith.'

Chapter Eighteen

Dominic was becoming increasingly frustrated with the slow progress of the investigation. It had been half an hour since the ex-Bow Street runner had left his study in Arlesford House and Dominic was musing over the scraps of information the man had delivered. Despite five days of intense questioning, tracking and bribing, it had proved impossible to find the silversmith who had crafted the unusual head of the walking cane. And all enquiries to discover its owner had so far met with a wall of silence.

Dominic's other lines of enquiries had been more fruitful. He knew that Smith had attempted to buy information concerning Arabella in her guise as both Miss Noir and Mrs Marlbrook from a variety of sources, including the servants both in his and Arabella's households. He knew that enquiries had been made concerning who was paying the rent on the town house in Curzon Street, who had ordered and paid for the furnishings and who had arranged for and paid the servants.

The missing manservant from Mrs Silver's had been found in a gaming house in Brighton, frittering away the last of his enormous bribe on the tables, with not a one of his debts cleared, and a very ugly posse of creditors at the door. Five hundred pounds was an extraordinary sum to have been paid for a description and confirmation of the fact that the Duke of Arlesford had bedded Miss Noir on her first night in the place and bought her the next evening from Mrs Silver. And although Dominic did not yet know the identity of Smith, he did know that someone very rich had gone to a lot of trouble to find Arabella.

The obvious next step was to go up to Amersham and speak to Arabella, but there was a risk that if he did she would tell him nothing, Smith would get word of it and then would discover her whereabouts. He needed to find this Smith first. And he wondered again why the hell Arabella had not come to him for help. No matter the threats Smith had made about revealing her identity, Dominic knew he could have protected her. He massaged the tightness from his temple and poured himself a brandy.

There came the sound of the front door being opened and then quietly closed again. Dominic barely noticed it. What he did notice was the light running footsteps that pattered quietly across the marble flags of his hallway. He felt the warning whisper against the back of his neck and goosepimple his skin. Dominic stopped lounging, sat upright and set his glass down on the desk. His hand was slipping within his desk drawer just as the door burst open and a small dark cloaked figure rushed into his study to stand before him.

She gave a small scream when she saw him sitting behind the desk. 'They said that you would not be—' The woman bit off what she had been about to say. 'That is, I—I….' She twisted her small black gloved hands tight together.

Dominic's fingers relaxed around the handle of his pistol for he recognised the voice and he knew who it was standing there before him. 'What are you doing sneaking into my study, Lady Marianne?' He raised one eyebrow and looked at her with his sternest face.

'Then you know that it is me,' she said softly and slipped the hood back to reveal her fair hair scraped back in a severe chignon. Lady Marianne Winslow stood there, her cheeks flushed with embarrassment, her eyes huge and frightened. She clutched the cloak to her as if he were a beast about to ravish her.

'You have not answered my question,' he said without the flicker of a smile.

Lady Marianne's face drained of all colour. She began to edge towards the door. 'I fear there has been a dreadful mistake,' she said and he could hear the slight tremor that shook her voice. 'I should not be here.'

'No, Lady Marianne. You should not.' He rose and in one swift motion was across the floor to block her exit.

Lady Marianne gave a gasp and stopped where she was. 'Please, your Grace. Let me leave unaccosted.'

'You may leave once you have told me what you are doing here.' His words were so cold and hard that she actually shivered.

She nodded her submission. 'I was told that you

would not be here, that I was to steal in unnoticed and leave a letter upon your desk. After which I must leave again as quietly as I had entered.' She slipped a hand into her pocket and held out a neatly folded letter. He could see the paper shaking between her fingers.

He took it from her, noting that the front was addressed to his name alone. 'Who sent you?' he asked as he broke the sealing wax.

Lady Marianne gave no answer.

He began opening up the letter. 'Spit it out, Lady Marianne, or rest assured I will keep you here until you do.'

The girl shook her head. 'I will not tell you,' she whispered.

He opened the last fold of the letter. And he knew then who had sent her and what this was about. For the paper was blank.

He moved swiftly to the bell and rang it. His butler appeared almost immediately.

'Escort this young lady out via the back door, Bentley.'

Bentley was experienced enough not to reveal anything of his surprise at finding a young woman alone in his master's study. 'Shall I summon a hackney carriage for the lady, your Grace?'

'No.'

Bentley glanced up at Dominic, the question clear in his eyes before his lowered them again.

'I am sure that she has her papa awaiting outside this house even as we speak,' he said to the butler, and then to Lady Marianne, 'Am I not right?'

Even if she spoke not one word, she was betrayed by the blush that stained her cheeks.

'Get her out of here as quickly as you can, Bentley,' he commanded, knowing that he was right about what had been planned for this night.

But it was too late.

Already he could hear the hammering of fists upon the front door and heard the men enter the house without the decency of waiting for an invitation.

'I will fetch Hillard and Dowd immediately, your Grace.' As Bentley opened the study door two men rushed in.

'There is no need, Bentley. I will deal with this. Leave us.'

The butler looked unconvinced, but he left all the same just as he had been told.

Dominic moved back to resume his seat.

'Good evening, gentlemen. I have been expecting you,' said Dominic as he surveyed the Earl of Misbourne and Viscount Linwood who were standing between him and Lady Marianne. 'What a nice family reunion.'

'Papa! Francis!' She cried and hurried to her father and brother. 'Thank goodness you are here. It has all gone horribly wrong!'

'No, Lady Marianne, I suspect it has gone entirely according to plan,' said Dominic grimly. He gestured to the two chairs on the other side of his desk. 'Do take a seat, gentlemen.'

Misbourne ignored him and stayed where he was. He puffed out his chest. 'Look here, you scoundrel, Arlesford. What do you think you are doing with my daughter? You have abducted her with the intention of seducing her.'

'What are you saying, Papa? You sent me here to deliver—'

'Silence, Marianne! Do not dare to utter another word, you foolish chit!' roared the earl.

The girl's face paled and she rapidly closed her mouth and backed away to stand by the door.

'Well, Arlesford?' demanded the earl.

'Well?' echoed Dominic.

'You must know that she is ruined just by being here—a gently bred innocent alone in the house of one of London's most scandalous rakes.'

'If it becomes known that she is here, then, yes, I agree, your daughter's reputation would not remain unscathed.'

'Then you will do the gentlemanly thing and save both her honour and your own by offering for her hand?' Misbourne's eyes glittered as he said the words. He could barely keep the smile from his face.

'Indeed not, sir. As you have already pointed out, I am known as a rake. Why should I care that Lady Marianne is ruined? She is *your* daughter.'

'Good Gad! Where is your sense of honour, sir?'

'In the same place as yours, Misbourne. I care not if you strip her naked and sit her upon my doorstep for all the world to see.' From the corner of his eye he saw Lady Marianne clutch a hand to her mouth and he felt sorry that she had to witness this. 'You may publish the story in every one of your newspapers and still I tell you most solemnly, sir, I will not marry her.'

Misbourne's face turned an unhealthy shade of puce. And then paled to an ashen shade as he realised his plan had failed. 'You have reneged on a contract that was agreed by your father. This betrothal has been in place since before my daughter was in her cradle.'

'As I told you before, Misbourne, I will not be bound by a contract that never existed. I thought that we could maintain some degree of civility between us because of our political association.'

'You led me to believe that you would consider taking her as your wife.'

'If I did, then I am sorry, sir, for it was never my intention.'

'You have made us a laughing stock before all of London, you damnable cur!' the earl growled. 'I should call you out!'

'I would be only too happy to oblige you, sir,' said Dominic coldly.

'No, Papa!' he heard Lady Marianne cry in the background.

'A moment, sir.' Viscount Linwood laid his hand upon his father's shoulder. 'We have not concluded our negotiation with his Grace.'

'On the contrary,' said Dominic, 'I consider the matter closed.'

'But we have not yet touched on Mrs Marlbrook, or should I call her Miss Noir? And then there is the consideration of the boy. I believe his name is Archie. What a startling resemblance he does bear his papa.' Linwood smiled a dark dangerous smile, and Dominic's gaze dropped to see the tiny glint of emeralds and the shape of a wolf's head in the handle of the walking cane beneath Linwood's palm.

Dominic's stomach turned over. He felt his blood turn to ice. 'It was you,' he said, hardly able to believe it. Smith. And in that moment all the answers slipped into place. Linwood part-owned his father's newspapers. He had journalistic connections. He had money in plenty. And an interest in seeing that Dominic did not marry Arabella.

'Think of what it would do to the boy were the truth of his mama and his most famous papa to be published throughout the capital. The duke, his doxy and their bastard—what a headline that would make!'

Dominic reacted first and thought later. His fist smashed hard against Linwood's jaw. It happened so fast the viscount did not see it coming and was left staggering and clutching a hand to his bleeding lip.

'That is what you used to threaten Arabella when you went to Curzon Street, is it not?' Dominic grabbed at Linwood's lapels and backed him against the wall.

'That and the threat of violence against your person if she told you. Did you think that I would just let you get away with how you have treated my sister?' snarled Linwood. 'The snub you have dealt us? You arrogant villain, Arlesford! Marry Marianne or I swear to you I will print every damn word of it.'

Dominic looked Linwood straight in the eye and watched the viscount pale. He allowed the deadly intent to show for the briefest of moments before masking it once more. And when he looked again at Linwood he was more under control and ready to play the biggest game of bluff of his life.

'Sit down, gentlemen. Let us discuss the matter.' He gestured once more to the chairs by his desk. 'I am sure you will forgive my outburst…given the provocation. The urge to protect one's blood is strong. I think we, all of us in this study, understand that. You have seen what young Archie's mother was prepared to sacrifice.

Can you expect his father to be any less protective?' He resumed his seat behind his desk.

Both Linwood and Misbourne still looked wary, but Dominic could see that they thought victory was at hand. This time they sat down as they were bid.

'A father has a duty to his son…and his daughter,' said Misbourne. 'By marrying my daughter you would be protecting your son. Only think if the scandalous story were to come out, what it would do to the child.'

'I do, sir, and thus I will do all in my power to avoid its publication.'

Misbourne nodded and could not quite hide the triumph in his smile. 'I am glad you begin to see sense, Arlesford.'

'Indeed.' Dominic returned the smile, but it was a smile that would have frozen the Thames. 'However, it does occur to me that the story Lord Linwood outlined is perhaps not the best one to fit the facts.'

'How so, sir?' Linwood's eyes narrowed slightly.

Dominic smiled again. 'Let us review the facts: firstly, there is the blonde masked courtesan, Miss Noir, whom, in contrast to my previous custom, I have gone to great lengths to keep secret. Secondly, there is the Earl of Misbourne's desperate insistence that I marry his daughter, his *blonde* daughter. And finally, there is the small matter of his daughter's presence here, at Arlesford House, the home of a dissolute bachelor, late at night.'

'What are you saying, Arlesford?' Misbourne demanded.

'Why, that the woman behind the mask of Miss Noir is none other than Lady Marianne Winslow, your daughter, sir.'

'Damnable lies, sir!' The words exploded from Misbourne as he jumped to his feet.

'So you say, but what would the *ton* make of it, I wonder?'

Linwood got to his feet too, staring daggers across the desk at Dominic. 'We have a witness to place Arabella Marlbrook as Miss Noir in Mrs Silver's brothel.'

'Do you? Have you tried to contact him lately?' Dominic's gaze was glacial and deadly. He rose and stood taller than the other two men. 'It seems you did not pay him quite enough for his creditors to be completely forgiving. I fear for his health. And as for the rest of Mrs Silver's household, I am sure that they will back my account of events.'

'People will see that you paid for their lies,' said Misbourne.

'People already know why a notorious rake would pay Mrs Silver and her girls. But why would an upstanding gentleman like Viscount Linwood be paying Mrs Silver, other than for her silence over his setting up his own sister as a doxy to trap a duke.'

Misbourne shook his head. 'That is too far-fetched for anyone to believe.'

'On the contrary, sir, people will see it as a bold and ambitious plot that will only enhance your already formidable reputation. Your daughter's reputation, I fear, will not fare so well.' Dominic smiled a cold hard smile. 'No, Misbourne, it is you who will be seen as the liar. And the blackmail of a respectable widow as a final act of desperation on your part.'

'Damn you, Arlesford!' Linwood's knuckles gripped white against the wolf's head handle of his cane.

Dominic glanced across at a white-faced Lady Marianne and felt the sting of his conscience. 'Thank you, gentlemen, I see that this business is now concluded. You may use the back door if you care to save the girl from further scrutiny.'

He watched while Bentley and two footmen escorted his unwanted guests away. The door closed behind them and Dominic relaxed back down into his chair. He would weather the storm if he had to, to protect Arabella and his son, but he doubted it would come to that; instinct told him that Misbourne and Linwood now realised they had overplayed their hand.

Dominic stared at the glass of brandy on the desk before him, the tawny amber of the liquid burnished red by the warm glow from the fire. He knew now why Arabella had refused to marry him. He knew now why she had lied and said that she did not love him. And he knew why she had not come to him and told him of Smith's threats. She had sacrificed herself to save him and their child.

He lifted the glass, and took a sip of the brandy, breathing his relief as the heat and strength of the alcohol burned his throat. He resisted the urge to run out to the stables, climb upon his horse and gallop off in the direction of Amersham. There were matters to be dealt with before he left London, matters that he would attend to at first light. He schooled his impatience and let his mind run to thoughts of Arabella.

'Archie is in fine health this morning, Mrs Marlbrook,' Doctor Roxby smiled.

Arabella was just about to speak when her mother rushed in there before her.

'Indeed, Doctor,' agreed Mrs Tatton. 'Your visits have made all the difference to my grandson's health.'

The doctor glanced away, slightly embarrassed. 'I am sure the improvement is down to Mrs Marlbrook's intervention at the school.'

'Miss Wallace is keeping a close eye on Archie and the boys who were taunting him.'

'Archie certainly seems to have taken a shine to you, Doctor,' said Mrs Tatton.

'And I, to him. He is a pleasant child, ma'am,' said Doctor Roxby politely. 'And a credit to his mother.'

'Would you care to stay for dinner, Doctor?' Arabella heard her mother ask and could have cringed in disbelief.

Doctor Roxby's eyes met Arabella's and she saw in their clear blue-green gaze both question and interest. She looked away, not wishing to encourage him.

'Thank you for your most kind offer, Mrs Tatton, but I am afraid I must decline upon this occasion. I have other patients to call upon and the hour grows late.'

'Perhaps another day, Doctor.' Mrs Tatton smiled.

'Indeed,' said Doctor Roxby and he smiled as his gaze once more went to Arabella. He gave a bow and, lifting up his black leather bag, he left.

Arabella waited until she heard the creak of the garden gate before she rounded upon her mother. 'Mama, what on earth did you think you were doing inviting him to stay for dinner?'

'It was a simple enough offer, Arabella,' her mother protested.

'I do not wish to give him the wrong impression.'

'Nonsense, Arabella,' said her mother brusquely. 'He is a respectable gentleman. I can see in his eyes that he is kind, and look how well he takes to Archie, and Archie to him.'

'He is only doing his job. Do not read more into it than there is.'

'Oh, stuff, Arabella. I am not yet in my dotage. I see the way he looks at you, and why not? You are still a young and comely woman. As a doctor within our community, young, handsome, and not yet married, he must be in want of a wife.'

'Mama, it is just a matter of time before he hears the village gossip about...' She could not bring herself to say Dominic's name. The pain was still too intense. 'About Archie's parentage. Indeed, I am surprised he has not heard already.' She knew she sounded bitter, but she could not help it. She just felt so miserable.

'You imagine the gossip to be something it is not,' chided her mother. 'And have I not already told you the truth? Of course there are whispers, but the villagers are our own people, and it was not as if you were left unwed with a child. They know you married Mr Marlbrook, and would have accepted you and Archie just the same. And, yes, it is unfortunate that the boy is the very image of...' her mother's voice hardened as it always did when she spoke of Dominic '...*that man,* but it was the old duke who forced us from this village, and nothing else.'

'Perhaps you are right, and indeed I pray that you are, for I want more than anything for Archie to be happy here.'

'And he will be.' Her mother patted her hand. 'The children will soon tire of their taunting.'

'I hope so,' said Arabella.

Her mother looked into her face. 'I can see that

you are unhappy and I do not blame you after all that you have been through with that villain Arlesford. But you must move on, Arabella, both for your own sake and for Archie's. The boy needs a father and you, a husband.'

'No, Mama,' Arabella objected. 'We are fine as we are. We do not need another man.' She knew her mother meant well, but Mrs Tatton did not know the truth. She did not know the terrible lies that Arabella had told. She did not know the guilt and the misery that weighed heavy on her heart.

'Will you hide yourself away here in this cottage for the rest of your life because he broke your heart? That is not you, Arabella. You have pride. You have spirit. You are a strong woman. A woman not unlike myself when I was younger.'

Her mother smiled at her, but in the smile was sadness and her eyes were filled with worry. Arabella felt all the worse, because it was her own fault. One lie upon another, and too many of those that she loved were suffering because of it.

'You must do what is best for Archie,' said Mrs Tatton.

'I always have,' said Arabella, 'and I always will.' No matter how hard that would be. No matter what it cost them all.

'And I am glad of it. I know you do not believe me when I tell you there will come a time, not so very far in the future, when the affection of a good and kind gentleman will heal your heart, Arabella, and make you forget all about Dominic Furneaux.'

No one and nothing would ever make her forget Dominic. She would never stop loving him. But she knew it would be a mistake to say this now to her mother. She did not want to talk any more about such a tender subject, especially one about which she could not tell her mother the truth. So she just smiled and gave her mother's hand a gentle pat.

'I know you have ever had my best interests at heart, Mama, and I thank you for it, but matters are still too raw. It needs to be just you, me and Archie for now.' And then she rose from the table and went to check on her son.

Dominic dealt with matters as speedily as he could the next morning. He visited the Archbishop of Canterbury, Moffat, his man of business, and finally Hunter, who, despite the afternoon hour, was only just up following an 'all nighter' at the gaming tables, but who nevertheless rallied to Dominic's request.

'And so Smith was really Linwood all along,' said Hunter as he stood there in his bedchamber with his chin up, letting his valet tie his cravat in some wonderful new knot. 'Damn the man. You should have run the villain through.'

'No doubt,' replied Dominic drily. Around them was a flurry of activity, as servants hurriedly took Hunter's clothes from their drawers and wardrobe and packed them in a travelling bag.

'Does Arabella know you are coming?'

'No. A letter would not arrive significantly before we do, and besides, I think what has to be said would be better in person.'

'I'll say,' said Hunter with a grin. He glanced at the coat that was being folded into his bag and spoke to his manservant. 'No, no, Telfer, my best one, man, the black superfine from Weston.'

In a matter of fifteen minutes Hunter was ready in his riding coat and breeches, his fully packed travelling bag strapped behind his saddle, and the two men geeing their mounts out on to the Aylesbury road.

Dominic waited until they had left London behind and were trotting along in the countryside before he spoke again.

'There is one other thing that I ought to tell you before we reach Amersham, Hunter.'

'What is that?' Hunter glanced across at him.

The small matter of his son. And Dominic told his friend all about Archie.

'Hell, Dominic, I had no idea. So Arabella married Marlbrook because she was—' He stopped himself just in time.

Dominic raised an eyebrow and drew him a droll look.

Silence, and then Hunter asked, 'Did Linwood know of the boy?'

'Most definitely.'

'Ah, I think I understand your feelings towards Linwood. Bad enough threatening your woman, but your son too?'

Dominic's eyes darkened at the memory. Linwood was lucky to have walked out of his house alive.

'Anything else you have not told me?' Hunter asked with a grin.

'Nothing you need know,' said Dominic, and smiled. 'Now, you'd better get that horse moving if we want to reach Amersham before midnight.'

Hunter laughed and kicked his horse to a canter. And Dominic thought of Arabella in the little Tatton cottage in Amersham, and he raced his mount past Hunter.

It was late by the time they reached Amersham. A waxing moon near to fullness hung high in the dark night sky and helped guide their way. The glow of light from the edges of windows shone in some of the cottages down in the village, but all was silent, all was still. Dominic glanced in the direction of the Tatton cottage, and although he was tired, travel stained and saddle sore he was restless to spur his horse down there and knock upon Arabella's door. Was she awake? Was she thinking of him as he thought of her?

'Do not even think it,' warned Hunter's quiet voice by his side. 'You want her to see you in your best light, Dominic, not when you are in need of a bed, a bath, a shave and some fresh clothes. Besides, I need a drink, very, very badly. I hope you have got some of that rather fine brandy of yours up here.'

Hunter was right. Dominic wanted everything to be readied and perfect when he saw Arabella again. He wanted to take her in his arms and tell her that everything was going to be all right. 'Come on then, five minutes to the Hall. And then you may have your brandy.' With one last longing glance towards the Tatton cottage he turned and spurred his horse along the road towards Shardeloes Hall.

At half past six the following evening Arabella bathed Archie. Once he had been dressed in his night-clothes with his hair dried by the fire and his supper of honeyed toast and warm milk long since eaten, she settled him in his little truckle bed. Then she drew the curtains across the small bedchamber window to block out the light, which was still bright. With the curtains closed the room felt dim and safe. Archie yawned as he snuggled down beneath the covers.

She bent to give him his goodnight kiss. 'Sleep tight, little lamb,' she said as usual, determined not to let her son see how miserable she felt.

'Mama,' he said quietly, 'I miss Dominic.'

'I miss him too, Archie.' She stroked his hair and kept her voice light.

'Will he come to visit us soon?'

'I do not know.' She forced the smile to her face. 'No more questions, my darling. You must go to sleep like a good boy, for it is Sunday tomorrow and we have church.'

'Not church, Mama,' he grumbled, but snuggled down and closed his eyes just the same.

Arabella walked down the stairs to the parlour, where her mother was sitting waiting for her.

'How is he?'

'Fine, because there is no school. I only hope he is well enough come Monday.' Arabella pinched the bridge of her nose and curbed the rest of her worries for Archie and his future.

'That Dominic Furneaux has much to answer for.'

Arabella did not feel strong enough to withstand another argument with her mother over Dominic. Her confidence felt shaken and her normal calm disposition ruffled. She was tense and anxious. 'Mama, please let us speak no more of Dominic.'

'No more? We have not spoken of him at all for

the sake of the boy. And I have held my tongue long enough.'

Arabella gave a sigh and sat down in the armchair by the window. She lifted her needlework. 'Mama, there is nothing to be gained by this.'

'He abandoned you, not once but twice, Arabella, and in the worst possible of ways. Publicly announcing a betrothal only to break it off again. Of all the cruel most humiliating ways that he might—'

'Mama!' Arabella said quickly. It had been cruel. It had been humiliating. But for Dominic, not for her. 'Remember that it is Dominic who gifted us this cottage and Dominic who is paying us an allowance that we may live a comfortable existence.'

'It is only right that a man should pay for his own child, Arabella. Especially a man who is now as rich and powerful as Dominic. Archie is his son; heaven knows he has done precious little else for the boy. Casting him off without a care—it breaks my heart to see it. The boy should be heir to a dukedom, not suffering the taunts of illegitimacy or begging for the crumbs Dominic deigns to spare him!'

Arabella felt the blood drain from her face. 'Cease this talk at once, Mama! I will not hear you say it.' *If only Mama knew the truth. I am guilty of all of these accusations, not Dominic.*

'I cannot, Arabella, for it needs to be said,' cried her mother. 'The spite of that man! The cruel arrogance! How you can still have a care for such a scoundrel defies logic.' Mrs Tatton was leaning forwards in her chair in full rant. 'I should have gone round to Arlesford House and given that man a piece of my mind before we left London. I should have told him exactly what I thought of him. That snake in the grass, that conniving, ill-mannered—'

Something snapped within Arabella. She could not hear her mother vilify Dominic for one minute more, blaming him for what she had done. The words blurted from her mouth,

'It was not Dominic who broke the betrothal, Mama, it was me. I did it, not Dominic.'

Silence followed her words. A great roaring loud silence.

Mrs Tatton gaped at Arabella in confusion and shock. She gave a strange little disbelieving laugh and then smiled. 'Come now, Arabella—'

'It is the truth. I told him that I did not love him and was leaving him and still he gave me this cottage and an allowance.'

The smile slipped from her mother's face. She looked as if she could not fully comprehend what Arabella was saying. 'But why would you do such a thing, Arabella? Why, when I know that you love him?'

'I do love him.' It was the first time she had admitted it aloud.

'Then why?' All vestige of colour had drained from Mrs Tatton's face. 'Why would you ruin it for yourself and for Archie?'

Arabella sat very still upon the chair; her hands lay slack. The floodgates had been opened, and there was no way to close them again. So she told her mother about Mr Smith and his threats. She told her everything, even of Miss Noir and Mrs Silver's.

'Oh, Arabella,' he mother whispered as she came to stand by her side. 'Why did you not tell me?'

'I could not risk that you would go to Dominic. Smith

will send his ruffians after him if you reveal any of this. Dominic's life hangs in the balance. And so too does Archie's, for Smith will publish the story and there will be no going back from that. I have hurt them both, terribly, but it was only to protect them from Smith. Dominic must never know. You do understand that, do you not?'

Her mother nodded.

'And as for Mrs Silver's, well…' Arabella fidgeted with her fingers and could not look up to meet her mother's gaze. 'I knew what the knowledge would do to you, and I could not bear to burden you with such shame.'

'I already knew, Arabella.'

Arabella glanced up at her mother. 'But how could you know?'

'Dominic told me where he had found you, that day he came to Curzon Street and you had taken Archie to the park.' There were tears rolling down Mrs Tatton's cheeks. 'You should have told me, Arabella. I would never be ashamed of you when all you have done has been to save those you love. You are the best of mothers to Archie. And you are the best of daughters to me.'

Arabella got to her feet and put her arms around her mother's shoulders, holding her and laying her cheek upon the top of her mother's head.

'Thank you, Mama, and bless you. Bless you for all that you have suffered because of me.'

Her mother looked drained and worried and Arabella felt more guilty than ever.

Mrs Tatton's health was too fragile. Arabella knew she should not have weakened and burdened her mother with the truth. It seemed to Arabella that however hard she tried, no matter what she did, she hurt the people she loved the most.

Dominic's voice echoed in her head. *I love you, Arabella.*

And she winced. The weight of the pain and the guilt was growing heavier with each passing day. And she wondered when Dominic would come, and she wondered how she was going to bear that meeting when eventually it happened. She felt as if she were suffocating from the weight of worry.

'Mama, I do not think that I will sleep feeling the way I do. Would you like to go for a walk along the woodland path, to help clear our heads a little?'

'I am tired, and would prefer to sit by the fire. But you go, Arabella.' Her mother took Arabella's hand in her own. 'Do not wander too far and be back before it is dark.'

'Yes, Mama.' Arabella dropped a kiss on her mother's head.

From outside she could hear the blackbirds calling and the soft rustle of leaves in the evening breeze.

Wrapping her shawl around her shoulders, Arabella slipped from the cottage out into the fresh air. She walked to straighten the thoughts in her head and to revive her resolve.

'What do you mean you are going out alone?' Hunter grumbled. 'We have not stopped all day. And we are supposed to be attending to other matters tonight, such as drinking and making merry and celebrating the joys of the bachelor life in all the most carnal of ways.'

Dominic threw his friend a speaking look.

'You are a changed man since you became reacquainted with Arabella, Dominic. A changed man, indeed.' Hunter shook his head in a sorrowful way.

'So you keep telling me. We will see how changed you are when you meet the woman you wish to marry.'

Hunter gave a disgusted snort. 'I assure you I have no plans in that direction for a good many years. And if I must eventually succumb to such a fate there will be no changing involved.'

'We shall see,' said Dominic.

'Indeed, you shall,' sniffed Hunter and helped himself to another brandy. 'All is ready for tomorrow?'

'Almost,' said Dominic and he thought again of Arabella.

'I shall be glad of the return to London. I do not know how you can stand it out here in the sticks. I bet they do not even know how to play faro or macao.'

Dominic laughed. 'I am sure they do not. Indeed, I doubt there is such an inveterate gambler as yourself within the whole village. You will have to wait for your return to London for that.'

Hunter sighed and sipped his brandy. 'Dear, dear London town, how I miss her sweet allures.'

Dominic laughed again and, gathering up his hat, gloves and riding crop, departed the Hall.

Chapter Nineteen

The evening sunlight filtered through the canopy of leaves and branches to spill in small pools and spots upon the woodland floor. There were still some patches of pale yellow primroses, although the heads of the bluebells had gone over. In their place were the tiny blue flowers of forget-me-not, bright splashes of colour amidst the earthy browns and greens of the soil and grass. A dove was cooing softly, sounding above the song of the smaller birds. Arabella walked on, small dry twigs crunching beneath her boots.

She followed the path as it curved its way around some mighty ancient oaks and then she hesitated, for there, coming closer and closer, was the shadowed figure of a horseman cantering along the pathway towards her. And there was something terribly familiar about the rider. As the seconds passed and as he came closer she recognised the dark clad man.

She stared and her heart seemed to cease beating and her lungs to cease breathing.

He was dressed impeccably in a dark tailcoat and buff-coloured riding breeches, with black highly polished top boots. His hat, gloves and riding crop were held together in one hand. The dappled sunshine touched red highlights to his hair and the breeze had stirred it to a sensual disarray.

'Dominic?' she whispered. *Was it really him? Or just a product of her own wishful mind?*

'Arabella.' His face had never looked more filled with love. There was no trace of the anger or hurt she remembered from their last meeting; he just looked glad and relieved to see her. He slipped down from his horse and came towards her, and there could be no mistake.

'Oh, Dominic!' She could not prevent herself from running into his open arms. She buried her face against his chest and he held her tight. 'Dominic.'

She heard the murmur of his voice and felt his kisses against her hair and the stroke of his hands against her back. And then she remembered. Smith. His threats. And she was suddenly desperately afraid of what she might have betrayed.

'Forgive my reaction. I was a little overcome by the shock of seeing you here.' Her voice, for all she was trying to sound sober and unaffected did not sound convincing even to herself. She made to pull back, to disengage herself from him, but Dominic's arms tightened around her so there was no escape. She dared not look at him, not trusting herself to play the role that was required to protect him.

'You have come to visit Archie.' Her throat was so tight the words sounded stilted, awkward, teetering too close to breaking down.

'I have come for *you,* Arabella.'

There was only the whisper of the wind through the green canopy of the leaves above.

Slowly, unable to fight against it any more, she raised her gaze to his. His eyes were a deep dark velvet. 'You cannot. You *must* not.' She clutched at the lapels of his tailcoat, in a silent plea. 'You do not understand!' She looked away, knowing she was handling this all wrong.

'Arabella, it is all right. I know about Smith.'

Her heart gave a flutter and fear twisted cold and hard in her stomach. 'You know?' She felt the blood drain from her face and Dominic's arms tightened around her. She looked up at him with dawning horror. 'You cannot,' she whispered. 'You cannot know. He will kill you, for pity's sake! Dominic, he will—'

But he placed a gentle hand at the nape of her neck, calming her panic and forcing her to look at him.

'Arabella, I have taken care of Smith. He will do nothing. You and Archie are safe.'

'It was not about me.'

'I know what it was about.' He stroked her hair. 'But I am safe too.'

'Thank God,' she cried and held him to her, and pressed fierce kisses to his neck, his chin, his cheek. 'I was so afraid—but how?' And the coldness of the thought that followed. 'Oh, my word, he did not publish, did he, all that he threatened?'

'He did not publish anything, Arabella, nor will he.' And then he told her. That Smith was not Smith at all, but Viscount Linwood. And why Linwood had done what he had done. He told her, and finally Arabella understood.

'You are certain?'

'Nothing can ever be certain, Arabella, but I do not

think that Linwood would risk the damage to his sister's reputation, nor Misbourne to his daughter's.'

She thought of the pretty, quietly spoken girl in the apothecary's shop in London, and this time it was sorrow that she felt for Lady Marianne. 'You would not really destroy her, would you, Dominic?'

'You know I would not. But as long as Misbourne and Linwood believe otherwise we are safe.'

She did not know how long they stood in each other's arms on that silent woodland path. Time lost all meaning. Arabella knew only that he was safe and her child was safe, and that, somehow, everything was going to be all right.

She looked into the eyes of the man that she loved and had so wounded. 'I have deceived you over so many things since that night in Mrs Silver's. And I am sorry for every one of them. I love you, Dominic.'

'I love you too, Arabella. And it is I who am sorry. I cannot forgive myself for what I did to you in Mrs Silver's, nor for what I did afterwards. I should have helped you, not made you my mistress.'

'Perhaps,' she nodded. 'But had we both chosen a different path it might not have led us to a better place. Would your father's deception ever have come to light? Would I ever have told you of Archie? We cannot know, Dominic.'

'We cannot,' he agreed and he looked at her with such tenderness that she could not doubt he loved her.

The sunlight had faded, casting the surrounding woodland in the mossy greens and deep browns of twilight. The air was growing chilled, but Arabella's heart was warm.

'The sun is sinking, Arabella. I had better get you

back to your mother before she thinks I have carried you off. She looked rather worried when I appeared at her door this evening, but she did tell me the direction you had taken.'

'Poor Mama. I am afraid I have not been very honest with her either.' And she explained the rest of it. 'So many lies.' She shook her head.

'But all are out in the open now.'

She nodded. 'No more dark secrets.' It was such a relief. She smiled. 'When did you arrive from London?'

'Late last night.'

'And you are only just come to find me?'

'There was much I had to organise this day.' He smiled in a mysterious way and then he lowered his mouth to hers and kissed her with a gentleness and care that mirrored the love in her heart.

'I have missed you so, Arabella.' His voice was low and guttural and filled with the same need that burned in her soul.

Their mouths merged, their lips revelling in the reunion. Her hand slipped beneath the lapel of his tail-coat, beneath his waistcoat to rest against his chest. Through the lawn of his shirt she could feel the warmth of his skin and the smattering of hair upon it, and she pressed her palm flat, feeling the strong steady beat of his heart. He eased back and looked into her eyes.

'I had better take you home, before I forget myself upon this woodland path and make us both the talk of the village.' His fingers brushed against Arabella's nipple and she gasped with the sensation that shivered through her.

'I fear we are already that,' she whispered. 'Everyone

has seen Archie. I fear they have guessed the truth, Dominic.'

'There is nothing to fear any more, Arabella. Everything is going to be fine.'

'Is it?' she asked.

'Yes, my love. It is.' And he kissed her again. A deep kiss. A kiss of passion and of love. A kiss that spoke of how he had missed her. She gave herself up to him, wanting to hold him for ever and never let him go, lest this all turned out to be a dream that would escape her on waking.

She felt him deepen the kiss, felt the warmth of his caress and the strength and safety of his arms. And then he stopped and looked into her eyes with such love and intensity.

'I must take you home now,' he murmured, 'or I *will* forget myself.' One swift last kiss and then he tucked her hand into the crook of his arm, grabbed the reins of his horse and began to walk her back in the direction of the cottage.

Arabella glanced down at his breeches at his obvious arousal and when she met his eyes again she was smiling.

'You, Arabella Tatton, are a very wicked woman. It is a good job you are going to church tomorrow morning,' he said and he smiled.

'Do hurry along, Archie, or we are going to be late,' Mrs Tatton scolded as they followed the woodland path the next morning in the direction of the church.

'Trojan is still eating his hay,' Archie explained to his grandmother, and gestured to his pretend horse. 'We shall soon gallop fast and overtake you.'

'Trojan?' queried Mrs Tatton to Arabella.

Arabella smiled. 'It is the name of Dominic's horse.' She smoothed down the skirt of pale blue silk and wondered if the dress was too much for the village church, but she knew Dominic would be there and she wanted to look her best for him.

Mrs Tatton smiled in return. 'I am glad you have sorted matters with Dominic.'

'I am too.' Arabella felt a warm glow of happiness.

'So, what is to happen between the two of you now?'

'In truth, I do not know, Mama. We have not yet discussed it.'

'Well, surely the betrothal will be reinstated and he will want to take you back to London?'

Arabella felt the smile fade from her face and some of the old tension was back. 'I am not so sure about that. The city does not hold such good memories for either of us. But I will do whatever it takes to be with you and Archie and Dominic.'

Her mother nodded, and as Archie galloped his imaginary Trojan past them they exchanged a smile.

There was not another soul about as they neared the church, and, indeed, the church door was closed.

'We must be very late.' Mrs Tatton took hold of Archie's hand, quickly smoothed the dark ruffle of his hair into some semblance of order again and hurried both him and Arabella towards the church.

Arabella pushed the heavy church door open and let her mother and son pass inside before her. After the bright sunshine outside it took a few moments for her eyes to adjust to the dim interior of the church porch.

'Arabella.' Reverend Martin sounded close by. 'My dear girl.' The vicar had a definite air of excitement about him and she wondered what had happened to make him so.

'Arabella!' She heard the catch in her mother's voice.

'Mama?' And then she looked through the open door into the nave where her mother was staring. The whole church was filled with flowers and greenery. At the end of every pew a large posy had been tied in place, so that the aisle was edged with flowers of pinks and purples and creams the whole way down to the altar. Garlands had been draped beneath the beautiful stained glass windows, and two massive matching floral displays stood on either side of the altar. Arabella stared in disbelief.

'What...?' she began to say and then she saw the two men dressed in their finest dark tailoring standing side by side at the front of the church. The low buzz of conversation increased as those at the back started to spread the word of her arrival and she saw the taller of the two men glance around and meet her eye.

The whole world seemed to stop. Her heart stuttered before racing off at a hundred miles an hour.

'Dominic,' she whispered and clasped her hand to her mouth as the significance of it all hit her.

'I know it is unusual, but in the absence of your dear papa and, if it is pleasing to you all, I thought that Mrs Tatton and young Archie might wish to walk you down the aisle and give your hand to the duke.' Reverend Martin was looking at her with a gentle expression of understanding upon his face.

'Thank you, Reverend,' said Mrs Tatton. 'If Arabella will have it, I would be proud to.'

'What is happening, Mama?' Archie tugged at her hand and stared up into her face.

She shook her head unable to believe this was real and not some dream.

'Mama?' Archie tugged harder.

She bent so that she might look him level in the eyes. 'Dominic is to become your papa and my husband. You are the man of the family and you must help Grandmama take me to him. Will you do that?'

'Yes, Mama. I would like Dominic to be my papa.'

Arabella smiled and she tucked her right hand into her mother's arm and took hold of Archie's little hand with her left. And with Reverend Martin following on behind them Arabella walked down the aisle.

Dominic had never seen her look more beautiful. There was such a look of wonder and surprise upon Arabella's face that he felt his heart swell with love. And when Mrs Tatton placed Arabella's trembling hand into his and stood back to leave her standing by his side, he had never felt so proud.

He knew that all of the village were filling the pews behind him. And that Reverend Martin was speaking the words of the marriage ceremony, but Dominic could think of nothing other than the woman standing so tall and beautiful by his side. He loved her completely and utterly. He had loved her since first he met her when she was a girl of fifteen. She was mother to his son, and when they left St Mary's she would be his wife.

Hunter cleared his throat and passed Dominic the wedding band to slip upon the third finger of Arabella's left hand.

'With this ring I thee wed. With my body I thee worship…' He swore his oath before God and all the village. And Arabella swore too.

'Those whom God hath joined together, let no man

put asunder…I pronounce that they be Man and Wife together.'

Arabella was smiling as he took her in his arms and kissed her.

She was his. At last.

It was such a glorious day of happiness for Arabella and it passed far too quickly. After the ceremony the villagers scattered rice over her and Dominic as they left the church, in accordance with tradition, and waiting outside were two gigs, one decorated in cream silken ribbons and pink roses and purplish-blue freesias, the other in pink and purple ribbons with white roses. Dominic lifted her up into the first gig with the cream ribbons, and she watched while Archie and her mother were helped up into the other gig. Then they were off to Shardeloes Hall, where long tables packed with food had been set out on the lawns of the front gardens and a band of musicians were already playing. A great party was just starting to which the whole of the village had been invited.

They ate and they drank and they danced, all the day through. And the sun shone from a cloudless blue sky and the breeze was gentle and soft, and the peacocks displayed the finery of their tails. And as Dominic took Arabella into his arms and waltzed her round the lawn Arabella thought there had never been a more perfect day and she told him so when he led her up the stairs to bed that night.

'Arabella,' he sat her down upon the bed. 'There is still something I must give you.'

She smiled and, taking his hands in hers, kissed his fingers. 'You have given me everything I could want—yourself and Archie. You have made me your wife. What more could I possibly want?'

He loosed his hands from hers and from a secret pocket inside his waistcoat he produced something she could not quite see, something golden that glinted in the candlelight. 'I have had it these weeks past; I always intended it to be one of my wedding gifts to you.' And then he unfastened the chain that was coiled in his hands and she saw it was the locket he had given her all those years ago. The same locket that had been stolen from the room in Flower and Dean Street and that she had never thought to see again. He moved behind her and draped it around her neck. Her skin shivered from the soft brush of his fingers against her skin as he fastened it in place.

'How on earth did you find it?' she asked.

'I hired a couple of very good thief-takers to recover it for you.' He smiled.

The golden oval lay warm against her breast. She opened it and there inside were the tiny miniature portraits of herself and of Dominic from all those years before when they had first fallen in love. And the curled lock from Archie's hair that she had placed between. The tears misted her eyes so she could no longer see the portraits properly.

'Oh, thank you, Dominic, thank you so very much.' She turned to him and kissed him.

'More tears?' he teased softly.

'I am just so happy,' she managed to say between sobs and the tears streamed all the more.

He took her face gently between his hands and wiped away the flow of tears with his thumbs, looking deeply into her eyes.

'I love you, Arabella. You are my duchess, my life, my very heartbeat. Without you there is nothing.' He kissed her so tenderly, so sweetly. She wrapped her arms around him and kissed him with all the love that was in her heart.

'I love you Dominic. I have always loved you. I will always love you, until the end of time.' She kissed him, and she knew theirs was a love that would never die. It had survived lies and mistrust and separation. Nothing would ever part them again. And when she felt his fingers against the laces of her bodice she rose to her feet and stood there while he stripped the dress and her undergarments from her body. And then slowly she teased the clothes from his body, brushing her breasts against the nakedness of his skin as she did so, delighting in the increasing harshness of his breathing and the tension that rippled throughout the toned muscles of his torso as she skimmed her fingers across it.

'Arabella…' He gasped as her fingers played with the buttons of his breeches without unfastening them. 'God help me,' he uttered and divested himself of his breeches at a speed unlike any she had seen before. And then his bare body was against hers, pressing her into the softness of the mattress. She was wet and warm and aching for him. She opened to him and felt him fill her, and she needed him to make love to her, wanted it, to complete their union of this day.

'Love me, Dominic,' she whispered to him as she nibbled at his ear lobe, and her hands slid to pull the firm muscle of his buttocks harder to her as if she would drive him deeper within her. They moved together, and he loved her and she loved him, loving and loving, their bodies worshipping each other, until they finally erupted in an exploding ecstasy of love and mutual pleasure and his seed spilled within her.

And when they had rested, they loved again—the whole night through.

A shaft of sunlight streaming through the window woke Arabella the next morning. She looked around her to make sure that yesterday and last night had not been some wonderful dream. But the heavy gold wedding band upon her finger and the large warm naked body snuggled next to hers reassured her it had been real.

'Good morning, *Wife,*' he murmured and her gaze flew to his to find the clear brown eyes awake and watching her.

'Good morning, *Husband.*' She smiled and felt his hand move upon her breast.

The sound of small running feet sounded in the passageway outside the duke's bedchamber in Shardeloes Hall.

'Mama? Where are you, Mama?' a small voice called.

Arabella laughed and rose, quickly pulling on her dressing gown that was lying across the carved wooden chest at the bottom of the bed. She threw the large dark coloured dressing gown by its side up to Dominic.

'You had best prepare yourself for your son, your Grace.' Then she hurried to the door and opened it to look out into the passageway where Archie was running. 'Here I am, little lamb, and your papa too.' She pulled him into her arms and kissed his forehead. 'Have you run away from your grandmama again?'

'Yes, Mama. I have been awake for ages and she is still snoring.'

So Archie came and climbed into the bed between Arabella and Dominic and the three of them snuggled down together.

'Are you going to let me see Trojan today?' he asked Dominic.

'Not Trojan,' said Dominic.

'Oh,' said Archie in a disappointed voice.

'I thought you might want to see Charlie instead.'

'Charlie?' Archie was staring at his father with great wide eyes. 'My Charlie, that Gemmell made for me?'

'Your Charlie, indeed, and from where do think Gemmell carved him? The real Charlie has been waiting here for you all along. He is your very own pony, Archie.'

Archie threw his arms around Dominic's neck. 'Oh, thank you, Papa! Can we go and ride him right now?'

'After breakfast,' said Dominic with a laugh and ruffled Archie's hair.

Arabella looked at her son and her husband and she knew that this truly was her happy ever after.

* * * * *

A Dark and
Brooding Gentleman

MARGARET McPHEE

For Isobel, and her Glasgow

Chapter One

The Tolbooth Gaol, Glasgow, Scotland—July 1810

'Blackloch Hall?' Sir Henry Allardyce shook his head and the fine white hair that clung around his veined, bald pate wafted with the movement. Upon his pallid face was such worry; it tugged at Phoebe's heart that her father, who had so much to endure in this dank miserable prison cell, was worrying not about himself, but about her. 'But I thought Mrs Hunter was estranged from her son.'

'She is, Papa. In all the months I have spent as the lady's companion I have never once heard her, or anyone else in the household, make mention of her son.'

'Then why has she expressed this sudden intent to travel to his home?'

'You know that Charlotte Street has been twice broken into in the past months, and the last time it was completely ransacked. Her most private things were raked through—her bedchamber, her dressing table, even her...' Phoebe paused and glanced away in embarrassment. 'Suffice to say nothing was left untouched.' Her brow furrowed at the memory. 'The damage was not so very great, but Mrs Hunter has arranged for the entire house to be redecorated. As it is, every room seems only to remind her that her home has been violated. She is more shaken by the experience than she will admit and wishes some time away.'

'And they still have not caught the villains responsible for the deed?' Her father looked appalled.

'Nor does it look likely that they will do so.'

'What has the world come to when a widow alone cannot feel safe in her own home?' He shook his head. 'Such a proud but goodly woman. It was generous of her to allow you to come here today. Most employers would have insisted upon you accompanying her to Blackloch Hall immediately.'

'Mrs Hunter asked me to run some errands in town before my visit to you.' Phoebe smiled. 'And she has given me the fare to catch the mail to the coaching inn on Blackloch Moor, from where I am to be collected.'

'Good,' he said, but he gave a heavy sigh and shook his head again.

'You must not worry, Papa. According to Mrs Hunter, Blackloch is not so very far away from Glasgow, only some twenty or so miles. So, she has agreed that our weekly visits may continue. As you said, she really is a good and kind employer and I am fortunate, indeed.' She took his dear old hand in her own and, feeling the chill that seemed to emanate from his bones, chafed it gently to bring some warmth to the swollen and twisted fingers. 'And she enquires after your health often.'

'Oh, child,' he murmured, and his rheumy eyes were bright with tears, 'I wish it had not come to this. You left alone to fend for yourself and forced to lie to hide the scandal of a father imprisoned. She still believes that I am hospitalised?'

Phoebe nodded.

'And it must stay that way. For all of her kindness, she would turn you off in the blink of an eye if she knew the truth. Anything to avoid more scandal, poor woman. Heaven knows, there was enough over her son.'

'You know of Mrs Hunter's son? What manner of scandal?'

He took a moment, looking not at Phoebe but at the shadowed corner of the cell, his focus fixed as if on some point far in the distance and not on his ragged fellow inmate who was crouched there upon the uneven stone flags. The seconds passed, until at last he looked round at her once more, and it seemed that he had made up his mind.

'I am not a man for gossip. It is a sinful and malicious occupation, the work of the devil, but…' He paused and it seemed to Phoebe that he was picking his words very carefully. 'It would be remiss of me to allow you to go to Blackloch Hall ignorant of the manner of man you will find there.'

Phoebe felt the weight of foreboding heavy upon her. She waited for the words her father would speak.

'Phoebe,' he said and his voice was so unusually serious that she could not mistake the measure of his concern. 'Sebastian Hunter was a rake of the very worst degree. He spent all his time in London, living the high life, gambling away his father's money, womanising and drinking. Little wonder that old Hunter despaired of him. They say his father's death changed him. That the boy is much altered. But…' He glanced over his shoulder at the cellmate in the corner and then lowered his voice to a whisper. 'There are dark whisperings about him, evil rumours…'

'Of what?'

He shook his head again, as if he could not bring himself to convey them to her. But he looked at her intently. 'Promise me that you will do all you can to stay away from him at Blackloch.'

She looked at him, slightly puzzled by his insistence. 'My job is with Mrs Hunter. I doubt I will have much contact with her son.'

'Phoebe, you are too innocent to understand the wickedness of some young men.' Her papa sounded grim and his implication was clear. 'So do as I ask, child, and promise me that you will have a special care where he is concerned.'

'I will be careful. I give you my word, Papa.'

He gave a satisfied grunt and then eyed the bulging travelling bag that sat by her feet. 'You are well packed. Does Mrs Hunter not transport your portmanteau with the rest of the baggage?'

She followed his gaze to the worn leather bag that contained every last one of her worldly possessions. 'Of course, but it does not travel down until tomorrow and I thought it better to take my favourite dresses,' she said with a teasing smile.

'You girls and your fashions.' He shook his head in mock scolding.

Phoebe laughed but she did not tell him the truth, that there was no trunk of clothes, that all, save her best dress and the one she was now wearing, had been pawned over the months for the coins to pay her father's fees within the gaol so that he would not be put to work.

'I have paid the turnkey the garnish money and more, so you should have candles and blankets, and ale and good food for the next week. Be sure that he gives them to you.'

'You have kept enough money back for yourself?' He was looking worried again.

'Of course.' She smiled to cover the lie. 'I have little requirement for money. Mrs Hunter provides all I need.'

'Bless you, child. What would I do without you?'

The turnkey had reappeared outside the door, rattling his keys so Phoebe knew visiting time was at an end.

'Come, Phoebe, give your old papa a kiss.'

She brushed his cheek with her lips and felt the chill of his mottled skin beneath.

'I will see you next week, Papa.'

The turnkey opened the door.

It was always the hardest moment, this walking away and leaving him in the prison cell with its stone slab floors and its damp walls and its one tiny barred window.

'I look forward to it, Phoebe. Pray remember what I have said regarding...'

The man's name went unspoken, but Phoebe knew to whom her papa was referring—*Hunter*.

She nodded. 'I will, Papa.' And then she turned and walked away, along the narrow dim passageways, out of the darkness of the gaol and into the bright light of Glasgow's busy Trongate.

On the right hand side was the Tontine Hotel and its mail coaches, but Phoebe walked straight past, making her way through the crowds along Argyle Street, before heading down Jamaica Street. She kept on walking until she crossed the New Bridge that spanned the River Clyde. Half of Mrs Hunter's coins for the coach fare were squirreled away inside her purse for next week's visit to her father. The rest lay snug in the pocket of one of the Tolbooth's turnkeys.

The road that led south out of the city towards the moor lay ahead. She changed the bag into her other hand and, bracing her shoulders for the walk, Phoebe began her journey to Blackloch Hall.

'Hunter, is that you, old man? Ain't seen you in an age. You ain't been down in London since—' Lord Bullford stopped himself, an awkward expression suddenly upon his face. He gruffly clapped a supportive hand to Hunter's shoulder. 'So sorry to hear about your father.'

Hunter said not one word. His expression was cold as he glanced first at Viscount Linwood standing in the background behind Bullford, and then at where Bullford's hand rested against the black superfine of his coat. He shifted his gaze to Bullford's face and looked at him with such deadly promise that the man withdrew his hand as if he had been burnt.

Bullford cleared his throat awkwardly. 'Up visiting Kelvin and bumped into Linwood. Thought we might drop in on you at Blackloch while we were here. The boys have been worried about you, Hunter. What with—'

'They need not have been.' Hunter glanced with obvious dislike at Linwood as he cut off the rest of Bullford's words and made to step aside. 'And visitors are not welcome at Blackloch.'

He saw Bullford's eyes widen slightly, but the man was not thwarted.

'Kelvin knows an excellent little place. We could—'

'No.' Hunter started to walk away.

'Stakes are high but the tables are the best, and the lightskirts that run the place...' Bullford skimmed his hands through the air to sketch the outline of a woman's curves '...just your type.'

Hunter turned, grabbed Bullford by the lapels of his

coat, thrust him hard against the wall of the building they were standing beside and held him there. 'I said no.' He felt rather than saw Linwood tense and move behind him.

'Easy, old man.' The sweat was glimmering on Bullford's upper lip and trickling down his chin. 'Understand perfectly.'

A voice interrupted—Linwood's. 'You go too far, Hunter.'

Hunter released Bullford, and turned to face the Viscount. 'Indeed?'

Linwood took one look at Hunter's face and retreated a step or two. But Hunter had already left Bullford and was covering the short distance to where his horse was tethered. The big black stallion bared his teeth and snorted a warning upon hearing his approach but, on seeing it was Hunter, let him untie his reins and swing himself up into the saddle. And as he turned the horse to ride away he heard Bullford saying softly to Linwood, 'Deuce, if he ain't worse than all the stories told.'

The July day was fine and dry; and Phoebe smiled to herself as, bit by bit, mile by mile, she left Glasgow behind her and passed through the outlying villages. The bustle and crowds of the city gave way gradually to quiet hamlets with cottages and fields and cows. The air grew cleaner and fresher, the fields more abundant. She could smell the sweetness of grass and heather and earth, and feel the sun warm upon her back, the breeze gentle upon her face.

Step by step she followed the road heading ever closer to Blackloch and its moor. Rolling hills and vast stretches of scrubby fields surrounded her, all green and yawning and peaceful. Sheep with their woolly coats sheared short wandered by the side of the road, bleating and gambling furiously ahead with their little tails bobbing as she approached. Overhead the sky was blue and cloudless, the light golden and bright with the summer sun. Bees droned, their pollen sacks heavy from the sweet heather flowers; birds chirped and sang and swooped between the hawthorn and gorse bushes. Two coaches passed, and a farmer with his cart, and then no more, so that as she neared the moorland she might have believed herself the only person in this place were it not for the two faint figures of horsemen in the distance behind her.

She walked on and her thoughts turned to Mrs Hunter's son and her papa's warning. *Dark whisperings and evil rumours,* she mused as she transferred the travelling bag from one hand to the other again, in an effort to ease the way its handles cut into her fingers. *You have no idea of the wickedness of some men...* Her feet were hot and her boots chafed against her toes as she conjured up an image of the wicked Mr Hunter—a squat heavy-set villain to be sure, run to fat with drink and dissipation, with eyes as black as thunder and a countenance to match. Living all alone on a moor miles away from anywhere. Little wonder his mother had disowned him. A man with a soul as black as the devil's. Phoebe shivered at the thought, then scolded herself for such foolishness.

Another mile farther and she stopped by a stile to rest, dumping the bag down upon the grass with relief and perching herself on the wooden step. She eased her stiffened fingers and rubbed at the welts the bag's straps had pressed through her gloves. Then she loosened the ribbons of her bonnet and slipped it from her head, to let the breeze ripple through her hair and cool her scalp, before leaning against the fence of the stile. She was quite alone in the peacefulness of the surrounding countryside, so she relaxed and let herself rest for a few minutes.

The clatter of the horses' hooves was muffled by the grass verge so that Phoebe did not hear the pair's approach. It was the jingle of a harness and a whinny that alerted her that she was no longer alone.

Not twenty yards away sat two men on horseback. Even had they not kerchiefs tied across their mouths and noses, and their battered leather hats pulled down low over their eyes, Phoebe would have known them for what they were. Everything of their manner, everything of the way they were looking at her, proclaimed their profession. Highwaymen. She knew it even before the men slid down from their saddles and began walking towards her.

She rose swiftly to her feet. There was no point in trying to escape. They were too close and she knew she could not outrun them, not with her heavy travelling bag. So she lifted her bag from where it lay on the grass and stood facing them defiantly.

'Well, well, what have we here?' said the taller of the two, whose kerchief obscuring his face was black. His accent was broad Glaswegian and he was without the slightest pretence of education or money.

Although she could not see their faces she had the impression that the men were both young. Maybe it was in the timbre of their voices, or maybe in something of their stance or build. Both were dressed in worn leather breeches, and jackets, with shirts and neckcloths that were old and shabby and high scuffed brown leather boots.

'A lassie in need of our assistance, I'd say,' came the reply from his shorter, slimmer accomplice wearing a red kerchief across his face.

'I have no need of assistance, thank you, gentlemen,'

said Phoebe firmly. 'I was but taking a small rest before resuming my journey.'

'Is that right?' the black-kerchiefed man said. 'That's a mighty heavy-looking bag you have there. Allow us to ease your burden, miss.'

'Really, there is no need. The bag is not heavy,' said Phoebe grimly and, eyeing them warily, she shifted the bag behind her and gripped it all the tighter.

'But I insist. Me and my friend, we dinnae like to see a lassie struggle under such a weight. Right gentlemanly we are.'

Gentlemen of the road, for they were certainly not gentlemen of any other description.

He walked slowly towards her.

Phoebe stepped back once, and then again, her heart hammering, not sure of what to do.

'The bag, if you please, miss.'

Phoebe's hands gripped even tighter to the handle, feeling enraged that these men could just rob her like this. She raised her chin and looked directly into the man's eyes. They were black and villainous, and she could tell he was amused by her. That fueled her fury more than anything.

Her own eyes narrowed. 'I do not think so, sir. I assure you there is nothing in my bag worth stealing unless you have an interest in ladies' dresses.'

He gave a small hard laugh and behind him the other highwayman appeared with a pistol in his hand that was aimed straight at her.

'Do as he says, miss, or you'll be sorry.'

'Jim, Jim,' said Black Kerchief, who was clearly the leader of the two, as if chiding the man. 'Such impatience. There are better ways to persuade a lady.' And then to

Phoebe, 'Forgive my friend.' His gaze meandered over her face, pausing to linger upon her lips.

A *frisson* of fear rippled down Phoebe's spine. She knew then that she would have to give them the bag, to yield her possessions. Better that than the alternative.

She threw the bag to land at their feet.

Black Kerchief swung the bag between his fingers as he gauged its weight. 'Far too heavy for a wee slip o' a lassie like you.' She could tell he was smiling again beneath his mask, but in a way that stoked her fear higher. 'Search it,' he instructed his accomplice and did not move, just kept his eyes on Phoebe. 'Best relieve the lassie of any unnecessary weighty items.'

Red Kerchief, or Jim as he had been called, lifted the bag and, making short work of its buckle fastenings, began to rake within. He would find nothing save her clothing, a pair of slippers, a comb and some toiletries. Thankfully her purse, and the few coins that it contained, was hidden inside the pocket of her dress.

Phoebe eyed the man with disdain. 'I have no money or jewels, if that is what you are after.'

'She's right; there's nothin' here,' Jim said and spat his disgust at the side of the road.

'Look again,' instructed Black Kerchief. 'What we've got here is a bona fide lady, if her accent and airs and graces are anythin' to go by. She must hae somethin' o' value.'

His accomplice emptied the contents of her bag out onto the verge and slit open the lining of her bag. Further rummaging revealed nothing. He dropped the bag with its ripped lining on top of the pile of her clothes and spat again.

'Nothin'.'

Phoebe prayed a coach would pass, but the road ahead

remained resolutely empty and there was silence all around. 'I did tell you,' she said. 'Now if you would be so kind as to let me pass on my way.' She held her head up and spoke with a calm confidence she did not feel. Inside her heart was hammering nineteen to the dozen and her stomach was a small tight knot of fear. She made to step towards the bag.

'Tut, tut, darlin', no' so fast.' The black-masked highwayman caught her back with an arm around her waist. 'There's a price to pay to travel this road, and if you've nae money and nae jewels...' His gaze dropped lower to the bodice of her dress and lower still to its dusty skirt before rising again to her face.

Phoebe felt her blood run cold. 'I have nothing to give you, sir, and I will be on my way.'

He laughed at that. 'I think I'll be the judge of that, hen.' He looked at Phoebe again. 'I'll hae a kiss. That's the price to continue on your way.'

She heard the other man snigger.

The villain curled his arm tighter and pulled her closer. The stench of ale and stale sweat was strong around him. 'Dinnae be shy, miss, there's no one here to see.'

'How dare you, sir? Release me at once. I insist upon it.'

'Insist, do you?' The highwayman pulled his mask down and leered at her to reveal his discoloured teeth. It was all Phoebe could do not to panic. Vying with the fear was a raging well of fury and indignation. But she stayed calm and delivered him a look that spoke the depth of her disgust.

He laughed.

And as he did she kicked back as hard as she could with her stout walking boots against his shins.

He was not laughing then.

A curse rent the air and she felt the loosening of his hands. Phoebe needed no further opportunity. She tore herself from his grip, hoisted up her skirts and, abandoning her bag, began to run.

The man recovered too quickly and she heard his booted footsteps chasing after her. Phoebe ran for all she was worth, her heart thudding fast and furious, her lungs panting fit to burst. She kept on running, but the highwayman was too fast. She barely made it a hundred yards before he caught her.

'Whoa, lassie. No' so fast. You and I havenae yet finished our business.'

'Unhand me, you villain!'

'Villain, am I?' With rough hands he pulled her into his arms and lowered the stench of his mouth towards hers.

Phoebe hit out and screamed.

A horse's hooves sounded then. Galloping fast, coming closer.

Her gaze shot round towards the noise, as did the highwayman's.

There, galloping down the same hill she had not long walked, was a huge black horse and its dark-clad rider— rather incongruous with the rest of the sunlit surroundings. He was moving so fast that the tails of his coat flew out behind him and he looked, for all the world, like some devil rider.

Black Kerchief's hand was firm around her wrist as he towed her quickly back to where his accomplice still stood waiting. And she saw that he, too, had pulled down his mask so that it now looked like a loose ill-fitting neckerchief. Jim grabbed her and used one hand to hold her wrists in a vice-like grip behind her back. She felt the jab of something sharp press against her side.

'One sound from you, lady, and the knife goes in. Got it?'

She gave a nod and watched as Black Kerchief stood between her and the road, so that she would be obscured from the rider's view as he sped past.

Please! Phoebe prayed. *Please*, she hoped with every last ounce of her will.

And it seemed that someone was listening for the horseman slowed as he approached and drew the huge stallion to a halt by their small group. Not the devil after all, but a rich gentleman clad all in black.

'Step away from the woman and be on your way.' Hunter spoke quietly enough, but in a tone that the men would not ignore if they had any kind of sense about them.

'She's my wife. Been givin' me some trouble, she has,' the taller of the men said.

Hunter's gaze moved from the woman's bonnet crushed on the grass by the men's feet, to the neckerchiefs around the men's collars, and finally to the woman herself. Her hair glowed a deep tawny red in the sunshine and was escaping its pins to spill over her shoulders. She was young and pretty enough with an air about her that proclaimed her gentle breeding, a class apart from the men who were holding her, and she was staring at him, those fine golden-brown eyes frantically trying to convey her need for help. He slipped down from the saddle.

'She is no more your wife than mine. So, as I said, step away from her and be on your way…gentlemen.' He saw the men glance at each other, communicating what they thought was a silent message.

'If you insist, sir,' the taller villain said and dragged

the girl from behind him and flung her towards Hunter at the same time as reaching for his pistol.

Hunter thrust the girl behind him and knocked the weapon from the highwayman's hand. He landed one hard punch to the man's face, and then another, the force of it sending the man staggering back before the villain slumped to his knees. Hunter saw the glint of the knife as it flew through the air. With the back of his hand he deflected its flight, as if he were swatting a fly, and heard the clatter of the blade on the empty road.

The accomplice drove at him, fists flying. Hunter stepped forwards to meet the man and barely felt the fist that landed against his cheekbone. The ineffective punch did nothing to interrupt Hunter's own, which was delivered with such force that, despite the villain's momentum, the man was lifted clear off his feet and driven backwards to land flat on his back. The shock of the impact was felt not only by the accomplice, who was out cold upon the ground, but seemed to reverberate around them. The taller highwayman, who had been trying to pick himself up following Hunter's first blow, stopped still and, as Hunter turned to him, all aggression evaporated from the scoundrel.

'Please, sir, we were only having a laugh.' It was almost a whimper. 'We wouldnae have hurt the lassie; look, here's her purse.' The highwayman fished the woman's purse from his pocket and offered it as if in supplication.

'Throw it,' Hunter instructed.

The man did as he was told and Hunter caught it easily in one hand before turning to the woman.

She was white-faced and wary, but calm enough for all her fear. In her hand she gripped the highwayman's knife as if she trusted him as little as the villains rolling and disabled on the ground before him.

Hunter's expression was still hard, but he let the promise of lethality fade from his eyes as he looked at her.

He held the purse aloft. 'Yours, I take it?'

She seemed to relax a little and gave an answering nod of her head. The man must have taken it from her pocket while they were struggling.

He threw the purse to her and watched her catch it, then barked an order for the highwayman, who was leaning dazed upon the stile, to pack the jumble of women's clothing lying in a heap at the side of the road into the discarded travelling bag. Only when the filled and fastened bag was placed carefully at his feet did Hunter move.

'To where are you walking?' His voice was curt and he could feel the woman's stare on him as he swung himself up into the saddle.

She glanced over at the highwaymen and then back at Hunter.

'Kingswell Inn.' A gentlewoman's voice sure enough. The pure clarity of it stirred sensations in Hunter that he thought he had forgotten.

He urged Ajax forwards a few steps and reached his hand down for her.

She hesitated and bit at her lower lip as if she were uncertain.

'Make up your mind, miss. Do I deliver you to Kingswell, or leave you here?' Hunter knew his tone was cold, but he did not care.

She took his hand.

'Place your foot on the stirrup to gain purchase,' he directed and pulled her up. As he settled her to sit sideways on the saddle before him the woman glanced up directly into his eyes. The attraction that arced between them was instant, its force enough to make him catch his breath. The shock of it hit him hard. For one second and then another they stared at each other, and then he deliberately turned his face away, crushing the sensation in its inception. Such feelings belonged to a life that was no longer his. He did not look at her again, just pressed the travelling bag into her hands and nudged Ajax to a trot.

'Did they hurt you?' The chill had thawed only a little from his voice.

Phoebe stared and her heart was beating too fast. 'I am quite unhurt, thank you, sir. Although it seems you are not.' She smiled to hide her nervousness. Clutching her bag all the tighter with one hand, she found her handkerchief with the other and offered it to him.

His frown did little to detract from the cold handsomeness of his face, but it did make it easier for Phoebe to ignore the butterflies' frantic fluttering in her stomach and the rush of blood pounding through her veins. The bright morning sunlight cast a blue hue in the ebony of his hair and illuminated the porcelain of his skin. Dark brows slashed bold over eyes of clear pale emerald. Such stark beautiful colouring upon a face as cleanly sculpted as that of the statues of Greek gods in her papa's books. A square chiselled jaw line and cleft chin led up to well-defined purposeful lips. His nose was strong and masculine, his cheekbones high, the left one of which was sporting a small cut that was bleeding. Phoebe could feel the very air of darkness and danger emanating from him and yet still she felt she wanted to stare at him and never look away. She ignored the urge.

'You have a little blood upon your cheek.'

He took the handkerchief without a word, wiped the

trickle of blood and stuffed the handkerchief into his own pocket.

She could feel the gentleman's arm around her waist anchoring her onto the saddle, and was too conscious of how close his body was to hers even though he had taken care to slide back in the saddle to leave some room between them. He might not care for manners, but Phoebe's papa had raised her well.

'Thank you for your intervention, sir.' She was pleased to hear that her voice was a deal calmer than she felt.

The pale eyes slid momentarily to hers and she saw that they were serious and appraising. He gave a small inclination of his head as acknowledgement of her gratitude, but he did not smile.

'They meant to rob me and steal a kiss.'

'That is not all they would have stolen.' She could almost feel the resonance of his voice within his chest so close was she to it, deep and rich and yet with that same coolness in it that had been there from the very start.

She looked up into those piercing eyes, not quite certain if his meaning was as she thought. She was so close she could see the iris, as pale and clear a green as that of glass, edged with solid black. She could see every individual dark lash and the dark wings of his brows. The breath seemed to lodge in her throat.

'If you have no mind to lose it, then you will not travel this road alone again.' He looked at her meaningfully and then he gee'd the horse to a canter, and there was no more talk.

As the horse gathered speed she gripped the pommel with her left hand, and held her bag in place with her right. The man's arm tightened around her and their bodies slid together so that Phoebe's right breast was hard against his chest, her right hip tight against his thigh, his hand holding firm upon her waist. Her heart was thudding too hard, her blood surging all the more and not because of the speed at which the great black horse was thundering along the road. It seemed that the man engulfed her senses, completely, utterly, so that she could not think straight. The time seemed to stretch for ever in a torture of wanton sensations.

He did not stop until they reached the coaching inn.

The high moorland surrounded them now, bleak and barren and vast, stretching into the distance as far as the eye could see. The breeze was stronger here, the birds quieter, the air that bit cooler.

And when he lowered her gently to the ground and she looked up at him to thank him again, the words died on her lips, for he was staring down at her with such intensity she could not look away. All time seemed to stop in that moment and it was as if something passed between them, something Phoebe did not understand that shimmered through the whole of her body. Finally he broke his gaze and turned, urging the great horse out of the inn's yard, out onto the road and, without a backward glance, galloped away across the moor.

Phoebe stood there with the dust caked thick upon her boots and the hem of her faded blue dress, the travelling bag in her hand, and she watched him until the dark figure upon his dark horse, so stark against the muted greens and purples and browns that surrounded him, faded against the horizon. And only then did she realise he had not asked her name nor told her his. She turned away and walked over to the small stone wall by the side of the inn and sat down in the shade to wait. The clock on the outside of the inn showed half past six.

Chapter Two

Out on the moor the land was washed with a warm orange hue from the setting sun. At Blackloch Hall Sebastian Hunter stood, sombre and unmoving, by the arched-latticework window of his study and stared out across the stretch of rugged moor. A cool breeze stirred the heavy dark-red curtains that framed the window and ruffled through his hair. The clock on the mantel chimed nine and then resumed its slow steady tick. He swirled the brandy in the crystal-cut glass and took a sip, revelling in the rich sweet taste and the heat it left as it washed over his tongue and down his throat. He was only half-listening as Jed McEwan, his friend and steward, sitting in the chair on the opposite side of the desk, covered each point on his agenda. Rather, Hunter was thinking over the day, of Bullford and Linwood's appearance in Glasgow, and more so over the happenings upon the road—of the highwaymen and the woman. Inside his pocket his fingers touched the small white-lace handkerchief.

'And finally, in less than a fortnight, it is the annual staff trip to the seaside. Do you plan to attend, Hunter?'

The inflection at the end of McEwan's voice alerted him to the question.

'I do.' It was a tradition passed down through generations of the Hunter family, and Hunter would keep to it regardless of how little he wanted to go.

'We have covered every item on the list.'

Hunter moved to top up McEwan's brandy glass, but McEwan put a hand over it and declined with thanks.

'Mairi been giving you a hard time?' Hunter asked as he filled his own glass.

'No, but I should be getting back to her.' McEwan smiled at the thought and Hunter felt a small stab of jealousy at his friend's happiness. The darkness that sat upon his soul had long since smothered any such tender feelings in Hunter. 'My father is arriving tonight.'

Hunter felt the muscle flicker in his jaw. He turned away so that McEwan would not see it.

But McEwan knew. And Hunter knew that he knew.

Through the open window, over the whisper of the wind and the rustle of the heather from the moor, came the faint rumble of distant carriage wheels.

Hunter raised an eyebrow and moved to stand at the window once more. He stared out over the moor, eyes scanning the narrow winding moor road that led only to one place—all the way up to Blackloch. 'Who the hell...?' And he thought of Bullford and Linwood again.

'Sorry, Hunter. I meant to tell you earlier, but I got waylaid with other things and then it slipped my mind.' McEwan picked up his pile of papers and came to stand by Hunter's side. 'That will be your mother's companion, a Miss Phoebe Allardyce. Mrs Hunter sent Jamie with the gig to Kingswell to meet the woman from the last coach.'

Hunter frowned. He did not know that his mother had a companion. He did not know anything of his mother's life in Glasgow, nor why she had suddenly arrived back at Blackloch yesterday, especially not after the way they had parted.

Hunter watched the small dark speck of the gig grow gradually larger and he wondered fleetingly what the woman would be like—young or old, plain or pretty? To the old Sebastian Hunter it would have mattered. But to the man that stood there now, so still and sullen, it did not. What did he care who she was, what she did? Hunter glanced at McEwan.

'My mother's companion is of no interest to me.' He felt only relief that it was not Bullford or any other of his old crowd. And gladder still it was not Linwood.

McEwan made no comment. He turned away from the window and its view. 'I will see you in the morning, Hunter.'

'That is Blackloch Hall, over there, ma'am,' said the young footman driving the gig and pointed ahead. 'And to the left hand side, down from the house, is the Black Loch itself, Mr Hunter's private loch, for which the house and the moor are named.'

Phoebe peered in the direction the boy was pointing. Across the barren moorland a solitary building stood proud and lonely, sinister in its bearing, a black silhouette against the red fire of the setting sun. And beyond it, the dark waters of the loch. The gig rounded the bend and the narrow track that had been winding up to this point straightened to become an avenue of approach to the house. At the front there was nothing to differentiate where the moor stopped and the house's boundary began. No wall, no hedging, no garden. The avenue led directly up to the house. With every turn of the gig's wheels Phoebe could see Blackloch Hall loom closer.

It was a large foreboding manor house made to look like a castle by virtue of its turrets and spires. As they drew nearer Phoebe saw the rugged black stonework transform to a bleak grey. All the windows were in darkness; not the flicker of a single candle showed. All was dark and still. All was quiet. It looked as if the house had been deserted. The great iron-studded mahogany front door, beneath its pointed stone arch of strange carved symbols, remained firmly closed. As the gig passed, she saw the door's cast-iron knocker shaped like a great, snarling wolf's head and she felt the trip of her heart. The gig drove on, round the side of the house and through a tall arched gateway, taking her round into a stable yard at the back of the house.

The young footman jumped down from the gig's seat and came round to assist her before fetching her bag from the gig's shelf.

'Thank you.' Phoebe's eyes flicked over the dismal dark walls of Blackloch Hall and shivered. It was like something out of one of Mrs Hunter's romance novels, all gothic and dark and menacing. Little wonder the lady had chosen to make her home in Glasgow.

The boy shot a glance at her as if he was expecting her to say something.

'What a very striking building,' she managed.

The boy, Jamie he said his name was, gave a nod and then, carrying her bag, led on.

Taking a deep breath, Phoebe followed Jamie towards the back door of the house. He no longer spoke and all around was silence, broken only by the crunch of their shoes against the gravel.

From high on the roof the caw of a solitary crow sounded, and from the corner of her eye she saw the flutter of dark wings…and she thought of the man against whom her father had warned her—Sebastian Hunter. A shiver rippled down her spine as she stepped across the threshold into Blackloch Hall.

Phoebe did not see Mrs Hunter until late the next morning in the drawing room, which to Phoebe's eye looked less like a drawing room and more like the medieval hall of an ancient castle.

Suspended from the centre of the ceiling was a huge circular black-iron chandelier. She could smell the sweetness of the honey-coloured beeswax candles that studded its circumference. The rough-hewn walls were covered with faded dull tapestries depicting hunting scenes and the floor of grey stone flags was devoid of a single carpet rug. A massive medieval-style fireplace was positioned in the centre of the wall to her left, complete with worn embroidered lum seats. A fire had been laid upon the hearth, but had not been lit so that, even though it was the height of summer, the room had a distinct chill to it. The three large lead-latticed windows that spanned the wall opposite the fireplace showed a fine view over the moor outside.

The furniture seemed a hodgepodge of styles: a pair of Italian-styled giltwood stools, a plainly fashioned but practical rotating square bookcase, a huge gilded eagle perched upon the floor beside the door, its great wings supporting a table top of grey-and-white marble, a small card table with the austere neoclassical lines of Sheraton, and on its surface a chessboard with its intricately carved pieces of ebony and ivory. Farther along the room was a long dark-green sofa and on either side of the sofa was a matching armchair and, behind them, in the corner, a suit of armour.

Mrs Hunter was ensconced on the sofa, supervising

the making of the pot of tea. She watched while Phoebe added milk and a lump of sugar to the two fine bone-china cups and poured.

'How was your father, Phoebe? Does he fare any better?'

'A little,' said Phoebe, feeling the hand of guilt heavy upon her shoulder.

'That at least is something.' The lady smiled and took the cup and saucer that Phoebe offered. 'And you attended to all of my matters before your visit to the hospital?'

'Yes, ma'am. Everything is in order. Mrs Montgomery will send your invitation to Blackloch Hall rather than Charlotte Street. I delivered the sample books back to Messrs Hudson and Collier and to Mrs Murtrie. As you suspected Mr Lyle did not have your shoes ready, but he says they will be done by the end of the week.'

'Very well.'

Phoebe continued. 'I collected your powders from Dr Watt and have informed all of the names on your list that you will be visiting Blackloch Hall for the next month and may be contacted here. And the letters and parcel I left with the receiving office.'

'Good.' Mrs Hunter gave a nod. 'And how was the journey down?'

'Fine, thank you,' she lied and focused her attention to stirring the sugar into her tea most vigorously so that she would not have to look at her employer.

'The coach was not too crowded?'

'Not at all. I was most fortunate.' A vision of the highwaymen and of a dark and handsome man with eyes the colour of emerald ice chips swam into her head. The teaspoon overbalanced from her saucer and dropped to the flagstones below where it bounced and disappeared out of sight beneath her chair. Phoebe set her cup and saucer down on the table and knelt to retrieve the spoon.

'I would have sent John with the coach, but I do not wish to be at Blackloch without my own carriage at my dispos—' Mrs Hunter broke off as the drawing-room door opened and the movement of footsteps sounded. 'Sebastian, my, but you honour me.' To Phoebe's surprise the lady's tone was acidic.

Phoebe felt a ripple of foreboding down her spine. She reached quickly for the teaspoon.

'Mother, forgive my absence yesterday. I was delayed by matters in Glasgow.' The man's voice was deep and cool as spring water...and disturbingly familiar.

Phoebe stilled, her fingers gripping the spoon's handle for dear life. Her heart was thudding too fast.

It could not be.

It was not possible.

Slowly she got to her feet and turned to face the wicked Mr Hunter. And there, standing only a few feet away across the room, was her dark handsome rescuer from the moor road.

Hunter stared at the young auburn-haired woman he had left standing alone at the Kingswell Inn. Her cheeks had paled. Her lips had parted. Her warm tawny eyes stared wide. She looked every inch as shocked as he felt.

He moved to his mother and touched his lips to her cool cheek. She suffered it as if he were a leper, shuddering slightly with distaste. So, nothing had changed after all. He wondered why the hell she was here at Blackloch.

'Sebastian.' His mother's voice was cold, if polite for the sake of the woman's presence. 'This is my companion, Miss Allardyce. She came down on the late coach last night.' Then to the woman, 'Miss Allardyce, my *son*, Mr

Hunter.' He could hear the effort it took her to force the admission of their kinship.

'Mr Hunter,' the woman said in that same clear calm voice he would have recognised anywhere, and made her curtsy, yet he saw the small flare of concern in her eyes before she hid it.

'Miss Allardyce.' He inclined his head ever so slightly in the woman's direction, and understood her worry given that it was now obvious she had palmed the money his mother had given her for her coach fare.

She was wearing the same blue dress, although every speck of dust looked to have been brushed from it. The colour highlighted the red burnish to her hair, now scraped and tightly pinned in a neat coil at the nape of her neck. His gaze lingered briefly on her face, on the small straight nose and those dewy dusky pink lips that made him want to wet his own. And he remembered the soft feel of her pressed against him on the saddle, and the clean rose-touched scent of her, and the shock of a desire he had thought quelled for good. She was temptation personified. And she was everything proper and correct that a lady's companion should be as she resumed her seat and calmly waited for Hunter to spill her secret.

Not that Hunter had any intention of doing so. After her experience with the highwaymen he doubted she would make the same mistake again. He watched as she set the teaspoon she was holding down upon the tray and lifted her cup and saucer.

His mother's tone was cool as she turned to her companion. 'My son has not seen his mother in nine months, Miss Allardyce, and yet he cannot bring himself into my company. This is his first appearance since my arrival at Blackloch.'

Miss Allardyce looked uneasy and took a sip of tea.

His mother turned her attention back to Hunter. 'Your concern is overwhelming. I think I can see the precise nature of the matters so important to keep you from me.' Her eyes were cold and appraising as they took in the small cut on his cheek and the bruising that surrounded it. She raised an eyebrow and gave a small snort.

'You have been brawling.'

He made no denial.

Miss Allardyce's eyes opened marginally wider.

'What were you fighting over this time? Let me guess, some new gaming debt?'

He stiffened, but kept his expression impassive and cool.

'No? If not that, then over a woman, I will warrant.'

A pause, during which he saw the slight colour that had washed the soft cream of Miss Allardyce's cheeks heighten.

'You know me too well, madam.'

'Indeed, I do. You are not changed in the slightest, not for all your promises—'

There was the rattle of china as Miss Allardyce set her cup and saucer down. 'Mrs Hunter...' The woman got to her feet. 'I fear you are mistaken, ma'am. Mr Hu—'

His mother turned her frown on her companion.

'Miss Allardyce,' Hunter interrupted smoothly, 'this is none of your affair and I would that it stay that way.' His tone was frosty with warning. If his mother wanted to believe the worst of him, let her. He would not have some girl defend him. He still had some measure of pride.

Miss Allardyce stared at him for a moment, with such depths in those golden-brown eyes of hers that he wondered what she was thinking. And then she calmly sat back down in her chair.

'Ever the gentleman, Sebastian,' said his mother. 'You

see, Miss Allardyce, do not waste your concern on him. He is quite beyond the niceties of society. Now you know why I do not come to Blackloch. Such unpleasant company.'

He leaned back in his chair. 'If we are speaking bluntly, what then has prompted your visit, madam?'

'I am having the town house redecorated and am in need of somewhere to stay for a few weeks, Sebastian. What other reason could possibly bring me here?' his mother sneered.

He gave a bow and left, vowing to avoid both his mother and the woman who made him remember too well the dissolute he had been.

After the awfulness of that first day Hunter did not seek his mother out again. And Phoebe could not blame him. She wondered why he had not told Mrs Hunter the truth of the cut upon his face or revealed that his mother's companion had not spent her money upon a coach fare after all. She wondered, too, as to why there was such hostility between mother and son. But Mrs Hunter made not a single mention of her son, and it was easy to keep her promise to her father as Phoebe saw little of the man in the days that followed. Once she saw him entering his study. Another time she caught a glimpse of him riding out on the moor. But nothing more. Not that Phoebe had time to notice, for Mrs Hunter was out of sorts, her mood as bleak as the moor that surrounded them.

Tuesday came around quickly and Phoebe could only be glad both of her chance to escape the oppressive atmosphere of Blackloch and to see her father.

The Glasgow Tolbooth was an impressive five-storey sandstone building situated at the Cross where the

Trongate met High Street. It housed not only the gaol, but also the Justiciary Court and the Town Hall, behind which had been built the Tontine Hotel. There was a small square turret at each corner and a fine square spire on the east side, in which was fitted a large clock. And the top of the spire arched in the form of an imperial crown. The prison windows were small and clad with iron bars, and over the main door, on the south side, was built a small rectangular portico on a level with the first floor of the prison, the stairs from which led directly down onto the street.

Phoebe arrived at the Tolbooth, glad of heart both to be back in the familiar cheery bustle of Glasgow and at the prospect of seeing her father. She hurried along the street and was just about to climb the stone steps to the portico and the main door when a man appeared by her side.

'Miss Allardyce?'

She stopped and glanced round at him.

He pulled the cloth cap from his head, revealing thick fair hair beneath. He was of medium height with nothing to mark him as noticeable. His clothes were neither shabby nor well-tailored, grey trousers and matching jacket, smart enough, but not those of a gentleman. Something of his manner made her think that he was in service. He blended well with the background in all features except his voice.

'Miss Phoebe Allardyce?' he said again and she heard the cockney twang to his accent, so different to the lilt of the Scottish voices all around.

'Who are you, sir?' She looked at him with suspicion. He was certainly no one that she knew.

'I'm the Messenger.'

His eyes were a washed-out grey and so narrow that

they lent him a shifty air. She made to walk on, but his next words stopped her.

'If you've a care for your father, you'll listen.'

She narrowed her own eyes slightly, feeling an instant dislike for the man. 'What do you want?'

'To deliver a message to you.' He was slim but there was a wiry strength to his frame.

'I am listening,' she said.

'Your father's locked up in there for the rest of his days. Old man like him, his health not too good. And the conditions being what they are in the Tolbooth. Must worry you that.'

'My father's welfare and my feelings on the matter are none of your concern, sir.' She made to walk on.

'They are if I can spring him, Miss Allardyce, or, should I say, give you the means to do so. Fifteen hundred pounds to pay his debt, plus another five hundred to set the pair of you up in a decent enough lifestyle.'

A cold feeling spread over her. She stared at him in shock. 'How do you know the details of my father's debt?'

The man gave a leering smile and she noticed that his teeth were straight and white. 'Oh, we know all about you and your pa. Don't you worry your pretty little head about that. Just think on the money. Two grand in the hand, Miss Allardyce, and old pop is out of the Tolbooth.'

'You are offering me two thousand pounds?' She stared at him in disbelief.

He threw her a purse. 'A hundred up front.' She peeped inside and felt her heart turn over as she saw the roll of white notes. 'The rest when you deliver your end of the bargain.'

'Which is?'

'The smallest of favours.'

She waited.

'As Mrs Hunter's companion you have access to the whole of Blackloch Hall.'

Her scalp prickled with the extent of his knowledge.

'There is a certain object currently within the possession of the lady's son, a trifling little thing that he wouldn't even miss.'

'You are asking me to steal from Mr Hunter?'

'We're asking you to retrieve an item for its rightful owner.'

The man was trouble, as was all that he asked. She shook her head and gave a cynical smile as she thrust the purse back into his hands. 'Good day to you, sir.' And she started to climb the steps. She climbed all of four steps before his voice sounded again. He had not moved, but still stood where he was in the street.

'If you won't do it for the money, Miss Allardyce, you best have a thought for your pa locked up in there. Dangerous place is the Tolbooth. All sorts of unsavoury characters, the sort your pa ain't got a chance against. Who knows who he'll be sharing a cell with next? You have a think about that, Miss Allardyce.'

The man's words made her blood run cold, but she did not look back, just ran up the remaining steps and through the porch to the front door of the gaol.

'Everything all right, miss?' the door guard enquired.

'Yes, thank you,' she said as she slipped inside to the large square hallway. 'If I could just have a moment to gather myself?'

The guard nodded.

Her hands were trembling as she stood aside a little to let the other visitors pass. She took several deep breaths, leaned her back against one of the great stone columns and calmed her thoughts. It was an idle threat, that was all. The villain could not truly hurt her father within the security of a prison as tough and rigorous as the Tol-booth. The man was a villain, a thief, trying to frighten her into stealing for him. And Phoebe had no intention of being blackmailed. She tucked some stray strands of hair beneath her bonnet, and smoothed a hand over the top of her skirts. And only when she was sure that her papa would not notice anything amiss did she make her way through the doorway that led to the prison cells. Once through that door she passed the guard her basket for checking.

He removed the cover and gave the contents a quick glance. 'Raspberries this week, is it?' With her weekly visits over the last six months Phoebe was on friendly terms with most of the guards and turnkeys.

'They are my papa's favourite.'

'Sir Henry'll fair enjoy them.'

'I hope so.' She smiled and followed him up the narrow staircase all the way up to the debtors' cells on the third floor in which her father was held.

But the smile fled her face and the raspberries were forgotten the moment she entered the cell.

'Papa!' She placed the basket down on the small wooden table and ran to him. 'Oh, my word! What ever has happened to you?' She guided him to stand in the narrow shaft of sunlight that shone down into the cell through the bars of the small high window. And there in the light she could see that the skin around Sir Henry's left eye was dark with bruising and so swollen as to partially conceal the bloodshot eye beneath. The bruising extended over the whole left side of his face, from his temple to his chin, and even on that side of his mouth his lower lip was swollen and cut.

'Now, child, do not fuss so. It is nothing but the result of my own foolish clumsiness.'

But the man's words were ringing in her head again. *Dangerous place is the Tolbooth. All sorts of unsavoury characters, the sort your pa ain't got a chance against.*

'Who did this to you?' she demanded; she did not realise her grip had tightened and her knuckles shone white with the strain of it. 'Who?' Her eyes roved over his poor battered face.

'I tripped and fell, Phoebe. Nothing more. Calm yourself.'

'Papa—'

'Phoebe,' her father said, and she recognised that tone in his voice. He would tell her nothing. He did not want to worry her, not when he thought there was nothing she could do.

Her gaze scanned the cell. 'Where is the other man, your cellmate?'

'Released,' pronounced her father. 'His debt was paid off.' Sir Henry nodded philosophically. 'He was interesting company.'

Who knows who he'll be sharing a cell with next?

Phoebe felt her stomach clench and a wave of nausea rise up.

'You are white as a sheet, child. Perhaps this travelling up from Blackloch Hall is too much for you.'

'No. Really.' She forced herself to smile at him brightly, so that he would not be concerned. 'I have been taking very great care to keep my complexion fair. A difficult proposition with red hair and the summer sun. I do not wish to end up with freckles!' She pretended to tease and managed an accompanying grin.

He chuckled. 'You have your mother's colouring, and she never had a freckle in her life, God rest her soul.'

Her eyes lingered momentarily on his bruising and she thought for one dreadful minute she might weep. It was such a struggle to maintain the façade, but she knew she had to for his sake. The smile was still stretched across her mouth as she took his arm in her own and led him back to the little table they had managed to save from the bailiffs. Her blood was cold and thick and slow as she pulled off the basket's cover to reveal the punnet of raspberries within.

'Oh, Phoebe, well done,' he said and picked out the largest and juiciest berry and slipped it into his mouth. 'So, tell me all about Blackloch Hall and the moor…and Hunter.'

'Oh, I have rarely seen Mr Hunter.' It was not a lie. 'But he seems to be a gentleman of honour, if a little cold in manner perhaps.' She thought of how Hunter had rescued her from the highwaymen and his discretion over the same matter.

'Do not be fooled, Phoebe. From all accounts the words honour and Sebastian Hunter do not go together in the same sentence. Why do you think his mother has disowned him?'

'I did not realise there was such…' she hesitated '… bad feeling between them,' she finished as she thought of the one interaction she had witnessed between Hunter and his mother. 'What is the cause of it, I wonder?'

'Who can know for sure?' Her father gave a shrug, but there was something in his manner that suggested that he knew more of the matter.

'But you must have heard something?'

'Nothing to be repeated to such innocent ears, child.' She saw the slight wince before he could disguise it. He eased himself to a more comfortable position upon the wooden stool and she saw the strain and pain that he was trying to hide.

She pressed him no further on the matter, but tried to

distract him with descriptions of the Gothic style of the house and the expansive ruggedness of the moor. And all the while she was conscious of the raw soreness of her father's injuries. By the time she kissed her father's undamaged cheek and made her way down the narrow staircase, her heart was thudding hard with the coldness of her purpose and there was a fury in her eyes.

The man was leaning against the outside of the gaol, waiting for her.

He pulled off his hat again as he came towards her. 'Miss Allar—' he started to say, but she cut him off, her voice hard as she hid the emotion beneath it. She looked at him and would have run the villain through with a sword had she one to hand.

'I will do it, on the proviso that no further harm comes to my father.'

There was a fleeting surprise in those narrow shifty eyes as if he had not thought her to agree so quickly.

'What is it that you want me to steal?'

And he leaned his face closer and whispered the words softly into her ear.

She nodded.

'We have been told Hunter keeps it in his study—in his desk. Bring it here with you when you visit next Tuesday. And keep your lips sealed over this, Miss Allardyce. One word to Mrs Hunter or her son and your old pa gets it…' He drew his finger across his throat like a knife blade to emphasise his point. 'Do you understand?'

'I understand perfectly,' she said and as the crowd hurried past, someone jostled her and when she looked round at the man again he was gone.

Her heart was aching for the hurts her father had suffered and her blood was surging with fury at the men who had hurt him. She knew she must not weaken, must not weep, not here, not now. She straightened her shoulders, held her head up and walked with purpose the small distance to the Tontine Hotel to wait for the mail coach that would deliver her to the moor.

Chapter Three

The moor was bathed golden and hazy in the late evening light. Behind the house, out over the Firth of Clyde, the sun would soon sink down behind the islands, a red ball of fire in a pink streaked sky. There was no sound, nothing save the steady slow tick of the clock and the whisper of the breeze through the grass and the heather.

Hunter remembered the last day of his father's life. When he closed his eyes he could see his father's face ruddy with choler, etched with disgust, and hear their final shouted exchange echoing in his head, each and every angry word of it…and what had followed. Thereafter, there had been such remorse, such anger, such guilt. He ached with it. And all the brandy in Britain and France did not change a damned thing.

The glass lay limp and empty within his hand. Hunter thought no more, just refilled it and settled back to numb the pain.

Phoebe struck that night, before her courage or her anger could desert her. Mrs Hunter was in bed when she arrived back in Blackloch, having retired early as was her normal habit.

Within the green guest bedchamber Phoebe went through the mechanics of preparing for bed. She changed into her nightdress, washed, brushed her teeth, combed and plaited her hair, brushed the dust from her dress and wiped her boots. And then she sat down in the little green armchair and she waited…and waited; waiting as the hours crawled by until, at last, Phoebe heard no more footsteps, no more voices, no more noise.

Daylight had long since faded and darkness shrouded the house. From downstairs in the hallway by the front door she heard the striking of the grandfather clock, two deep sonorous chimes. Only now did Phoebe trust that all of Blackloch was asleep. She stole from her room, treading as quietly and as quickly as she could along the corridor and down the main staircase.

The house was in total darkness and she was thankful she had decided to bring the single candle to light her way. Its small flame flickered as she walked, casting ghostly shadows all around. There was silence, the thump of her heart and whisper of her breath the only sounds. Her feet trod softly, carefully, down each step until she reached the main hallway. She could hear the slow heavy ticking of the clock.

The hallway was expansive, floored in the same greystone flags that ran throughout the whole of the lower house and roofed with dark disappearing arches reminiscent of some ancient medieval cathedral. She held up her candle to confirm she was alone and saw a small snarling face staring down at her from the arches. She jumped, almost dropping her candle in the process, and gave a gasp. Her heart was racing. She stared back at the face and saw this time that it was only the gargoyle of a wolf carved into the stone. Indeed, there was a whole series of them hidden within the ribs of the ceiling: a pack of wolves, all watching her. She froze, holding her breath, her heart thumping hard and fast, waiting to see if anyone had heard her, waiting to see if anyone would come. The grandfather clock marked the passing of the minutes, five in all, and nobody arrived. She breathed a sigh of relief and looked across at the study.

Not the slightest glimmer of light showed beneath the doorway. No sound came from within. Phoebe crept quietly towards the dark mahogany door, placed her hand upon the wrought-iron handle and slowly turned. The door opened without a creak. She held up her candle to light the darkness and stepped into Sebastian Hunter's study.

Hunter was sitting silently in his chair by the window, his eyes staring blindly out at the dark-enveloped moor when he heard the noise from the hallway outside his study. The waning half moon was hidden under a small streak of cloud and the black-velvet sky was lit only by a sprinkling of stars, bright and twinkly as diamonds. His head turned, listening, but otherwise he did not move. His senses sharpened. And even though he had been drinking he was instantly alert.

Someone was out there, he could feel their presence. A maidservant on her way down to the kitchens? A footman returning to bed following a tryst? Or another intruder, like the ones who had tried before? He set the brandy glass down and quietly withdrew the pistol from the bottom right-hand drawer of his desk, then turned the chair back to face the moor so that he would not be seen from the doorway; he waited, and he listened.

He listened to the light pad of footsteps across the

stone flags towards his door. He listened as the handle slowly turned and the door quietly opened, then closed again. Within the small diamond-shaped lead-lined panes he saw the reflection of a bright flicker of candlelight. The soft even tread of small feet moved towards the desk behind him. He waited until he heard the clunk of the brass candlestick being set down upon the wooden surface of the desk behind him, then he cocked the pistol and swivelled his chair round to face the intruder.

She was standing with her back to him, looking over his desk.

'Miss Allardyce.'

She started round to face him, gave a small shriek and stumbled back against the desk. Her mouth worked, but no words sounded.

He rose to his feet.

Her gaze dropped to the pistol.

He made it safe and lowered it.

'Mr Hunter,' she said and he could hear the shock in her voice and see it in every nuance of her face, of her body and the way she was gripping at the desk behind her. 'I had no idea that you were in here.'

'Evidently not.' He let his gaze wander from the long thick auburn braid of her hair that hung over her shoulder, down across the bodice of the cotton nightdress which, though prim and plain and patched in places, did not quite hide the figure beneath. His gaze dropped lower to the little bare toes that peeped from beneath its hem, before lifting once more to those golden brown eyes. And something of the woman seemed to call to him so that, just as when he had first looked at her upon the moor, an overwhelming desire surged through him. Had this been a year ago... Had this been before all that had changed him...

He saw her glance flicker away before coming back to meet his own and, when she did, he could see she had recovered herself and where the shock and panic had been there was now calm determination.

'Mrs Hunter is having trouble sleeping. She sent me to find a book for her, in the hope that it would help.' She made to move away and he should have let her go, but Hunter stepped closer, effectively blocking her exit.

'Any book in particular?'

Miss Allardyce gave a little shrug. 'She did not say.' The backs of her thighs were still tight against the desk, her hands behind her still gripping to its wooden edge.

He leaned across her to lay the pistol down upon the smooth polished surface of the desk and the brush of his arm against the softness of her breast sent his blood rushing all the faster.

Miss Allardyce sucked in her breath and jumped at the contact between their bodies. He saw the shock in her eyes…and the passion, and knew she was not indifferent to him, that something of the madness of this sensation was racing through her, too.

He was standing so close that the toe of his left boot was beneath the hem of her nightdress. So close that the scent of roses and sunlight and sweet woman filled his nose. His gaze traced the outline of her features, of her cheekbones and her nose, down to the fullness of her lips. And the urge to take her into his arms and kiss her was overwhelming. A vision of them making love upon the surface of the desk swam in his mind, of him moving between the pale soft thighs beneath the thick cotton of her nightdress, of his mouth upon her breasts…

Desire hummed loud. He had never experienced such an immediacy of feeling like that which was coursing between him and Miss Allardyce. Hunter slid a hand behind that slender creamy neck and her lips seemed to call to his. All of his promises were forgotten. He lowered his face towards hers…

And felt the firm thrust of Miss Allardyce's hands against his chest.

'What on earth do you think you are doing, Mr Hunter?' Her chest was rising and falling in a rapid rhythm, her breath as ragged as if they had indeed just made love.

It was enough to shatter the madness of the moment. He realised what he was doing.

She was staring at him, her eyes suddenly dark in the candlelight, her cheeks stained with colour.

'Forgive me.' He stepped swiftly back to place a distance between them. He was not a rake. He damn well was not. Not any more. He did not gamble. And he did not womanise. 'A book, you say?'

'If you please.' A no-nonsense tone, unaffected, except that when she picked up the candlestick he could see the slight tremor of it in her hand.

'Be my guest.' He gestured to the books that lined the walls and moved away even further to the safety of the shelves closest to the window. '*Evelina* used to be a favourite of my mother's,' he said and drew the volume from its shelf. He offered it to her, holding it by the farthest edge so that their fingers would not touch.

She accepted the book from him, said 'Thank you', and made her way to the door where she paused, hand resting on the handle, and glanced round at him.

'And thank you for both your assistance upon the moor and your discretion over the matter.' She spoke with hesitation and he could feel her awkwardness at both the situation and the words, but there was a strength in her eyes that he had not seen in any other woman before. 'I will catch the coach in the future.' And before he could utter a word she was gone, leaving Hunter staring at the softly closed door of his study with a firm resolve to keep a distance between Miss Allardyce and himself for the weeks that remained of his mother's visit.

Inside the green bedchamber Phoebe leaned heavily against the door. Her legs felt like jelly and she was shaking so badly that the candlelight flickered and jumped wildly around the room. She set the candlestick down upon her little table and tried to calm the frenzied beat of her heart, to no avail.

Her heart was hammering as hard as it had been when she had faced Hunter in his study. Standing there in just his shirt and breeches. No coat, no waistcoat, no neck-cloth. The neck of his fine white shirt open and loose, revealing the bare skin beneath, a chest that she knew was hard with muscle from the hand she had placed upon it. Memories of his very proximity that made it difficult for her to catch a breath. She closed her eyes and in her mind saw again that piercing gaze holding hers, driving every sensible thought from her head, making her stomach turn a cartwheel and her legs melt to jelly. Images and sensations vivid enough to take her breath away, all of which should have shocked and appalled her. She *was* shocked. Shocked at the spark the mere brush of his arm had ignited throughout her body. Shocked that for the tiniest of moments she had almost let him kiss her. Phoebe had never experienced anything like it. She clutched a hand to her mouth and tried to stop the stampede of emotion.

What on earth was he doing sitting in there in the dark in the middle of the night anyway? And she remembered the rich sweet smell of brandy that had clung to his breath and the way his chair had been positioned to face out onto the moor. A man who did not sleep. A man who had much to brood upon.

She walked to the window and pulled the curtains apart. Unfastening the catch, she slid the window up and stared out at the night beyond. The bitten wafer of the moon shone silver and all around, scattered across the deep black velvet of the sky, were tiny stars like diamonds. Cool fresh air wafted in and she inhaled its sweet dampness, breathing slowly and deeply in an attempt to calm herself. Not so far away she could hear the quiet ripple of the Black Loch, its water merging with the darkness of the night. She thought of her father's warning about Hunter and his wickedness. And no matter how much she willed it, her heart would not slow or her mind dismiss the image of a raven-haired man whose eyes were so strangely and dangerously alluring.

In the cool light of the next morning after a restless night Phoebe could see things more clearly. Hunter had discovered her about to search his desk in the middle of the night. No doubt any woman's thoughts would be in such disarray and her sensibilities so thoroughly disturbed were a gun levelled at her heart by a gentleman with Hunter's reputation. The important thing was that he had appeared to believe her excuse and for that she could only be thankful. Phoebe had bigger matters to worry about. She could not let the incident in the night deter her from securing her father's safety.

Phoebe tried again the next night and the night after that, but each time she stole down the stairs it was to see the faint flicker of light beneath the door to Hunter's study and she knew he was alone within, drinking through the night, as if he could not bear to sleep. As if he were haunted. As if he carried a sin so dark upon his soul that it chained him in perpetual torment. She shivered and forced the thoughts away, knowing that the days before Tuesday and her visit to the Tolbooth were too few. There had to be a way to search the study. Phoebe was in an agony of worry.

It was Mrs Hunter who solved the problem…when she told Phoebe of the Blackloch outing to the seaside planned for Saturday.

The morning of the trip was glorious. The sun shone down on a sea that stretched out in a broad glistening vastness before him. To the right was the edge of the island of Arran, and to the left, in the distance, the characteristic conical lump on the horizon that was the rock of Ailsa Craig. A bank of grass led down to the large curved bay of golden sand. It was beautiful, but nothing of the scene touched Hunter.

He and McEwan dismounted, tying their horses to a nearby tethering pole. The maids and footmen were milling around the carriages, chatting and laughing with excitement. McEwan looked to Hunter for his nod, then went to organise the party, to see that the blankets were spread upon the sands before collecting the picnic hampers and baskets containing the bottles of lemonade and elderflower cordial. Hunter stood there for a moment alone, detached, remote from the good spirits, and watched as the men peeled off their jackets and the women abandoned their shawls and pushed up their sleeves. There was such joviality, such happiness and anticipation amongst the entirety of his household that Hunter felt his very presence might spoil it. He moved away towards his mother's coach where her footman was already assisting her down the steps.

She threw him a grudging nod. 'I am glad that at least you have not let the old customs slip.'

He gave a nod of acknowledgement, his face cold and expressionless to hide the memories her words evoked.

His mother took her parasol from the maid who appeared from the carriage behind her. There was a silence as she surveyed the scene before her, a small half-smile upon her mouth there not for Hunter, but for the sake of the staff.

Hunter glanced round, expecting Miss Allardyce, but his mother's companion did not appear.

'The book was to your satisfaction?' he enquired.

'The book?' His mother peered at him as if he were talking double Dutch.

'Evelina,' he prompted.

'I have not seen that book in years,' she said and turned her attention away from him.

Hunter turned the implication of her answer over in his mind and let the minutes pass before he spoke again.

'Your companion does not accompany you,' he said, as if merely making an observation. His face remained forward, watching the staff as they carried the hampers down onto the sand.

'Miss Allardyce is feeling unwell. I told her to spend the day in bed, resting.' His mother equally kept her focus on the maids and the footmen.

'The timing of her illness is unfortunate.' *Or fortunate, depending on whose point of view one was considering,* he thought grimly.

His mother nodded. 'Indeed it is—poor girl.'

Once everyone was settled upon the blankets, his mother in pride of place upon a chair and rug, he and

McEwan removed their coats, rolled up their sleeves and served plates of cold sliced cooked chicken, ham and beef to the waiting servants. There were bread rolls and cheese and hard-boiled eggs. There were strawberries and raspberries, fresh cooled cream and the finest jams, sponge cakes, peppermint creams and hard-boiled sweets. And chunks of ice all wrapped up and placed amongst the food and drink to keep it cool. Expense had not been skimped upon. Hunter wanted his staff to have a good time, just as his father had done before him and his father before him.

This was duty. He knew that and so he endured it, even though the laughter and light that surrounded him made him feel all the darker and all the more alone. Hunter stood aside from the rest and watched the little party, his mother in the centre of it, good humoured, partaking in the jokes and the chatter; the few staff that remained at Blackloch were as warm with her as if she had never left.

He slid a glance at his pocket watch before making his way over to his mother. The laughter on her face died away as soon as she saw him. And he thought he saw something of the light in her expire.

'There are matters at Blackloch to which I must attend. I will leave McEwan at your disposal.'

She smiled, if it could be called that, but her eyes were filled with disdain and condemnation. She made no attempt to dissuade him. Indeed, she looked positively relieved that he was leaving.

McEwan appeared by his side as Hunter pulled on his coat.

'Attend to my mother's wishes if you will, McEwan. I will see you back at Blackloch later.' Hunter brushed his heels against Ajax's flank and was gone, heading back along the road to Blackloch Hall.

* * *

Phoebe did not know where else to look in the sunlit study. All six desk drawers lay open. She had searched through each one twice and found nothing of what she sought. There were bottles of ink, pens and pen sharpeners. There was also a packet of crest-embossed writing paper, books of estate accounts, newspapers and letters, a brace of pistols and even a roll of crisp white banknotes, but not the object she must steal. She had searched all of the library shelves, even sliding each deep red leatherbound book out just in case, but behind them was only dark old mahogany and a fine layer of dust.

The faint aroma of brandy still hung in the air, rich and sweet and ripe, mixed with the underlying scent of a man's cologne—the smell of Hunter. She thought of him sitting in this room through the long dark hours of the night, alone and filling himself with brandy. And despite her father's words, and whatever it was that Hunter had done, she could not help but feel a twinge of compassion for him.

She slumped down into Hunter's chair, not knowing what to do. The man had said it would be in Hunter's study. But Phoebe had been looking for over an hour without a sight of it. She leaned her elbows on the dark ebony surface of Hunter's desk and rested her head in her hands. *Where else to look? Where?* But there were no other hiding places to search.

The sun was beating through the arched lattice windows directly upon her and she felt flustered and hot and worried. A bead of sweat trickled between her breasts as she got to her feet, her shoulders tense and tight with disappointment and worry. There was nothing more to be gained by searching yet again. The Messenger, as he called himself, had been wrong; she could do nothing other than tell him so.

She thought of Mrs Hunter, and the man who was her son, and of all the staff down at the seaside, with the cooling sea breeze and the wash of the waves rolling in over the sand, and up to the ankles of those who dared to paddle. Her fingers wiped the sweat from her brow and she felt a pang of jealousy. And then she remembered the loch with its still cool water and its smooth dark surface. She rubbed at the ache of tension that throbbed in her shoulders as she thought of its soothing peacefulness and tranquillity.

She knew she should not, but Mrs Hunter had said they would not be back until late afternoon, and there was no one here to see. Phoebe felt very daring as she closed the door of Hunter's study behind her.

The glare of the mid-day sun was relentless as Hunter cantered along the Kilmarnock road. He would not gallop Ajax until he reached the softer ground of the moor. Sweat glistened on the horse's neck, but the heat of the day did not touch Hunter, for he was chilled inside, chilled as the dead. In the sky above it was as if a great dark cloud covered the sun, the same dark shadow that dogged him always.

He thought of Miss Allardyce and he spurred Ajax on until he reached Blackloch.

Hunter stabled his horse and then slipped into the house through the back door. All was quiet, and still; the only things moving were the tiny particles of dust dancing in the sunlight bathing the hallway. He made his way into his study, his refuge. And, dispensing with his hat and gloves, scanned the room with a new eye.

Nothing looked out of place. Everything was just as he

had left it. The piles of paperwork and books perched at the far edge of his desk, the roll of banknotes in the top drawer, the set of pistols in the bottom. He pulled out the money, counted the notes—not one was missing. Upon the shelves that lined the room the books, bound in their dark red leather with gold-lettered spines, sat uniform and tidy. No gaps caught the eye. His gaze moved to the fourth shelf by the window, to the one gap that should have been there. *Evelina* sat in its rightful place.

Hunter poured himself a brandy and sat down at the desk. She had been in here. He mused over the knowledge while he sipped at the brandy. Returning a book that she had lied about needing to borrow. His gaze moved over the polished ebony surface of his desk, and he saw it—a single hair, long and stark against the darkness of the wood. A hair that had not been there this morning, on a desk that she had no need to be near in order to return the book to its shelf. He lifted it carefully, held it between his fingers and, in the light from the window, the hair glowed a deep burnished red. Hunter felt a spurt of anger that he had allowed his physical reaction to the woman cloud his judgement. He abandoned his brandy and made his way to find Miss Allardyce.

It was no surprise to find the bedchamber empty and the bed neatly made. He undertook a cursory search of her belongings, of which it seemed that Miss Allardyce possessed scant few. A green silk evening dress, the bonnet she had been wearing upon the moor road the day he had encountered her with the highwaymen. A pair of well-worn brown leather boots, one pair of green silk slippers to match the dress. A shawl of pale grey wool, a dark cloak, some gloves, underwear. All of it outmoded and worn, but well cared for. A hairbrush, ribbons, a toothbrush and powder, soap. No jewellery. Nothing that he would not expect to find. And yet a feeling nagged in his gut that something with Miss Allardyce was not quite right. And where the hell was she?

He stood where he was, his gaze ranging the room that held her scent—sweet and clean, roses and soap. And then something caught his eye in the scene through the window. A pale movement in the dark water of the loch. Hunter moved closer and stared out, his eye following the moorland running down to the loch. And the breath caught in his throat, for there in the waters of the Black Loch was a woman—a young, naked woman. Her long hair, dark reddish brown, wet and swirling around her, her skin ivory where she lay beneath the surface of the water, so still that he wondered if she were drowned. But then those slim pale arms moved up and over her head, skimming the water behind her as she swam, and he could see the slight churn where she kicked her feet.

He stood there and watched, unable to help himself. Watched the small mounds of her breasts break the surface and fall beneath again. He watched her rise up, emerging from the loch's dark depths like a red-haired Aphrodite, naked and beautiful. Even across the distance he could see her wet creamy skin, the curve of her small breasts with their rosy tips, the narrowness of her waist and the gentle swell of her hips. She stood on the bank and wrung out her hair, sending more rivulets of water cascading down her body before reaching down to pull on her shift. Hunter felt his mouth go dry and his body harden. He knew now the whereabouts of Miss Allardyce—she was swimming in his loch.

Chapter Four

Phoebe hummed as she hurried up the main staircase, carrying her petticoats and dress draped over her arm. She resolved that once she was dressed she would retrace her route and wipe the trail of wet footprints she was leaving in her wake. The tension had eased from her shoulders; she was feeling clear-headed and much more positive about tackling the Messenger on Tuesday. She was padding down the corridor towards her bedchamber when one of the doors on the left opened and out stepped Sebastian Hunter.

Phoebe gave a shriek and almost dropped her bundle of clothes. 'What on earth...? Good heavens!' He seemed to take up the whole of the passageway ahead. She saw his gaze sweep down over her body where the thin worn cotton of her shift was moulded to the dampness of her skin; she clutched her dress and undergarments tight to cover her indecency.

'Mr Hunter, you startled me. I thought you were gone to the seaside with the rest of the house.' She could feel the scald of embarrassment in her cheeks and hear the slight breathlessness of shock in her voice.

'I returned early.' His expression was closed and unsmiling as ever.

'If you will excuse me, sir,' she said and made to walk past him, but to Phoebe's horror Hunter moved to block her way.

'My mother said you were ill abed.' His tone was cold and she thought she could see a hint of accusation in his eyes.

'This is not the time for discussion, sir. At least have the decency to let me clothe myself first.' She looked at him with indignation and prayed that he would not see the truth beneath it.

Hunter showed no sign of moving.

'I would hear your explanation now, Miss Allardyce.' His gaze was piercing.

'This is ridiculous! You have no right to accost me so!'

'And you have no right to lie to my mother,' he countered in a voice so cool and silky that it sent shivers rippling the length of her spine.

'I did not lie.' Another lie upon all the others. She could not meet his gaze as she said it.

'You do not look ill and abed to me, Miss Allardyce. Indeed, you look very much as if you have been swimming in the loch.'

She could not very well deny it. She stared at her the bareness of her feet and the droplets of water surrounding them, then, taking a deep breath, raised her eyes to his. And in their meeting that same feeling passed between them as had done on the moor and that night in his study. Hunter felt it, too, she could see it in his eyes. And standing there, barely clothed before him, at this most inopportune of moments she understood exactly what it was. An overwhelming, irrational attraction. Her mind went blank; she could think of not a single thing to say.

'I…'

Hunter waited.

With a will of iron she managed to drag her gaze away and close her mind to the realisation.

'I felt somewhat feverish and took a dip in the loch to cool the heat.' The excuse slipped from her tongue and, feeble though it was, she was thankful for it. 'As a result I am feeling much recovered.'

He gave no sign that he did not believe her, but neither did he look convinced. The tension hummed between them. The seconds seemed to stretch for ever.

'Sir, I am barely clothed! Your behaviour is reprehensible!' She forced her chin up and eyed him with disdain.

Hunter did not move. 'You were in my study today, Miss Allardyce.' That pale intense gaze bored into hers as if he could see every last thought in her head.

Phoebe's heart gave a little stutter. The tension ratcheted tighter between them. She swallowed hard and kept her eyes on his, as if to look away would be some kind of admission of guilt. She thought of her father and his poor battered face and the memory was enough to steel every trembling nerve in her body. She knew what was at stake here.

'I returned your book.' She could feel the water dripping from her hair over her shoulders, rolling down over her arms, which were bare to Hunter's perusal if he should choose to look, but his gaze did not stray once from her own.

'How did my mother enjoy *Evelina*?'

'Well enough, I believe.' Phoebe spoke calmly, and stayed focused.

He said nothing, but there was a tiny flicker of a muscle in his jaw.

She shivered, but whether it was from the cooling of

her skin or the burning intensity of Hunter's eyes she did not know. 'And now, if you will excuse me, sir.'

His gaze shifted then, swept over her bare shoulders, over the dress she clutched to her breast, down to her bare feet and the puddle of loch water that was forming around them. And she blushed with embarrassment and anger, and most of all with the knowledge that she could be attracted to such a man.

'Really, Mr Hunter! How dare you?'

Hunter's eyes met hers once more. He did not look away, but he did step aside to let her reach the door.

She edged past him, keeping her back to the door so that he would not see the full extent of her undress. Her hand fumbled behind at the door knob.

The door did not open.

Phoebe twisted it to the left.

The door did not yield.

Then to the right.

Still nothing happened.

She rattled at the blasted knob, panicking at the thought she would have to turn round and in the process present Hunter with a view that did not bear thinking about.

Hunter moved, closing the distance between them.

Phoebe gave a gasp as his hand reached round behind her. He was so close she could smell his soap, his cologne, the very scent that was the man himself. Her heart was thudding so hard she felt dizzy. And as Hunter stared down at her she could see the sudden darkening blaze in his eyes, could sense the still tension that gripped his large powerful male body, could feel the very air vibrate between them. The edge of his sleeve brushed against her arm. And part of her dreaded it and, heaven help her, part of her wanted to feel the touch of those strong firm lips. To be kissed, to be held by such a strong dangerous man.

She squeezed her eyes closed and clutched the dress all the tighter.

Cool air hit against her skin and she heard the sound of booted steps receding along the passageway. She opened her eyes to find Hunter gone and the door to her chamber wide open behind her.

Hunter paused as the clock upon his study mantel chimed eight and then looked across his desk at McEwan, who was sitting in the chair opposite and waiting with the air of a man much contented. Hunter swallowed back the bitterness.

'You are up and about early this morning, Hunter.' Hunter saw McEwan eye the still half-full brandy decanter, but his steward was wise enough to make no comment upon it.

'I have things on my mind,' said Hunter and frowned again as he thought of Miss Allardyce.

'What do you make of my mother's companion?'

'I cannot say I have noticed her,' McEwan confessed.

'Hell's teeth, man, how could—?' Hunter stopped, suddenly aware of revealing just how much he had noticed Miss Allardyce himself. In his time he had known diamonds of the *ton*, actresses whose looks commanded thousands and opera singers with the faces of angels, all of whose beauty far exceeded that of his mother's companion. And yet there was something about Phoebe Allardyce, something when she looked at him with those golden-brown eyes of hers that affected Hunter in a way no woman ever had. He took a breath, leaned back in the chair and looked at McEwan.

'She seems much as any other lady's companion I have met,' McEwan offered. 'Why are you asking?'

Hunter hesitated.

The clock ticked loud and slow.

'I do not trust her,' he said at last.

McEwan's brows shot up. 'What has she done?'

'Nothing…at least nothing solid I can confront her with.' He thought of her visits to his study, and the telltale hair upon his desk so vibrant against the polished ebony of the wood. He glanced up at McEwan. 'Let us just call it a gut feeling.'

'Is it a question of her honesty?'

'Possibly.' Hunter thought of her lies about the coach fare, *Evelina*, her absence at the seaside trip, all of which were trivial and might be explained away by a myriad of reasons. But his instincts were telling him otherwise. And that was not all his damnable instincts were telling him of Miss Allardyce. A vision appeared in his mind of her standing in the upstairs passageway, her shift clinging damp and transparent, and the pile of clothing that hid little, and he almost groaned at the pulse of desire that throbbed through him. He closed his eyes, clenched his teeth to martial some control and felt anger and determination overcome the lust. When he opened his eyes again McEwan was staring at him.

'Everything all right?'

Hunter schooled himself to dispassion. 'Why would it be otherwise?' He saw the compassion that came into McEwan's eyes and hated it. 'We are talking of Miss Allardyce,' he said and knew he should curb the cold tone from his voice. Jed McEwan was his friend and the one who had helped him through those darkest days. The man did not deserve such treatment. 'Forgive me,' he muttered.

McEwan gave a single nod and the expression on his face told Hunter that he understood. 'What do you want to do about Miss Allardyce?'

Hunter narrowed his eyes slightly. 'Find out a little more about her. There is a man I know in Glasgow who should be able to help.' A man he had used before for less honourable pursuits. 'Would you be able to act on my behalf?'

'Of course.'

Hunter scribbled the man's details on a sheet of paper; while he waited for the ink to dry, he opened the drawer and extracted one of the rolls of banknotes. 'The sooner, the better.' He pushed the money and the paper across the desk's surface to McEwan, who folded the paper before slipping both into his pocket.

'And while you are gone I will see what I can discover from my mother.'

Hunter waited until his mother and her companion had finished their breakfast and were playing cards within the drawing room before he approached.

His mother was dressed as smartly as ever, not a hair out of place in her chignon, her dress of deep purple silk proclaiming her still to be in mourning for his father, although it had been nine months since his death. Miss Allardyce sat opposite her, wearing the same faded blue dress he had last seen clutched raggedly against her breast, on the face of it looking calm and unruffled, but he saw the flicker of wariness in those tawny eyes before she masked it.

'If you would excuse me for a few minutes, ma'am.' Miss Allardyce set her cards face down upon the green baize surface of the card table and got to her feet. She smiled at his mother. 'I have left my handkerchiefs in my bedchamber and find I have need of them.'

His mother gave a sullen nod, but did not look pleased.

'Well?' she asked as the door closed behind her companion. 'What is it that you have to say to me?'

Hunter walked over to Miss Allardyce's chair and sat down upon it. 'How are you finding it being back at Blackloch?'

'Well enough,' she said in a tone that would have soured the freshest of milk. She eyed him with cold dislike. 'There are no amends that you can make for what you did, Sebastian. You cannot expect that I will forgive you.'

'I do not,' he said easily and lifted Miss Allardyce's cards from the table. He fanned them out, looking at them. 'Is Miss Allardyce to play?'

His mother gave a grudging nod.

Hunter gestured for another card from the banker's pile. And his mother slid one face down across the baize towards him. He noticed the arthritic knuckles above the large cluster of diamonds that glittered upon her fingers, and the slight tremor that held them.

'I did not know you had taken on a companion.'

'There is much you do not know about me, Sebastian.'

'You did not advertise the position in the *Glasgow Herald*; I would have seen it.' He narrowed his eyes and stared at the cards as if musing what move to make. His attention was seemingly focused entirely upon the fan of cards within his hand.

'Miss Allardyce came to me recommended by a friend. She is from a good family, the daughter of a knight, no less, albeit in unfortunate circumstances.'

'Indeed,' murmured Hunter and played his card.

His mother nodded appreciatively at his choice. She sniffed and regarded her own cards more closely, then filled the silence as he had hoped. 'She is left alone while her father, a Sir Henry Allardyce, is hospitalised. I offered my assistance when I heard of her situation.'

'You are too good, Mother, taking in waifs and strays.'

'Do not be sharp, Sebastian. It does not suit you.'

He gave a small smile of amusement.

She played a card.

Hunter eyed it. 'Your card skills have improved.'

His mother tried not to show it, but he could tell she was pleased with the compliment.

'Did she offer a letter of recommendation, a character?'

'Of course not. I told you, she is a gentleman's daughter with no previous experience of such a position.' His mother's eyes narrowed. 'You are very interested in Miss Allardyce all of a sudden. Do not think to start with any of your rakish nonsense. I will not stand for it. She is my companion.'

'Miss Allardyce is not my type,' he said coolly. 'As well you know.'

Her cheeks coloured faintly at his reference to the light-skirts in whom he had previously taken such interest. 'There is no need for vulgarity.'

'I apologise if I have offended you.' He inclined his head. 'My concern is with you, Mother, and if that warrants an interest in those you take into your employ, particularly in positions of such confidence, then I make no apology for that. What do you really know of the girl? Of her trustworthiness and her background?'

'Oh, do not speak of concern for me, for I know full well that you have none,' she snapped. The disdain was back in her eyes, their momentary truce broken. 'And as for Miss Allardyce, or any of my staff, I will not be dictated to, nor will I have my choice vetted by you. To put it bluntly, Sebastian, it is none of your business.'

'On the contrary, I owe it to my father—'

'Do not dare speak his name! You have no right, no damned right at all!' And she threw the cards down on the table and swept from the room.

Phoebe spent the next hour trying to pacify her employer in the lady's rooms.

'Come, cease your pacing, Mrs Hunter. You will make yourself ill.' Already the older woman's face was pale and pinched. She ignored Phoebe and continued her movement about the room.

'How dare he?' she mumbled to herself.

'Mr Hunter has upset you,' Phoebe said with concern.

'My son's very existence upsets me,' muttered Mrs Hunter in a harsh voice. 'I rue the day he was born.'

Phoebe masked her shock before it showed. 'I am sure you do not mean that, ma'am. Let me ring for some tea. It will make you feel better.'

'I do not want yet another cup of tea, Phoebe,' she snapped. 'And, yes, when it comes to Sebastian, I mean every word that I say.' She stopped by the window, leaning her hands upon the sill to stare out of the front of the house across the moor. 'I hate my son,' she said more quietly in a tone like ice. 'It is an admission that no mother should make, but it is the truth.' She glanced round at Phoebe. 'I have shocked you, have I not?'

'A little,' admitted Phoebe.

She turned to face her fully. 'If you knew what he has done, you would understand.'

Phoebe felt her blood run cold at the words. *Tell me,* she wanted to say.

Mrs Hunter looked at Phoebe for a moment as if she had heard the silent plea, then the anger drained away. In its place was exhaustion and a fragility that Phoebe had never before seen there. Her face was pale and peaked and as Phoebe looked she realised Mrs Hunter looked old and ill.

'Do you wish to speak of it?'

There was silence and for a moment, a very small moment, Phoebe thought she would. And then Mrs Hunter shook her head and closed her eyes. 'I cannot.' And then she pressed a hand to her forehead, half-shielding one eye as if she might weep.

Phoebe moved to take Mrs Hunter's arm and guided her to sit in an armchair. She knelt by her side and took one of the lady's hands within her own. 'Is there anything that I might do to help?'

Mrs Hunter gave a little shake of the head and a weak smile. 'You are a good and honest girl, Phoebe.'

Phoebe felt the guilt stain her cheeks. She glanced down uneasily, knowing that she had been less than honest and that thieving made her very bad.

Mrs Hunter sighed as her hand moved to her breastbone and she rubbed her fingers against the silk of her dress, feeling the golden locket that Phoebe knew lay hidden beneath. 'My head aches almost as much as my heart.' Her voice was unsteady and there was such an underlying pain there that Phoebe felt the ache of it in her own chest.

'I could make you a feverfew tisane. It should relieve the pain a little.'

'Yes. I would like that.' Mrs Hunter patted Phoebe's hand, then she rose and walked from the little sitting room towards her bedchamber. 'And send Polly up. I wish to lie down for a while.'

Phoebe nodded and quietly left. Yet she could not stop wondering at the terrible deed in Hunter's past that had made his mother hate him so.

* * *

McEwan came to him that evening with the information he had discovered.

'Are you certain?' Hunter demanded.

McEwan glanced up at him. 'Absolutely. Sir Henry Allardyce was sent to gaol for an unpaid debt of fifteen hundred pounds some six months ago. He has been imprisoned in the Tolbooth ever since.' McEwan tasted the brandy. 'It seems that your instincts concerning Miss Allardyce were right, Hunter.'

Hunter said nothing, just toyed with the glass of brandy in his hand.

McEwan lounged back in the wing chair by the unlit fire. 'I suppose it is understandable that she would lie over the matter. She is unlikely to have found a decent position otherwise.'

'Indeed.' Hunter took a small sip of brandy.

'Will you tell Mrs Hunter?'

'My mother will not thank me for the knowledge.'

'Then we will leave Miss Allardyce to her secret.'

'Not quite,' said Hunter and set his glass down on the drum table between him and McEwan. He thought of Miss Allardyce in his study and of the lies she had spun, and he could not rid himself of the notion that there was more to the mystery surrounding the girl than simply hiding her father's fate.

McEwan listened while Hunter told him his plan and then left to rush back to his Mairi. Hunter lifted his glass and stood by the window, looking out over the moor. In all these months not once had he even looked at a woman. He was the man his father had wanted him to be. And yet it was all too little, too late. The past could not be undone. Some sins could never be washed clean. And Hunter would have to live with that knowledge for the rest of his life. All he had were the vows he had sworn and his determination to honour them. And now it seemed even they were to be tried.

Fate was taunting him, testing him. Throwing temptation in his path, and such a temptation that Hunter could never have imagined, wrapped in the guise of a plain and ordinary girl, except there was nothing plain or ordinary about Phoebe Allardyce. For the sake of his mother there could be no more thought of avoiding Miss Allardyce. He sipped at the brandy and knew he would have to take an interest in the girl, whether he liked it or not. And in him burned a cold steady anger and a determination to honour the promises he had sworn.

Mrs Hunter was still in bed as Phoebe hurried down the main staircase two mornings later, reticule in hand, shawl around her shoulders. Through the window she could see the sky was an expanse of dull grey filled with the promise of rain, and all around her the air held a nip that boded of the end of summer. Phoebe's normally bright spirits on a Tuesday morning were clouded by the prospect of meeting the Messenger empty-handed. Ahead of her the front door of Blackloch lay open, rendering the house all the more chilled for the cold seeping breeze. But Phoebe barely noticed; her mind was filled with thoughts of her father as she crossed the smooth grey flags of the hallway.

She was through the doorway, down the stone steps and out onto the driveway before she realised that Jamie was not wearing his normal clothes, but a smart black-and-silver livery. Where the gig should have stood was a sleek and glossy black coach complete with coachman in a uniform to match Jamie's.

'Miss Allardyce.' The voice sounded behind her; his

booted footsteps came down the steps, then crunched upon the gravel. And she did not need to turn to know who it was that had spoken for the whole of her body seemed to tingle and her heart gave a flutter.

She turned, showing not one hint of her reaction to him. 'Mr Hunter.'

'Forgive me for borrowing Jamie when you had asked him to drive you to Kingswell, but I have a meeting in Glasgow and as we are both travelling the same way I thought we might travel together.'

For just one awful moment Phoebe felt the mask slip and something of her horror show. They could not possibly travel together, not when she was going to the Tolbooth gaol. But she could think of not a single excuse to extricate herself from the situation. She forced the smile to her face and looked at him perhaps a little too brightly so that he would not fathom anything of her real thoughts on the matter.

'I thank you for your offer, sir, but I could not possibly put you to such inconvenience.'

'It is no inconvenience, Miss Allardyce.' He was standing close to her, looking down into her face with the same brooding intensity he always wore. Those stark ice-green eyes, the gaze that seemed to see too much. She glanced away, feeling uncommonly hot and flustered, and pretended to fix the handle on her reticule.

'Indeed, I insist upon it, the roads being as unsafe as they are these days.'

'I...'

But he was already walking the few steps to the coach.

Jamie had already opened the door and pulled down the step.

Hunter reached the door and turned to her. 'After you, Miss Allardyce.'

She stared at the coach, consternation filling her every pore, for she knew there was no means to escape this. Phoebe took a deep breath, thought of her father and climbed into the coach.

The interior was as dark as the outside. Black-velvet squabs upon black-leather upholstery. And at each window matching thick black-velvet curtains tied back to let in the daylight.

The ride was comfortable and smooth, but Phoebe could not relax, not with Hunter sitting opposite, his long black pantalooned legs stretched out by her side, so that his booted feet were close to the hem of her skirt; too close, she thought and she remembered the feel of him standing so near when she was half-naked, clutching the pile of clothes to her breast. She blushed and pushed the memory away.

His boots looked as if they were new, as black and gleaming as the horses that pulled the coach. Her eyes travelled up to his thighs, noting that the pantaloons did little to disguise the muscles beneath. Phoebe realised what she was doing, blushed again and averted her eyes to look out of the window at the passing moorland. But even then she was too conscious of him, of the sheer size of him, of his strength and his very presence. The coach seemed too small a space and the atmosphere held a strain. Her hands clasped tighter together.

'To which hospital do I deliver you?'

She ignored his question. 'Mrs Hunter has then told you something of my situation?' she said carefully.

'She has. If it is not too delicate a matter, may I enquire as to your father's ailment?'

'The doctors are not sure yet. Until they are, he must be confined.' She stuck to the story her father had devised.

'Confined, you say?'

She glanced up to find Hunter's gaze upon her. And it did not matter how many times she had told the story previously without the slightest betrayal, sitting there in the coach before him, Phoebe felt guilt scald her cheeks. 'Indeed. It is a most worrying situation.' At least that was truthful. 'I fear for him.' She glanced away out of the window, thinking of her father's poor swollen face the last time she had seen him and the threats so vilely uttered against him. 'More than you can imagine. Without these visits I do not know how either of us would survive the time.' Her words halted as she realised just how much of the truth she had revealed and when she looked back she found Hunter was watching her with a strange expression upon his face.

'What of your mother?'

'She died when I was a child.'

'And you have no other family?'

'My sister died almost two years past.' Phoebe could almost speak of Elspeth now, but it had taken such a long time.

'I am sorry for your loss,' he said and something of the chill had thawed from his voice.

She glanced round at the change in his voice, met his eyes once more. And something unspoken seemed to pass between them, some kind of shared experience that bound them together.

'And you, sir?' she asked. 'Do you have any other family?'

'None.'

'Your father, he—?'

'I do not speak of my father, Miss Allardyce.' And the coldness was back again just as if it had never gone.

'Please forgive me. I did not intend to stir painful memories.' Phoebe understood what grief felt like, how, just when you were not even thinking upon it, the smallest, most unexpected thing could trigger a rush of emotion so intense you were plunged into the depths all over again and the ache in your heart caught the breath from your lungs and made you weep. And she did not imagine a man like Hunter would wish to reveal such emotion. It was only nine months since his father had died.

She watched the blur of earthy colours through the carriage window, content to let the silence grow between them. And even though her focus was on the passing moorland she could feel the weight of Hunter's gaze heavy upon her. She did not look round. She wanted no more questions about her father.

The minutes passed.

'You do not know, do you?' he said at last, his voice softer than normal. And when she looked round at him there was almost disbelief on his face. And then as if to himself, 'She has not told you. I did not think—' He stopped himself.

Phoebe shook her head. 'I do not know of what you are talking, sir.'

He smiled; it was a cold smile, a mirthless smile and in his eyes there was an anguish he could not quite hide. 'I suppose that at least is something.' Their gazes held and for that brief moment there was such pain in his eyes that Phoebe could not help herself from reaching her hand towards him.

Hunter's gaze dropped to her hand and then slid back up to meet her eyes and the same stony control had slotted into place.

She froze, suddenly conscious of what she was doing, and pulled her hand back as if it had been bitten.

'You did not answer my question, Miss Allardyce—in which hospital is your father being treated?'

Only then did she realise that he was the only person since she had started as Mrs Hunter's companion to ask her that question.

'The Royal Infirmary.' It was the closest hospital to the Tolbooth. She dreaded what more he would ask and where his questions would lead. Her nervousness around him made it hard to think straight and she feared what she might be tricked into revealing. But to her relief Hunter made no further comment and the journey continued in silence. Part of her was willing the journey to be over, longing only for safety and to see her papa. And another part, a small perverse part that Phoebe did not understand, did not want it to end. Paradoxically, the minutes were both too long and too short until they reached Glasgow's Royal Infirmary.

She thanked Hunter and bade him good day as if she felt nothing of the roaring attraction to a man against whom she had been warned, a man she knew to be thoroughly wicked.

Phoebe stood and waited until the black luxurious carriage disappeared out of sight and only then did she release the breath she had been holding. Hunter was gone. Her secret was safe. *She* was safe.

She watched for a moment longer, thinking of the dark man in that dark carriage, then she turned and hurried off down Castle Street towards the gaol.

Chapter Five

The Messenger arrived at the Tolbooth's steps five minutes after Phoebe. He glanced around nervously before placing his hand on her arm and pulling her into the shadowed arches of the adjoining coffee rooms.

'You have it?' She could see the eagerness in his narrow grey eyes and felt a wave of revulsion and anger for him and the threat he posed to her father.

She had not time for preamble, and this man, whoever he was, deserved nothing of politeness. 'It was not where you said it would be.'

'You are lying.' His face hardened.

'It is the truth.' She stepped closer to him, the fury blazing in her eyes. 'Do you honestly think I would jeopardise my father's safety any more than it is already?' she demanded. 'I searched the whole of the study—every place I could find. Your information is wrong, sir. The item is not there.'

'You'd better be telling the truth, lady.' His voice was ugly.

'I assure you I am.'

They faced each other, Phoebe defiant and glaring, the Messenger suspicious and thinking. The drone of voices and traffic went on around them as if nothing was wrong.

'Everything all right, Miss Allardyce?' It was the one of the turnkeys who looked after her papa's cell, on his way home having finished his shift. His eyes flitted to the Messenger.

The Messenger's gaze met Phoebe's and it was filled with unspoken warning; not that she needed any reminders of what was at stake.

'Everything is fine, thank you, Mr Murray. I will be in to see my papa shortly.'

The turnkey gave a nod and was on his way, leaving them alone again.

'Good girl,' said the Messenger and smiled.

Phoebe narrowed her eyes and made no effort to hide her contempt. 'I have done as you asked and I trust that my father will be safe.'

'Old pop's safety can't be guaranteed till you deliver the goods, Miss Allardyce.'

'But—'

'Where else would a man keep such a thing?' When Phoebe did not respond the man answered his own question. 'In his bedchamber, perhaps?' The Messenger raised his eyebrows and looked at her expectantly.

'No,' she said firmly. 'You cannot expect me to—'

'If you care about your *dear papa*,' he emphasised the words horribly, 'then you will be as thorough with Hunter's bedchamber as you were with the study. The item is somewhere in that house, Miss Allardyce. And until you have found it and it is safely in my pocket then who knows when it comes to Sir Henry…?'

'You are a villain, sir!' she said quietly through gritted teeth. 'A rogue of the worst degree!'

He smiled. 'I've been called worse.'

'I cannot search the entirety of the house unseen in a week. I will have to wait until no one will catch me and that will take time.'

He looked at her, weighing up her words. 'At the start of September Mrs Hunter'll be travelling down to London to visit a friend, no doubt taking her trusty companion with her.'

'She has no such plans. I would know—'

But he cut her off. 'Bring the item with you to London. I will contact you there. And remember, Miss Allardyce, I'll hear if you've talked. One word to Hunter or his mother and you know what'll happen…' His eyes narrowed in threat and glanced meaningfully at the prison building behind her. 'Best go and see how your pa is farin'.' He smiled and then turned and walked away, leaving Phoebe standing there looking after him. The Tolbooth clock struck eleven.

'I thought you were planning to confront her at the prison?' McEwan lounged back in his chair across the desk from Hunter.

'There was a change of plan.'

McEwan arched an eyebrow and transferred the calendar of appointments and notebook from his knee to the desk's surface so that he might concentrate on what Hunter was saying all the better.

'Miss Allardyce met with a man outside the gaol. It was a planned meeting. She waited for him before he showed.'

'An accomplice?' asked McEwan.

'Possibly.' Hunter's jaw tightened as he remembered the man's proprietorial grip on Miss Allardyce's arm. 'Miss Allardyce went with him readily enough to hide beneath the arches and sent the turnkey away when he ventured near them.' He wished he had been able to see her face or hear something of their words. 'Accomplice or not, I suspect there may be more to Miss Allardyce's deception than meets the eye.'

'You mean more than her guise to hide the truth of her father?'

'I believe so.'

'You do not think she means to harm Mrs Hunter, do you?' McEwan's eyes were serious with concern, his voice quiet.

'I hope for Miss Allardyce's sake that she does not,' said Hunter in such a steely voice that McEwan actually flinched. He softened his tone. 'But I doubt that is her intent.' He thought of her visits to his study and the insistent notion that she was looking for something. 'I think Miss Allardyce may have another purpose altogether.'

'Such as?'

'Theft, perhaps.' He looked at McEwan. 'I believe she has searched this study.' He made no mention of when he had found her here, or of what had so nearly passed between them.

McEwan gave a small shake of the head and a low whistle. 'Who would have thought it of Miss Allardyce? She seems so...'

Hunter raised a brow. 'So...?'

'So upstanding, so innocent, so honest,' finished McEwan.

'I think we have already established that whatever Miss Allardyce is, it is not honest. And as for the rest...'

'We should warn Mrs Hunter about the girl.'

Hunter thought of his mother's reaction to his enquiries over Miss Allardyce. 'Such an action would only make my mother all the more determined to keep Miss Allardyce.'

'What, then, can we do?'

'We must find another way to discover the nature of Miss Allardyce's game.' Hunter's face was grim. 'And in the meantime when she next visits the Tolbooth we will follow the man she meets with. Find out where he goes, who he is.'

McEwan gave a nod. Then the two men moved to discuss matters relating to the estate.

The door had not even closed behind McEwan when Hunter turned his chair round to face the moor once more. He left his brandy untouched, and as he looked over the windswept heather he brooded not upon his father, but upon Miss Phoebe Allardyce.

The window of the green guest bedchamber overlooked a garden that had been walled to gentle the harshness of the moor's wind and allow Blackloch to grow some of its own fruit and vegetables. To the right-hand side stood the stables and to the left, the still water of the loch where Phoebe had swum in the heat of the summer's day. She knew all that was there even though the darkness rendered it invisible. Dark shadows in a dark landscape beneath a sky of charcoal cloud. There was no moon to light the night, no stars to pretty the sky. Phoebe wrapped the shawl more tightly over her nightdress and stared out at the darkness, worrying about her father. Her eyes squeezed closed at the memory of what the Messenger had done to him and in her stomach was the familiar twist of horror.

Poor Papa who was gentle and kind and had never hurt so much as a fly, who was so lost in his science he barely knew the day of the week, and who could not even look after himself let alone offer a defence against such a savage assault. And she felt angry and frustrated and helpless, knowing there was nothing she could do to protect him from the Messenger's men if they chose to make good on their threats. Nothing save steal from Hunter just as the Messenger wanted. Steal from a man whose reputation was dark and dangerous as the devil's, and who, with one glance from those cool green eyes, could unnerve Phoebe completely.

It was that simple…and that difficult.

By midnight Blackloch was all silence. There was only the hush of the wind whispering against the glass of her window and the soft ripple of water. Everyone would be in bed, all save one. She shrugged off her shawl and, taking up her candle, Phoebe crept halfway down the staircase and peered over the banister at the darkened hallway below. A faint glow of light showed beneath the door to Hunter's study. She sighed with relief and made her way back up the stairs.

Hunter's bedchamber was opposite Phoebe's, but twice the size and with the door positioned as if it were one room up. She crept quietly past Mrs Hunter's room and stopped outside the bedchamber of the master of Blackloch.

McCabe would not be there. She had been careful to make her enquiries as to Hunter's valet. She supposed the man was too used to a master who, it seemed, did not sleep. Taking a deep breath, Phoebe opened the door and slipped into Hunter's bedchamber.

The room was lit only by the glow of coals upon the hearth. She closed the door softly behind her; even though she knew Hunter was downstairs in his study drinking alone through the night, her heart was racing as she held the candle aloft and scanned her surroundings.

It was undoubtedly a masculine room, as dark and sombre as Hunter himself. Dark curtains, dark covers, dark pillows. Every piece of furniture had been carved in ebony or deep mahogany or blackened oak. A huge four-poster bed, both wide and high, too luxuriant for a man who barely slept, sat between the two arched windows, facing into the room. The curtains framing the windows were thick and long, their hems just brushing against the polished floorboards. There was a large rectangular rug on the near side of the bed, the pattern a jumble of dark colours beneath the light of her candle. Her gaze swept around the bed, taking in the unlit wall sconces nearby, the matching chests of drawers on either flank and the large heavy studded chest at the foot. She moved her attention back to the room, her gaze moving over the large solid dark furniture and the internal doors on opposing walls. One she knew led to the bedchamber of the lady of the house, in which Mrs Hunter was currently sleeping. The other she guessed would be a bathroom.

Behind her was a heavy mahogany fireplace, above which hung a large painting of a dark-cowled man with a pet dog guarding its master. A monk and his dog. Such a peculiar choice of painting for a bedchamber that Phoebe peered closer, and gave a small breathy gasp when she realised that the dog was not a dog at all, but a wolf watching her with warning in its eyes. There were so many wolves at Blackloch that they must hold some significance to the Hunter family. She shivered, the sensation rippling right through her as if someone had walked over her grave, and such was her sudden overwhelming fear that it was all she could do not to turn and flee. But Phoebe could not run away from this, no matter how much she wanted to. She knew what she had to steal. And she knew, too, that, for the sake of her papa, there could be no room for failure. She turned away from the painting and forced herself to begin a calm, methodical search.

The bathroom contained a large oval bath with a shower device fixed above it, a screened water closet, a looking glass and a shaving accoutrements, and a comfortable armchair. Nothing in which the object was likely to be hidden.

She carefully searched each piece of furniture, one by one, every shelf, every drawer, every cupboard. By half past midnight she had reached the second set of drawers closest to the main door. As she set her candle down upon the surface she looked up and the curtains swaying in the draught caught her attention; she saw the looking glass and her own pale reflection staring back at her. And in that moment it seemed she felt the cold breath of foreboding whisper against her cheek. Phoebe ignored it, telling herself it was just her imagination at work, and pulled open the top drawer. And there, at last, was Hunter's jewellery casket.

He did not seem to be a man who favoured jewellery for there were few enough pieces. A diamond cravat pin, a gold-and-onyx signet ring engraved with the same crest that adorned the cushions of the dining-room chairs and the seats in the hall, a gold pocket watch and two silver snuff boxes, enamelled with such scandalous paintings of women upon their lids as to bring a blush to Phoebe's cheeks. She ran her fingers against the velvet lining of the casket's interior, searching insistently for something that was not there.

A sound whispered from the passageway, the soft tread of footsteps. Phoebe started and quickly piled all of the jewellery back into the casket, thrust the lid on and shoved the drawer shut. Last of all she grabbed her candle and turned to leave, just as the door to the bedchamber opened and in walked Sebastian Hunter.

He stilled, the intense gaze trained on her, the dark impassivity of his expression gone, replaced with surprise.

Phoebe could not move, could not speak, could not breathe. Everything in the world stopped.

She stared at Hunter.

'Miss Allardyce,' he said quietly and his voice was smooth and cool as silk.

She dropped her gaze to take in the tall black riding boots, the tight buckskin breeches and the coat slung haphazardly over his shoulder. His waistcoat and cravat were unfastened and his shirt gaped open at the neck, revealing something of the pale muscled skin beneath. The door closed behind him without a sound. As Hunter walked slowly towards her, relieving himself of the coat and cravat upon the armchair on the way, Phoebe's stomach dipped.

'I was about to ask what you are doing here.' He kept on walking until he was standing directly before her. 'But I suppose that would be a foolish question, when the answer is so obvious.'

She knew she had failed and she knew, too, the cost of that failure for her papa; the thought of it made her want to weep. There was nothing she could say, nothing she could do. She pressed her lips firm and waited for her dismissal.

'For why else does a woman come to a man's bedchamber in the night?'

Such was her anguish that it took a moment for his words to register. Phoebe blinked up at him in confusion. And as she looked up into his eyes she understood what it was he thought. Her heart skipped a beat and she felt the kindling of hope.

'Unless I am mistaken and there is some other reason that you are here...?' He waited, and everything about him seemed to still in that waiting.

She glanced down. Such a tiny second to make such a momentous decision, and yet, there was no decision to be made, not when her father's life was at stake. Time slowed. All that had happened with her papa and the Messenger ran through her head as she stood there.

'Miss Allardyce...?' Hunter pressed.

Phoebe knew what Hunter was offering her—the chance to save her papa. She raised her gaze to look through the soft flickering candlelight at the stark handsome man who so fascinated her. 'You are not mistaken,' she said and she heard the words as if they had been spoken by someone other than herself.

She saw something flicker in Hunter's eyes, and she could not tell whether it was surprise or anger or something else altogether. He made not one move and his expression was hard and thoughtful. 'But that night in my study...'

'I have changed my mind.'

The silenced hummed loud between them. The very air seemed to crackle as if there were a storm waiting to unleash.

'Do you even know what you are asking?' His voice had dropped to barely more than a husky whisper.

'Of course,' Phoebe lied. She remembered Elspeth's whispered warnings from so long ago and wished she had asked more. 'As you said, why else would I be here?' Her heart was thudding so loud she wondered that he could not hear it.

He stepped closer and stroked his fingers against her

cheek, sliding them down to touch against her lips. Phoebe's breath shook. Her blood pounded all the harder.

'I am not sure that I believe you,' he said softly and let his hand fall away.

Her heart stuttered at his words—she knew just how close to the edge she was treading. Her father's life hung in the balance. She knew she had to persuade Hunter. Slowly she reached her face up to his and brushed her lips against his cheek.

His skin was rough with the stubbled growth of beard. The scent of him encompassed her, both familiar and enticing. It was such a very wicked thing to do, and Hunter must have thought so, too, for she heard his sudden intake of air and saw the sharpening of his gaze.

The candle in her hand began to tremble and she could not still it. He took it from her and set it down upon the chest of drawers, beside the looking glass.

'Miss Allardyce,' he said and his voice was so soft and so very sensual that it made her tremble all the more.

He lowered his face to hers, his mouth so close yet not quite touching. She felt the warmth of his breath caress her hair, her eyelids, the line of her cheek and everywhere that it touched her skin blossomed and tingled. His breath swept a kiss against her mouth and the sensation of it shimmered through her body, even though his lips had not yet touched to her own. The breath caught in her throat in anticipation.

'One last chance...' he whispered softly against her ear. A shiver stroked all the way down Phoebe's spine and the breath she had been holding rushed from her lungs. 'To change your mind...' His mouth hovered just above her own, so close she felt his words rather than heard them. She shivered again and felt her nipples tighten.

His eyes were dark in the candlelight, dark and dangerous and utterly beguiling.

'Miss Allardyce...' he whispered and his gaze swept slowly, sensually down to fix upon her lips. 'Phoebe...' and she quivered at the hunger in his voice.

She shook her head and reached her mouth towards his, and as Hunter finally claimed her lips she closed her eyes and gave herself up to him.

The kiss was more than Phoebe could ever have imagined a kiss to be. Gentle yet possessive. Enticing yet demanding. His lips courting hers to make her forget that anything else even existed. It seemed that she had waited all her life for this moment and this man. Nothing had ever felt so right, nothing ever so wonderful. She felt his arms around her, moulding her against his body, breast to breast, thigh to thigh, as his mouth worked its wonder upon her own. Phoebe yielded to him and all that he offered, splaying her hands against the hard muscle of his chest so she could feel the warmth of his skin through the fine linen of his shirt, pressing herself closer to feel the heat in his long muscular thighs.

She heard the rasp of Hunter's breath, a sound that mirrored her own. She was his, completely, utterly, just as he was hers. He deepened the kiss, his lips inviting hers to so much more, and she did not even think of not following. His tongue led hers in a dance that both fed and consumed, with such intimacy and passion as to scorch away all that was in its path. And the blood was rushing in her veins and desire was pounding in her soul, and everything was hot and reckless and overwhelmed with her need for Hunter. She felt she had known him for a thousand lifetimes, that he was her alpha and omega, that for her there would never be any other man.

He threaded his fingers through the length of her hair, teasing and mussing and stroking.

'Phoebe,' he whispered her name and she answered his call with everything that she was and everything that she would be.

The touch of his hand scorched through her nightdress, caressing her breast, her hip, her stomach, touching her as she had never been touched before, lighting a fire in her thighs and belly. She burned for him, ached for him, arched against him, wanting this and everything that could be between them. Then she felt his hand slip inside the nightdress, to the bare skin of her breast, his fingers teasing against its hardened sensitive peak, touching the very core of her being, rocking the world on its axis. She gave a moan and, as her legs buckled beneath her, stumbled back against the tall wooden bedpost even as Hunter caught her.

Phoebe glanced up, her gaze falling directly at the looking glass. The woman she saw there was dark-eyed and flushed with passion, her hair long and wanton, her nightdress gaping to expose small pale breasts and she was in the arms of a tall dark-haired man. And even then it did not hit her, not until the man turned his face to follow her gaze and she saw that it was Hunter.

Hunter stared at the reflection and the shock of it cooled his ardour in an instant. Only then did he realise just what he was doing—ravishing Phoebe Allardyce with all the thoroughness of a rake. He stared, appalled at himself, and released her, stepping away to open up a space between them.

He saw the daze clear from her eyes, saw the sudden awareness and the shame and horror that followed in its stead. She looked as shocked as he felt, staring at him with great wide eyes as if she could not believe what had just passed between them. He could hear the raggedness of her breathing, see the tremble in her hands as she clutched her nightdress to cover herself.

'Phoebe—'

But she turned and fled, silent as a wraith.

Hunter made no move to stop her. Just stood where he was until he heard the quiet closing of the door. His heart was still thudding with a sickening speed. He raked a hand through his hair and wondered what the hell had just happened between him and Phoebe Allardyce. Such untutored passion, such connection and depth of desire. Hunter had never experienced anything like it before. And yet he had known she was an innocent from that very first tentative touch of her lips.

God help me, he thought. *God help me in truth.*

Her candle still sat upon his chest of drawers. Hunter lifted it, noting that his hand was not quite steady as he did so. His blood was still surging too hard, his heart beating too strong. He took a deep breath, and struggled to control himself. And then his eye caught the glint of something on the Turkey rug before his feet. He crouched to retrieve his diamond cravat pin, and by its side found the dark silken ribbon he had slid from Phoebe Allardyce's hair. He rose and surveyed the room.

Nothing was missing. Nothing else had been moved. He slipped the diamond pin into its place and threaded the ribbon through his fingers. And the look in his eyes was brooding, for he knew most assuredly that she had not come to his room to wait for him.

Miss Phoebe Allardyce had been searching through his jewellery casket…and had taken not one item.

Chapter Six

Phoebe stood by the window in her bedchamber, staring out over the walled garden and the still, dark water of the loch. The brightness of the morning sun hurt her eyes and she felt tired and groggy from a night devoid of sleep. Behind her the bed was a tumbled mess of sheets and blankets, where she had tossed and turned and worried through the hours of darkness.

The memory of what had happened between them, the clear knowledge of what she had done, made her cringe. She leaned her forehead against the glass and closed her eyes, knowing that the hours that had since passed relieved nothing of the fury of emotion that pulsed through her. Shame and embarrassment, guilt and desire.

She had led him to kiss her, to touch her in ways Phoebe could never have imagined. And the most terrible thing of all was the wickedness of her own feelings. That she had wanted his kiss, that in some deep instinctive way she had needed it. Hunter had awakened something within her that she had not even known existed, something she did not understand and that, standing here alone in the cold light of day, seemed very far away. She wondered how on earth she was going to be able to face him again, after what had passed between them, after what she had led him to believe. And yet if she was to hide the truth of what she had been doing in his bedchamber she knew she would have to do precisely that.

When she opened her eyes and looked out again the moor looked cold and bleak beneath the white-grey sky and the wind keened low through the panes of her window. And she seemed to hear again the echo of her father's words, *There are dark whisperings about him, evil rumours...* Phoebe shivered and forced her thoughts away from Hunter. There was the whole of Blackloch to be searched, and she could not balk from it. She turned and moved to face the day.

Phoebe and Mrs Hunter worked side by side on the tapestry. Each day they filled in a little more of the still-life vase and flowers sketched upon the canvas, their needles flashing fast in the sunlight of the drawing room. Mrs Hunter brought the roses to life with threads of dusky pink while Phoebe stitched at the freesias with a violet thread. They worked together in comfortable silence.

Mrs Hunter tied off her thread and searched in their thread basket for a skein.

'Oh, bother!'

'What is wrong?' Phoebe stopped stitching to glance round at Mrs Hunter.

'I am about to start the leaves and have left the pale green thread in my bedchamber. Would you be a dear and run and fetch it, Phoebe?'

'Of course.'

'I think it is on my bedside table,' she called as Phoebe exited the drawing door.

The green-coloured thread was not upon the bedside table. As Phoebe scanned around the room she realised the opportunity that had just presented itself. This was her chance to search the bedchamber, not for the thread, but for something else altogether.

It felt so wrong, so sordid, that she hated to do it, but one thought of her papa was enough to push such sensibilities aside. Phoebe began a systematic and speedy search. She started with Mrs Hunter's jewellery box, moved on to her trinket box and the drawers of her dressing table, then the drawers of the bedside cabinet. The minutes passed too quickly. She found the thread, a cool pale green reminiscent of Hunter's eyes, but nothing else that she was seeking, and knew that she could take no more time. Mrs Hunter was waiting. She gathered up the skein of thread and left.

'There you are, Miss Allardyce, or perhaps, as we are alone, I may call you Phoebe.' Hunter moved from his position leaning against the wall outside his mother's bedchamber. 'I thought you were never going to come back out of there. I believe my mother is in the drawing room if you are looking for her.'

Miss Allardyce gave a start and a tint of peaches coloured her cheeks. 'Mrs Hunter sent me to fetch some thread.' She handed him the skein as if offering her proof. 'It was not where it was supposed to be. I had to search for it and, well, it took an age in the finding.' Her voice was calm enough, but she was talking too much, revealing her nerves and, Hunter suspected, her guilt. 'If you will excuse me, sir, I fear I have kept Mrs Hunter waiting long enough.' He saw the calm determination slot back down over her ruffled poise.

He stayed her with a hand to her arm, and felt her jump

beneath his touch. 'Only fifteen minutes, Phoebe, what are a few minutes more?'

'You were timing me?'

'In my eagerness to see you.' And it was only half a lie.

'Mr Hunter!' She sounded breathless.

'Sebastian,' he insisted, and told himself he was doing this for the sake of his mother's safety, and not because he had wanted Miss Allardyce since first setting eyes on her. Not that he would allow matters to progress anywhere near as far as taking her; unlike last night, now he was prepared. Hell, but the kiss had shaken him enough; he could not doubt what it had done to Phoebe Allardyce. What the hell was she looking for in the rooms of Blackloch? A little more pressure and she would reveal the truth in one way or another.

'Really, I must go.'

But Hunter slid his hand down her arm to take her hand in his. 'Are you forgetting our arrangement, Phoebe?'

'Arrangement?' Her expression was innocent and artless, her eyes filled with wariness she could not quite disguise.

'Surely you have not forgotten last night?' he murmured.

Her blush intensified. 'Last night...' And just for a moment something of the strength in her eyes faltered. Her hand slipped out of his and she backed away until the wall blocked her retreat. She dropped her gaze, hiding beneath the sweep of those tawny-red lashes so that he thought she would cease her pretence.

'Phoebe?' he said more gently.

She looked up at him then and he saw that he was wrong. They stared at one another across the width of the passageway and in her eyes was nothing of capitulation, only caution and, beneath it, a steadfast resolve that bordered on defiance. He wondered what she would do if he took her in his arms and kissed her as hard and thoroughly as he wanted to. What would it take to make her confess the truth of what she had been doing in his bedchamber last night, of what she had been searching for in his mother's rooms just now? Would she let him carry her into his bedchamber, throw her on bed and bury himself inside her? He made not one move, but something of his thoughts must have shown in his face for she paled, but she still did not back down.

'Sebastian...' The sound of his name upon her lips made his pulse kick. 'We will speak of this later. But for now I must not keep your mother waiting.' Her voice was all calmness and control. She turned to leave, but he caught hold of her elbow, preventing her departure. He felt her start beneath his touch, heard the slight catch of her breath, saw the frenzied leap of the pulse in her neck, and he knew she was not so unaffected as she was feigning. Her eyes locked with his, and in their depths he thought he saw the flash of guilt and fear and desire.

'I have already told you—'

He said not one word, just pressed the pale green thread into her hand and walked away.

Over the next few days Phoebe found it impossible to continue her search of Blackloch. Hunter was always around, brooding, silent and yet present. For all the animosity that existed between him and his mother, since the night she had gone to his bedchamber he had been spending more and more time in Mrs Hunter's company. And in his presence Phoebe felt a constant awareness of their 'arrangement' as he had called it. Every time their eyes met the memory of that night was between them, of his mouth possessing hers. The feel of his arms holding her close, of being pressed against the long hard length of his body. She denied the thoughts, pushed them away, knowing that she could not afford to let herself weaken, feeling a guilt at this unbidden attraction. Responsibility sat heavy on her shoulders. And the fear for her papa drove her on.

Beneath the shade of a crab apple tree in the walled garden Phoebe and Mrs Hunter sat reading.

'This was always my favourite spot,' Mrs Hunter told Phoebe, 'for it is nicely tucked away out of the wind.'

'Mother.' Hunter appeared through the arched gateway, making Phoebe start and lose her place in her book. He gave a grave bow. 'I am need of your company today to assist with the tenant visits.'

Mrs Hunter peered at him with irritation. 'I thought your steward, McEwan, did that.'

'The visits involve matters that would be better dealt with by a woman—the distribution of linens and such.'

Mrs Hunter frowned. 'What of Mrs Dawson?'

'Mrs Dawson left Blackloch shortly after you did.'

'And you did not replace her? It is little wonder the place is in such disarray without a housekeeper.'

Hunter said nothing, but it seemed to Phoebe, as mother and son stared at one another with expressions that boarded on glacial, the comfortable temperature within the sheltered garden spot seemed to drop a few degrees.

Mrs Hunter gave in first. 'It seems I have little option,' she complained with a scowl, which she then turned upon Phoebe. 'Come along, Phoebe, you may return the books to my room and ready yourself.'

'Ready myself?' Phoebe repeated and looked at her

employer. 'But shall you not be attending with Mr Hunter alone?'

'No, I shall not,' snapped the lady. 'It is bad enough that I am being dragged around the countryside visiting one smelly peasant after another, but I am certainly not enduring the day alone.' And with a final glare at her son Mrs Hunter marched from the garden.

Phoebe met Hunter's gaze briefly, but a *frisson* of awareness tingled between them and she had a horrible suspicion as to the reason Hunter was suddenly desirous of his mother's company. She turned away before he could fathom anything of her thoughts and followed in Mrs Hunter's wake.

Hunter rode on his great black horse. Mrs Hunter and Phoebe sat in Hunter's fine coach, Mrs Hunter not wishing to ruin hers by trailing it through, as the lady put it, the mud of all the moor. The baskets of linens and food were fastened in the boot.

Within each farmstead Hunter spoke to the man of the house, he who was holding the tenancy to farm the land, and eke some measure of living from it. From what Phoebe could hear their conversations seemed to centre on breeds of sheep, trout in the lochs, deer and the maintenance of the farm buildings. While Hunter dealt with that side of it, Mrs Hunter was in her element bestowing sheets, blankets and great hampers of food on the wives. Between each farm she moaned incessantly about the mud dirtying her shoes and the wind ruining her hair. But once in the farms Phoebe could see that Mrs Hunter was secretly enjoying herself.

One of the farmsteads, the closest to Blackloch and located on a particularly bleak stretch of the moor, housed a family of eight children, all girls, the oldest of which looked to be only ten or eleven years of age. The younger girls, dressed in clothes that looked worn and shabby, were running about the yard when the carriage drew up. The older girls were helping their mother peg wet washing to a drying line. All activity ceased as the coach rolled into the yard.

The woman's husband, the tenant sheep farmer, was a thin, grey-haired man with a kind but work-worn face. He looked as if life on the moor was not an easy existence. Hunter and the man must have been talking of the barn for the pair of them were looking and pointing in that direction before walking off towards the small wooden building.

The small girls gathered round Mrs Hunter and Phoebe in silence, their little faces in awe of their visitors, their hands and fronts of their smocks revealing that they had been busy playing in the dirt.

'Oh, Mrs Hunter, ma'am.' The mother hastened to greet them, pink cheeked and breathless, and Phoebe saw the wash of embarrassment on Mrs Hunter's face as her gaze dropped to the woman's heavily swollen belly. Mrs Hunter glanced around almost as if checking that her son was not witnessing the woman's condition. And now Hunter's request for his mother's presence seemed to make sense and Phoebe felt ashamed at her thoughts over his motive.

'Such a pleasure, ma'am. I was just doing the washing for it is a fine drying day.'

'Indeed,' said Mrs Hunter and smiled as if she understood completely, even though Phoebe doubted whether Mrs Hunter had ever had to give a thought to the washing and drying of clothes in the whole of her life.

'Our Martha loves working in the big house. She

cannae speak highly enough of you and Mr Hunter, ma'am,' the woman gushed.

Mrs Hunter smiled magnanimously and said to Phoebe, 'Martha Beattie is a maid of all at Blackloch.'

Phoebe thought of the freckle-faced young girl who lit the fires and drew the water and swept the stairs.

The footman carried over two baskets, setting them down upon a bench in the yard and opening the lids for the farmer's wife to see the linens in one and food in the other, before leaving to answer Hunter's summons.

'Oh, bless you, ma'am, bless you. I've never enough baby linens to go round. Rosie and Meg are still in nappies, and I didnae ken how I was gonnae manage wi' the other wee one on her way.' She patted her hugely rounded stomach.

The children's eyes lit up when they saw the hamper of food. Soon their curiosity overcame their awe and they edged closer.

'Can I offer you some water, or a little ale?' Mrs Beattie asked.

But Mrs Hunter declined graciously.

'Let me get this emptied so that you can take the baskets away back wi' you.' And the woman lifted both baskets.

Mrs Hunter frowned. 'Should you be…?'

Phoebe stepped forwards. 'Please allow me to help you with that, Mrs Beattie.'

'Ocht, they're no' heavy, no' next to a load of wet wash. Never be botherin' yoursel', miss.'

But Phoebe had taken hold of the baskets, which were, she could confirm, most definitely too heavy to be carried by a woman in Mrs Beattie's condition.

She carried the baskets into the cottage and set them down where Mrs Beattie directed, before helping the woman to unpack their contents. The cottage was clean, scrubbed and well swept, but the rooms were small and the bedroom in which they were piling the linens was tiny with barely room for more than the bed.

Phoebe and Mrs Beattie made their way back outside just in time to see toddler Rosie fall over beside Mrs Hunter. The toddler began to cry and tried to right herself, reaching with little muddy hands for the lady's fine silk skirt.

'No, Rosie!' shouted her mother, trying to rush forwards and prevent the calamity that everyone standing there in the yard could see unfolding before their eyes.

Phoebe reacted in an instant, sprinting and scooping the child up into her arms just in time, cuddling her in close so she would feel safe and secure. 'Oops a daisy, Rosie. Up you get.'

The little girl looked at her, fat tear drops balancing on the end of her lashes, her little nose all pink and wet.

'Have you been making some lovely mudpies?'

Rosie nodded.

Phoebe smiled at Rosie, 'And what's all this wet all over your face?' she asked.

Rosie sniffed back a sob.

'Shall we wipe it all nice and clean?' She set the little girl carefully on her feet out of reach of Mrs Hunter's dress; taking out her handkerchief, Phoebe wiped the child's nose and tucked the handkerchief in the pocket of the little mud-smeared smock. 'Just like a big girl,' she whispered.

Rosie patted her pocket. 'A big girl,' she said with a shy smile.

'I'm ever so sorry, ma'am, miss.' Mrs Beattie was looking from Mrs Hunter to Phoebe.

'There was no harm done,' said Mrs Hunter, but she

lifted her skirts and started to make her way back to the carriage. 'And now we must be moving on. We are visiting quite a few of the farmsteads this afternoon.'

Phoebe smiled to reassure Mrs Beattie, who had taken a firm hold of Rosie's hand. 'Good luck for the baby when it comes,' she said quietly.

'There's a month to wait yet, but thank you, miss.' Mrs Beattie smiled and then her eyes shifted to Phoebe's side. 'Mr Hunter, sir.' She bobbed a curtsy and hurried away to catch hold of another small child.

'Mrs Beattie.' Hunter nodded and Phoebe jumped at the sudden sound of his voice beside her. He leaned closer and said quietly to Phoebe, 'You will have no handkerchiefs left at this rate.' And she remembered their first meeting upon the moor when he had rescued her. Their eyes met just for the briefest of moments, but it was enough to send a myriad of shimmering sensations racing through her body just as if he had pulled her into his arms and lowered his mouth to take her own. She blushed and quickly averted her gaze.

'Phoebe!' called Mrs Hunter with impatience.

Fortunately for Mrs Hunter there was only one more tenant to be visited and he was without children, muddy or otherwise. He was an old man, tall and thin, but slightly bent, his hands large and ruddy, his knuckles enlarged with age and too many years of hard living. Dressed in his brown overalls and an old woollen work jacket patched at the elbows, he walked forwards to meet Hunter's horse, pulling a cloth cap from his head to reveal some sparse white hair as he did so.

Phoebe was surprised to see Hunter dismount and grip the man's hand in a warm greeting. The coldness had vanished from his face. Indeed, he was smiling so warmly and sincerely that it quite transformed his face, lighting all of the darkness to reveal something very different in its place. Phoebe stared and could not look away, shocked at the difference in him. And she felt a warmth steal over her heart.

She blushed at the feeling and at her staring, and glanced round at Mrs Hunter to see if she had noticed, but Mrs Hunter was also watching Hunter, and with a less-than-convivial expression. Her face was thoughtful, her mood sombre as if seeing him like this brought back memories that saddened her.

'I am sure Sebastian can manage this one by himself, Phoebe. McInnes lives alone so there can be no need here of female sensibilities. Besides, I am feeling a little tired.'

Hunter glanced round at the carriage at that moment, expecting to see his mother and Phoebe alighting.

Mrs Hunter looked away, but not before Phoebe had seen that the lady's eyes were blinking back the tears.

And when she looked at Hunter again he was making his way towards the carriage with a grim expression upon his face.

'Is there a problem?'

'I have a headache. I believe I shall return to Blackloch,' Mrs Hunter said without even looking round at Hunter.

'This is the last farmstead. We are for home after this.'

'I cannot wait; I am leaving now.'

'Will you not at least step out of the carriage and show your face to McInnes? He will be insulted if you do not.'

'What do I care for McInnes's thoughts?' Mrs Hunter glared at her son. 'He is a tenant. Little more than a peasant grubbing in the dirt with his sheep and his hens. Lord, Sebastian, you always did treat him better than your own fath—' She bit off the word but even to Phoebe it was obvious what she had intended to say. Mrs Hunter set her face straight ahead, stubbornness and fury was etched into its every line.

Hunter stilled. Phoebe saw the tightening in his jaw as if he was clenching his teeth, controlling some strong emotion.

'He is an old man.' Hunter said quietly so that McInnes would not hear. 'Put aside your personal grievances for me in this one instance. He has a mare not long foaled. Come, ask him about it.'

But Mrs Hunter's face remained front facing and stubbornly defiant as if she had heard not a word her son had spoken.

'He is ill,' Hunter said, and then added, 'Mother... please.' Phoebe could see what it cost him to plead.

'He is ill?' Mrs Hunter turned to him, anger and hurt blazing in her eyes. 'Your father was ill! What care had you about him?'

Hunter's face seemed to bleach while his eyes darkened. His lips pressed firm. He turned and walked away without another word.

Phoebe knew she had to act quickly. 'Ma'am, you are unwell, and little wonder when you have suffered a headache the day long and still undertaken all with a smile for the sake of those who admire and respect you.' She paused, knowing that she might be risking too much in what she was about to say, but she spoke the words anyway. 'I could make your apologies to Mr McInnes and see to the linen and the food...if you so wish.'

Mrs Hunter looked at her for a moment and Phoebe could see the anger and jealousy still simmering, and, behind that veil, the hurt and the grief.

'Thank you Phoebe, that is what I was about to ask.' Mrs Hunter looked away before the tears could betray her completely.

Phoebe nodded.

Hunter started to talk to McInnes, again, drawing the old man away from the carriage and his mother. McInnes was no fool—Hunter knew he would realise the truth. Then he saw the old man's gaze shift back to the carriage and he heard the crunch of footsteps; when he turned there was Phoebe Allardyce walking beside the footman and his hamper, carrying an armful of linen.

'Good afternoon, Mr McInnes. I am afraid that Mrs Hunter is quite unwell with a headache, but she has sent you some linen and some small extras, too, and she asked if I would be so kind as to enquire as to your mare. Mr Hunter was telling us that she recently foaled.' Miss Allardyce smiled a tremulous smile at the old man.

'Very kind of Mrs Hunter. Please be sure to thank her for me.' McInnes kneaded the cloth cap between his hands and gave a respectful nod and a tug of his forelock towards the shadowy figure of the woman within the carriage.

And Hunter watched with surprise as a gloved hand appeared through the carriage window in an acknowledging wave.

'This is Miss Allardyce, my mother's companion,' said Hunter, and his eyes met those of Phoebe Allardyce both in warning and question.

Then McInnes took the linen and the small hamper and disappeared with them into his tiny stone cottage, only to reappear in the doorway a minute later with a stone bottle in his hand. 'Will you be taking a dram, Mr Hunter?'

'Not today, thank you, McInnes. Mrs Hunter is unwell, I should be returning her to Blackloch. I will drop in when I am passing tomorrow.'

The old man nodded, then shifted his rheumy gaze to

Miss Allardyce. 'Do you want to see the foal so that you might tell Mrs Hunter?'

'Could I?'

He had to admit that Miss Allardyce's acting skills were of the first order. She managed somehow to make her face glow with delight; her eyes were bright and her smile broad and warm as she looked at McInnes.

McInnes gave a chuckle. 'Just a quick peek, mind, so as no' to keep Mrs Hunter waitin'.'

And just like that, Alasdair McInnes was won over by the girl who was lying to her employer, and who was steadily working a search through Blackloch by stealth, no doubt with a view to theft. She was dangerous, Hunter thought. And not only with her lies and her subterfuge. She was dangerous enough to tempt a man, to make him forget what it was that drove him through every hour of every day. Even now he was too aware of her, of her slender neck with its soft velvet skin that he had nuzzled and mouthed, of the small dimple that appeared in the corner of her mouth when she smiled, and the sweep of her long dark-red eyelashes, and the depths in those clear brown eyes.

He watched her absorbed in what the old man was telling her, with her shabby plain blue dress and her prim pinned hair, and that most wonderful warm smile. Yes, Miss Phoebe Allardyce was definitely the most dangerous woman he had ever met. The sooner he discovered what she was up to and she was out of his house, the better.

Chapter Seven

The sunset had lit the moor in a fire of red hues but, for once, Sebastian Hunter was paying no attention. He had not seen Phoebe Allardyce since their return to Blackloch the previous day, yet he had been thinking of her and the mystery she presented without respite.

'You are sure that she met with no one either before or after her visit to the Tolbooth?' Hunter asked as he leaned against the mantel above the fireplace.

McEwan made himself comfortable in one of the winged chairs before the empty fireplace and sipped at his brandy. 'Quite sure. The only time she was out of my sight was when she entered the building of the gaol itself. There was no man.'

Hunter's thumb toyed absently with the cleft in his chin and his eyes narrowed in thought. 'How the hell are we going to find him?' he murmured almost to himself.

'How goes your side of the campaign? Has she searched any of the other rooms?'

'The bedchambers—mine and my mother's. Nothing was taken that I can see.'

'But if nothing was taken? You are certain she was searching the rooms?'

'Oh, I am sure of it,' said Hunter grimly.

'What can she be looking for?' McEwan frowned in puzzlement.

'I suspect the answer to that question is the key to solving the whole damn mystery.'

'And how are we to find the answer? Short of catching the girl in the act with the Hunter family silver in her pocket?'

'I suppose I will have to keep an even closer eye on Miss Allardyce than I have been doing.' Hunter made no mention of just how close an eye he had been keeping on his mother's companion, or of how the prospect both compelled and taunted him. 'My mother's safety is paramount.'

'Absolutely. We should stop at nothing to discover Miss Allardyce's scheme.'

The pounding of the wolf's-head knocker woke Phoebe in the night. Over the sound of heavy rain drumming against the peat land outside there was the sound of footsteps running up and down the stairs, of hushed voices, and small scrapes and bangs from Hunter's room as if he were opening and closing drawers or cupboards. Phoebe rose from her bed, pulled a shawl around her shoulders and peeped out into the hallway. A couple of wall sconce candles had been lit, casting the passageway in a dim flickering light.

And just at that same moment Hunter emerged from his bedchamber, pulling his great caped riding coat over his dark coat and breeches. His hair was ruffled and dark as a raven's wing, and over his cheeks and chin Phoebe could see the shadow of his beard's growth. He looked piratical, wicked and dangerously handsome. His gaze met hers and that same tremulous feeling fluttered right through her.

'A coach has come off the road. Assistance is required at the scene of the accident.'

'There may be ladies present amongst the passengers. I will come with you and help, if you will give me but a moment to dress.'

'You offer is appreciated, but unnecessary. The moor is difficult to negotiate in the dark and rain. As I said, I will deal with the matter. Go back to bed, Miss Allardyce.' He glanced towards his mother's door, which remained shut.

'Mrs Hunter has taken one of her sleeping draughts. I doubt the rumpus will wake her.'

A nod of the head and he was gone, his great coat swirling out behind him and only the sound of his booted steps running down the stairs. She heard the distant thump of the back door as she returned to her room to dress.

Downstairs a few servants were huddled in the hallway, discussing the possible severity of the coaching accident and what they should be doing.

'Oh, Miss Allardyce, Mr Hunter told us no' to waken you,' McCabe, the oldest of the group and Hunter's valet, said.

'Rest assured, you did not waken me,' she said with a smile, knowing that Hunter had no housekeeper and that his mother was in no fit state to oversee what needed to be done. 'Now, tell me, what instruction has Mr Hunter left?'

'He's no' left any instructions. The master went out in such a hurry, there wasnae time,' said Jamie. 'And Polly told us that Mrs Hunter's had her powder the night so there'll be no wakenin' her.'

'We thought we would wait up for the master to return,' added Polly.

'Where are the rest of the servants?'

'Most dinnae live in, miss, but come over fae Blackloch village in the morning,' said a dark-haired maid by the name of Annie, standing beside Martha Beattie.

'Well, I am sure we will manage as we are,' said Phoebe. 'Jamie and Gavin, fetch some more coal in and up to the guest bedchambers and then lay the fires ready to be lit. Lay the fire in my room, too, as I may need to move elsewhere if a large enough number of injured persons are brought to Blackloch. And light the fire in Mr Hunter's bedchamber.'

'Yes, miss.'

'Tam and Stewart, check the accommodation in the stables for extra horses and carriages and then return to your room above the stables. Get what sleep you can before Mr Hunter returns.'

'Polly and Annie, prepare a pile of the oldest linen that would be suitable to be used as dressings and bandages, and some drying cloths, too. Mr McCabe, are there any old clothes suitable for gentlemen and lady passengers to borrow?'

'I will check, miss.'

'And you had best set out some drying cloths and night clothes for Mr Hunter in his chambers; he will need them upon his return.' As if to emphasise her point the rain drummed harder against the great front door and the wind gave a howl as if moaning across the moor.

'Martha and Sally, come with me. We will boil up plenty of water. There may be wounds to be cleansed or

baths required. And prepare a pot of soup for the simmer.'
Phoebe began to roll up her sleeves.

'Cook doesnae come in until the mornin',' said Martha.

'I am sure we will manage between us.' Since the loss
of Papa's money Phoebe had become adept at managing
their household on the most meagre of coins. She could
make a very palatable pot of soup, even if she did say so
herself.

Phoebe and the servants worked hard, but when two
hours later there was still no sign of Hunter she sent
the servants back to bed, telling them to get some sleep
and that she would wake them upon Mr Hunter's return.
Phoebe wrapped her shawl around her shoulders and sat
down in the night-porter's chair in the hallway to wait
for Hunter.

The first hint of dawn was lighting the charcoal from
the sky as Hunter and his men handed their horses and
the gig across to the grooms in the stable. The rain was
still falling, albeit lightly, and Hunter could feel the heavy
ache of fatigue in his muscles as he entered Blackloch
through the back door with the rest of his menservants.

The smell of the broth hit him as soon as he opened
the door. His stomach growled its response. They peeled
off their sodden coats and over-garments and left them to
dry in the scullery. Not a single maid was in evidence so
Hunter and his men helped themselves to the soup, ladling
the broth into bowls, gulping down the warming liquid.
The great pots of water were still warm to the touch
although they had been moved off both the range and the
open fire. On the long table at the side of the kitchen sat
piles of linen sheets and some of his old clothes neatly
folded. The big kitchen clock on the wall showed a little

after four. All of Blackloch slept. Hunter left his men to find their quarters and went to seek his own bed.

He did not doubt that Miss Allardyce would have used his absence and his mother's sleeping draught to continue her search. Would he find her in his bedchamber again? Part of him hoped it would be so. And right at this moment he was too tired to be angry or to fight the temptation she embodied.

His boots made no noise upon the stairs up from the kitchen. But when he reached the hallway and glanced across at the porter's chair, he knew he had been mistaken. Phoebe Allardyce was not conducting a search of any room in Blackloch, for she was curled up fast asleep in the chair.

In the faint light of the dawn she looked very young, her face creamy pale and unlined in sleep, her lips pink and infinitely kissable, her auburn lashes long against the unblemished skin of her cheeks. She was dressed in the same blue muslin dress as ever, but her hair snaked over her shoulder in the long thick braid that she wore for bed. And from beneath the hem of her skirts, tucked up on the chair, peeped her stockinged toes, where she had curled her legs beneath her on the seat of the chair. His gaze dropped lower to the worn boots that sat neatly by the chair's wooden leg. He stepped closer, his own boots making a small noise against the stone flags of the floor and she stirred, her eyes fluttering open, yet still heavy-lidded with sleep.

'Mr Hunter,' she whispered sleepily, and the sound of his name on her lips was as if she had trailed her fingers teasingly down the length of his spine. She uncurled herself, yawned and stretched, the thin muslin stretched tight across her breasts. Hunter's mouth went dry.

'What happened with the accident?' She rose from the

chair and stood in her stocking soles on the cold stone of the floor before him. 'Were there many injuries?' She looked up at him, her face filled with concern and he thought he had not realised just how much smaller than he she was. The top of her head barely reached his chin.

'Mr Hunter?' she prompted, and he realised he was staring.

'It was a town coach travelling too fast in the rain, the driver misjudged the corner and overturned the coach across the road. There were two young gentlemen passengers, both shaken, but neither of them hurt.'

'Do they return to Blackloch with you?'

He shook his head. 'They were in a rush to reach Glasgow—one of them is the bridegroom in a wedding this morning. I sent them on in my coach.'

She met his eyes before her gaze shifted to take in the dirty wet state of his clothes. 'I thought you were wearing your greatcoat...'

'The coach had to be cleared from the road to prevent another accident.'

Her gaze dropped lower to take in the scrapes and cuts and dirt on his hands where he had been helping to lift the carriage and change the wheel.

'Your hands...' She took his hands into hers, her fingers small and slender beside his, her touch gentle as a caress. And when she looked up at him there was something in her eyes that made him think he had got Phoebe Allardyce all wrong.

'They should be cleansed.'

Her fingers felt chilled to his touch. He pulled his hands away, feeling suddenly confused.

'It is late, Miss Allardyce, go to bed,' he said and he knew that his voice was too hard.

He saw the small flicker of hurt before she masked it

and walked away without a word, and he wished he could call back the harshness.

In his bedchamber, McCabe was snoozing in the corner chair.

'Mr Hunter, sir.' The valet wakened and got to his feet.

'What are you doing here, McCabe?'

'Beggin' your pardon, sir, but Miss Allardyce sent me.'

Hunter's eyes scanned the room that appeared so different to the one he had left earlier that night. The fire had been lit, casting a warm glow to cheer the darkness. A nightshirt was hanging over the second fireguard to warm and his bed had been neatly made.

McCabe saw the direction of his gaze. 'She thought as how you might be feeling the cold upon your return… wi' the weather and all.'

'Miss Allardyce organised this?' Hunter could not keep the sharpness from his voice.

'Aye, sir. She organised everything—the guest chambers, the linens in case there was a need for bandages and dressings, the hot water. On account o' Mrs Hunter havin' taken one of her pooders. She made the soup with Martha and Sally, too—in case there was a need for it.' McCabe removed a warming pan from the bed as he spoke.

Hunter could scarcely believe what he was hearing.

And later, after McCabe had gone and he finally found sleep, the thought on his mind was not the coaching accident or the moor, or the usual nightmare that haunted him, but Miss Allardyce…liar and would-be thief…who had held his household together for him this night.

In Mrs Hunter's dressing room Phoebe and the lady stood before the opened wardrobes trying to select a dress suitable for the rout that evening.

'Polly informed me there was something of an incident in the night.'

'Indeed.' Phoebe related the details of the carriage accident.

'I am surprised that Sebastian could drag himself from his slumber to attend the scene.'

'Ma'am, Mr Hunter not only relayed the gentlemen passengers to Glasgow in his own equipage, but personally participated in righting the damaged vehicle and removing it from blocking the road.' She thought of the cuts and scrapes upon his hands, of how wet his clothes had been and the fatigue that had shadowed beneath his eyes. And of the strange expression in his gaze before the dark pensive chill had returned.

Mrs Hunter waved away her words with an airy hand. 'Forgive me if I find that difficult to believe.'

'It is the truth, ma'am.' Whatever dark deeds Hunter had committed, his mother deserved to know that he had acted most honourably last night.

'And you would know this how precisely?' Mrs Hunter peered at her.

'I was wakened by the knocking at the front door of those who came to fetch Mr Hunter.' Phoebe hesitated over admitting her part in the night's proceedings.

Mrs Hunter peered more closely at her. 'Indeed, you look as if you have not slept a wink.'

'I did have some trouble finding sleep once more,' she offered and was saved from further explanation by Polly's arrival with Mrs Hunter's breakfast tray.

'Miss Allardyce, Cook was wondering if she might have a word with you in the kitchen,' said Polly.

Phoebe thought of the pot of soup that Cook must have come in to find this morning. She glanced at Mrs Hunter.

'Go on, girl, go and see what she wants,' said Mrs

Hunter in a grumpy tone. 'And let us hope that I feel a deal better after my chocolate. I shall see you in the drawing room in an hour.'

Cook wished to know the recipe of the soup. Phoebe smiled and was only too happy to share. She was heading back up the stairs to her own chamber when she met Hunter coming down.

'Miss Allardyce.' He bowed.

'Mr Hunter.'

'I owe you thanks for all that you did last night,' he said stiffly. 'It was much appreciated.' He sounded ill at ease. He did not speak of their arrangement, nor did he try to take her hand or to kiss her. She wondered at the change in him.

Those pale haunting eyes held hers and there was something different in them this morning, as if he were looking at her for the first time. A footman passed in the hallway below. Hunter gave her a little nod of the head and carried on down the stairs, but a few steps later she glanced back at Hunter at exactly the same time as he looked back at her. A feeling of recognition and something shared, something binding, passed between them.

Hunter leafed through the pile of newly delivered letters.

The day was warm and sunny; the sky outside his window, blue and cloudless. There were two letters for his mother and all the rest were addressed to himself, all save the one at the bottom of the pile. The small neat handwriting on the front had directed it to Miss Phoebe Allardyce, care of Blackloch Hall. Both the handwriting and the slight scent of violet perfume indicated a female sender. He turned the letter over, and on the reverse written in small script at the top right-hand corner was the sender's name.

Hunter stilled. The shock kicked in his chest. The rest of the letters tumbled forgotten to the floor. He read the name again and again, and still the taste was bitter in his mouth and his stomach felt a small tight knot. *Miss Emma Northcote.* All he saw of the name was *Northcote.* It had been the start of the whole of this sorry mess. And the nightmare played again through his mind and he gripped so hard to the letter that his knuckles shone white. And then, quite deliberately, carefully, he set it down upon his desk. It sat there, a small pale square stark against the ebony; he reached for the brandy decanter and filled his glass, and with his eyes still fixed upon the letter, he drained it just as quickly. And outside the clouds moved across the sky to block the sun, and all of the darkness had returned.

Chapter Eight

'Damnation!' Mrs Hunter cursed. 'There is never a servant to be found in this wretched place when I need one. Should I have to run my own errands? Have I not reached the stage in my life when I warrant a little comfort and ease? And instead I find myself in this…this mausoleum of a house.' Mrs Hunter winced and rubbed her fingers against her forehead. 'Perhaps it is time that we went back to Charlotte Street, even if the decorating is not yet complete.'

'No!' Phoebe said a little too forcefully and found her employer peering round at her. She forced a smile and picking up Mrs Hunter's shawl draped it around the lady's shoulders. 'What I mean to say is, would it not be better to wait just a week or two more? You know how sensitive your head is to strong vapours. The smell of the paint would not be good for you, ma'am. Perhaps you should wait until it has dispelled somewhat before returning to Charlotte Street.'

Mrs Hunter nodded, but her face was all discontentment. 'You are probably right, Phoebe.'

'And Polly is preparing you a sleeping draught so you should rest well tonight.'

'For that, at least, I am thankful. Be a dear, Phoebe, and fetch my fashion journals from the drawing room. I left them in there earlier.'

'Of course.'

Phoebe was passing Hunter's study with the journals in her hand when he appeared in the doorway. She started, but then smothered the butterflies in her stomach to walk past him. He could not kiss her here in broad daylight where anyone might chance to see them.

'Miss Allardyce,' he said and her heart gave a little somersault. His face was paler than normal, his eyes glittered in the sunlight and there was something very cold and very dangerous in the way he was looking at her.

'I have a letter for you.'

'A letter?'

A movement of his hand and she saw the small folded parchment there. He held it out to her.

'Thank you.' The cool brush of his fingers against hers as she accepted the letter made all of the butterflies and tingles reappear. Her heart began to thud as ever it did when Hunter was around. She turned to hurry away, desperate to escape the madness of the feelings surging through her body.

'I could not help but notice the sender,' he said and beneath his usual coolness was an edge of something else. 'I did not know you are an acquaintance of the Northcote family?'

She glanced at the back of the letter and saw Emma's name. 'Miss Northcote is a friend of mine. We were at school together.' She folded the letter and slipped it into her pocket.

He stepped out into the corridor, walked closer until he was standing right before her, staring down into her eyes. 'So many things I do not know about you, Phoebe Allardyce.'

And there was something in his voice that sent a shiver down the full length of her body. She swallowed, feeling her stomach dance at his proximity, both wanting and dreading his kiss.

She grasped around for something to say. 'Are you acquainted with Miss Northcote, or perhaps one of her brothers?' She knew the moment the words were out of her mouth that she had chosen wrongly. Gone was the cool quiet intensity and in its place was pure and unadulterated anger. She saw the sudden tension that ran through Hunter's body, saw the tightening of his jaw, the sudden flare of fury that darkened his eyes. She edged away until her spine touched against the stone of the corridor wall. But Hunter saw the move, and in an instant his hands were leaning against the wall on either side of her head, his body so close to hers yet not touching, effectively trapping her where she stood.

'What manner of game are you playing with me, Miss Allardyce?' he demanded and his voice was low and guttural and tortured.

Her heart was racing in earnest now, thudding so hard she could feel the vibration of it throughout her body. She shook her head with the tiniest motion. 'I do not know what you mean.'

He leaned so close she could feel the warmth of his breath against her cheek and smell the sweet rich aroma of brandy. 'If you do not already know it, I give you fair warning, Phoebe.'

Her heart stuttered to a halt before racing off at full tilt again. He could not know, could he? She stared up into his eyes, and the intensity that was in them, the anger, and such tortured pain made her forget all about her own fears. 'Sebastian,' she said softly.

He squeezed his eyes closed as if aware he had inadvertently revealed too much, and when he opened them again the hurt was gone, hidden well away, and his anger was reined under some measure of control.

'Do you not know that you are playing with fire?' he said and his voice was harsh. 'If you are such good friends with Miss Northcote, you must know what I am.'

She shook her head. 'I...' she said, but something in his eyes stopped her.

He took her lips and this time there was nothing of gentleness, only of urgency and a need so overwhelming that it razed everything in its path. His mouth was hard and possessive as it claimed hers. He took her without mercy, his tongue plundering, his lips pillaging, ravishing her with his kiss as thoroughly as in the dreams that plagued her nights. It was a kiss that should have frightened, a kiss that should have punished, but in it she felt the measure of his desperation and hurt.

She knew she should have resisted, despite their 'arrangement'. All that was right and proper decreed that she should have made some excuse to escape him, but Phoebe reacted instinctively, responding to Hunter and the hurt in him. She wrapped her arms around his neck and gave herself up to his onslaught, salving his pain with her gentleness, meeting his passion with her own. Losing herself in the ecstasy and power of his kiss.

When he eventually raised his face from hers, he retreated, breathing heavy, leaning against the wall and staring at her with an unreadable expression upon his face. And Phoebe stared back, as aghast at what she had just done as Hunter looked. Her heart was thudding fit to burst. Her body felt molten from his touch. Everything was in tumult, everything, wild and overwhelming.

She picked up the journals from where they had fallen and walked away while she could, her head held high as if she were not trembling from the force of what had just exploded between her and Hunter. And not once did she look back at him.

'Phoebe, there you are. I was just about to send out the search party. What on earth took you so long?' Mrs Hunter demanded.

'Forgive me, ma'am, I…' Phoebe could not meet the lady's eyes. 'I had a little difficulty in locating them.' She set the fashion journals upon the table before Mrs Hunter and tried to mask the riot of emotion still pounding through her blood.

Mrs Hunter peered at her. 'Are you feeling quite yourself?'

No! she wanted to cry. *I have not been feeling myself since the moment I looked into your son's eyes.* She was still reeling from the hurt in Hunter's eyes and the fury that she had done nothing to provoke, still reeling from the wantonness of her response to him. She felt frightened by her feelings and how very little control she seemed to have over them. But Phoebe hid her fears and feelings and forced herself to look calmly at her employer.

'Perfectly,' she lied.

But Mrs Hunter was not convinced. 'Come and sit down beside me.' She patted the sofa seat by her side.

Phoebe had no choice but to obey.

'You look positively feverish, my girl, and breathless.' Mrs Hunter took Phoebe's hand in her own. 'And you are trembling.'

Phoebe quickly withdrew her traitorous hand from Mrs

Hunter's, and felt the blush of guilt and embarrassment and turbulent emotion heat her cheeks all the hotter. 'I rushed up the stairs too fast so as not to keep you waiting any longer.'

'I should not need to remind you, Phoebe, that young ladies never run.'

'I am sorry, Mrs Hunter.'

Mrs Hunter gave a nod of conciliation. 'It is fatigue, Phoebe. I can see it in your eyes. And little wonder with having been awake half the night with the storm and the hullabaloo surrounding the coaching accident. I think I have been a little selfish in my demands of you today.'

'Not at all, ma'am,' said Phoebe.

'I am sending you to bed. You need to rest.'

'But it is Mrs Montgomery's rout this evening.' She thought of what Mrs Hunter's absence would mean—she would be alone at Blackloch with Hunter.

'Exactly—we both know what Amelia's routs are like. If it runs on as late as the last one, I shall stay overnight and travel back in the morning. Believe me, Phoebe, you are in no fit state for such an evening and I shall manage very well alone. And you need not fear to be left in Sebastian's company. My son will be gone to McEwan's house to dine with him and Mairi, so there will be no one here to disturb you.'

No one to disturb her.

All of her protestations died on her lips. Phoebe swallowed. She would be free to search Blackloch.

'Now, off with you, girl. I will not hear another word on the matter.'

The evening was still light, but the curtains were closed in Phoebe's bedchamber. Phoebe lay in the bed and listened to the faint chimes of the grandfather clock down in the hallway, and the crunch of Mrs Hunter's carriage as it rolled down the gravel of the driveway. Hunter was long gone, but Phoebe was thinking of him, just as she had been thinking of him all of the previous hours.

In all her three-and-twenty years no one had ever made her feel the way he did. She had never questioned her life. Not the loss of a mother so young, or the years spent keeping house and caring for a father who, for all his brilliant mind, had not the slightest notion of how to care for himself. Not the loss of a sister so beloved or the tragedy that went with it. Not even the loss of all their money and the gaoling of her father. She loved her papa, Mrs Hunter was more than kind and Phoebe had been content with her life. But now that she had met Hunter, everything up until that moment on the moor felt as if she had been existing rather than living.

He did not look at her as a daughter, a carer or a servant. Hunter looked at her as a woman. And no one had ever done that before. For the first time in her life she felt attractive and desirable and alive. He made her feel excited. He made her feel like she was glowing inside. And all of this while her papa was locked in gaol with a face beaten black and blue.

It was so wrong, for Phoebe loved her papa, and she could not understand the selfishness of her feelings, or how she could even be thinking of Hunter in such a way. And she wept with the guilt and confusion and she knew she could not allow this madness to continue. The Messenger wanted one thing. Phoebe knew she must focus only on that and her papa.

She dried her tears and slipped silently from the bed.

Hunter handed the reins of Ajax over to the groom and slipped into Blackloch. The dinner with McEwan and

Mairi had been pleasant enough, but he could not dislodge the feeling of guilt over the way he had treated Phoebe Allardyce. He thought of last night, of her standing before him in the darkened hallway with that look of concern and tenderness in her eyes. The coaching accident had presented her with the perfect opportunity to continue her search of Blackloch, yet Miss Allardyce had forgone it in order to help him and his household. And he thought of how pale she had looked this morning, of the shadows that had pinched beneath those warm golden-brown eyes. Little wonder after everything she had done through the night. But all of Hunter's gratitude had been forgotten the moment he had seen that name upon the letter. Even if she had been sent here by the Northcotes to remind him of what he had done to them, or to exact some measure of revenge, she had not deserved the harshness of his treatment. And he thought of the passion of her response, of its gentleness and strength. Remorse moved over his heart.

Hunter did not go to his study, pour himself a brandy and sit staring out over the moor. Instead, he walked up the stairs and headed straight for Phoebe Allardyce's bedchamber.

Chapter Nine

Phoebe had almost finished searching the last of the guest bedchambers when she heard the tread of feet upon the main staircase. Her first thought was that it was one of the servants taking advantage of the family's absence to use the main stairs. But even before she recognised the sound of the footsteps a shiver tingled through her body and her heart leapt—she knew it was Hunter. She quietly closed the cupboard door and stood where she was, listening. Her heart was galloping. If Hunter caught her in here, what feasible excuse could she give?

Hunter's bedchamber was at the end of the corridor. But the footsteps stopped short. She heard the nearby knock, the pause, the tread of his feet as he entered Phoebe's own bedchamber.

The room was empty. The covers on the bed were thrown back as if she had only just climbed from it.

Hunter moved forwards, pressed his hand to the sheets and found they were cool. He glanced around the room, seeing the curtains still drawn and Miss Allardyce's blue dress hanging over the door of the wardrobe.

His eyes narrowed and his mouth tightened. He crushed the tender feelings he had been harbouring, and strode out of the bedchamber to discover just which part of Blackloch Phoebe Allardyce was engaged in searching, and found her standing, still in her nightdress, outside the door to the next guest chamber.

'There you are, Miss Allardyce.'

She stilled. 'Mr Hunter. I thought you were having dinner with Mr McEwan and his wife.'

'I was.' Hunter did not elaborate. 'I thought you were abed.'

She gave a nervous swallow. 'I…I have been in bed since this afternoon. I was merely stretching my legs.'

Hunter moved his gaze to the door of the guest chamber immediately behind her before shifting it back to the woman.

Her stance did not waver, but he saw the tiny flicker in her eyes, that moment of doubt, and the flush of guilt that coloured her cheeks. He was angry, partly at Miss Allardyce, but mainly at himself. He had had enough of women's games.

'Why are you and my mother really here at Blackloch?'

Her eyes widened slightly, but whether it was a response to the question or the cold demand in his voice he did not know, nor did he care.

'The town house is being decorated.'

'Forgive me if I find it difficult to believe that my mother's desire to change her wallpaper would bring her back here. She left Blackloch the day we buried my father and swore she would never return,' he said harshly. 'My mother loathes the very sight of me.'

'No!' Miss Allardyce took a small involuntary step towards him and shook her head. 'You are quite wrong. Mrs Hunter—' She caught herself back from saying what she would have, but the concern was still etched upon her face. She bit at her lower lip as if weighing up a decision. 'I am not supposed to tell you, but I think perhaps Mrs Hunter is wrong in keeping it from you.' She looked at him, her expression serious. 'If I confide in you, you must keep it secret.' She waited for his reassurance.

Hunter just looked at her. 'Miss Allardyce.'

'She would be very angry if she thought you knew. I could lose my position.'

Still Hunter would make no promise.

Phoebe Allardyce's eyes regarded him steadily. 'I would have your oath on this, sir, or I will tell you nothing.' And from the strength in her gaze Hunter knew it was no idle threat.

'Very well, you have my oath.'

Her eyes met his and he knew she would tell him. 'There have been two break-ins at the town house in Charlotte Street. The first was some months ago, not long after I first started as Mrs Hunter's companion, and the second was only a matter of weeks ago. Mrs Hunter would never admit to it, but the last break-in distressed her greatly. Nothing was left untouched. All of our most personal possessions were rifled through. She did not sleep well before the last break-in, and since then, well...' She raised her eyebrows and Hunter could only guess at how bad things had become. 'That is why she makes such use of sleeping powders. In answer to your question, Mr Hunter, I believe that your mother is here because she is frightened.'

Her words hit him hard. 'She should have told me,' he ground out.

She touched her fingers to his sleeve. 'Mrs Hunter is too proud. As I think are you,' she said softly.

His eyes met hers and he saw the sympathy that was

there. It hardened his heart. He stepped back out of her reach.

'What was stolen?'

'That is the strange thing. Nothing was actually stolen, but they made something of a mess in their searching. I think that is why Mrs Hunter is having the house redecorated, that and, I suspect, as a way of wiping away the intruder's presence.'

The significance of what she was telling him slotted into place. 'There have been two break-ins at Blackloch since my father's death, both of which revealed nothing was taken.'

'How very peculiar.' She frowned.

'Break-ins in both properties in which nothing was taken, but the rooms turned over as if they have been searched most thoroughly... It sounds as if someone is looking for something very particular that they believe to be in my mother's or my possession.' He looked at Phoebe Allardyce.

She was staring not at him, but at some point in the far distance, a look of sudden realisation and horror in her eyes. The blood drained from her face so that she was pale as a ghost.

'What do you think, Phoebe?' he asked quietly.

She tried to mask her shock before she looked at him, but not very successfully. 'I do not know.' She swallowed and her gaze fluttered nervously around the corridor. 'It seems...unlikely. I mean, what on earth would such a person be looking for?'

'I was hoping you might be able to enlighten me as to that.'

Her eyes shot to his and he saw that they were filled with fear, more than just the fear of discovery. She was standing against the wall, holding her breath, her body rigid with dread. And Hunter had the sensation that something much more was going on here. He backed off a little.

'You witnessed the evidence of the break-ins in Charlotte Street so I am interested to hear your thoughts on the matter. Your insight could be valuable.'

She swallowed again and the small smile was forced. 'What are thieves normally after—money, plate, paintings…jewellery?' She gave a shrug. 'Anything of value, I would think.'

He nodded and came to stand opposite her, leaning back against the wall to mirror her stance. 'You know that I cannot stand by and allow a threat to my mother, Phoebe.'

She nodded and closed her eyes, but not before he had seen the unshed tears.

'Threats are such a terrible thing,' she said and her voice was barely more than a whisper. The clear brown eyes flickered open and how she managed to prevent the swell of tears from falling he did not know. 'And now if you will excuse me, sir, I must return to bed.'

She was so pale that Hunter thought she might swoon where she stood. But Phoebe Allardyce held her head high and walked the small distance to her bedchamber to disappear inside.

Phoebe could not sleep that night. The implication of what Hunter had said, that the Messenger was behind the break-ins and the violent ruthlessness of his search through Mrs Hunter's home and personal possessions, played in her mind. And for the first time she realised the significance of the Messenger having spoken of 'we' rather than 'I'. How many of them were involved in this and who were they that such a small seemingly inconsequential item could mean so much to them? Phoebe feared the strength and force of the men and what they could do to her papa. She feared she had allowed her attraction to Hunter and all that he made her feel distract her from the importance and urgency of what they had set her to do. And she knew that she must find what they wanted very soon.

She tossed and turned for hours, unable to find comfort, and had almost given up on sleep when a knock sounded on her bedchamber door. The maid Martha Beattie, who Phoebe had seen leave for home after dinner, slipped through the doorway wearing a dark shawl and with a lantern in her hand.

'Oh, Miss Allardyce, I'm so sorry to waken you.' The girl sounded breathless as if she had been running. Phoebe could smell the damp night air coming from her and see the girl's face was taut and pale and so filled with worry that it made Phoebe forget all of her own.

'Martha, what is wrong?'

'Oh, Miss Allardyce, it's my ma.' Martha began to sob and the lantern trembled in her hand.

'Take a deep breath, calm yourself and tell me what has happened.' Phoebe placed a steadying hand on the girl's arm.

'The baby is coming and my pa hasnae come back from Glasgow the day. I cannae run all the way to the village for the midwife and my ma says there's something wrong. I—I dinnae know what to do, miss.'

'Stay here, Martha, while I wake Mr Hunter. Then we will have someone fetch the midwife before we set off for your cottage.'

'Oh, miss…'

'We will do everything that we possibly can to help your mother.' She patted the girl's shoulder. 'Stout heart,

Martha. I will be as quick as I can.' She lit her candle from Martha's lantern and hurried to fetch Hunter.

Hunter's face was not peaceful in repose. Whatever dreams he had did not look to be pleasant. He murmured and his head rolled against the pillow. In the flicker of the candlelight Phoebe could see the slight sheen of sweat upon his pale skin and the pain that racked his features and felt a surge of compassion for him. From the wall above the fireplace the dark-cowled man and the wolf looked down on her and this time when she looked at the monk, she had the strangest notion that he was not a monk at all, but something altogether more sinister. Such a painting could not help Hunter's nightmares. She turned her back on the twin watchers and touched a hand to Hunter's arm.

'Mr Hunter...Sebastian.'

His eyes were still drugged with sleep as he squinted into the lantern light. 'Phoebe?' And he reached for her, pulling her to him.

She placed a hand against his chest to restrain him and felt the warm firm muscle of bare skin. 'No, you must wake up. It is an emergency. Mrs Beattie's baby is coming, a month before it should. Martha is here for our help.'

Her words reached him and the drowsiness was gone in an instant.

'Mr Beattie has not returned from Glasgow and Martha has no means to reach the midwife.'

Hunter sat up and Phoebe saw that he wore no night-shirt. His chest, arms and stomach were pale and as defined with the taut lines of muscles as if he were a Greek god carved in marble.

'I will fetch the midwife and bring her to the Beatties' cottage.'

Phoebe dragged her eyes away from his nakedness, appalled that she could be staring at him, even at a time like this. 'If you are amenable I will have Jamie take Martha and me in one of the carriages back to her cottage while we wait for you to arrive. She ran all the way here, poor girl.'

'Take Jamie and the gig. It's easier to handle in the dark.'

She nodded and turned to leave.

'And, Phoebe...' he called after her.

She glanced back at him, and their gazes locked.

'Have a care.'

She nodded and hurried back to Martha.

When Hunter arrived at the Beatties' cottage with the midwife there was no sign of either Phoebe or Mr Beattie. A large pot of hot water was simmering over the fire. In the front parlour the children were red-eyed with tiredness and crying, their little faces streaked with tears and the smear of runny noses. The smallest one, Rosie, who was little more than a baby herself, had fallen asleep curled in a little ball on the floor. A terrible moaning was coming from the downstairs bedroom and every time it sounded the children's crying renewed. The midwife did not pause to remove her cloak, just disappeared into that bedroom. Hunter did not dare to even look through the door. He retreated into the hallway, feeling useless, not knowing what to do in this women's world.

Phoebe appeared from the bedroom, her sleeves rolled up, her cheeks pink from heat and exertion. 'Oh, Mr Hunter, thank goodness,' she whispered as her fingers brushed against his hand. Her relief at his presence was like a gentle touch against his heart.

'What can I do to help?'

'Look after the children.'

Hunter looked at her helplessly.

'Put your arm around them, cuddle them when they cry. Put a blanket over them when they are cold. Tell them that everything will be fine and that they must be good girls for their mother.' Then, to the young footman who was hovering ashen-faced by the kitchen door as if he would rather be outside, 'Into the kitchen, Jamie, scrub your hands, then fill another pail of water and set another pot on to boil. Once it has boiled, take it off the heat and let it cool.'

'Yes, miss,' Jamie mumbled dutifully.

And then she was gone, bustling towards the kitchen to return with a bowl of hot water and a pile of linen.

'Go,' she urged Hunter. 'You can do it.'

Hunter nodded, knowing that he had to help, and walked into the parlour of crying children.

The hours passed slowly, painfully, and still the baby had not been born. Mrs Beattie was in so much pain she did not know who was in the room with her and who was not. The low dull moan was now constant, and every so often she cried and wept for her husband. Phoebe closed off her emotions so that she could get through this night. She had seen this same scene before, and she knew how it would end. And yet even so, through those hours she mopped Mrs Beattie's brow and held her hand and willed the woman to keep going. And when the midwife went into her bag and brought out a large pair of metal spoon-shaped tongs, Phoebe understood.

'She's no' gonnae manage hersel', miss. We'll have to pull the babe out into this world.'

Phoebe nodded and went to scrub the tongs in hot water.

It was just like Elspeth, except that when the midwife handed her the baby, still warm from Mrs Beattie's body, the boy breathed and moved, a cry erupting from his little gummy mouth. Phoebe wiped him clean and swaddled the tiny body in fresh linen as his loud wails filled the air. And it seemed to Phoebe that she had never heard such a glorious noise.

Mrs Beattie raised her head from the pillow, looking for the baby.

'A boy, ma,' said Martha. 'A fine healthy boy.'

Phoebe rested the tiny bundle into the woman's outstretched arms.

Mrs Beattie smiled and tears of joy were streaming down her face. 'At last,' she whispered. 'And Malcolm not here to see it.'

Hunter stirred as Phoebe entered the parlour. Her eyes scanned the room, taking in the girls sleeping on the rug before the fire with Hunter's coat laid over them as a blanket. Hunter was on the sofa, a small girl snuggled into him on either side, and baby Rosie sprawled over his chest, his hand gently cradling the child. His hair was dishevelled and the shadow of beard growth darkened his cheeks and chin.

'Phoebe?' he whispered. 'I heard the babe's cries.'

'A boy, alive and well.'

'Beattie will be pleased.'

Together they carried the children upstairs into the bedroom and snuggled them into their beds, shooshing them with soft words when they stirred.

Phoebe spoke to Hunter in the little parlour. 'The midwife is almost finished, but someone needs to stay with Mrs Beattie and the baby. Martha is exhausted. She will be needed here tomorrow so I have sent her to bed and assured her that I will watch over her mother most carefully until the morning. There is nothing more that you can do here, Mr Hunter. You may as well go back to Blackloch and get some sleep.'

'Jamie can take the midwife back to the village. I will stay here—with you.'

'Mr Hunter—' But the look on his face was resolute and she did not have the energy to argue. Besides, she could not deny that she was glad of his presence. She felt the reassuring squeeze of his fingers against hers before she turned and walked away.

Malcolm Beattie returned some time in the wee small hours. His horse had thrown a shoe and the man had walked all the way home from Glasgow in the darkness. Hunter clapped Beattie on the back.

'Congratulations, Beattie, you have a fine son.'

'A son?' The tears were streaming down Beattie's cheeks, rolling unashamed, so incongruous a sight for the man. 'And Rena?'

'Your wife has had a night of it. She is tired, but the midwife assures us that she will be fine.'

'Thank God! Thank God!' wept Beattie.

Yet still Phoebe would not desert her post. She insisted Mr Beattie got a few hours sleep.

At eight o'clock two women from the village appeared at the cottage door armed with baskets of bread and eggs, cheese and ham and offers of help.

Only after speaking to them did Phoebe agree to leave.

Hunter took her arm in his and led her out to the phaeton, climbing up before her and then reaching down to help her up to sit beside him.

The early morning mist had not yet burned away. The

moor seemed very still, a hushed quiet so that even the wind was but a breath upon his face.

'Jeanie and Alice from the village will take the girls to their own homes and care for them for a few days, and there will be others that will come later to help both Mr and Mrs Beattie,' she said.

'They are good people, all of them.'

'Yes.' Her face was pale, with blue shadows smudged beneath her eyes.

He twitched the reins and the two horses moved off slowly, the wheels crunching against the gravel and soil as they travelled along the narrow track.

Neither of them spoke, just sat in a silence that seemed comfortable to Hunter. There was only the song of the blackbird and the sparrows. He slowed the phaeton so that she would not be jarred with the roughness of the track and thought he saw a glimmer of moisture upon her cheeks.

'Phoebe?'

She turned her head away so that he would not see her face.

He stopped the carriage where it was and gently captured her face to bring it round to his. Her tears were wet beneath his fingers. It was the first time he had seen her cry and he felt moved by the sight of it.

'The night must have been difficult for you.'

She tried to turn away, but he did not release her.

'A birthing...when you are innocent of the knowledge of such matters...'

'No.' She gave a small choking sound, half-laughing, half-sobbing. She squeezed her eyes shut, but the tears leaked through to stream down her cheeks.

'Phoebe...'

'I am just tired, that is all. I will be fine once I have slept.' She sniffed and rummaged for her handkerchief.

Hunter was not sure he believed her. He passed her the clean one from his pocket. 'In settlement of my debt.'

She gave him a wobbly smile, took the handkerchief, dried her cheeks and blew her nose.

'You did magnificently,' he said quietly and stroked his thumb against her cheek.

She looked up at him and there was something in her eyes that mirrored what was in Hunter's soul: a sadness, a sense of loss that quite smote Hunter's heart. 'I did what had to be done,' she said. 'I always do what has to be done.' And he had the feeling that she was talking about so much more than the Beattie baby.

Tendrils of auburn hair had escaped to curl around her face; the long thick plait was messy as it snaked over her shoulder and down onto her breast. Her dress was stained with blood and other marks and her eyes were red-rimmed and glistening with tears. And Hunter did not know why there was such a tight warm feeling in his chest or why he had such a need to comfort her and take away her pain. He touched his lips to hers in the smallest and gentlest of kisses and when he drew away he knew that something had changed between them, something from which there would be no going back. He wrapped his arm around her waist so that she was snug by his side, and gave a tug at the reins in his other hand. And he took her back to Blackloch.

Chapter Ten

'What on earth were you thinking of letting her attend a birthing, Sebastian?' his mother demanded the next day. She was seated on the sofa in the drawing room, staring at him imperiously and ignoring the plate of luncheon sandwiches on the table before her. Phoebe Allardyce, about whom they were talking, was upstairs fast asleep in her bedchamber.

Hunter was standing by the fireplace, leaning an arm against the mantel.

'Not only is she unmarried and a young gentlewoman…' And such was her agitation that she rose to her feet and came to stand before him that she might deliver the full weight of her displeasure all the better. 'Lord, Sebastian!' His mother's face crumpled. 'Phoebe's sister died in childbirth not two years since. Did she make no mention of the matter?'

He stared at his mother in horror. 'She spoke not a word of it.' And he thought of how hard Phoebe had fought to keep from weeping and he understood now that look in her eyes—it was grief, raw and unadulterated.

It was as if a hand had reached into his chest and twisted his heart. 'Forgive me,' he uttered. 'I never would have let her go had I known.' But even as he said it he knew that he could not have stopped Phoebe from going to help Beattie's wife. The girl was as stubborn as himself. Stubborn, and damned courageous.

When Phoebe arrived in the drawing room later that day, ready to attend to Mrs Hunter's plans, she was surprised to find Hunter present. He was standing by the window, staring out over the moor, the usual brooding expression upon his face. Mrs Hunter was working on the tapestry. The room was in silence, but there was not the same chilled tension in the air between them that had been there in those early days of their arrival at Blackloch.

'Ah, Phoebe, my dear.' Mrs Hunter smiled and patted the sofa next to her. 'Come and sit by me and tell me how you are feeling.'

'I am well, ma'am, thank you. How was Mrs Montgomery's rout?'

'It was as we expected, Phoebe.' Mrs Hunter sniffed in a superior way, but her eyes were kind. 'I have been hearing of last night's events.'

Phoebe glanced over at Hunter, unsure of just how much he had told his mother. His eyes met hers.

'News of Mrs Beattie's emergency is all round the village. Mrs Fraser, the local busybody, called upon my mother this morning,' he said.

'She is wife to Sir Hamish Fraser of Newmilns,' corrected Mrs Hunter in an irritated tone, 'although I will admit to her being a bothersome woman.'

Hunter moved from his stance at the window to take the seat furthest from Phoebe and his mother.

Mrs Hunter frowned at him, but there was nothing of malice in it. Her face softened again as she turned to Phoebe. 'Now, you are not to worry, Phoebe. I soon set Eliza Fraser straight once Sebastian had explained the whole of it to me.'

Phoebe stared in amazement. Her gaze shifted from Mrs Hunter to her son and back again. 'Thank you.'

'I never did like that woman,' Mrs Hunter confided.

Hunter stayed for the next hour, and in truth, although Phoebe was glad to see the thaw in relations between him and his mother, she was relieved when he left. She was too aware of last night, and the emotion that still echoed from it. Too aware that Hunter had not left her, but stayed with her until the end at the Beattie cottage, too aware of the tenderness in his eyes at the weakness of her tears. The gentle brush of his lips had meant more than either of their previous passionate exchanges. That one small kiss had somehow shifted what lay between them, deepening it, calling to her all the more. And Phoebe was afraid that she might betray something of her feelings for him before Mrs Hunter.

The maid had brought Phoebe's freshly laundered blue dress to her chamber the next morning.

'Most of it came out in the cold-water soak, but there is still some staining, miss,' the maid's voice sounded beside Phoebe.

The two women stared at the bodice as Phoebe held it up to the light. The brownish marks sat like dark islands within a sea of faded blue muslin.

'Some ribbon and lace might hide the marks. I could sew some pieces across,' Phoebe said.

The maid chewed at her lip. 'It'll need a fair old length

of ribbon but, aye, I think you're right. Do you want me to do it, miss?'

Phoebe smiled and shook her head. 'I will manage myself, but thank you for the offer.'

The maid bobbed a curtsy and turned to leave. 'Oh, miss.' She stopped, turned back to Phoebe and produced a letter from within her apron. 'I checked your pockets before I put your dress through the wash and found this.'

'Thank you, Agnes,' she said, but the maid had already left.

It was the letter Hunter had given her the day before yesterday—Emma's letter about which he had been so angry. The scene in the corridor outside his study seemed a lifetime ago.

Her fingers broke the sealing wax, unfolding the paper and even before she began to read a shiver of foreboding had rippled down her spine. And the words that Emma had written upon the paper made her sit down hard upon the bed.

I am much worried by the news that you are to accompany Mrs Hunter on her visit to Blackloch and her son, for there is something that you should know of Mr Sebastian Hunter. An ominous feeling was forming in the pit of Phoebe's stomach. Her eyes raced on, skimming Emma's neatly penned words.

You are already aware of the great folly that Kit perpetrated and thus the current most unfortunate circumstances in which my family finds itself. Kit, Emma's brother, had bankrupted the family at the gaming tables so that Emma and her family had lost their home, their money and their reputation. Their lives had been ruined.

Sebastian Hunter was chief amongst the pack of rakes who beguiled Kit into their gang. Kit looked up to Hunter, admired him, as if there was anything about the man to be admired, hung on his every word. It was Hunter who took Kit to that gaming den the night he lost our fortune and Hunter who goaded him to such recklessness. He cares nothing for anyone other than his own selfish pleasure. Indeed, my dear friend, Hunter would ruin you without so much as a second thought. Thus, I implore you, Phoebe, with all my heart, to heed my warning and guard yourself most carefully from Hunter.

A cold shadow moved over her heart. Phoebe stared at the words that Emma had written, words so similar in vein to the ones her papa had spoken. The same warning issued from the two people that she loved and trusted the most. A warning that so contrasted with all she had seen of Hunter. She thought of the man who had cared enough about his tenants to visit them in person, gifting money and food and linens. The man who had ridden out in the dead of night in the driving rain to help those involved in a carriage accident. He had saved her from the highwaymen, fetched the midwife for Rena Beattie, and she did not think she would ever forget the sight of him in the parlour with the Beattie children snuggled all around. But most of all she thought of the small tender touch of his lips against hers when the memory of Elspeth had threatened to overwhelm her.

She moved to stand by her bedchamber window, staring out over the moor and the darkness of the loch. The day was cool and grey as if summer had already left. She closed her eyes, not knowing what to believe.

Hunter had to wait until that morning to follow Phoebe down to the scullery, where she was mixing up a pot of face cream.

He chased out the maid who was washing dishes and closed the door behind her.

'Sebastian!' Phoebe whispered in a scandalised tone. 'You will have the staff gossiping.'

'It is the only way that I may speak to you alone.'

'You should not be down here.' She turned away and resumed her pounding of the pestle against the mortar.

'You should have told me of your sister, Phoebe.'

She stilled, the pestle loose within her fingers.

'If I had known…' The words petered out. 'The night before must have been a torture for you.'

She shook her head, but still did not look at him.

He moved to her, taking the mortar and pestle from her hands and pulling her gently round to face him.

'The birthing itself was not so bad,' she said. 'I did not let myself think of anything save Mrs Beattie and the baby.'

'And on the moor afterwards, when all the clamour was over and all of the thoughts were there in your head?'

'That was hard,' she admitted.

'Why did you not tell me, Phoebe, when we were alone? I would have understood.'

'I have never spoken of Elspeth or the baby. It distressed my papa so much when she died that he would not hear her name mentioned in the house again. It was… terrible.' She pressed her hands to her face, covering her eyes. 'I must not speak of it, I must not even think of it, for I cannot start weeping, not here, not like this.'

He took her in his arms and held her to him, stroking a hand over her hair.

'I am here if you wish to speak of it. You may come to me, Phoebe, and you may speak of it and think of it and weep about it as much as you will. There is no wrong in that. I understand your pain, Phoebe, I know what it is like to feel such grief.'

'Your father,' she whispered.

'Yes.'

'Of whom you do not speak either.'

'No.'

'We are a fine pair.'

'We are, Phoebe Allardyce, a fine pair indeed.' He traced a finger over the line of her cheek.

'You should go now,' she said. 'I promised Mrs Hunter that I would make up this beautifying lotion for her.' She gestured to the mortar and pestle and the recipe in the opened fashion journal on the table top before it. 'She is waiting.'

'Let her wait a little longer.' And he lowered his mouth to hers and he kissed her, tenderly, gently, to salve the hurt that was in her heart.

Hunter and McEwan began installation of the new drainage system at the lower end of the moorland the next day. It was an important event, for the land was in a sheltered spot close to McInnes's farmstead and, if the operation proved successful, the land might be used for crops instead of lying as useless bog for most of the year. Phoebe was thankful that Hunter's attention was engaged elsewhere for it was Tuesday and she feared he would have insisted upon driving her to Glasgow, and she could not face lying to him over her father. But when she had gone to leave for Kingswell, she had discovered that Hunter had left instructions for Jamie to both take her to Glasgow and bring her back again in the gig. She had the young footman let her out at the Royal Infirmary and told him to spend the next hour down at the Green while she pretended to enter the hospital. Then she ran all the way down to the Tolbooth.

* * *

'Phoebe. You are pink-cheeked and puffing. Come and sit down.'

She sat in the chair across the table from her father in his prison cell.

'The day is warm.' She smiled as she gave the excuse, but her gaze was busy studying his face, checking that his bruises were fading and that he had taken no new hurts.

'You look radiant, child,' he observed. 'Just like your mother when she was young and in love.' He smiled and his eyes took on a faraway look as he remembered her mama from across the years. 'Something of the moor air must be agreeing with you.'

Phoebe's heart gave a little flutter as she thought of Hunter and realised that her father was not so very far away from the truth. She glanced away so that he would not see it in her eyes.

'How are you enjoying Blackloch Hall?' he asked.

'Very well, indeed.' Phoebe relayed something of her days at Blackloch, rambling on, telling her papa all the small details of the farmsteads and the tenants and the coaching accident that she knew he would be interested to hear. She made no mention of Mrs Beattie or the baby.

'So Hunter went to the gentlemen's assistance?'

She nodded. 'He cleared the road of the damaged vehicle and had the shaken passengers transported to Glasgow in his own coach.'

Her papa looked at her with such an expression of surprise on his face that she wondered if she had said too much of Hunter.

Her gaze dropped, moving over the sheets of paper strewn in piles across the table's surface between them. Her papa's writing was small and cramped and he had filled the sheets one way, before turning the paper at a right angle and writing across the lines of words already there, making a lattice of words that utilised every available space on the paper.

'I am sorry that I could not bring more paper with me today,' she said to change the subject from Hunter. Indeed, there had barely been enough to pay to the turn-key.

'You are here, and that is all that matters to me. To see your face, Phoebe, it gladdens my heart.'

'Dearest Papa,' she whispered and felt the emotion sweep over her. 'How does your book come along?'

Sir Henry nodded. 'Nicely enough, although I have had a new thought concerning one of my hypotheses.' A distant look came into his eyes. Phoebe recognised it well. Her father was thinking of his chemistry. 'I might need to write to young Davy on the matter. I wonder...'

She felt a measure of reassurance that her papa must be feeling his old self if he was so absorbed in his science.

'Mmm...' And it was some minutes later before Sir Henry remembered that she was sitting there before him.

She laughed aloud; so did he and the sound of his laughter eased the worry from her heart.

'I did not tell you, did I, my dear? I am to have a new cellmate.'

The laughter died upon her lips. 'A new cellmate?'

'Before the week is out. Wonderful news, is it not? I do like some company.' He stopped, staring at her with eyes laden with concern. 'What is wrong, child? You look as if you have just heard a death knell. Is it something I said?'

'No. No, of course not. Nothing is wrong.' She shook her head and forced a smile. 'It is wonderful news indeed, Papa.' And all of the danger and the threat was back in the space of a moment, all that she had not thought of in these past days with Hunter. 'Now tell me all about your book,' she asked to distract him.

Her father smiled and began to tell her all about his latest theory.

If her visit to the Tolbooth had not been enough to remind Phoebe that the Messenger meant what he said, there was no room for doubt the following morning. When Phoebe met with Mrs Hunter in her little sitting room at ten o'clock, the lady was positively beaming, a sight that in Mrs Hunter was rare indeed.

'We are going to Glasgow today to order ourselves some new dresses.'

'New dresses, but—' Phoebe thought of the few coins in her purse.

But Mrs Hunter rushed on. 'For London. Caroline Edingham, Lady Willaston, has written to me, insisting that I visit her at the start of next month, and do you know, Phoebe, I am going to go. It is exactly what I need.' Mrs Hunter flicked a finger at Polly to pass her the fashion journals from the table in the corner. 'And, of course, it goes without speaking that, as my companion, you will be coming with me.'

Phoebe stared at Mrs Hunter, speechless as the memory of the Messenger's words ran through her head: *At the start of September Mrs Hunter'll be travelling down to London to visit a friend, no doubt taking her trusty companion with her.*

'I know,' said Mrs Hunter, quite misinterpreting Phoebe's shock. 'Is it not just too too good? And I am sure that your papa, even with his current state of health, would not wish you to miss such an opportunity.'

'I am not sure,' said Phoebe weakly. The Messenger was setting everything in motion just as he had promised.

'Well, I mean to convince him, even if I have to go up to that hospital and tell him myself.' Mrs Hunter smiled.

Phoebe could barely keep the horror from her face. It was the nightmare come true.

'La, I declare I have not felt so excited in an age. In two weeks, Phoebe, we shall be in London,' she said. 'Only two weeks. And there is so much to be done.'

'So much indeed,' murmured Phoebe. Two weeks to find what she sought. Two weeks to evade Hunter and her feelings for him. Two weeks to save her papa's life.

Hunter made his way towards the drawing room. A week had passed since his mother's announcement of her trip to London, during which Phoebe had successfully avoided him thanks largely to his mother spending all day every day shopping in Glasgow.

'A strong box is a splendid idea for the town house, Phoebe,' Hunter heard his mother saying as he approached the half-opened door. 'At least I know my jewellery would be safe.'

'Maybe you should use one here. Does Blackloch Hall possess such a thing?' She was trying to sound casual, but he could hear the slight tension beneath the façade. Hunter's eyes narrowed. He stopped where he was and listened in.

'Not as far as I know.' His mother did not seem to notice anything amiss with the question. 'My husband had one in our town house in London, but never here. I believe Edward never thought Blackloch at risk of break-ins.'

'He was most probably right,' he heard Phoebe say in a reassuring tone. 'Blackloch is a most secure place.'

He felt a small measure of relief that at least she had not frightened his mother by revealing her knowledge of Blackloch's burglaries. There was a pause and then she said, 'Mrs Hunter, I could not help but notice the preponderance of wolves in the decoration of Blackloch. It is most unusual.'

'And quite frightful, I know, my dear, but the wolf is the Hunter family emblem. I believe it stems from some play on the name; the original Hunters must have been hunters in the true sense of the word, just as much as the wolf. Men and their silly games!' His mother gave a small laugh. 'But enough of this talk, Phoebe. We have more important matters to discuss, such as your stubborn refusal to permit me to buy you more than one new dress.'

'Your offer was most kind and I thank you for it, but I have more than enough serviceable dresses.' Hunter thought of the bloodstains that had marred the bodice of her dress the night he had brought her back to Blackloch. 'And you have already been more than generous to me.'

He turned and quietly retraced his steps away from the drawing room.

The day grew more dismal as it progressed. There was a dampness in the air, a dull grey oppression that brought on one of Mrs Hunter's headaches and lowered everyone's spirits. At three o'clock the lady took a tisane of feverfew and went to lie down, leaving Phoebe to brood alone in her bedchamber.

Phoebe paced the room. She could not rest, could not even sit still. And she dared not go down to the drawing room, for Hunter was about and she had no wish to let him see her, not when she felt so worried and anxious and desperately ill at ease. She did not doubt that he would fathom something of her distress, and what could she tell him when he asked the reason?

Events were slotting into place, all of them engineered by the Messenger. He would be waiting for her in London, waiting for what she was supposed to have found, except that she had searched everywhere in Blackloch that she could think of and discovered nothing. And when she arrived in London he would find her and learn that truth. She knew what the consequences would be for her papa. Her palms grew clammy and she felt queasy. She had not found what the Messenger wanted. And she knew she was falling in love with Hunter. It was all of it a mess, a terrible dangerous mess.

Phoebe stood by the window and stared out at the black water of the loch, and the great dark heavy sky, and the wild bleakness of the moor, and felt something of its dark beauty touch her spirit. She leaned her forehead against the window pane so that its coolness soothed the heat from her head, and let the moor calm her.

'So we are no closer to solving the mystery of Miss Allardyce?' McEwan asked as he stood by the fireplace of Hunter's study, watching the golden lick of flames devour the coal.

'Further investigation is required,' said Hunter. He did not look round at McEwan, just stood by the window staring out over the moor. It was dark today beneath an ominous leaden sky. Not a breath of breeze to stir the slow creeping stillness. He did not want to tell McEwan how much he had learned of Phoebe Allardyce in these few short weeks and how much he had come to feel for her. None of it mattered. She was still a would-be thief. He had not yet discovered what she was looking for.

'The man has never shown for any of her prison visits.

I followed her each time. There has been no one. And your contact in Glasgow could turn up no further information upon her. Perhaps you were mistaken, Hunter. Perhaps you should just let it be.'

'No.'

'You are spending much time with Miss Allardyce.'

'It is a necessary part of my investigation.' Hunter turned to look at McEwan.

'People are beginning to notice.'

Hunter narrowed his eyes ever so slightly. 'She is a would-be thief.'

'She is also your mother's companion, a lady and a young and comely one at that.'

'And what is that supposed to mean?'

'That you should be careful if you do not wish to find yourself having to offer for her.'

'I am intent on discovering the truth, not bedding her.' Yet the thought of bedding Phoebe Allardyce was dangerously arousing. 'I have not had a woman these nine months past. I have not gambled. I am not a damned rake.' He was keeping the promises he had sworn.

'I know, Sebastian.' McEwan clapped a hand against his shoulder. 'Just have a care, that is all I am saying.' And McEwan left, leaving Hunter sitting alone.

The wind tapped against his window, moaning softly, stirring the deep red of the curtains. He thought of Phoebe and all he had not said to McEwan: that he wanted her, that he cared for her, even knowing that she was a liar and had searched his home. He stroked at his chin, his fingers toying with its cleft. She had even quizzed his mother. And now he was sure she was avoiding him. Hunter pushed aside his emotions, deadened them, just as he had all of the months past. This was about a threat to his mother's safety. He could not afford to let his feelings for Phoebe sway him.

He rang the bell for a footman, and summoned Miss Allardyce.

Chapter Eleven

'You wished to see me, Mr Hunter.' Phoebe was determined to keep matters on a formal footing. She faced him with a feigned serenity, showing nothing of her worries, nothing of the feelings that roared in such turmoil. Behind her the study door remained open as was only appropriate for a single lady alone in a room with a gentleman.

'Close the door and come and sit down.'

'I do not think that is—'

'Just do it, Phoebe.' The tone of his voice was almost weary.

She turned to close the door and there it was. Facing her. On the wall beside the door. A portrait of a man with the same brilliant green eyes as Hunter, a man whose face had the same classical features, but aged by the years. Instead of the dark ruffle of ebony hair, the man's hair in the painting was a dark peppered silver. But upon his face was the same brooding expression that Hunter wore. She saw all these things in a second, but none of them was why she was staring at the painting. Her heart began to beat very fast.

'Phoebe?'

She knew she should turn away and answer Hunter, but she could not. She walked closer to the painting, peering up at its every detail as the tension coursed through her body.

'My father,' he said and she could hear the slight change in his voice.

All was quiet in the room. She heard the spit of logs on the fire, as the flames licked around the wood to release the subtle scent of pine throughout the study, and the slow ticking of the clock. Phoebe knew how difficult this might be for Hunter. She did not want to hurt him, but she had to ask the question.

'The ring he is wearing…'

She did not hear Hunter move, but felt his sudden close presence. The words she spoke were calm and quiet, a stark contrast to the roar of tension through her body. 'A silver wolf's head with emerald eyes.' It matched precisely the description the Messenger had given her. 'A most unusual design,' she said and did not dare to look round at him.

'One of a kind, so my father told me.' Hunter answered, his voice so close behind her she felt the nape of her neck and shoulder tingle.

'I wonder what became of the ring…?' There did not seem to be enough air in the room. The clamminess prickled upon her palms.

'It was my father's,' said Hunter, 'and now it is mine.'

'You must consider it to be the most precious of keepsakes.'

'I do. It was the last thing my father gave to me, the last tangible link between us.'

His words made her falter—she remembered how very much it had hurt to part with Elspeth's possessions.

And it seemed that from across the years she heard again the sound of her father's grief, sobbing in the depth of the night when he thought there was none to hear. Papa. The thought of him was enough to push her to the task. The quiver of her nerves stilled.

'The ring,' she said quietly, and her eyes never left the portrait. 'Where is it now?'

She felt Hunter's hand rest upon her right shoulder and schooled herself not to react. He moved, turning her as he did so, so that they were standing face to face. She kept her eyes trained upon his cravat, on the knot he had used to tie it. The minutes stretched and still Hunter was waiting and she knew she must meet him head on over this. She raised her gaze to meet his.

They looked at one another across that tiny divide and the very air seemed to crackle between them.

'Guarded most carefully,' he said, 'close to my heart.'

Phoebe's focus dropped to Hunter's chest.

The wind howled across the moor and the branches of the old clambering rose tapped against the study window.

Slowly she reached her hand out to lay it very gently against his black superfine lapel. Through all the layers of shirt and waistcoat and coat Phoebe could feel the strong steady beat of his heart. Inch by tiny inch, as if dragged by a will that was not her own, Phoebe raised her eyes to look into Hunter's, and they were the colour of a Hebridean sea. As they stared into one another's eyes the distance between them seemed to shrink.

She knew she should look away, drop her fingers from where they touched him, change the subject to talk of small trivial matters. She knew all of that, yet she did none of them. And when Hunter took her mouth with his own she met his lips with a passion that flared through the entirety of her being. Her hand slid up his lapel to the nape of his neck. She felt his arms close around her, felt him pull her so that their bodies stood snug together, her breasts crushed against the hard muscle of his chest. She kissed him with all the need that was in her soul.

There was a slight tap at the door as it swung fully open. Hunter and Phoebe jumped apart.

'Forgot to leave these—' McEwan stopped, the shock evident upon his face. 'I do beg your pardon,' he said and retreated as quickly as he had entered, the thin pile of papers still gripped within his hand. The door closed firmly behind him.

Phoebe stared, horrified at what she had just done. She glanced at Hunter. His normally pale cheeks held a faint touch of colour. His hair was dishevelled where she had threaded her fingers, and there was a slight elevation in his breathing. And in his eyes was shock and desire and anger. She said not a word, just turned and fled.

McEwan did not let the matter lie.

'What the hell are you thinking of, Hunter?' His steward ceased his pacing, raked a hand through his hair and stared across the study at Hunter in disbelief. 'You were supposed to be keeping an eye on her, not seducing the girl.'

'I was not seducing her,' Hunter said stiffly and wondered if he had not set out to seduce Phoebe Allardyce from the very start.

'Then she was seducing you? To get her hands on whatever it is that she is supposed to be seeking?'

Hunter's jaw tightened.

'Or is all of this just an excuse that you might have her?'

'Be careful, McEwan. You go too far.' His voice was cold and hard-edged.

McEwan stopped pacing and came to stand before him. 'I am sorry, Sebastian, but I am worried for you. I thought at first this business with Phoebe Allardyce was a blessing in disguise. It drew you out of your megrims, gave you a purpose, a task on which to focus.'

'No.' Hunter shook his head in denial.

'Yes, Hunter,' McEwan affirmed. 'When was the last time you sat in this study the whole night through? When was the last time you drank a bottle of brandy in one sitting? Do you observe no correlation with Miss Allardyce's arrival?'

McEwan was right, Hunter realised, but he was not about to admit it.

'But in the space of a few weeks that has changed. You are obsessed with the girl.'

'Hardly,' murmured Hunter and knew it was a lie.

'Do you deny that you want her?'

'I make no denial,' said Hunter coldly. 'I have wanted Phoebe Allardyce since the moment I set eyes on her.'

McEwan gave a nod as if Hunter was confirming all that he knew.

'But it does not mean that I will act upon it,' finished Hunter.

McEwan gave a cynical laugh. 'If you were not acting upon it, what then was it that I interrupted this evening?'

'It is not as you think, McEwan. Everything is under control,' he lied. 'I know what I am doing.'

'Whatever else you suspect her of, whatever else you think her, she is still your mother's companion. Think what would happen had it been Mrs Hunter who had walked in that door instead of me.'

'My mother never comes in here. Besides, the whole reason I am doing this is to protect my mother.'

'Are you certain of that, Sebastian?' McEwan said softly.

Hunter did not answer the question. Instead he walked away to stand by the window and stare out over the moor. The clock marked the passing seconds. 'I know what Phoebe Allardyce is searching for.'

Hunter heard the change in McEwan's tone. 'What is it that she means to steal?'

'My father's ring.' He turned and gestured towards the portrait of his father on the wall.

McEwan walked right up to the painting and studied the artist's rendition of the wolf's-head ring upon his father's finger. Then he shook his head and when he looked round at Hunter his face was crinkled in puzzlement. 'Of all the possibilities... It is not even gold. Why on earth would she want it?'

'I do not yet know.'

McEwan came to stand before him. 'You will have a care over how you do this, won't you, Sebastian? You know if this goes wrong that it will touch your mother's reputation as well as your own.'

'It will not go wrong.' He saw the concern on his friend's face. 'I know what I am doing, Jed,' he said again quietly.

'I pray that you do, Sebastian. You have been through enough these past months. I do not wish matters to go worse.' He struck the top of Hunter's arm in a manly gesture of support and then left.

Hunter stood there alone, but he did not turn back round to the window and the moor. Instead he walked up to where McEwan had stood, and Phoebe before him. Hunter stood in the same spot and looked up at the portrait. His eyes focused on the ring in the painting and he felt the same strong sweep of emotion as ever he did when he looked at it. If it had been any other item in the whole of this house... Hunter wished with all his heart that it were so. For Phoebe Allardyce was trying to steal the one thing he had sworn to guard with his very life. A shiver rippled down his spine as he remembered his father's words—tenacious and insistent, even when Edward Hunter was dying. And Hunter could not suppress the feeling that something sinister was at work here. He moved his gaze up to his father's face, so sober and serious.

'What is the significance of the ring, Father, that she will risk all to steal it?' he whispered quietly.

But his father just stared down at him with the same disapproval that had been there every time he looked at Hunter. And the room was silent save for the beat of Hunter's heart.

Phoebe was not surprised to find Hunter's coach, rather than Jamie and the gig, waiting when she exited the front door the next morning. The sky was a thick lilac-grey blanket of cloud, imbuing the light with a peculiar acute clarity and washing the landscape with that same translucent purple hue. For once, perhaps the only time since Phoebe had arrived at Blackloch, there was not a breath of wind. The air hung heavy and still and the atmosphere seemed pregnant with foreboding, but whether that was just a figment of Phoebe's own guilty conscience she did not know. Hunter's coach, a deep glossy black, luxurious and sleek, sat before her. Jamie in his black-and-silver livery pulled the step down into place. She could see the coachman already up on his seat at the front.

'Miss Allardyce.' She heard the crunch of Hunter's boots across the gravel and her pulse leapt.

'Mr Hunter.' She hoped that nothing of the flurry of

emotion showed upon her face. In the strange light of this day the contrast of his pale skin, dark dark hair and clear emerald eyes was striking. To Phoebe, Hunter had never looked more handsome or his eyes more intriguingly beautiful. Nor had he looked so worryingly dark and brooding. His gaze met hers and she felt a shiver of sensation touch her very core.

He gestured towards the waiting coach, but did not make the excuse of attending some meeting in Glasgow or the dangers of highwaymen upon the road. Neither did Phoebe make any attempt to decline his invitation. They both knew that matters were beyond that. She climbed in without a word.

Her head was thick from lack of sleep. Her eyes stung with it. The hours of the night had been filled not with rest, but with worry—over the wolf's-head ring and her papa and Hunter.

She knew that they needed to talk, but she did not know what she could say. *Give me the ring so that the villains will not kill my papa?* Hardly. She could tell no one, least of all Hunter. And she was afraid that she might have roused his suspicions, that he might question her interest in the ring. She was afraid, too, of what might happen between them closed together and alone in the coach all the way to Glasgow. But Hunter did not mention the ring. Indeed, he hardly spoke at all. He spent his time staring out of the window, although she had the impression that he was not seeing anything of the passing countryside, but wrestling with some great problem that tortured him. He appeared to have such a weight of worrisome thought to dwell upon that she tried to draw him into light conversation, but Hunter would not be drawn and when he looked at her it seemed to Phoebe that he could see too much, of her, of her lies, and her feelings for him. She could not risk him seeing the truth so she left him to his brooding and turned her gaze to the other window.

There was the sound of the wheels rumbling along the road, and the horses' hooves pounding in their rhythm... and the strange heavy silence that hung in the air. The moorland passed in a blur of colours, all grey sky and purples and earthy browns. And with every mile that passed Phoebe grew more conscious of the tension within Hunter. He had not spoken, had not moved, other than to cast the odd intense glance in her direction.

By the time the coach crossed over the River Clyde and made its way along Argyle Street the rain was drumming softly against the roof, and Phoebe could only be relieved that she would soon be at her destination. But as they reached the Trongate Hunter banged his cane on the roof and stuck his head out of the window to say something to his coachman. Reminding the man to follow up High Street to the Royal Infirmary, or so Phoebe thought. But a matter of minutes later the coach did not turn left as it should have done, but stopped directly outside the Tolbooth.

Phoebe's heart stuttered before thundering off a reckless pace. Her blood ran cold. Deep in the pit of her stomach was a horrible feeling of dread. Through the window of the coach she could see the great sandstone blocks of the building, the rows of windows and the steps that led up to the portico over the front door. She turned her gaze to Hunter's, trying to hide the truth from her face.

'Why have we stopped here?'

'Because you have come to visit your father.'

She gave a small laugh as if this was some jest he were playing. 'My father is in the Royal Infirmary.'

'Sir Henry Allardyce has been a prisoner in the Tolbooth gaol these past seven months,' Hunter said.

'You know?' she said in a low voice from which she could not keep the horror.

'Of course I know.'

'For how long have you known?'

'Long enough,' he said.

She closed her eyes as if that could block out the nightmare of what was happening.

'Why did you not tell me, Phoebe?'

She opened her eyes and stared at him. 'Why do you think?' she demanded, incredulous that he even needed to ask the question, then shook her head. 'I did not want to lose my position as your mother's companion.' She turned her head to stare out at the gaol building, raising her eyes to the tiny barred window of the third floor room in which she knew her papa waited. 'Does Mrs Hunter know, too?'

'She does not.'

Her gaze jumped to his.

'Fifteen hundred pounds on a failed medicinal chemistry company…'

She balked at how much of the detail he knew.

'Your father's debt is nothing of your doing, Phoebe. Do you not already suffer enough for it?'

She stared at him. 'You cannot mean that you do not intend to tell your mother the truth about me?' she said carefully, not sure that she had understood what he was saying.

'That is precisely what I mean, Phoebe.'

There was a dangerous swell of emotion around her heart, and then the penny dropped and she realised what he really meant. 'Oh…I understand,' she said and there was an ache in her heart. 'Because of our arrangement. You wish to—'

Hunter's eyes flashed a vivid green with anger. In one swift fluid movement he had their hands entwined and their faces barely two inches apart.

'There is no arrangement. There was never any arrangement.'

'But...'

'If I were the rake you think me, you would have been in my bed the very first day that we met.'

She sucked in her breath.

'We both know it is the truth.' They were so close she could see each and every black lash that lined his eyes, and all of the tiny hairs that made up the dark line of his brows. Some strange force seemed to be pulling them together.

Phoebe fought against it.

'What other secrets are you hiding, Phoebe?' he whispered, and his breath was warm against her mouth, his lips so close yet not touching.

She stared into his eyes and she wanted to tell him, indeed, longed to tell him. To share that terrible burden that had weighed on her all of the weeks she had been at Blackloch Hall. For a moment the temptation almost overcame her, but at the back of her mind were the words the Messenger had spoken, words that haunted her every hour of every day, *One word to Hunter or his mother and you know what'll happen... I'll hear if you've talked.* Phoebe did not doubt that the villain would hear, for he had already more than proven the extent of his knowledge. Much as she wanted to tell Hunter, she knew she could not risk her father's life.

She gave the tiniest shake of her head. 'None that I

can share,' she said softly, and with a will of iron and a heavy heart she turned her face away.

Hunter did not move. She felt the weight of his eyes upon her for minutes that were too long. Until finally, at last, he turned away and opened the door and would have climbed out had she not stopped him.

'Do not! I mean, it would be better if you are not seen here...outside the prison...with me.' Her gaze darted to the street beyond, checking the passing bodies for a sight of the Messenger and feeling relief that he was nowhere to be seen.

She saw his eyes shift to follow where she had scanned before coming back to hers. She saw, too, the speculation in them and the hard edge of anger.

'The visiting time is already waning. If I am to see my papa...'

He gave a nod. 'I will wait here for you, Phoebe.'

Hunter stood with McEwan at the study window, watching the thick sheet of rain that had shrouded the moor for the last few hours since he had brought Phoebe back to Blackloch. The light was so dim that the room was grey and shadowed as if night were already falling, even though it was only six o'clock.

'The roads will flood if this does not ease soon,' Hunter said.

'Most of the servants elected to leave early,' said McEwan, 'just as you said.'

'They will need to work fast to gather in the livestock and secure their houses. The storm will hit tonight.'

'Cook has left a cold collation.' McEwan looked worried as the intensity of the rain seemed to increase as they stood there. 'Mrs Hunter is not yet returned from her visiting,' he noted with concern.

'My mother is not fool enough to travel in such weather. She will stay overnight with the Fraser woman in Newmilns.'

There was a pause before McEwan said, 'I could take Miss Allardyce to stay with me and Mairi tonight.'

'And why should you do that?'

'You know fine well why, Hunter,' said McEwan softly.

Hunter looked steadily at McEwan. 'Mairi will be worrying about you, McEwan. You should be heading back to her.'

Blue gaze held green as McEwan challenged what he was saying. The seconds passed, until at last Hunter raked a hand through his hair and glanced away.

'I have...' He tried again. 'I feel...' But he could not form the words. 'It is none of it as you think, McEwan. I would not hurt her. I...' Again the words tailed off.

Hunter felt his friend's eyes scrutinising him, seeing too much. He turned his gaze away, but it was too late.

'Lord, Hunter,' McEwan said softly. 'I had no idea...' He paused, seemingly absorbing the magnitude of what Hunter had just revealed, then he met Hunter's gaze once more. 'I'll leave you alone with Miss Allardyce, then.'

Hunter gave a nod and watched his friend leave.

Chapter Twelve

Phoebe was not asleep when the first clap of thunder resonated in the dark hours of the night. Indeed, she had not slept since climbing into the bed despite the fatigue that hung heavy upon her. Her mind was too active, running with images of her papa and of Hunter, and her legs were so restless that it was a discomfort to lie still.

She slipped from the bed and parted her curtains to look out over the garden and the loch and the moor. But the rain was so heavy and the darkness so complete that she could see nothing at all, not even her own reflection. She stood for a while and listened as the thunder rolled closer, its crash exploding through the air louder each time it sounded, shaking the very foundations of the moor and Blackloch and Phoebe herself.

Using the red glow of the fire ashes, she found the remains of her candle and lit it from the embers. Her dinner tray still sat on the table by the door, her single plate with its remnants of cold ham and chicken upon it. And she thought of Hunter eating alone in his study while she ate alone up here, while all of Blackloch was empty save for the two of them. And as the thunder crashed and rolled around the heavens, Phoebe pulled her shawl around her and, with her candle in her hand, moved quietly towards the door.

Hunter was not in his bedchamber. His bed had not been slept in. She made her way down the stairs and knocked lightly against the study door before letting herself in.

Hunter was standing by the window, a glass of brandy in his hand, watching the storm. The room was warm. The remains of a fire glowed on the hearth.

'Phoebe.' He turned to her, and she saw that he was wearing only his buckskin breeches and shirt pulled loose and open at the neck.

A fork of lightning struck out on the moor, the flash flickering momentarily to illuminate the study and Hunter in its stark white light. His hair was dark and dishevelled, and his chin and jaw shadowed with beard stubble. She walked to stand by his side.

Hunter sat his glass down on the windowsill and did not touch it again.

The curtains stirred where they hung on either side of the window. The chill of the draught that slipped through the edges of the panes prickled her skin. The candle guttered and extinguished. Between the peals of thunder the rain drummed loud and hard, and the soft moan of the wind sounded.

Phoebe and Hunter stood side by side, not touching, not looking at the other, but only out over the moor at the storm. The lightning forked, blinding and white against the darkness of the sky, stabbing down into the land. And the thunder crashed as if the gods were smashing boulders in the heavens.

'It is magnificent,' she breathed. 'The storm, the moor...'

'Truly,' he replied.

And neither moved their gaze from the view beyond the window.

Another strike of lightning. Another roll of thunder. And Phoebe began to speak. Her voice was quiet. She did not look at Hunter, only at the moor.

'My father is a scientist. His interest lies in medicinal chemistry, the discovery of compounds that may be used to cure or relieve disease states. He has had a small laboratory within our house for as long as I can remember and is never happier than when he is working at his research. A year or so ago, he met a man who said he could take one of his ideas, an antimonial compound for the treatment of various toxic conditions, and manufacture it in large quantities in the factory that he owned, that they should start a company. My papa is a clever man, but his head is full of science, and when it comes to business...' She let the words peter out. 'The gentleman said he would look after all of that side of matters. The antimony was a great success. But the company was not. The gentleman took the monies and ran off to the East Indies, leaving all of the debts and no money to pay them. In the paperwork it all came down to my papa. There was nothing we could do.'

'And so your father was sent to the Tolbooth,' Hunter said.

'To stay there until the debts can be paid.'

'I am sorry, Phoebe.' She felt his hand take hers, but neither of them shifted their stance or their gaze.

'An old friend of my papa has a sister who heard that Mrs Hunter was seeking a companion. There was nowhere for me to go and no money to keep me. Your mother's position seemed the ideal solution. We had to lie, of course, for no lady would wish to take on a companion with the hint of scandal, let alone a papa imprisoned.'

'I am afraid that my mother has been sensitised through the years to gossip and scandal. All of it my fault.' His fingers were warm and supportive. 'You must miss your father.'

'Very much indeed. He worries about me out here without him, and I worry about him inside the Tolbooth gaol.'

'You are fortunate indeed to have his love.' She heard the pain in his voice and her heart went out to him.

'Mrs Hunter...' Phoebe hesitated, aware of the sensitivity around the issue. 'Relations between you and Mrs Hunter seem a little improved of late.'

'I do not delude myself. My mother will never forgive me, nor do I ask her to.'

And she remembered Mrs Hunter's words from across the weeks. *If you knew what he had done...* She brushed her thumb against his. 'For what crime must you seek her forgiveness?'

Outside a crash of thunder rolled across the sky.

He turned to her, looking down into her face through the darkness. The thunder was fading as he gave his answer. 'She believes that I killed my father.'

A gasp of breath escaped her. Whatever dark family secret she had imagined it was not this. All of the warnings came flooding back. All of the whispers and gossip to which her papa had alluded. 'And did you?' she asked.

Another fork of lightning flickered across the sky, revealing Hunter's face in flashes of bleaching light. And upon his face was such an agony of grief and of guilt that she knew what his answer would be even before he uttered the words.

'Yes.'

'I do not believe you,' she whispered.

He pulled her to him with nothing of gentleness, his hands angling her head so that their faces were almost touching. 'I killed him, Phoebe,' he said and his voice was raw. 'And I must live with that knowledge for every day of the rest of my life.' He backed away and she could see the horror in his eyes before he looked away.

Phoebe moved quickly, taking hold of his arms and guiding him down into his chair. 'Tell me,' she said. 'Tell me all, from the very beginning.'

And Hunter did. He told her the story of how he had been a rake and a dissolute in London, running with a crowd that included one of Emma Northcote's brothers. Of how Northcote had ruined himself and his whole family, and Hunter had been blamed, chief amongst his friends, for leading the boy astray.

'He was too young,' said Hunter. 'I did not realise my influence upon him. I had no idea he would go so far. It was the tipping point for my father. When he heard of the Northcotes' ruin he cut off my allowance, called me back to Blackloch, said I was hedonistic, selfish, immature, indulged by my mother and a disappointment to him. All of it was true, of course. But my father was an exacting man and I never felt that I could live up to his expectations. I gave up trying when I was still a boy. I turned to McInnes, spent much of my youth hanging about his farmstead.' Hunter smiled a little at the memory of his time with the old man.

Phoebe understood what she had seen on the moor that day when Hunter and his mother had visited McInness on the moor. 'And your father's death?' she urged.

'It was here in this study. We argued, my father and I, over Northcote. Everything he said was the truth, but I did not want him to see how much his words flayed me. I walked away from him, even knowing that he had been feeling unwell for those few days. I am ashamed to even think about it.'

She sat on the arm of the chair and took his hand in her own. 'Go on.'

'He hauled me back, gave me the rollicking I deserved. But the strain of it, the physical exertion, was too much. He collapsed. It was his heart, you see. As he lay dying he ordered me to change my ways, to take responsibility for the family.' The lightning flickered and Hunter seemed to hear again the echo of those disjointed words that his father had struggled so hard to speak: *...order...wolf... take responsibility for...* 'Ten minutes later he was dead.'

'Oh, Sebastian,' she whispered and leaned down to take him in her arms.

'It was all my fault, Phoebe, both Northcote's ruin and my father's death.'

'No,' she said, but he would not look at her. 'Sebastian,' she said more firmly, and took his face in her hands and forced him to do so. 'You made mistakes, heaven knows, we all do. You might have been selfish and imbued with all of those vices which you admit, but what occurred was not your fault. Emma's brother made his own choices. And as for your father, you said yourself that his heart was weak.' Her thumbs stroked against his jaw line. 'You are a good man, Sebastian Hunter.'

Their eyes clung together and in the flash of lightning she saw that his glistened with unshed tears. 'You are grieving. Your mother is grieving. You feel enraged and lost and despairing all at the same time. I felt the same for my sister. I still feel it. A soul can bear such grief, but guilt and blame and bitterness—these are what destroy a heart. You must stop blaming yourself, Sebastian.' She felt his tears wet against her fingers.

'Oh, Sebastian.' She slipped from the chair arm to kneel astride him and pull him to her and she held him against her breast while he silently wept.

She held him until the thunder was just the faintest rumble in the distance and the lightning no longer flared across the sky. And when he moved to look into her face it seemed the most natural thing in the world to kiss him. Gently. Tenderly. As if her lips could mend the wound that was in his soul.

'Phoebe,' he whispered, and there was such a heartfelt plea in that one word. She kissed him with all the love that was in her heart. And Hunter kissed her back. There was no need for words. They needed one another. And when he unfastened the ribbon of her nightdress and let it slip low to uncover her breasts she revelled in his gentle touch. His fingers stroked and caressed, and when his mouth replaced his fingers, so that he was tasting her, kissing her, laving her, she clutched his head to her and wanted him all the more. He lifted her slightly, adjusted her position upon him, moving her nightdress to bare her before settling her down to straddle his groin. She could feel the soft buckskin of his breeches against her most intimate of places.

'Sebastian,' she breathed. And then he began to rock her, in a steady easy pace, so it seemed as if she were riding him. She could feel the press of his manhood straining through his breeches, could feel herself rubbing against it. And all she knew was that she needed him and he needed her. And the need was in the white-hot heat in her thighs and the slick moisture between her legs, and the ache of her breasts; all feelings that Phoebe did not understand, just as she did not understand what was happening between them except that it was right, except that there was such a warmth and love and understanding that it almost overwhelmed her.

She groaned aloud at the glorious sensation that was growing in her. Such pleasure, such need. She wanted it never to stop and yet she was poised on a knife edge of passion, reaching for something more. She rode him harder, faster and when his mouth closed over her breast to suckle her nipple an explosion of sensation burst throughout the whole of Phoebe. Such a flood of exquisite delight as if she and Hunter were lifted from the dark storminess of Blackloch and the moor to a place of golden sunlight and paradise.

She collapsed onto him, planting a myriad of butterfly kisses over his temple and eyes and cheeks. She kissed his mouth and whispered his name a thousand times over. And all she felt for him was love, pure and complete. He rolled her round so that they lay together upon the chair, her back snug against his chest, his arms around her stomach, and now that the thunder had subsided there was only the steady drum of the rain against the moorland. Hunter pulled his coat to cover them and kissed her hair and her ear and the edge of her forehead. They slept and when the slow grey dawn came they watched together while it crept across the moor.

Hunter watched his mother and Phoebe across the drawing room as Phoebe poured the tea the maid had just delivered.

'Apparently Eliza Fraser was down in London for the Season and delighted in telling me all of the latest *on dit*. She was talking down to me as if I were some country bumpkin. Indeed! Well, I can tell you that the wind soon dropped from her sails when I told her that I was for London this very weekend. "Oh, but London will be quiet this time of year. 'Tis such a shame you missed the Season."' His mother impersonated Mrs Fraser's patronising tone. 'On the contrary, says I, only the best of the families will have returned for the Little Season. That quieted her.'

'I am sure it did.' Phoebe smiled and passed the first cup to his mother. He noted how careful she was not to look at him today and he could not blame her. It was only months of practice that enabled Hunter to sit there and show nothing of the fury of conflicting emotions that were vying in his breast.

'She has a new wardrobe of gowns from Mrs Thomas of Fleet Street and insisted on telling me the vast sums that each had cost. So not the done thing!' His mother sipped at her tea. 'I told her I prefer Rae and Rhind of Glasgow for my dresses. When one finds a talented dressmaker I always feel it is important to retain them and not float on a whim to another.'

'Absolutely,' agreed Phoebe, who managed to pass the next cup of tea to Hunter without meeting his eye.

'Talking of which, we are for Glasgow tomorrow to try on and collect our new dresses.' His mother smiled broadly, the first time in over a year that he had seen such a sight. 'I simply cannot wait to reach London. You have not visited the city before, have you, Phoebe? You must be in a veritable frenzy of excitement over our little trip.'

'Quite,' said Phoebe, but to Hunter's eye she seemed to pale and there was a look of pure dread in her eyes before she masked it. He was quite certain he had not imagined it.

His mother peered closer at Phoebe. 'You are looking a little pale and tired, my dear. I expect you did not sleep well because of the thunder.'

'The thunder did waken me,' Phoebe admitted and a faint peach blush washed her cheeks. She added a lump of sugar to her tea and concentrated on stirring it.

'It is always worse out here on the moor.' And fortunately his mother began talking of her plans for London again.

'I thought I might come with you to London, Mother.' Hunter nonchalantly dropped the news into the conversation.

He heard the quiet rattle of china of Phoebe's cup against its saucer before she set them down upon the table.

His mother frowned. 'I do not think that is a good idea, Sebastian.'

'On the contrary, I am quite convinced of its merit.'

'I see,' said his mother, tight-mouthed. All of her animation had vanished. The cold haughty demeanour was resumed. 'I had intended staying in the town house, but if you mean to—'

'I shall stay with Arlesford if it suits you better,' he said, cutting off her protestation.

She sniffed. 'I suppose London is a big enough place.'

'I am sure that it is.' As Hunter rose to leave, Phoebe's eyes came at last to his for just the smallest moment. All that was between them seemed to roar across the room before she looked away again.

The worst of the weather had passed by Thursday when Phoebe travelled with Mrs Hunter to collect their new dresses from Glasgow. The day was mild, with grey-white skies and a stiff breeze, but at least it was not raining, and the puddles still remaining from Tuesday's storm soon dried.

They had spent an hour with the dressmaker and left with the promise to return later that same afternoon as there were only two small alterations to be made to an evening gown and a walking dress for Mrs Hunter. There were so many shops to be visited, shoes to be collected, stockings and reticules to be bought, fascinators, feathers and ribbons to be perused, soaps and perfumes to be selected. And Mrs Hunter's full set of luggage to be sent down to Blackloch ready to be packed.

Phoebe had been glad of the activity; at least then she could not dwell and worry over her papa and Hunter... and the ring. Her feet had been aching by the time Mrs Hunter's heavily laden carriage was making its way back towards the moor. Mrs Hunter had been tired, too. She had closed the curtains and laid her head back on the squabs and, lulled by the rocking of the carriage, dozed. And then there was nothing to distract Phoebe from the confusion of worries and fears that crowded her mind.

They had not long turned onto the road beyond Kingswell that would take them across the moor to Blackloch when the carriage came to a halt.

'Stand and deliver!'

The voice was rough and horribly familiar.

Mrs Hunter's head rolled and she came to her senses. 'Phoebe? Are we home?'

Phoebe reached across the carriage and took the lady's hand in her own. 'We have not yet reached Blackloch, Mrs Hunter. I fear that we are being held up by highwaymen.'

'Be away with you, you fiends!' roared John Coachman and then there was the crack of pistol fire, and yells and shouting and an ominous thud upon the ground outside as if something heavy had fallen upon it.

'Oh, my word!' Mrs Hunter clutched instinctively to

the locket that Phoebe knew lay beneath all of the layers of her clothing.

'Stay calm, ma'am. I will not let them harm you.'

'Phoebe!' Mrs Hunter's face drained of all colour as the door was wrenched open and Phoebe saw the same masked highwaymen that she had met on a journey from a lifetime ago.

Chapter Thirteen

'Out you come, ladies. Just a brief interruption of your journey. Heading over to the big house, are yous? All nicely laden up.'

Black Kerchief grabbed first for Mrs Hunter. Phoebe swatted his hand away. 'We need no assistance, thank you, sir. I will help the lady.' The highwaymen stood back and watched while Phoebe jumped down, kicked the step into place and helped Mrs Hunter down onto the road.

'Well, well, well, Jim,' Black Kerchief said when he saw Phoebe in the full light of day and she knew that he recognised her just as readily as she had recognised him. 'If it's no' the lassie that escaped without payment the last time. This here bit of the road is dead. No passing coaches or carts. No horsemen or walkers. There's no gent to come galloping down the road to save you this time.'

'What is he talking about, Phoebe?' Mrs Hunter turned to her.

'Oh, now that's interesting. You didnae tell her of our wee encounter the other week.'

'The first day I came to Blackloch these men tried

to rob me. Mr Hunter arrived and saved me. That was why he had the bruising upon his face that first night at dinner.'

'Hunter himself, was it?' said Red Kerchief Jim. 'Hell, I would have wet m'breeks if I'd known.'

'Why did you not tell me, Phoebe?' demanded Mrs Hunter. 'Why did he let me think—?'

'Save the questions and explanations for later, ladies,' interrupted Black Kerchief. 'For now, there are other more pressing matters to be dealt with.'

'Such as relieving yous of your purses and jewels,' said his accomplice and slammed the door of the carriage shut.

Only once the door was closed did Phoebe realise the full magnitude of their situation, for on the ground ahead lay John Coachman groaning faintly, a bullet in his shoulder. Jamie lay trussed on the ground, blood trickling from a gash on his forehead.

Mrs Hunter clutched a trembling hand to her mouth. 'Oh, my good lord! You have killed him!'

'Not quite, but that's what happens when you dinnae do as you're asked,' said Black Kerchief.

'Aye,' said Jim and aimed a pistol at Mrs Hunter. 'You've been asked for certain items and I dinnae see you doing much to deliver them. Purses and jewels, now, if you please!'

Mrs Hunter was so white Phoebe thought she would faint.

'Jim, such impatience. Have I no' told you before that there are better ways of persuading ladies?' Black Kerchief said.

But Mrs Hunter had already extracted her purse and lady's watch from her reticule and was passing them to the black-masked highwayman. She slipped the pearl earrings from the lobes of her ears and the rings from her fingers, hesitating only over her wedding band.

'Come on,' growled Jim as he took the jewellery from her. 'All of it.'

'For pity's sake! She is a widow. Will you not even leave her her wedding ring?' demanded Phoebe.

'A nice weighty piece of gold like that? I dinnae think so, miss.'

Mrs Hunter pressed her lips together and Phoebe knew it was to control their tremble. She eased the ring from her finger and handed it to the fair-haired highwayman. 'That is all I have with me.' Her fingers fluttered fleetingly to touch her dress where the locket lay hidden.

Jim checked the purse for its contents and, satisfied with what he saw, threw it to Black Kerchief, who was standing a little back.

'Now we move to you, miss, and you better have something with which to pay the price this time.' Jim moved towards her.

'No' so fast.' The taller highwayman came to stand before Mrs Hunter. 'You're hiding something, lady.'

'I have given you all that I have,' Mrs Hunter affirmed again.

Black Kerchief's eyes dropped to the exact spot on her chest against which her fingers had strayed. 'Give me it willingly, lady, or I will take it from you.'

Whatever was within the locket must be precious to Mrs Hunter. Indeed, Phoebe had long suspected it to be a miniature of her husband. She moved to distract the highwayman.

'She has nothing more to give you. Leave her be.'

But Black Kerchief ignored her and levelled his pistol at Mrs Hunter's face.

Mrs Hunter swallowed and with fingers that were visibly shaking unfastened the gold chain at the back of her neck to slip the locket from its hiding place. The chain coiled like a snake into the highwayman's open palm and she laid the large golden oval body on top of it.

He opened the locket.

Mrs Hunter squeezed her eyes shut as the villain looked upon her most precious of secrets.

'Looks rather familiar, wouldn't you say, miss?' Black Kerchief held the locket up to show Phoebe its contents, so that she learned at last Mrs Hunter's secret. Inside were two miniature portraits, a dark-haired handsome man with pale emerald eyes, and a boy that could only be the man's son. For a moment Phoebe thought she was looking at Sebastian and his son, then she realized that Sebastian was the boy and the man was the same one she had looked upon in the large stern portrait within Hunter's study—Hunter's father. The two people Mrs Hunter loved best in the world—her husband and her son. And Phoebe knew in that moment that for all her accusations, for all that she had said, Mrs Hunter had never stopped loving Sebastian.

'You have everything else. Will you not leave her this one thing at least?' Phoebe asked the highwayman.

He gave a callous laugh. 'What do you think?' And he closed the locket body with a snap and threw it to his accomplice.

'And now for you, miss. What have you got to offer me? A coin or two?' He pushed her hard against the polished burgundy-gloss body of Mrs Hunter's carriage and pulled the mask down from his face to dangle around his neck. She recognised too well his face and the lust that was in it. He grabbed hold of her wrists, holding them above her head with one of his hands while the other found the pocket of her dress and rummaged. He dropped the two small plain white handkerchiefs that he found there onto the road and spat in disgust.

'No purse.'

His fingers raked roughly against her own. 'No rings.'

His large bulky body crowded against hers and his hand roved boldly over her bodice and down farther over the tops of her thighs, licking his lips as he did so. 'Nothing concealed.' Phoebe struggled against him, but he just smiled.

'What payment are you going to offer me? I'll have you know the price has gone up since the last time.'

'You are a villain, sir!' she hissed through her teeth. 'A veritable villain. Unhand me this instant!'

'Oh, little Miss Vixen, I'm nowhere near to unhanding you just yet.' And his mouth descended hard upon her own. His kiss was nothing like Hunter's. He tasted of tobacco and ale. He reeked of horses and sweat. She kicked out at his shins, tried to bite the thick furred tongue that invaded her mouth.

Black Kerchief drew back, releasing his grip on her wrists to dab at the trickle of blood over his lips. 'You shouldnae have done that, lassie.' And his hand gripped hard to her throat, pinioning her in place against the coach door so that she could not move, could not scream, could barely breathe.

Mrs Hunter began to sob. 'Please do not hurt her, I beg of you.'

'Tie the old lady up, strip the luggage of anything valuable and check the inside of the coach.'

Jim's eyes flickered towards Phoebe. 'We havenae the time for this. Bring the lassie wi' us. We can both hae our fun o' her then.'

'I'm havin' her and I'm havin' her now. So get on and do as I say, Jim. This'll no' take me long.' Black Kerchief slipped the pistol into his pocket with his free hand and produced a knife in its stead. The blade was short but wicked as he held it pointed straight at Phoebe's heart.

Phoebe said nothing, just looked directly into the highwayman's evil black eyes and thought it ridiculous that he could just extinguish her life so easily upon the moor. He leaned closer, then slashed the length of Phoebe's bodice.

Mrs Hunter screamed at the top of her lungs.

'Hell, Jim, gag her before they hear her in Blackloch.'

'No!' yelled Phoebe. 'Leave her be, you fiend! She paid what you asked.'

But Black Kerchief released her and landed her a blow across the face, so that her head cracked against the door of the carriage. The moor breeze was cool against her skin as the highwayman ripped the remaining material open, and his hands were rough and calloused against her breasts. His mouth fastened upon hers once more, his rancid breath filling her nose so it was all she could do not to gag. The knife dropped, its handle bouncing against Phoebe's boot, but Black Kerchief had other things on his mind. She ceased her struggle, let him think that he had cowed her, as her fingers crept into the pocket of his jacket and fastened upon the pistol. She extracted it quick as a flash, wrenched her mouth from his and pressed the muzzle hard against his belly.

'Stand away, sir, or I will shoot.'

Black Kerchief's eyes narrowed. 'I bet you havenae the first idea of how to fire a pistol,' he sneered.

'Shall I just pull back the cock, squeeze the trigger and see what happens?' She did not take her eyes from his as her thumb pulled back the cock lever as far as it would go.

Black Kerchief felt the motion and backed away, raising his hands, palms up in a gesture of submission. 'Easy, lass, no need to get excited.'

'Leave the locket, then get on your horses and ride away while you still can.'

He laughed, but there was nothing in his eyes save wariness and malice. 'Jim'll have a bullet through you before you can pull the trigger.'

From the corner of her eye she could see Red Kerchief with his pistol aimed right at her. He started to move towards her.

'Stop where you are, sir, or I will shoot your friend,' she shouted to him without taking her eyes off Black Kerchief.

'And I'll shoot you and then the old lady.' The pistol was in his right hand. With his left he produced a knife from the leather bag slung across his chest. 'You might no' have a care for your own life, but I could make a right mess of her before I finally put a bullet between her eyes.'

Phoebe did not doubt that he would do it, too. Black Kerchief's eyes were waiting and watchful. She knew she had no choice. She lowered the pistol and the highwayman snatched it from her, the victory plain on his face.

'Now where were we?' He grabbed her and threw her onto the ground; standing over her, he unfastened the fall on his breeches.

Hunter's big black stallion came flying over the road.

His first pistol killed the red-masked highwayman outright. Black Kerchief ducked towards the carriage and fired, the ball catching the top of Hunter's arm as he charged up to them. But Hunter kept on coming, his second pistol's shot hitting Black Kerchief in the chest. The highwayman tried to stagger away before crumpling to his knees and slumping face first onto the ground.

Hunter leapt from his horse, shrugging out of his coat

as he ran towards Phoebe. The blood was stark against the white of his shirt, a dense crimson stain spread across his left arm and shoulder.

Phoebe gave a little cry and ran to him.

He swirled his coat around her to cover her nakedness.

'Sebastian! There is so much blood!' The oozing wound clearly visible through the tear in the sleeve of his shirt. Her eyes widened in terror.

'The bullet has scratched my skin only, not torn through the muscle. It does not signify.'

His hands gripped the sides of her upper arms. 'Phoebe,' he whispered and there was such anguish upon his face. 'My God, I thought…'

'I am unharmed. But they have shot John Coachman,' she said, 'and tied up Mrs Hunter and Jamie.' She gestured towards where his mother lay bound and terrified. 'Go to her. I will free Jamie.' She stooped and picked up Black Kerchief's knife where it still lay upon the soil and when she stood with the knife in her hand, she saw the sudden uncertainty on Hunter's face.

'I will see to Jamie. My mother will want you, Phoebe.'

'No, you are wron—' she started to say, but he was already gone, walking away to help the young footman.

Phoebe hurried to Mrs Hunter and dislodged the gag from the older woman's mouth, then cut away the ropes that bit into her wrists and ankles.

'Mrs Hunter,' she began, but the lady was not even looking at Phoebe. Her eyes were trained on a spot beyond where Phoebe was kneeling.

'Sebastian is bleeding,' Mrs Hunter said. 'Oh, Phoebe, he is hurt.'

'The bullet grazed him. There is much blood, but he is not badly wounded,' Phoebe tried to reassure Mrs Hunter, but it seemed that the lady could not hear her. Her face was ashen, her eyes wide and staring.

'He is hurt,' she said again.

And then Phoebe felt Hunter by her shoulder.

'Mother,' he said and the bag of jewellery and money was in his hand.

'Oh, Sebastian!' Mrs Hunter sobbed and she clutched him to her. 'My son,' she cried. 'My son!'

Phoebe took the loot bag from him and recovered the locket. 'Mrs Hunter has worn this locket day and night for all the months that I have known her.' Phoebe opened the locket and showed the paintings within to Hunter. 'She has never stopped loving you,' she whispered, and, pressing the locket into his hand, she rose and went to help Jamie.

'Should you not be sitting down, Hunter? Come take a seat.'

Hunter glanced round at his friend from where he stood by the study window and gestured to the black arm sling he was wearing. 'You saw the wound, McEwan; it is a scratch. I am only wearing the damn thing to pacify my mother.' Two days had passed since the incident on the moor and in that time his mother had given him little peace.

'She is most concerned over your health.'

'She has not stopped fussing over me since we returned to Blackloch. She has even postponed her trip to London.'

'At least matters seem resolved between the two of you.'

'I am glad of it, McEwan, truly I am, but she is taking such an interest in my affairs that it has proven nigh on impossible to speak to Phoebe alone.'

'Hunter, should you be...?'

'When I saw that villain strike her...' Hunter shook his head.

'Your reaction is understandable,' said McEwan.

'I should have killed him the last time and none of this would have happened.'

'You could not have known, Sebastian.'

'She has no one to protect her, Jed. Her mother and sister are dead. Her father is imprisoned through a mess of debts that were no fault of his own. She is three-and-twenty years of age and alone.'

'How is Miss Allardyce subsequent to the attack?'

'As far as I can tell she is bruised, but otherwise uninjured. The bastard meant to rape her, McEwan.'

'Hell,' muttered McEwan.

'I will speak with her.'

'And say what?' McEwan laid his hand upon Hunter's good shoulder. 'Hunter, no matter what has happened, she is your mother's companion and there is this other business of your father's ring to consider.'

'There is an enemy at work here, Jed, but I cannot believe that it is Phoebe.' He met McEwan's eyes. 'There has to be some other explanation behind it.'

'Maybe,' said McEwan but he did not sound convinced.

'I mean to confront her over it, to hear her side of the story.'

Phoebe came down the stairs and was about to cross the hallway on her way to the drawing room when she saw Hunter walking towards the bottom of the stairs. A week had passed since the highwaymen's attack on Mrs Hunter's carriage, a week in which Phoebe's love for Hunter had grown. Her eyes scanned over him, noting that he was no longer wearing the black arm sling and she gave a little sigh of relief that his arm was healing so well. He looked so strong and devastatingly handsome and her heart swelled with love and warmth when she saw him.

He stopped where he was on seeing her, and such a determined look came over his face that Phoebe's heart turned over. There was no way she could avoid him.

'Mr Hunter.' She gave a polite nod and made to pass him, but he captured her and pulled her into the shadows of the servants' corridor at the side of the hallway.

'Phoebe, we need to talk.' His hands were gently around her waist, his body close to hers as he stared down into her face.

'Mrs Hunter is waiting.' She tried to break away, but Hunter did not yield.

'Meet me tonight. Come to my study once my mother is in bed.'

'I cannot,' she whispered.

'Why not?' His green gaze bored down into hers.

Because I love you. Because if I let myself be alone with you I do not think that I can hide that truth from you, and they will kill my papa. Because if you were to learn what I am, what I would do to you, you will hate me. But Phoebe spoke none of those truths.

'I have duties to which I must attend.'

'Tomorrow morning then, first thing, before breakfast.'

'No, Sebastian. We cannot meet alone, not then or any other time.'

She saw the muscle flicker in his jaw.

'Why not?'

'I…I have my position to consider. And you have yours.'

There was a flash of fierce green fire in his eyes. 'Damn it, Phoebe, this is nothing of positions. You know there are matters of which we must speak.'

'No,' she forced herself to say. 'I do not.' She could not let herself conduct an affair with him. She had to find the ring and steal it, to save her papa. But she loved Hunter. And she had not found the ring. And she did not know what she was going to do.

Their eyes clung together, her heart was aching, but she could not let herself weaken. The distance between them seemed to shrink. His face was only inches from hers. She could smell his scent, feel his warmth. The little hairs on the back of her neck stood up at the feel of his breath against her cheek. She ached for his kiss, longed to wrap her arms around his neck and press her lips to those of this kind, strong, glorious man whom she loved.

'You must let me go,' she whispered.

'For now,' he said and pressed a fierce kiss to her lips. It was a kiss of possession, a kiss that seemed to seal all that was between them. And then he released her.

Phoebe walked across the stone flags of the hallway just as a maid appeared on the stairs leading from the kitchen and scullery.

'Mrs Hunter rang from the drawing room,' the girl said.

'I am on my way to her at this very moment.' Phoebe smiled and hoped that nothing of Hunter's kiss showed upon her lips. But the maid did not seem to notice any-thing awry. Phoebe tucked a loose strand of hair into her chignon, and accompanied the girl towards the drawing room.

Hunter had not moved. She did not need to look back to know that he was still standing there in the shadows watching her.

A few days later Hunter was sitting opposite his mother and Phoebe in the breakfast room, sipping at his coffee and thinking. The day was bright, a last throw of summer. Sunlight filled the room, lighting Phoebe's face and showing too well the shadows beneath her eyes. She looked as if she were sleeping badly, and when she thought that no one was watching there was a worry in her eyes. And she had been avoiding him most successfully.

A footman brought the mail in, setting the silver salver down by Hunter's elbow.

Two letters for himself. One from his tailor, the other with Dominic's writing on the front. Three for his mother. And one for Phoebe, not from Emma Northcote; indeed the handwriting looked masculine and simplistic as if someone had taken pains to disguise their hand—the sender's details were not recorded upon the back of the letter.

He passed them across, threw the tailor's letter aside unopened and broke the wax on Dominic's note. Hunter's eyes scanned over Dominic's words. He smiled at the news.

'Be a dear and run and fetch my reading glasses will you, Phoebe.' Hunter felt a pang of irritation at the way his mother treated Phoebe.

'We have servants for that sort of thing,' he said drily and set Dominic's letter upon the table before him.

His mother looked up at him in surprise.

A hint of colour washed Phoebe's cheeks. 'It is no inconvenience, I assure you, sir.' And she slipped away before he could reach for the bell.

There was the cracking of wax and rustle of paper as his mother unfolded her letters. She picked up the first and held it at arm's length, peering at it with screwed-up eyes. 'Writing the size of an ant. Cannot see a word of it. Read it to me, Sebastian.'

'Hawkins writes to inform you that the decorators have finished at the town house in Charlotte Street. And that all is order for your return.'

Phoebe came back into the breakfast room just as he was reading the words. He saw her stiffen, saw that she understood the implication of that news just as well as he. But she did not look at him, just smiled at his mother and delivered the spectacles.

'So soon.' His mother seemed surprised.

'You do not have to leave,' he said. 'Indeed, I insist that you stay.' He thought of what Phoebe had told him of the break-ins at Charlotte Street and of his mother's fears. And he thought, too, of Phoebe.

'You are a young man, Sebastian.' His mother smiled. 'You are already burdened with an old woman's overlong visit.'

'You are neither old nor a burden. And I insist that you stay.'

'I will not hear of it,' his mother said, but she laughed and there was a sparkle in her eye that he had not seen since before his father's death.

From the corner of his eye, where he was surreptitiously watching Phoebe open her mail, he saw her fold the letter away almost as soon as she had opened it. Hunter glanced across at her, just as she looked up and met his gaze, and what he saw in her eyes was a fleeting glimpse of fear before she glanced down, and when she looked up again all of that was hidden and she was quite herself again.

'Good news?' his mother enquired and gestured to the letter clutched tight in Phoebe's hand.

Phoebe's smile was almost convincing. 'Nothing important,' she said. 'Now, what plans do you have for today, ma'am?'

* * *

Hunter rode Ajax hard across the moor. The wind was harsh against his cheeks, the sky a bright white-grey, lighting all of the moor with that clarity that he loved. In the distance he could see a pair of eagles soaring high in the sky, the birds huge and majestic. Hunter noticed it all, even though his mind was fixed most firmly on Phoebe Allardyce.

The letter had to be linked in some way with her search for his father's ring, its address penned by a male hand. And he thought of the man he had seen her meet outside of the Tolbooth, and the fear that flashed in her eyes as she saw the letter's contents. He had no intention of just letting her walk out of Blackloch, out of his life. There was too much that he still did not know. He needed answers. He needed her.

Hunter rode faster, harder, longer. And by the time he walked Ajax into Blackloch's stables he knew what he would do.

Chapter Fourteen

In the privacy of her bedchamber Phoebe stared again at the letter that had been delivered that morning. A letter that comprised only three words: *We are waiting*.

And whatever she might have been hoping, that the postponed trip to London might have in some way meant that the nightmare had vanished, those three words told her that she was wrong. Whether she went to London or not, whether she was here at Blackloch, or in Mrs Hunter's house in Charlotte Street, the Messenger would find a way to reach her…and, more importantly, her papa. She did not have the ring. Indeed, she was no closer to finding it now than she had been the first day she had arrived at Blackloch. Hunter had it, guarded most carefully as he had said. Maybe not even in Blackloch. Maybe in a bank or safety deposit box. Wherever it was, Phoebe had almost given up hope of finding it. And when she thought of what that meant she wanted to weep.

The clock had just chimed five when she heard Mrs Hunter's bedchamber door open and the lady's slippered steps across the passageway.

Phoebe screwed the letter to a ball and threw it onto the fire, watching the flames consume the paper and burn it to a cinder. Then she straightened her back, held her head up and went to follow Mrs Hunter down for dinner.

Hunter waited until both his mother and Phoebe were seated before he took his own seat. Hunter was at the head of the table, Mrs Hunter at the foot; Phoebe sat in between the two, her back to the windows and facing the door.

'Such fine salmon,' commented Mrs Hunter. 'I must compliment Cook.' Phoebe watched her clearing her plate. Such a marked change for the lady who, in all the months that Phoebe had worked for her, had only ever picked at her food. The lines of Mrs Hunter's face were no longer gaunt and sharp looking; she looked softer, happier, more agreeable. In contrast, Phoebe was feeling tense and worried. She had not the slightest appetite and there was a tinge of nausea in her stomach. She poked her salmon around her plate to make it look as if she were eating it, and cut her beef into small pieces, only one of which passed her lips.

'Indeed,' agreed Hunter.

The conversation passed on around her. Phoebe made small noises of agreement, but otherwise said little. Plates were delivered and removed. All she could think of was her papa.

'But you are not recovered enough to endure the rigours of such a journey, Sebastian.' Mrs Hunter's exclamation brought her from her reverie. Phoebe noticed that the last of the plates had been removed.

'Mother, I am perfectly recovered and the injury was the merest scratch in the first place.'

'I am not sure.' Mrs Hunter sounded doubtful.

'Besides, Arlesford has written to me. He is expecting

an addition to his nursery. He and Arabella are planning a ball to celebrate the good news and we are invited.'

Hunter rose from his seat and walked down the side of the table opposite to Phoebe, pausing just past her. He produced a letter from the pocket of his dark tailcoat and passed it to his mother with his right hand. His left hand leaned flat upon the table as he did so.

Mrs Hunter slipped her spectacles from around her neck onto her nose and read the opened letter. 'How delightful! And I suppose it would be such a shame to disappoint Lady Willaston. It was so kind of her to invite me and she was to have thrown a card rout in my honour.' Her eyes moved to Phoebe and they were filled with concern. 'What say you, my dear? Given what happened upon the moor, I would understand perfectly if you do not wish to travel to London.'

Phoebe barely heard the question. She was too busy staring at Hunter's hand leaning upon the crisp white tablecloth, at his long, square tipped fingers. Her heart began to race. She bit her lip and slowly raised her gaze to his.

Hunter's eyes glittered as green and intense as the emeralds in the silver wolf's-head ring that he wore.

'Phoebe?' Mrs Hunter prompted.

She drew her gaze away from Hunter's. 'London sounds delightful. It is exactly what we need at this moment in time.' She did not know how she managed to keep her voice so calm and level when everything of her emotions was in such chaos.

'I am so glad that you think so, my dear.' Mrs Hunter smiled and returned the letter to her son. 'When shall we leave?'

'As soon as possible,' said Hunter as he slipped the

letter into his pocket. 'Unless Miss Allardyce has any objection.'

'I have no objection whatsoever.' She tried to feign a smile, but could not do it. The relief was sour, tainted by deep sickening dread. In her ears she heard only the whisper of betrayal and in her heart felt a deep pulsating ache.

'In that case, come along, Phoebe, we shall leave Sebastian to his port and organise the maids to our packing.'

As she followed Mrs Hunter out of the dining room Phoebe could not help glancing back at Hunter. He was still watching her, his gaze intense. And Phoebe shivered at the prospect of all that lay ahead.

They travelled to London in Hunter's sleek black travelling coach, after Phoebe had visited the Tolbooth gaol to bid her papa farewell. Hunter himself insisted upon riding, despite all of his mother's protestations, and, although she worried about whether his arm was healed enough, Phoebe was glad. There was such a tension of feelings between them; she feared that, once they were enclosed within such a small space, his mother would be aware of it.

They broke the journey twice, staying in expensive and comfortable inns, Phoebe and Mrs Hunter sharing a room, Hunter in his own. And with every hour that passed, and every mile that took them closer to London, Phoebe felt as if she were travelling to some sort of inevitability that could not be stopped. Hunter treated her just as a gentleman should treat his mother's companion, nothing more, but when he drew near, when his glance met hers, her whole body flared its response and her heart glowed with love. And from the look in his eyes she knew that he felt it, too.

Every day her eyes scanned his fingers for the ring: she saw it only once more and then thereafter, when he removed his gloves, his hands were bare. And even if he were to wear it, there was only one way she could think of to glean it from him and she could not bear the thought of tricking him, of seducing him, of stealing from him. Soon they would be in London, and soon the Messenger would make contact. Phoebe tried not to think of what was coming.

The town house, in Grosvenor Street, held many memories for Hunter. The smart terraced house of golden sandstone had belonged to his father the last time Sebastian had stayed here, and now it belonged to Sebastian. The paintwork around the door and Palladian windows still appeared a fresh glossy black, the window panes sparkled and the steps were scrubbed and clean, just as if the house had not lain empty for almost a year. Even the door knocker had been replaced for their arrival by Trenton, Hunter's caretaker butler, and Mrs Trenton, his housekeeper-wife.

They had been in London for four days. Four days of shopping and excursions, routs and musicales, none of which had seen Hunter alone with Phoebe.

He stood in the empty echoing hallway. The black-and-white chequered marble floor gleamed a reflection of the crystal-and-obsidian-tiered chandelier that hung suspended from the high ceiling. To the right-hand side, close to the door that led into the drawing room, stood a circular table inlaid with mother of pearl and obsidian, and upon which was a silvered glass vase containing a huge bloom of white flowers. On the wall on the left, above the black chinoiserie chairs lined with their backs to the wallpaper, was a large elaborate gold-framed mirror. The décor of the house, in all rooms save for the study, was elegant, sophisticated and in stark contrast to the sturdy old comfort of Blackloch. The smell of the place filled his nostrils, Mrs Trenton's own beeswax polish mix and the echoes of his father and the years he had spent here.

He stood there in the silence, absorbing it all, letting the memories of last year and all that had been wash over him. There was still a sadness, but the terrible eroding guilt had lessened since the night of the thunderstorm with Phoebe. She believed in him. She did not blame him.

From the drawing room came the tinkling of women's laughter: his mother and her friends…and Phoebe. A vision of Phoebe played in his head. For all that they had not been alone, that was not due to Phoebe. She was no longer avoiding him. She had seen the ring. It was just a matter of time before she came to his room.

He lifted his hat, gloves and cane and went off to spend another afternoon at the home of his friend, Dominic Furneaux, the Duke of Arlesford.

'So let me get this straight. This Miss Allardyce has ignored rolls of bank notes and bags of sovereigns, your mother's diamonds and the priceless paintings hung in your drawing room to search exclusively for a ring.'

Hunter could see the way Arlesford was looking at him across the library. He glanced away so that his friend would glean nothing of the depth of his feelings over the matter.

'Most peculiar.' Arlesford frowned as he thought. 'And there is nothing in particular about this ring?' The Duke picked up the brandy decanter and poured a measure into each of two glasses, passing one to Hunter before sipping from the other himself. 'Aside from the fact it was your father's and thus has significance to you,' he added more gently.

'The ring is indeed precious to me, more so than you can imagine, but why it should be so to any other is a mystery. There is nothing exceptional about it apart from its unusual design. I have only seen its like once before, on a cane belonging to our favourite viscount.'

Arlesford's frown deepened.

'But quite what that means I do not know. Silver and chip emeralds are hardly worth a mint.' Hunter took the brandy with a murmur of thanks. He took a single sip and then set it down on the occasional table. 'And then there was the man she met with outside the gaol.'

'He might have been a lover, rather than an accomplice.' Arlesford arched an eyebrow. 'Or maybe even both.'

Hunter felt himself tense. The muscle flickered in his jaw. 'He was not her lover.'

'How can you be so sure?'

'Just a gut instinct,' he said, keeping his voice flat and without emotion so that Arlesford would not guess the truth.

'And the letter she recently received?'

'Whatever was written within it frightened her for all that she tried to hide it.'

'What are you thinking?' Arlesford sipped at his brandy.

'Intimidation.'

'Not that some collector with an eye for the unusual, perhaps even Linwood himself, has found himself a little thief willing to steal for him?'

'She is not like that.'

'She certainly has you on her side.' Arlesford smiled

in a suggestive way. 'Pretty little thing, is she? Captured your fancy?'

Hunter's eyes narrowed. He stopped pacing and came to stand directly before Arlesford in a warning stance. 'Have a care over how you speak of Miss Allardyce.'

'What aren't you telling me, Hunter?'

'There is nothing else you need to know.'

Arlesford's eyes were too perceptive as he looked down into Hunter's face. 'She is a thief and your mother's companion,' he said.

'My mother's companion maybe, but Phoebe is no thief.'

'Phoebe?' Arlesford arched an eyebrow.

'Damn it, Dominic,' snapped Hunter.

A knock sounded at the door and Arlesford's wife, Arabella, entered. She smiled a radiant smile at her husband, before speaking to Hunter.

'I thought I heard your voice, Sebastian.'

'Arabella.' Hunter bowed.

'So glad to see you again. Now, tell me, are you and your mother attending Lady Routledge's ball this evening?'

'We are.' He thought of Phoebe.

'How lovely. Please tell her I am so looking forward to seeing her again.'

'I will.' Hunter nodded. 'If you will excuse me, I must head back to Grosvenor Street.'

As Hunter made his way down the stone steps outside Arlesford House, the Duke and Duchess of Arlesford stood by the library window and watched him. Arabella leaned back against her husband as he wrapped his arms around her.

'He is more changed than I realised, Dominic. He seems a man with something pressing upon his mind.'

'Indeed he is, my love,' said the Duke. 'And from the looks of it, a deal more than he is willing to admit.'

At Lady Routledge's ball that evening Phoebe sat with Mrs Hunter and a group of her friends, two of whom were accompanied by their own companions. She was only half-listening to the chatter going on around her; she was too aware of Hunter leaning against a nearby Doric column, of the brooding expression upon his face and the way his gaze came too often to rest upon her face.

'Is that not so, Miss Allardyce?' Mrs Hunter asked.

'Indeed, yes, ma'am,' she answered as if she had been following the conversation most carefully. And when she slid a surreptitious glance across at Hunter again he was still watching her.

She turned her gaze away and looked longingly at the dance floor, where Hunter's friend the Duke of Arlesford was dancing with his wife. Arabella Furneaux, Arlesford's duchess, was by far the most beautiful woman in the whole ballroom. Tall and elegant, she wore her hair piled in a mass of golden shining curls high at the back of her head, several of which had escaped to trail artlessly around her perfect throat. The dove-grey silk dress overset with silver gossamer must have cost a small fortune if its cut and fit and richness of material were anything to judge by. Next to Arabella, Phoebe felt drab and old-fashioned in her old green-silk evening gown. But the duchess was also kind and warm and had included Phoebe completely in her conversations with Mrs Hunter. And when the dance was over, and Arlesford delivered her back to the seat she had taken beside Phoebe and Mrs Hunter, Phoebe saw Mrs Hunter glow with pride at her favour with a duchess. And soon the ladies were all of a-chatter again.

* * *

Across the ballroom behind the pillars, Hunter was standing beside Arlesford, talking to Bullford and feeling ashamed of his shoddy treatment of his old friend at their last meeting in Glasgow.

'Think nothing of it, old man,' Bullford waved away Hunter's apology. 'Just glad to see you are feeling better.'

Hunter nodded. 'You enjoyed your visit with Kelvin?' Over Bullford's shoulder he had a good view of Phoebe. Arabella was sitting by her side and the three ladies seemed deep in conversation.

'Grand to see the old boy again. Had a splendid time. Even if it was m'father that forced me to make the trip. Can't upset the old man.'

'Quite,' said Hunter curtly.

'Sorry, didn't mean to…' Bullford blushed. Hunter relaxed a bit, knowing that it was his own sensitivity and not Bullford that was causing the problem.

'I know, Bullford.'

'Damned good at putting my foot in it these days.'

Hunter shook his head. 'My fault, not yours.'

Bullford gave a nod and smiled in his usual good-natured way. 'Your mother in good health, Hunter?' Bullford turned to look across at Mrs Hunter.

'She is.' The three men's gazes moved across the room to where Mrs Hunter was sitting. But Hunter was not looking at his mother.

'Who is the pretty girl with Mrs H.?'

Hunter frowned. 'That is Miss Phoebe Allardyce, my mother's companion.'

'Looking at the dance floor as if she'd like to be up there. Mind if I ask her to dance, Hunter?'

Mind? Hunter felt a burst of fury just at the thought. He did not think that he could very well ask Phoebe to dance without raising a few eyebrows, notably those of his mother. But he would be damned if he'd see her being handled around the dance floor by some other man.

'She is here to accompany my mother, not to spend the evening dancing,' he said stiffly.

'You're dashed hard on the girl, Hunter. Mrs H. seems to have plenty of company at the minute, but naturally I would ask the lady's permission first before stealing her companion onto the floor.'

Arlesford drew Hunter a meaningful look.

Hunter remained stubbornly tight-lipped.

Arlesford trod on his toe.

'When you put it like that, Bullford...' Hunter said grudgingly.

'Knew you wouldn't be so unreasonable as to see the poor girl sat in a ballroom full of dancers and music the whole night, without so much as a chance to take a turn upon the floor for herself. Girls do so enjoy a dance. Should ask her up yourself, old man.'

Hunter resisted the urge to plant Bullford a facer right there and then, and had to stand and watch as Bullford made his way around the edge of the dance floor towards Phoebe.

'Damnable rake!' muttered Hunter. 'He need not think to get any of his ideas about her.'

'Bullford has cooled his heels much as you, Hunter. He is behaving himself these days. Besides, he is right; she has been looking at the dance floor as if she would care to take a spin upon it.'

Hunter clenched his jaw to stopper the reply he would have made.

Arlesford appeared oblivious. 'Linwood is here.'

Arlesford did not make one movement, yet Hunter felt the tension emanate from his friend just at the mention of the viscount's name. For all intents and purposes it appeared that Arlesford's gaze was fixed on Bullford handling Phoebe up onto the dance floor, but Hunter knew that his friend's attention was elsewhere.

'Left-hand corner, opposite side of the room,' said the duke quietly.

Hunter's eyes sought out Linwood and found him standing behind the chairs where his mother and sister were seated. 'He was with Bullford when I met him in Glasgow.'

'I did not know the two of them were on such good terms,' said Arlesford.

'I believe their fathers are old friends.'

'Then more pity Bullford.'

Hunter did not give a damn about Linwood right at this moment. He was staring at Phoebe and Bullford and wondering how he was going to endure the rest of the night.

By one o'clock in the morning Phoebe and Mrs Hunter were making their way down the stone steps outside Lady Routledge's house towards the carriage. Arlesford had called Hunter back into the hallway to say something to him.

For all of the tension between herself and Hunter, Phoebe had still enjoyed the evening. Not only had she made a new friend of Arlesford's duchess, Arabella, but she had actually danced three times; once with the Duke of Arlesford and twice with another of Hunter's friends, Lord Bullford. And for all that she had longed for it, Hunter had not asked her and she knew that he was right not to have done. Indeed, he had barely spoken a word to her all night, just watched her with that same intense brooding expression and more than a hint of anger in his eyes.

They were almost halfway down the steps when Phoebe's reticule slipped from her fingers. She turned to lift it, but someone else was there before her: a gentleman, dark-haired, olive-skinned and handsome.

'Your reticule, miss.' He handed it to her.

Phoebe's heart began to beat too fast. Her eyes met his that were black as the night that surrounded them.

He lingered for only the briefest of moments, then bowed and walked away into the night.

Mrs Hunter had almost reached the carriage, but Phoebe stood, staring after the gentleman, not at the lithe confident way that he moved, or even at the dark eyes as they glanced back at her.

'Come along, Phoebe, stop wool gathering, girl,' Mrs Hunter called.

Phoebe made her way towards her employer, but her mind was still filled with an image of the gentleman's walking cane—an ebony stick, mounted with a silver wolf's head handle in which she had seen the glow of two emerald eyes.

Chapter Fifteen

Mrs Hunter slept late the next day. And Hunter had taken Ajax out into Hyde Park for a gallop with Arlesford. Phoebe realized that this might be the opportunity she needed. She tried not to think about what it was she was doing, stealing from the man she loved, and concentrated on the technicalities of performing the act itself.

She broke her fast alone in her bedchamber with a tray of coffee and a bread roll spread with marmalade. When the maid came to remove the tray Phoebe waited until she heard the girl disappear down the servants' stairs, then crept out into the corridor. As she passed Mrs Hunter's room, the one through the wall from her own, she paused and listened, but from inside came only silence. Hunter's room was across on the other side of the main staircase. Phoebe made her way quietly towards it. She was just crossing the landing when, ahead of her, the door to Hunter's bedchamber opened and a maid carrying an armful of bed linen appeared. Through the open door Phoebe could see another maid still within the room.

'Beggin' your pardon, ma'am.' The maid bobbed a

curtsy and hurried away with her load, towards the servants' stairs at the far end of the corridor.

'Good morning, Betsy.' Phoebe forced a smile and made her way down the main staircase as if that had been where she was headed all along. She went into the drawing room to worry and to wait and to wonder how, amidst this carousel of balls and routs and visits, she could keep on pretending that everything was normal.

Only twelve hours later and Phoebe was sitting by Mrs Hunter's side at Lady Willaston's card party. The ladies were all playing in one room and the gentlemen in another. Phoebe partnered Mrs Hunter, and played against Arabella and Mrs Forbes, and then the forthright Lady Misbourne who bossed her daughter, the Honourable Miss Winslow, terribly, and who was exceptionally skilled at the game, much to Mrs Hunter's annoyance. Phoebe was relieved the game was over and Mrs Hunter, having realised that if she was to progress anywhere in the evening she would require a partner more talented in the whist stakes than Phoebe, had allied herself with Mrs Dobson. Phoebe watched for a while, then wandered off to the ladies' withdrawing room to powder her nose. She made her way back, thinking of the wretched wolf's-head ring, and wondering if she dared feign a headache to return to the town house in Grosvenor Street and search Sebastian's bedchamber. As she rounded the corner just past the stairs, heading into the foyer between the two card rooms, she walked right into a gentleman.

His hands closed around her arms, steadying her, but drew back as soon as he knew that she would not stumble.

'I beg your pardon, miss.'

She looked up into the dark eyes of the gentleman who had returned her reticule the previous evening.

'Miss Allardyce, I believe.'

'I...' Her gaze dropped to the walking cane in his right hand, to its silver wolf's-head embedded with emerald chips, before returning once more to that dark, handsome face. And her heart was pounding and she felt the cold hand of fear touch to her blood. 'We have not been introduced, sir,' she said primly and made to walk on.

But he shifted his stance ever so slightly to block her path. 'Then permit me to introduce myself. I am Linwood. You played cards with my mother and sister earlier this evening, I believe—Lady Misbourne and Miss Winslow.'

'They are most talented players,' she said carefully and glanced again at his walking cane, which was identical in every detail to the ring that she had seen upon Hunter's finger. It could be no coincidence. If the wolf's-head symbol held some significance for him, it might well explain why a man would go to such lengths to possess the ring.

She waited for the question that would follow, tried to frame her explanation within her mind as to why she did not have the ring in her possession.

'They are much practiced. It is my mother's favourite pastime.'

She gave a nod and looked away. Knowing the power that this man held over her father made her feel sick to her stomach and desperately afraid.

'Miss Allardyce?' He leaned closer, a folly of concern across his face.

She stepped back to keep a distance between them and felt her spine bump against the plaster of Lady Willaston's wall.

'You appear to be a little unwell, Miss Allardyce. Perhaps I should fetch Mrs Hunter to you.' He turned away to leave.

'Please do not, sir,' she said quickly and placed a hand upon his arm to stop him. 'I am quite well, I assure you.' She hesitated, 'And able to answer any questions you may wish to ask of me...'

He shook his head and took her hand from his sleeve, holding it before him as if he would kiss it. 'I fear you are under a misapprehension as to—'

'What the hell do you think you are playing at, Linwood?' Hunter's low growl interrupted whatever the viscount had been about to say.

Phoebe jumped at Sebastian's sudden appearance.

'Hunter,' Linwood inclined his head '...always a pleasure to see you.' But the smile on his face was one of sarcasm. 'Thought you would be busy keeping Arlesford company.' Linwood's face was filled with such a burning contempt that Phoebe felt shocked to see it.

'Take your hands off her.' Sebastian spoke quietly, slowly, every word controlled, but it did not disguise the menace of the threat that lay beneath that harsh control. His skin was white as marble beside the dark looks of the viscount, his eyes a clear cold green...and deadly.

Linwood released her hand and said silkily, 'I had no idea you had such an interest in Miss Allardyce.'

Sebastian stepped right up to Linwood until they were too close. As he towered over the slighter man he stared down into Linwood's face. 'Miss Allardyce is my mother's companion and, as such, I consider any insult dealt her an insult against my family. Do not think to start your games with me or mine.'

The word 'mine' seemed to hang in the air. Linwood's gaze shifted to Phoebe's face and she felt herself blush before he turned back to Sebastian.

Linwood smiled a dark mocking smile. 'Is it true?' he asked. 'What they say about you and your father's death?'

There was a roaring silence.

She saw the tiny telltale flicker in Sebastian's jaw, saw the sudden change in his eyes.

'Mr Hunter.' She stepped quickly between Sebastian and Linwood. And then more softly, 'Sebastian.' His whole body hummed with violence. She knew she had to stop him before it was too late. She laid her hand against Sebastian's lapel. 'Please…do not do this, I beg of you.'

And then Arlesford was there beside Sebastian.

'Miss Allardyce.' Linwood bowed at her as if they had just conducted a civilised and polite conversation.

Bullford appeared at the other side and murmured something to both Sebastian and Arlesford so that the three men walked off into the Marquis of Willaston's library.

Phoebe glanced up to find Mrs Hunter standing not ten feet away in the doorway of the ladies' card-playing room, and from her pale shaken face she knew that the lady had heard Viscount Linwood's question.

'I seem to have developed something of a headache. I wonder if you would mind, Mrs Hunter, if we were to leave a little early this evening.'

'Not at all, my dear,' said Mrs Hunter, and she allowed Phoebe to lead her away in the direction of the front door. Phoebe did not look back towards the library.

It was not surprising that Mrs Hunter slept late the next morning. And, according to Trenton, Sebastian had gone out, although the hour of the morning was so early that Phoebe rather suspected, perhaps, that that meant he had not come back to the house at all. Knowing how Sebastian blamed himself for his father's death Phoebe could only guess at just how very deeply Linwood's words must have cut. She felt his pain, and felt a rage that Linwood could deal such an underhand barb.

Supposing he had gone after Lord Linwood. Supposing the two of them had fought, or, worse still, duelled. Sebastian might at this very minute be lying wounded on a common. He might even be dead. Phoebe pressed her palm to her mouth, trying to quell the unbearable thought. And her heart was swollen and aching, for she knew that she loved him. Utterly. Completely.

She paced the drawing room, knowing she would not rest until she was certain Sebastian was safe. And she thought of his veiled claim on her. *Do not start your games with me or mine.* Of course people would expect him to have an interest in the reputation of his mother's companion—should she lose it Mrs Hunter would be affected. But Phoebe knew there was so much more to it than that. Linwood guessed it, too, if that look upon his face had been anything to go by. And she worried all the more about the ring and why he had not asked her for it, and what that might mean for her papa.

She paced and she worried—about the ring, and her papa, and Sebastian. The thoughts were running round and round, until she thought her head might explode.

She could not settle to her needlework. She read the same page of her book three times before abandoning it upon the sofa and toyed with the jet-and-ivory carved chess pieces neatly lined up upon their board in the corner, before abandoning them to stand by the window and look out on to the street. The road was quiet; only one carriage passed and a milkmaid carrying her wooden churns across her shoulders. Phoebe raised her eyes to the sky, the same white-blue sky that Blackloch sat beneath.

A flock of starlings flew by and she thought of the great black crows that cawed and the golden eagles that soared over the moor. She closed her eyes and in her mind she could see that wind-ravaged land with its bleak hills and its hardy sheep and the black curve of the narrow road that snaked across it. Standing there in the drawing room of the London town house, Phoebe thought she could smell the clear fresh scent of the wind and the sweetness of the heather and the tangy pungent peat smoke that curled from the farmstead chimneys. The storm of thoughts calmed to settle as still and cool as the deep dark water of the Black Loch itself.

She could not steal from Hunter. She loved him. And she was sure that he harboured some measure of affection towards her. There was no right or wrong answer. No simple black and white, only a world washed in tones of grey. But now that she had made the decision Phoebe felt strangely calm. She sat down upon the sofa, picked up her embroidery and settled back to wait for Hunter's return.

In the morning room of Arlesford House Hunter rubbed at his head and accepted the coffee that Dominic offered. The two men sat alone. The servants had been dismissed and Arabella had not yet woken.

'I should have called him out.'

'Maybe,' said Arlesford. 'Lord knows the bastard deserves it. But you have more than your own reputation to consider in this, Hunter.'

'My mother does not remain unaffected by the insult dealt.' Hunter sipped at the coffee and tried to shake the brandy-induced ache from his head.

'I was not referring to your mother.'

Hunter glanced up from his cup.

'Miss Allardyce…' said Arlesford.

'Miss Allardyce has no bearing on this.'

'On the contrary, Hunter, your mother's companion may have prevented you and Linwood brawling in possibly the worst of places, but at some cost to her own reputation.'

Hunter thought of Phoebe's hand in Linwood's and frowned, making the pain ache all the more in his head. 'She did nothing untoward.'

'Hunter, London does not know what Linwood did to Arabella. They do not understand why you and I should despise him so. Last night they saw only you cutting in on his conversation with Miss Allardyce. She called you by your given name, Hunter, and restrained you in a way that suggested a degree of familiarity between the two of you.'

Hunter winced. 'I would not have her reputation sullied.'

'Even though she would thieve from you?'

Hunter said nothing, but his jaw was clenched and stubborn.

'Is she your mistress?'

'Certainly not! Hell's teeth, Dominic, I would not... I am not... Not any more!'

'Then what is between the two of you?'

Hunter shook his head as if to deny the question.

'Hell, Sebastian, any fool with eyes in his head can see the way you look at each other. You love her.'

Hunter dropped his head into his hands.

'You love a woman who has lied to both you and your mother, who has abused her position and is intent upon stealing from you,' said Arlesford.

'Phoebe Allardyce is courageous and warm of heart. She is compassionate and kind.' Hunter did not say that she had suffered as he had suffered, that she understood him, that she forgave him. 'I cannot bear that she should suffer, Dominic. I would take her every hurt upon myself to free her from it. My mind longs for her. My heart aches for her. And, yes, my body wants her, all of her, in every way possible. Knowing that she lied, knowing that she would steal the ring—it makes no difference to any of it. If that is love, then I am guilty of it.'

Arlesford gave a gruff reassuring pat against Hunter's shoulder. Then the two friends sat in silence for a few minutes.

'What do you mean to do about it?'

'I mean to discover why she is trying to steal the ring.'

'And the rest of it?'

'One step at a time, my friend.'

Phoebe was alone in the drawing room when Hunter returned to Grosvenor Street. He dismissed Trenton and closed the door behind him.

She came to her feet, hurried to stand before him, her eyes scanning his body before rising to search his face. 'You are unhurt?'

'Quite unhurt. Why would you think otherwise?'

'Last night with Lord Linwood, and then it seemed this morning that you had not come home and I thought… I have been so filled with worry that he might…that you would be…'

And he knew exactly what she thought and her concern touched his heart. He took her hands in his. 'Phoebe.' He stroked a hand to her cheek. 'I stayed the night at Arlesford House. I was angry after my encounter with Linwood and wished to cool my temper before returning here. I am sorry, I did not think you would be worried about me.'

She glanced away, embarrassed.

'You have my gratitude for preventing me from

brawling with Linwood last night. I dread to think what it would have descended into had you not acted so promptly.'

She gave a little nod.

'When I saw you with Linwood...you were white as a sheet. What did he say to you to frighten you so?' His thumbs moved over the backs of her hands where he held her.

She shook her head. 'Not what I thought he would say. In truth, I do not even know if—' Then she stopped herself, and looked up into his eyes. 'Sebastian, there is a matter on which I would like to seek your help, but...' She bit at her lip.

'Phoebe, you must know that you can come to me with anything, anything at all, and I will do all within my power to help you.'

'Even if it is something you do not like or a matter that is most dishonourable?'

'I will help you, Phoebe. I give you my most solemn word.'

She nodded and moved her hands within his. 'I pray you can understand the difficulty of the position I find myself in. I cannot do as they ask, yet nor can I not do it.'

From the hallway came the sound of Mrs Hunter's voice quizzing Trenton, then her footsteps treading towards the drawing room.

Phoebe glanced nervously at the door. A furrow of worry marred her brow.

Hunter kissed the furrow away. 'Meet me here in the drawing room, at eight o'clock tomorrow morning. We will speak then.'

She nodded and hurried back to the sofa to pick up her embroidery. By the time his mother entered the room,

Phoebe was calmly stitching and Hunter was standing braced by the window, watching the world go by.

And as to the events of the previous evening, his mother said not one word.

Phoebe and Mrs Hunter spent the afternoon shopping, while Sebastian went to his club to meet with Arlesford and Bullford, only returning to Grosvenor Street at half past four.

'I am going for a nap, Phoebe, and I recommend that you do likewise. Remember that we have the theatre at seven.'

Phoebe gave a nod.

Then Mrs Hunter spoke to the butler hovering discreetly in the background. 'Trenton, has m'son returned yet?'

'He has not, madam.'

Then back to Phoebe. 'I do hope he remembers that he is supposed to be accompanying us.'

'I am sure that Mr Hunter will return in time.'

'We do have to make a stand after last night.'

Phoebe nodded.

'And if we see Lord Linwood tonight, Phoebe, you had best hold me back as well.' Mrs Hunter smiled and then retired to her bedchamber, leaving Phoebe alone in the drawing room.

She had only been sewing for a few minutes when a knock sounded on the drawing room door and Trenton, appeared. 'A message for you, Miss Allardyce.' He handed her the sealed note. 'Delivered by hand, miss— the lad did not wait for a reply.'

She recognised the carefully formed handwriting in which her name upon the letter's front had been written and a wave of nausea swept through her. She dismissed the butler before sliding a finger along the edge of the paper to break the sealing wax. On the note within the instructions were concise:

Head towards Davies Street on foot immediately. Come alone. Tell no one. Bring what is required.

There was no signature, but Phoebe did not need one to know who the letter was from—the Messenger.

She shivered and moved quickly to the window, knowing that whoever had sent this must be watching the house to know that she was alone and able to leave this house at this moment. A gentleman rode past on his horse. A cart carrying coal rumbled over the cobbles and a carriage was almost out of sight in the opposite direction. An old man hobbled along the pavement and a couple of urchins were cheeking the coachman of the chaise waiting outside the house three doors down. No sign of the Messenger... or of Lord Linwood.

She moved away again, folding the letter into the pocket of her new fawn day dress. A chill seemed to touch to her blood and a shadow cloud over all of her hopes. She shivered again and hurried to fetch her bonnet.

'Shall you be requiring the carriage, miss?' enquired Trenton as she stood in the hall with her bonnet tied in place.

'No, thank you, Mr Trenton.' Phoebe fitted the gloves onto her fingers. 'If Mrs Hunter should enquire, please tell her that I have gone for a short walk. It is such a fine day.' She smiled, but the smile felt stiff upon her lips and more like a grimace. She did not have the ring. Hunter was gone from home. And she dare not ignore the summons.

Chapter Sixteen

She had been walking in the direction of Davies Street for only some five minutes when the black closed carriage stopped beside her. The door opened and the Messenger jumped down, pulling the door shut again behind him.

'Miss Allardyce, we meet again, just as I promised.'

'Sir.' She looked at him and felt fear and that same overwhelming sense of dislike and anger.

He waved his hand towards the coach. 'Your carriage awaits, miss.'

'I am not getting in there with you. We may discuss what you will out here just as well.'

'May be, miss, but there's someone who wants to meet you.'

A vision of Lord Linwood appeared in her mind.

The Messenger added, 'I must insist, Miss Allardyce. Or maybe you've forgotten all about your pa since you've been down here in fair old London town?'

Phoebe met the Messenger's sly gaze squarely. 'The carriage it is then, sir.'

He opened the door, kicked down the step and bundled

her inside before following. The door slammed shut and, before her eyes could adjust to the dim light of the interior, a dark hood was thrust over her head. She fought to free herself, but rough hands clasped hers, wrenching them behind her back and holding her tight.

'Unhand me, you villain!' she demanded, the hood muffling her words.

'Calm yourself, Miss Allardyce. I have a mind to speak with you without revealing my identity, that is all.' The voice, which came from the seat directly opposite, was not that of Lord Linwood. It sounded like that of an older gentleman and there was something vaguely familiar about it, although she could not place it.

The Messenger's grip tightened unbearably and Phoebe ceased her struggles.

'That is better.' The gentleman took a breath. 'Now, let us not prevaricate, Miss Allardyce. Do you have the ring?'

'I…' Her stomach clenched at the thought of revealing the truth to this man. She knew he must be very powerful. She knew just what he could do to her father. 'It is not yet in my possession.' The hood was a thick heavy black material that smelled faintly of sweet tobacco and sandalwood. It not only rendered her effectively blind, but made it hot and difficult to breathe.

'Not yet, you say?' the gentleman said. 'And yet you have had ample time in which to recover it, Miss Allardyce. Perhaps you do not have so much care for your father as we had thought?'

'I have every care for my father, but it has been difficult. At first I could not find the ring at Blackloch Hall—'

'At first, implies that you have now discovered its location.'

'I…' To admit it felt like a betrayal of Hunter.

'Miss Allardyce.' The man's voice was harsh with warning.

'The ring is in Mr Hunter's possession.'

'You have seen it?'

'I have, sir.'

'Where precisely, Miss Allardyce?'

'It was upon Mr Hunter's finger.'

'He wore it?' The man sounded shocked.

'He did, sir.'

There was a small cogitative silence.

'Does he have it with him here in London?'

Phoebe was loathe to tell them.

The silence within the carriage seemed very loud.

'Your father is in danger and yet still you hesitate to co-operate.'

'Sir, I am co-operating fully. Have I not searched every last room in Blackloch Hall for you? I...I am not certain as to the ring's precise whereabouts since we have come to London.'

Another loaded silence stretched between them, in which Phoebe could only hear the sound of her own breath loud within the hood.

'I have heard a whisper that you harbour tender feelings for Hunter,' he said at last.

'No.'

'And from what I saw of Hunter's little display last night he is certainly not indifferent to you.'

'You are wrong, sir.'

'Having an affair with his mother's companion while pretending to us all that he has reformed his rakish tendencies after a year spent brooding upon his lonely moor.'

'Such scurrilous accusations are false! There is nothing between Mr Hunter and myself.'

The man laughed at her protestations. 'That is why

you do not have the ring, is it not, Miss Allardyce? You cannot bear to steal from him.'

'No!' she lied. 'I have already told you the reason I do not yet have it.'

'That was no doubt true at first, before Hunter seduced you.'

'He did not seduce me, sir. I will not hear you say it of him.'

The man let another silence open up so that Phoebe did not know whether he believed what she said or not. The seconds stretched to minutes.

'If you have a notion to confide in Hunter, or anyone else for that matter, Miss Allardyce, I will arrange for him to follow the same fate as your father.'

'You would not dare to threaten him.'

'Oh, I assure you, Miss Allardyce, we will do more than threaten. We are very powerful. There is no one who can hide from us.'

'Who are you?' she whispered.

'No one that a young lady should concern herself with.'

'Do not hurt him. I have told him nothing.'

'Then let us keep it that way. I will know if you tell him. Nothing escapes me, Miss Allardyce. Believe me when I tell you I have eyes and ears everywhere.' She could hear the smile in his voice. 'And so now to the ring once more, my dear. My patience wears thin with the wait. I require that the matter be concluded by the end of this week.'

'Impossible, sir,' Phoebe protested.

'If the ring is not within your possession by then, Miss Allardyce, I shall make arrangements for Hunter to be relieved of it by violent means. And, of course, then there is the little matter of your papa to be dealt with… Both their lives will be extinguished.'

'No! I beg of you, sir!'

'The end of the week, Miss Allardyce. Not a day longer. When you have secured it, wear this red shawl and stand by a front window of Hunter's town house. We will then send you instructions of how to proceed.' He passed her a small thin red shawl. 'Go now, my…associate…will assist you out of the carriage.'

She heard the slide of a window. 'All clear, gov,' said the Messenger and then he manhandled her to what she presumed must be the door, standing behind her and pulling the hood from her head as he opened the door and tipped her out onto the footpath. The door slammed and the carriage pulled away at a brisk pace, leaving Phoebe blinking in the sudden strong sunlight.

Hunter had arrived in the drawing room of his town house in Grosvenor Street at five minutes before eight the next morning. The curtains were open and the early autumn sunlight filled the room. He was still waiting at nine o'clock when he enquired of Trenton as to his mother and Miss Allardyce, and was told they were both not yet risen for the day. He took Ajax for a gallop in Hyde Park, and returned two hours later to find both ladies in the drawing room entertaining Lady Chilcotte and her daughters. He had endured an hour of Lady Chilcotte thrusting her eldest daughter beneath his nose in far too obvious a manner, but Phoebe did not once meet his eye.

After luncheon, when his mother had decided to go shopping, again, Hunter accompanied them, carrying parcels once the footman's arms became full. And again Phoebe would not meet his eye, even when she had perforce to take his hand when he assisted the ladies into and out of the coach. At the fashionable hour of five o'clock his mother expressed a desire to take a drive in Hyde

Park. And again Hunter accompanied them. And still everything of Phoebe was closed against him, almost as if their conversation of the previous day had never occurred, so that he grew increasingly convinced that something had happened between then and now, something to make her change her mind.

At dinner in the town house Hunter gave up waiting and addressed her directly.

'You seem a little preoccupied today, Miss Allardyce. Is all well with you?'

'Everything is fine, thank you, sir,' she answered and it seemed she had to force herself to look at him. Her eyes were dark and troubled, her face pale with a haunted expression she could not quite hide. Hunter resolved to speak to Trenton to discover if Miss Allardyce had received any new letters.

'Then you will be accompanying my mother to Arlesford's ball tonight?'

'I…um…' She hesitated. 'I do have something of a headache.'

'A headache, Phoebe?' asked his mother.

'Perhaps I would be better to stay at home tonight— that is, if you could manage without me tonight, ma'am.' Phoebe looked at his mother and not once at him. But Hunter knew exactly what she was doing. She knew this was the ball to which both his mother and himself had been especially invited. She wanted to be alone in the town house, and Hunter had a good idea as to the reason.

'How very peculiar,' he said. 'I feel the stirrings of an ache in my own head.' Hunter touched a hand to his forehead. 'Perhaps it is a contagious headache, Miss Allardyce.'

'Well, I cannot very well go alone,' said his mother,

'and if both of you are struck down with it, perhaps it is only a matter of time before I, too, am likewise affected. And I was so looking forward to the night. I have my new grey-silk ball gown especially for the occasion.'

'Now, ma'am, we cannot have that,' said Phoebe quickly. 'If you will excuse me, I will go and lie down for half an hour and I am sure that will help diminish the headache.'

'Very well, Phoebe,' said his mother.

Phoebe sat by Mrs Hunter's side at the Duke of Arlesford's ball and tried not to look at Hunter. She had successfully eluded him the whole day through, but the strain of it had frayed her nerves and she was feeling tense and miserable. Her eyes roved through the throng of people, remembering the man in the carriage's words that he had eyes and ears everywhere. Was the man here himself, watching her and Hunter even now?

On the other side of the ballroom she saw Emma Northcote, but Emma's eyes moved to where Hunter was standing behind Phoebe's chair and when she looked at Phoebe again she gave a small shake of her head as if to tell her that there could be no friendship while Phoebe was allied with the Hunters. Emma turned her attention back to her mother. Phoebe glanced round and saw that Hunter had seen the interaction between Emma and herself.

He waited until his mother was fully engaged in conversation before leaning forwards and saying quietly, 'Phoebe—'

'Ah, there you are Hunter, old man, and Miss Allardyce, too.' She was mercifully saved by Lord Bullford's interruption. Hunter shot his friend a look of irritation. And then, after speaking to Mrs Hunter, Lord Bullford had her up on the dance floor for the next two dances, and by the time he returned her to her seat Hunter was over talking to Arlesford.

'You are sure about this?' Arlesford asked.

Hunter nodded. 'I know it is a big favour to ask of you, but it is the only way that I can see of getting her alone.'

'Very well,' Arlesford gave a nod. 'Only do not cause a scandal at Arabella's ball.'

'I will guard against it most carefully. Thank you, Dominic. You know I would not ask were it not important.'

'I am well aware of the importance of Miss Allardyce to you.'

Hunter turned to leave.

'Sebastian,' his friend said softly.

Hunter glanced back.

'Good luck.'

Hunter gave a grave nod, then made his way nonchalantly from the ballroom.

Phoebe was making her way back from the ladies' withdrawing room as the Duke's footman approached her.

'Miss Allardyce?'

'Yes?'

She saw the letter as he slipped it from his pocket and her heart began to race. She thought of the Messenger and his master in the carriage. 'I was asked to deliver this note to you, miss.' He slipped it to her surreptitiously and, with a bow, was gone.

She hid it in her pocket and headed a little farther up the corridor, away from the withdrawing room and ballroom, before ducking in to an alcove to read it. The hand in which her name was written was none that she recognised. It was not in the careful font of the Messenger, but the wax seal had been smudged just like those on his notes. Nor was it in the strong black spikes of Hunter's writing. She broke the seal and opened out the letter to find one short message written in the centre of the paper:

Come alone to the Duke's rose conservatory. There have been further developments since yesterday.

There could only be one person who would write such a message. He was here, watching her. She crumpled the paper and pressed a hand to her head. The end of the week, he had said. There were still two more days to go. What could possibly have happened? She drew a deep breath and smoothed the letter out before folding it neatly and placing it in her pocket. Then she braced her shoulders and went to find Arlesford's rose conservatory.

The footman led her down an unlit narrow corridor lined its length with closed mahogany doors. The man ignored every door and kept on walking. The farther they walked from the ballroom the darker it became. Darker and darker until Phoebe had to strain her eyes to see what was before them.

Phoebe knocked once upon the door and then she pushed it slowly open to reveal a room illuminated by soft silver moonlight. The sweet perfume of roses seeped from within. She stepped inside.

There was no messenger waiting to pounce and slip a hood over her head this time. Indeed, on first impressions the room seemed empty. Three sides of the conservatory and the roof were part constructed from glass. The silver moonlight flooded through the wall of windows to light the collection of beautiful blooms housed within. The perfume of the roses was more intense in here; it seemed heady and intoxicating. She walked into the centre of the room. There was no one…and then she heard the door close behind her and her heart stuttered as she turned to face the villain once more. It was not the Messenger who was standing there leaning back against the door, but Sebastian.

'You?' The moonlight revealed him in full.

'Who were you expecting, Phoebe?'

'I…' She shook her head. 'I have to go. I cannot leave Mrs Hunter waiting.'

'Not yet, Phoebe.' He walked slowly towards her.

Her eyes measured the distance to the door, but he seemed to take up all the space and she knew she would not make it past him without capture.

'You did not keep the meeting we had arranged for this morning.'

'I…' The music floated through from the ballroom, faint but still audible. 'I could not.'

'And all day you have avoided me most studiously.'

'You are mistaken.'

'I am sure that I am not.'

She swallowed hard and her heart was thudding so loud she was sure Sebastian must hear it in the quietness of the room.

'Yesterday you asked for my help.'

'The matter has resolved. I have no need of your help.'

'If it had, you would have simply told me such. What changed between our last meeting and this morning?'

'Nothing changed.'

'Save the letter you received.'

'I received no letter.'

'Hand-delivered by an urchin paid a copper to do so, or so Trenton informs me.'

'Oh, *that* letter.' She wetted her suddenly dry lips. 'I had quite forgotten about it.'

'Who was its sender, Phoebe?'

'Sir!' she exclaimed pretending to be shocked.

'Phoebe,' and his voice was something of a growl.

'A…friend.'

'The same friend whom you left almost immediately to meet.'

'I met with no one. I went for a walk, that is all.'

'In the evening and alone?' he persisted.

'It was not so late.'

'Late enough that when you returned some half an hour later your hair was in disarray.'

'Trenton exaggerates. The wind coupled with the vigour of my walking may have loosened a few of my pins.'

'Who is he, Phoebe?'

'I do not know what you are talking about.'

'The man you met last night.'

'I told you, I met no one.' She set a determined look upon her face and tried to walk right past him. 'If you will excuse me, I must attend to Mrs Hunter. She will be wondering where I have got to.' But he caught her arm and pulled her to him.

'Why will you not trust me, Phoebe?' he whispered and the underlying pain in his voice echoed that in her heart.

'I trust you, Sebastian. You must know that.' She stared up into his eyes.

'Then tell me what is going on.'

She glanced away in despair. 'I cannot.'

'Cannot or will not?' he demanded.

She looked up at him, took his face between her hands. 'Sebastian, I trust you with my very life, truly I do. But this matter of which we speak, this is the one thing I cannot tell. Please believe me, were there any other way...'

'You do not have to do this, Phoebe. I can help you. I can keep you safe, if that is what you fear.'

She dropped her hands and tried to turn away, knowing the irony of the situation. 'This has nothing to do with my safety.'

But he would not let her go. 'Who are you protecting?'

You, she wanted to cry. *My papa.* But she said nothing, just shook her head.

'Phoebe.' His fingers stroked soothingly against her cheek. 'Do you not know I would lay down my life for you?'

She turned her head to kiss the tips of his fingers. 'And I, for you.'

'But still you will not tell me?'

She shook her head sadly. 'Forgive me, Sebastian,' she whispered and reached up to touch her lips briefly against his.

'Phoebe...' She could hear the torture in his voice.

They stared into one another's eyes. And when his mouth moved slowly to hers she kissed him with all the love and all the tenderness that was in her heart. Telling him with her actions what she could not tell him in words. She threaded her hands through his hair, pulling him closer, pressing herself to him, needing his strength, needing his passion.

She shivered in delight as his hands swept over her body, stroking over the swell of her hips, her buttocks, up over her ribcage. Their bodies clung together. They breathed the same breath. They kissed until she no longer knew where she ended and he began. And Phoebe knew she would never love anyone the way she loved Hunter.

A knock sounded. By the time the door opened, Hunter had thrust Phoebe behind him and turned to face the door.

'So sorry to intrude, old man.' Lord Bullford was glancing away in obvious embarrassment. 'Came to warn you that Mrs H. has noticed her companion is missing.' He cleared his throat several times and did not look once in Phoebe's direction.

Hunter scowled at his friend, but his words when uttered were civil enough. 'Thank you, Bullford.'

Lord Bullford disappeared into the darkness of the corridor, his footsteps fading to merge with the low lilt of the music.

'I must go,' she said.

Hunter nodded. 'I will follow in a while so it is not apparent we have been together.'

She walked away and left him, to follow down the dark corridor all the way back to the ballroom.

The morning after the ball Phoebe and Mrs Hunter sat in the morning room, drinking coffee and eating toast. Sebastian had not yet emerged from his bedchamber.

'And how is your head this morning, Phoebe?' enquired Mrs Hunter.

'Much recovered, thank you, ma'am.' Phoebe sipped at her coffee and ignored the slice of toast that lay on her plate.

'You should have told me you were taken unwell with it last night. I was quite worried when you disappeared for such a while.'

'I am sorry to have worried you. I thought only to step away from the heat and bright lights and music for a while.'

'Well, as long as you are recovered now.'

'Completely,' said Phoebe. She drank some more

coffee to try to dispel the thick blanket of fatigue that seemed to cloak her brain this morning. She had slept little. All the thoughts in her head were of Sebastian and her papa, of the Messenger and the gentleman in the carriage. And the words that kept running through her head were Sebastian's: *Do you not know I would lay down my life for you.*

'I plan a day of rest and recovery today, so that we will be fresh for tomorrow. I thought an afternoon visit to Mrs Stanebridge, then an early night,' said Mrs Hunter.

'A good idea, ma'am.' Yet, in truth, Phoebe knew that she could settle to nothing. Her nerves felt frayed, her mind in turmoil; her body ached for a sleep that would not come no matter how long she lay upon a bed. Time was running out. Phoebe had only one more day to steal the ring.

Hunter did not leave the house, yet he stayed away from Phoebe and his mother, seeking instead the comfort of his father's library. Trenton had been given instructions to deliver any letters that might arrive addressed to Miss Allardyce to Hunter himself. And when the ladies went visiting in the afternoon, he sent two footmen to follow discreetly to guard their safety. He stared out onto the London street that was so different from his moor and he waited for the day to pass and the night to come.

He sensed the flare of emotion in Phoebe when she saw him enter the drawing room after the ladies' return, but she hid it well. Her attention stayed fixed on his mother and the stories she relayed of their afternoon at Mrs Stanebridge's. She smiled in all the right places, made the right agreements and nodded frequently, yet beneath the façade of normality there was such an air of tension about her that he did not know how his mother could fail to notice it.

'I am having dinner with Fallingham tonight and will probably stay there overnight.'

His mother gave a nod. 'But you will be back tomorrow to take Miss Allardyce and me to Colonel and Mrs Morely's as you promised?'

'Of course.' Hunter smiled, then toyed with the wolf's-head ring, twisting it in small rotations around his finger in an abstract manner.

His mother did not miss the movement. She peered across at his hand. 'Is that your father's ring you are wearing?'

He glanced down at the ring, and the wolf's eyes stared back up at him. 'It is. I had forgotten that I was wearing it,' he lied. He rang the bell, then twisted the ring from his finger and held it upon the flat of his palm for a moment.

'I never did like it,' said his mother, 'but Edward would not be without it.'

When Trenton arrived Hunter handed him the ring. 'Please see that it is placed in the jewel casket in my bedchamber.'

'Very good, sir.'

'I will see you tomorrow, Mother.' He gave her a small bow and then turned to Phoebe, who was sitting as still and pale as a statue, her eyes trained on the ring. 'Miss Allardyce.' Her eyes moved to meet his, and there was such a look in them that Hunter's resolve almost broke— relief, disbelief, sorrow and guilt.

'Mr Hunter,' she said softly and gave him a curtsy.

Chapter Seventeen

By midnight the last of the servants had retired for the night. Mrs Hunter had long since been abed and Phoebe was standing fully dressed in her faded blue muslin by the window of the guest bedchamber. The night sky was clear, the moon waning, shrinking towards the crescent it would soon become, and the street lamps still burned, their orange glow lighting the darkness. The opportunity for which she had prayed and hoped and waited all of these weeks past was finally here. And the moment was bittersweet. She both dreaded and longed to hold the ring in her hand, to slip it into her pocket and walk away. Tomorrow she would wear the red shawl by the window and await the Messenger's instructions. And finally she would give him the ring. It would be done. She would be a thief and a traitor, and Sebastian and her papa would be safe.

She knew she could not stay as Mrs Hunter's companion after that, not when she had abused her trust, and not with all that lay between her and Sebastian. To face him knowing what she had done would be a torture she did not think she could bear. She would give notice, travel back to Glasgow, find some other way to survive. She had her health. She was fit and strong and not afraid to work, even as a maid if needs be.

With trembling fingers she struck the tinderbox and lit her candle, then quietly made her way to Sebastian's bedchamber.

The curtains had been closed so the room was in darkness. Her heart was beating in a fast thudding fury as the door clicked shut behind her. The room still held Sebastian's scent, his cologne and soap and the smell of the man himself. She stopped where she was, allowed herself to breathe in that familiar scent and felt her heart and her body tingle in response. She bit her lip as the sensations washed over her, and she heard again the whisper of his voice: *Do you not know I would lay down my life for you?* She forced herself to the task. Holding the candle aloft, she surveyed the dim shadowed room by its tiny flickering light.

It was not so large a room, indeed barely larger than the guest room in which she was ensconced and very much smaller than the lady's room in which Mrs Hunter now slept. She wondered why Sebastian had not taken the room designated for the master of the house. But maybe this had been his room as a boy, and maybe there were too many associations with the room that had been his father's. On the right-hand side of the room a large four-poster bed faced out from the wall. Even in the candlelight she could see the undisturbed bedding was a deep rich claret to match the curtains that covered the window. She let her gaze linger a moment there, imagining Hunter's dark head against the pillow, and his body naked beneath the sheets. She felt her heart swell with love for him.

There was a small bedside cabinet to the left of the bed and, on the right, a dressing screen. On the wall to her immediate left-hand side, the mahogany-framed fireplace was dark and empty. Ahead of her, on top of the chest of drawers, sat the same ebony wooden casket that she had searched at Blackloch, not hidden away this time but sitting proudly on display. She took a deep breath, moved forwards and set her candlestick down by its side.

The lid raised easily and without a single sound; she searched the top black velvet-lined tray. There was Sebastian's diamond cravat pin and his signet ring. She lifted the tray out and sat it down beside her candlestick while she returned to the casket. Beneath where the tray had lain were the two saucily painted snuffboxes she had seen before and Sebastian's gold pocket watch. But the wolf's-head ring was not there. She began to rake again through the items of the tray. And then she heard the noise. She glanced around and the diamond pin fell from her fingers as she gasped and backed away, for there in front of the dressing screen stood Sebastian.

'I thought that you had…' she whispered.

'I know what you thought, Phoebe,' he said softly as he came to stand before her.

'I…' There was nothing she could say, not a single explanation that would excuse her presence in his bed-chamber, rummaging through his jewellery casket. She stared at him in horror, knowing what this meant for both him and her papa.

'You will not find it in there.' He slipped his fingers to the watch pocket of his waistcoat. At the end of the chain dangled not a watch, but the wolf's-head ring. He freed it from its anchoring and sat it upon his palm before holding his hand out before her. 'As I said, I keep it close to my heart.'

She looked from the ring to Sebastian's face. 'How could you know?'

'From the time you looked upon my father's portrait in the study at Blackloch I have known, Phoebe,' he said with such gentleness that it made her want to weep.

'I'm so sorry, Sebastian.' She placed her hands over her face, covering her eyes, knowing that all was lost.

'You may as well tell me about it now.'

'I cannot,' she whispered, frightened that if she did it would only make matters worse for both Sebastian and her father.

There was a small silence and then she heard him move, felt him take her in his arms. 'You know that I love you, Phoebe.'

'You must not love me.'

'It is too late,' he said softly against her ear. 'My heart is already yours as yours is mine. Do you deny it?'

She shook her head.

'Then tell me what this is all about.'

'Please do not ask me.' She touched her fingers to his mouth to stop his words.

He kissed them before drawing them away. 'You know I cannot do that.' And there was such a determination in his eyes that she feared her own resolve. 'What power has this man over you?'

But she just shook her head and spoke with a certainty she did not feel. 'I will not tell you, Sebastian, no matter how many times you ask me.'

'Then you leave me no alternative, Phoebe.' He stared down into her eyes. 'I will wear my father's ring to Lady Faversham's rout tomorrow. Flaunt it to whomsoever it is that is pulling your strings. And set the whisper that you have told me all.'

'No! Please Sebastian, I beg of you, do not!' Phoebe

felt the blood drain from her face. She stared at him in horror and mounting panic.

'But I must, Phoebe…if you will not tell me.' And the look on his face was so adamant that she knew that he would do it.

'They will kill you, if you do,' she said in a voice that was all of despair. And she could not stop the tears that leaked from her eyes. 'And they will kill my papa, too.'

'They threatened your father.' Sebastian placed his hands upon her upper arms and she could see the concern and the anger on his face. 'I should have realised.'

She nodded.

'But he is in the Tolbooth.'

'They have already beaten him and I do not doubt their threats to take the matter further. They are very powerful, Sebastian. The gentleman who held me hooded yesterday told me he has eyes and ears everywhere.'

'Held you hooded?' She saw something change in his face. Saw the clenching of his jaw and the danger in his eyes. 'I think you had better start at the beginning, Phoebe, and tell me all.'

And Phoebe did. She told him of the Messenger at the Tolbooth and how at first the threats had been directed only against her papa. She told him of the letters and of her meeting in the carriage with the gentleman. And of the threats to Hunter…of what they were willing to do to have the ring. Of how she was to steal it and the means of communication. Every last little detail there was to tell.

'Now do you understand why I could not tell you?' she asked. 'I could not risk my father's life. I could not risk yours.' She took his face in her hands feeling the rasp of the beard stubble beneath her fingers. 'What is so special about this ring that it would cost two men their lives?'

'It should hold significance for me alone, Phoebe. My father entrusted it to me as he lay dying.'

'I know what the ring means to you, Sebastian, truly I do.' And her heart was aching with his pain. 'But you must let me give it to them.'

'Never.' The word was unyielding. 'With his last breath my father made me swear to guard the ring with my life. I will not break that oath, Phoebe.'

'Please! Your father would have understood.'

'I will not part with it.' There was such vehemence in his voice that she knew he would not be persuaded and all the fear and panic bubbled up to overflow.

'They will kill you, Sebastian! And they will kill my father, too! Do you not understand?'

He slipped the ring back into his pocket and took her hands in his own.

'Phoebe, trust me in this. I will find another way. Have no fear—for I will see that your father is safe. And I will discover who is behind this and deal with them for what they have done to you.'

He did not understand the power and reach of the men who wanted the ring. She stared up into his eyes, felt a terrible despair roll through her and wept in earnest.

Hunter gently wiped away her tears and pulled her to him. 'Hush, my love, do not be afraid. All will be well.' He held her to him and stroked her hair and whispered words of reassurance. She cried until there were no more tears, cried until she felt empty, then just stood there in his arms, her face hidden against his chest.

Beneath her cheek she could feel the strong steady beat of his heart and, in the arms that surrounded her, the warmth of his love. He was everything to her: her heart, her love, her life. She raised her eyes to look up into his beloved face.

'I love you, Sebastian. I love you so very much.' She cupped his cheek with her hand, caressing the fine stubble.

'I love you, too, Phoebe.' He turned his face to kiss her fingers and then slid his hand against her scalp, holding her to stare down into her eyes, and there was such love and absolute integrity in his gaze that she could not doubt the truth of it.

Sebastian reached her mouth to his and kissed her with such tenderness. His hands trailed down over her arms to take her hands in his, entwining their fingers as surely as their hearts were entwined.

'You were always my love, Phoebe,' he whispered. 'And you always will be.' And he kissed her again, slowly, meaningfully, as if to substantiate the words of his promise. They kissed and in their kiss there was a merging of their hearts, a merging of their souls. They kissed and she did not let herself think of the danger and darkness and hopelessness that surrounded them. She did not look beyond to all that lay ahead. She loved him. She loved him, and she knew there would only ever be this one night.

All of her joy was in that kiss, and all of her sorrow. All of her passion and despair. Everything she had found and everything she would lose. And as the flame that had burned between them always flared and raged she laid her heart open to its blaze.

He kissed her eyelids, her cheeks, the line of her jaw, capturing her hands to the small of her back and holding them there to support her as he arched her to him. Her head lolled back, exposing her neck all the more to his mouth. He trailed kisses all the way down her throat, nuzzling the hollow in its base, lapping against her, tasting her, kissing her until her breasts were straining against the blue muslin, aching for his touch, longing for it. His lips slid lower over her décolletage, his breath hot and moist through the muslin.

She squirmed, willing him to mouth her breasts, but Sebastian followed back the same route, tilting her upright, claiming her mouth again with his own. He freed her hands and slid his fingers up her back, pulling her to him, deepening the kiss to share his very soul. She knew his gift, knew her life would never be the same again and she clung to him, until at last the kiss ended and they stood there staring into each other's eyes in the soft shadowed candlelight.

'Phoebe.' His voice was strained with emotion.

'Yes,' she said and reached her fingers to stroke down his jawline, feeling the rasp of his beard stubble all the way down to his chin, all the way to dip the tip of one finger into the cleft that nestled there. 'Please, Sebastian,' she whispered; looking up into the dark intensity of his eyes, she grasped his chin and touched her tongue to the cleft, probing it gently, kissing it. She felt the tremor that ran through him and slid her fingers lower, down over the abrasive skin of his neck, over the lump of his Adam's apple and the stiff collar of his shirt. The knot of his cravat parted easily enough and the linen strip fluttered to land forgotten on the floor. Her hands were trembling as she unfastened the collar of his shirt and felt it fall away as she leaned in to touch her mouth to the hollow of his throat, just as he had done to her. Beneath her lips she could feel the fast hard thrum of his pulse.

Sebastian's touch was so light against her back she did not realise that he had unbuttoned her bodice until the dress gaped away from her breast and began to slide from her shoulders. He eased it down her arms and she helped him until the muslin slid with a soft rush to pool around her ankles. One tug of a lace and the white froth of her petticoats tumbled to the same fate. His eyes glittered and smouldered in the flicker of the candlelight as their gaze meandered from her legs, over her shift, all the way up to her stays and the tops of her breasts that it exposed.

'You are beautiful, Phoebe,' he murmured.

And her heart leapt to hear the words even as it was tinged with the shadow of sadness. The kiss was deeper now, giving all the more, worshipping her with the slide of his lips, the tease of his tongue, the graze of his teeth. His hands caressed her hips as he pulled her snug to him so that she felt the press of him low against her belly. She wanted him so much, all of his love, all that could be between them. It felt as they were made to be together, that she had been waiting only for him all of those long lonely years. He completed her. He was the other half of herself. And she told him so in her kiss.

Hunter felt the tremble of her fingers as they struggled with the buttons of his waistcoat and he thought that he had never known such love. It filled his heart to overflowing. Nothing in his life had been right until he found Phoebe. Nothing could ever be right without her. She was his destiny, and part of him had known it from the very first moment their eyes met. He worked the buttons open for her and felt the slide of her hands over the lawn of his shirt, skimming the muscle that lay beneath, and his manhood throbbed for her, and his heart ached for her. And all that he had ever longed for in his life was the woman before him.

'Phoebe,' he whispered, and her eyes were dark and filled with such love and passion. 'Phoebe,' he said, and there were no words to express what he felt, the enormity of it, the towering brilliant force of it. He knew only one way to show her how much he needed her, how very much he loved her.

He stripped off his tailcoat, let his waistcoat fall away to the floor. His shirt slipped easily over his head so that his chest was bared to her and he shivered with the sweet caress of her fingers against his naked skin. And then he took her in his arms once more and pressed kisses to her forehead, her eyelids, her cheeks and ear.

'My love,' he said as he tongued the soft sweet lobe of her ear. 'My sweet love', as his teeth grazed gently against her throat and followed round to taste the skin at the nape of her neck.

One by one he plucked the pins from her hair, placing them in a pile beside her candle. He revelled in the loosening of that heavy auburn coil, unwinding it to hang loose against her shoulders; slid his hands into its soft length, pressed his nose to it, inhaling its scent. He kissed all the way down those lengths, his hands anchoring around her waist as his mouth caressed the pale mounds of her breasts that peeped from her stays. A soft moan escaped her and in it he heard both her pleasure and her need.

She moaned again as his mouth left her; when he looked in her eyes they were dark and dazed with desire. 'Sebastian,' she pleaded as he turned her away from him.

But he reassured her with soft whispers nuzzled against the edge of her shoulder. Still she did not understand, not until his fingers touched to the laces of her stays. He schooled himself to patience, knowing that she was a virgin, knowing how very much he wanted to pleasure her, for this to be the most wonderful experience of her life. His fingers were shaking as he worked his way slowly, methodically down, unlacing the ribbon one stretch at a time, watching the stiff-boned underwear temptingly slacken and teasingly gape until at last it tumbled to land with a thud on the rug.

She turned to face him and he could see the outline of her breasts through the thin worn material of her shift. And she came into his arms and he kissed her, questing gently at first, then deepening the kiss as he felt the measure of her desire. He rejoiced in the feel of her body, stroking her, touching her to stoke her pleasure all the higher. Beneath his hands her breasts were firm, her nipples nosing at his palms. He rolled their pebbled tips between his thumb and fingers, tugging at them gently until she was gasping out loud.

Hunter knelt before the woman he loved, circled her waist with his arms and then he took one breast into his mouth. Her moan was low and deep and guttural. He kissed her slowly and sensually, flicking his tongue against her hardened nub. She gasped and quivered with the force of sensation, threading her fingers through his hair, and clasping his head to her as if she would suckle him. He licked her, sucked her, mouthed her, caressing her hips as he did so. And everywhere his mouth had been the cotton of her shift clung tight and translucent to the bead of her nipple.

'Phoebe,' he groaned, knowing both torture and delight. He was shaking with his own need for her, his manhood so aroused and aching for release that the pain throbbed with an escalating intensity through his body. Yet he wanted her to be ready. He wanted her pleasure at the moment of their coupling to obscure her pain.

He reached for the ribbon of her shift and the soft worn material slid off her shoulders and down her arms, catching on her nipples before slipping all the way down her legs. She stepped out from it, naked save for her stockings and shoes.

'Phoebe,' he whispered as his mouth slid kisses against her stomach, her abdomen, and lower still until his mouth teased over the auburn triangle of hair between her legs.

'Sebastian,' she gasped and dug her fingers into the muscle of his shoulders.

He gazed up from where he knelt, his eyes sweeping over her with all of the fierce possession and adoration that was in his soul.

'You are mine, Phoebe, now and for ever.' And never taking his eyes from where they locked with hers he stroked his hands against her ankles. 'Just as I am yours.'

'Yes,' she whispered, as his fingers began to edge slowly up the inner edge of her stockings. His caress was soft, the lightest trail of his fingers against the silk, against her calf, over her knee and up farther to the pale blue ribbons of her garters tied. She thought he would untie the bow and let the stockings slide down her legs, but he left them intact, kissing each ribbon so that she felt the warmth of his breath against the bare skin of her thigh as he untied the bows and let the stockings slide down her legs.

His hands stroked her hips, cupping her buttocks, his eyes clinging to hers as he moved his mouth to meet what lay between her legs.

'Sebastian!' she gasped, but he did not release her, just worked magic on that most intimate and secret of places, until she was clutching his head to her, pulling his hair, crying out as pleasure exploded throughout her and her body convulsed and throbbed and her legs were so weak that she would have collapsed had he not stood up and swept her up into his arms.

He carried her to the bed and laid her down on the sheets.

She watched while he stripped off the rest of his

clothes, stared at his nakedness, at his strength and his beauty, at a body that was so different in every way from her own. Such pale white skin, such hard defined muscle in his arms and shoulders, abdomen and thighs. His manhood was long and thick and rigid and the sight of it sent a pulsing ache through her woman's core.

He covered her with his body and kissed her, his tongue penetrating her mouth in thrusting strokes that had her gasping and pressing her hips to him, and arching to drive her breasts against the granite of his chest. And then his fingers played upon her where his mouth had worked such magic, where she was wet and throbbing for him, her body pleading its invitation. She shuddered her pleasure again, gasping, reeling, floating, so that she barely noticed the pain amidst the shimmering ecstasy as his manhood pierced her. Two bodies became one.

She clung to him as he held her and kissed her mouth and stroked her face. And when he moved, slowly at first, sliding so gently, she knew that this was their journey, their place, the nearing of their final destination. He moved and she met each driving stroke of his body, pulling him into her all the deeper, needing this union, wanting this man. They moved together in what was always meant to be between them. Walking, then running. Running to reach the place that each could only find with the other. Glorying in their union. Striving for the end, yet prolonging the journey in every way that they could. Until he spilled his seed within her and she was truly his and he was truly hers. A sharing of bodies. A communion of souls. A merging of hearts and minds and beings. And nothing would ever be the same again.

He eased down to lie by her side, breathless, reeling from the wonder of her and the love and passion that was between them. His mouth touched hers with all the reverence and joy and love that he felt. She snuggled against him and he wrapped her in his arms, knowing he would protect her from all the world. Phoebe Allardyce, the woman he would make his wife.

Lying there in the darkness of the night and the warmth of his arms, Phoebe wished she could stop time and make this perfect night last for ever. But the hours were passing too quickly and her mind dreaded what the morning would bring. Sebastian turned in his sleep and the moonlight revealed his pale stark handsome features. He looked so peaceful, vulnerable almost, and her heart welled with love for him.

She knew what the men would do to him, for all his strength and resolution; they were many and he was but one man. And it seemed in the quietness of the night she heard again the whisper of his words.

Do you not know I would lay down my life for you?

And she would lay down hers for him. The thought came unbidden, a quiet certainty that it seemed had never not been there. With it came the knowledge that she could not let them harm him. She could not risk his life. And in that moment Phoebe knew that there was more than one way to lay down a life.

Her heart shrivelled at the thought of what she must do and how much it would hurt him. To think of that hurt was almost unbearable, but better that than what the men would do to him. To lose his love and gain his hatred was a price she would pay for a lifetime to save him.

'Phoebe?' he murmured, half-waking as she stole from beneath the sheets.

'It will soon be dawn and I must not be found in your bed,' she whispered. She brushed a kiss against his lips and the pain squeezed all the tighter in her heart. 'Go back to sleep, Sebastian. I love you. Remember that, whatever should happen.'

'I love you, too, Phoebe,' he said and caught her hand in his own as if to keep her with him. She squeezed it gently, one last touch to last a lifetime, before releasing him. Then she moved quietly through the darkness to where their clothing lay upon the floor.

Chapter Eighteen

Hunter woke in a shaft of early autumn sunshine. He felt bathed in warmth and happiness. He could still smell the scent of Phoebe upon his skin, could almost still feel the softness of her body pressed to his. She was his woman in truth, his one true love. The knowledge made his heart glow and his face smile. And as he lay there a plan formed in his head of how to deal with the men who had blackmailed her.

It involved a certain amount of risk and ingenuity, but Hunter knew it would work. It would protect Phoebe and her father, and flush out the bastards who would steal his father's ring. And he wondered again why anyone else would want the ring so very badly. Not that they had a chance in hell of taking it from him.

The note made no noise as it slipped beneath his door. Hunter saw it and thought again of Phoebe. He smiled and rose to fetch it. Once all this was done and Phoebe was safe, then he would speak to his mother.

Only his given name was written on the outside of the folded paper and the ink smeared beneath his fingers so he knew that she had only just written it and passed it to him with her very own hand. He smiled again at the intimacy of it and at the love they shared, and opened the note to read her secret message.

There were only two words. Two words, and the smile wiped from his face and the dread and the disbelief churned in his stomach. *Forgive me.* So black and stark against the pale paper sheet.

His gaze moved to the pile of abandoned clothing, now devoid of all trace of Phoebe, and his blood ran cold with premonition.

The chain coiled alone in the pocket of his waistcoat. He did not need to search anywhere else to know that the ring was gone. Her words of the night whispered again in his head and he understood their meaning and that last breath of a kiss.

Hunter pulled on his breeches and stormed from the room.

Her bedchamber was empty, just as he had known it would be.

He ran down the stairs, yelling her name.

A maid gave a yelp at the sight of him and scurried away, but Trenton appeared in the hallway.

'Miss Allardyce went out five minutes ago, sir.'

Hunter opened the front door and stepped outside to scan the street. There was no sign of her.

He saw the embarrassment in his butler's face and in his urgency to find her he did not care if the whole world knew he had spent the night loving her.

'Where did she go?' he barked the question.

Trenton shook his head. 'She didn't say where, just that she was going out for a walk.'

'Did she receive any messages this morning?'

'Yes, sir. A letter was delivered for her not ten minutes since. The lad said it was urgent. I took it up to her myself.'

Hunter gave a nod. 'Have Ajax saddled and brought round to the front.' And then he took the stairs two at a time back to her room.

The cupboards and drawers were empty and her travelling bag, the same one mauled by the highwaymen on a moor so long ago, sat fully packed by the foot of the bed. Hunter stood and scanned the room.

The smell of burning hung in the air, yet no fire had been lit. He glanced over at the blackened empty fireplace, then moved closer and saw the paper upon the grate. In her haste to leave she had not stayed to watch its burning. The familiar writing was charred, but still readable.

The corner of Red Lion Street with Paternoster Row at Spitalfields Market. Come by hackney carriage immediately and wear the red shawl. Tie the ring inside a white handkerchief and hold it in your hand.

Five minutes later Hunter was dressed and galloping Ajax down the street. She had a fifteen-minute start on him, but he knew the shortcuts that a hackney carriage could not take, and he knew he could reach Spitalfields first. His face was grim with determination and he spurred his horse all the faster.

Phoebe did not look out at the passing buildings, but kept her eyes upon the white-handkerchief pouch clutched so tightly within her hand. The carriage rumbled and lurched over the road, taking her ever closer to Spitalfields. The day was mild and the red woollen shawl was wrapped around her shoulders, but Phoebe was so cold her teeth chattered from it. She felt numb, frozen, sick with the knowledge of what she was doing. And yet not once did she contemplate turning back. It had to be done, to save Sebastian and to save her father.

She dreaded the moment the betrayal would be complete, and she dreaded even more returning to Grosvenor Street to face Sebastian and all that would stand where love had been. Wrath and hurt and contempt. And she would not blame him, not one little bit, not when she had taken everything of him and betrayed him.

She glanced down at the faded blue muslin of her skirt and she remembered the very first time she had met Sebastian, when he had rescued her from the highwaymen on the moor. All of what was between them had been there from the moment she had looked up into his eyes; she just had not known it.

She loved him. She loved him enough to betray him. And the price of her treachery was her own heart.

From his vantage point beneath the portico of Christ Church, Hunter had a clear view of the junction between Red Lion Street and Paternoster Row. Thursday was market day at Spitalfields and despite the early hour the market place was busy and the streets thronged with people. The villains had chosen well, he thought. No one would notice what was happening, and even if they did they would not care.

This was the East End and, although it had once been the affluent quarters of the Huguenot silk weavers, the area had fallen on hard times so that the faces Hunter saw milling around the market were sharp-eyed and lean-cheeked and rough, and he feared all the more for Phoebe. He could hear the cries of the hawkers and stallholders advertising the bargains and quality to be had. Fruit and vegetables, from blackberries and apples to potatoes and lettuce. Carts and gigs and hackney carriages lined the roads, and there were no sweepers here so the horses had left their business free and plenty afoot. He stayed hidden by the church's great stone columns and he watched and waited and a few minutes later saw the woman he loved step out of the hackney carriage.

The scarlet shawl marked her amidst the dark drabness all around. Something of her stance suggested a woman going to her doom, something of her very stillness was all speaking and the pallor of her face was stark against the brightness of the shawl. Hunter slipped from his hiding place and made his way through the crowd.

He threaded his way steadily closer, never once losing sight of the red shawl. He had almost reached her when he saw the figure move behind her, a fair-haired man with his cap pulled down low over his eyes—the same man he had last seen outside the Tolbooth in Glasgow.

He was so close and yet the throng of people between them barred his way, and he knew he would not reach her in time.

'Phoebe!' he shouted, 'Do not do it!' He saw her face turn to him, saw her shock and her anguish.

'Sebastian!' She began to move towards him just as the man struck, snatching the white handkerchief from her hand.

Phoebe stared in disbelief and wondered for a moment if Sebastian were real or just a figment of her imagination.

She had never seen his eyes look so dark or his face so white with fury. He grabbed hold of her, staring down at her and there was such darkness, such danger and intensity about him to raze all else in its path. Phoebe trembled at the promise she saw in his eyes.

'Are you all right?'

She nodded, not trusting herself to speak.

'Take a carriage home and wait for me there. And do not dare run away from me, Phoebe Allardyce.' He pressed his purse into her hands and then sped off in pursuit of the Messenger.

The man knocked people flying as he fled from Hunter, cutting a swathe through the crowd to reach the road where he dodged through the mêlée of carriages and carts. Hunter did not hesitate, running between the carriages, chasing down his quarry. He ran with a cold determination that made his legs pump all the faster. The man glanced back over his shoulder and Hunter knew the villain was tiring. He pressed on harder. Another glance back and this time it cost the man his footing. The bastard slid in a pile of horse dung and almost fell, before catching his balance and running on. A third glance and Hunter caught him as he ducked into the alleyway.

The man bounced against the brick of the building as Hunter's punch landed hard against the villain's jaw.

'You bastard!' Hunter snarled and made to move in.

But the man cowered away and as he did so Hunter felt a flash of recognition as if he knew this man from somewhere, but could not place him. 'Don't hurt me! Please! Just take it...' the coward pleaded and threw the small white parcel.

Hunter felt the hardness of metal as he caught it, but he had to be sure. He ripped through the cotton of Phoebe's handkerchief and there inside, with its emerald eyes looking up at him, was his father's wolf's-head ring.

He glanced up to see the man sloping away. Their eyes met and the man sprang to action and ran for his life.

Hunter tucked the ring safely away and then started after him.

The man sped from the alley, turning left to nip out onto the street just before a procession of carts and a surge in the crowd.

Hunter cursed, then realised that the villain was heading west towards Bishopsgate and for the first time in a year Hunter was glad of his rakish past, of his misspent nights in the low-life gaming dens of Spitalfields and Whitechapel. He knew the lanes round here like the back of his hand. He slipped into Duke Street and then cut along Artillery Lane, taking a short cut to bring him out on Bishopsgate only twenty yards behind the man who was no longer running, but hurrying. Hunter did not close the distance, just stayed amidst the crowd and followed. And as the market crowd thinned and they entered the banking area of London, Hunter knew the man would lead him to whoever was behind this villainy.

The man hurried on until he came to a quiet leafy street lined with a few large houses, a street down which Hunter had never travelled. Hunter hung back, knowing that in the emptiness the man would be sure to see him if he followed too close, then used the ancient sycamores that lined the road as cover to close the distance.

The man hesitated outside the largest of the houses and, with a furtive glance around him, ran up the front steps and disappeared inside the opened door. Upon a black stone plaque on its wall the words *Obsidian House* had been carved and beneath the words were the same symbols that were carved into the lintels above the front doors of both Blackloch and his town house in Grosvenor Street. And Hunter felt the stirring of something dark.

Only once the man was inside the house did he follow. The main doors stood open, caught back and secured with a hook. There was a small porch area followed by a set of glass interior doors that led into the hallway. The glass doors were closed, but Hunter was up the stairs and his back pressed flat against the wall at the edge of the outer doors that he might inch his head round and gain a view.

Inside in the hallway, the man was talking to a gentleman. And now Hunter knew why the fair-haired villain's face had seemed so vaguely familiar. He was a footman. And the gentleman at his side was his master. A gentleman Hunter knew very well. A gentleman Hunter had considered a friend: James Edingham, Viscount Bullford.

There were more men appearing in the hallway now. Men that Hunter or his father had counted friends. Rich men, powerful men. A high court judge, an archbishop, a member of the cabinet, even a member of the royal family. A duke clapped his hand against Bullford's back in a gesture of friendship. And they began filing down a corridor that led straight ahead.

They were smiling. And they were all of them wearing long black ceremonial robes identical to that of the man in the painting in Hunter's bedchamber at Blackloch.

His eyes dropped from the receding black figures to the floor of the porch. Not tiled or wooden, but a mosaic and depicting the same hunting scene from classical antiquity as was carved into the stone fireplace of his study in his town house.

Hunter saw the footmen that came to close the outer doors. He dodged back out of the way and jumped down behind the bushes that grew in the narrow soil strips on either side of the house. Once the doors were closed he made his way back to Grosvenor Street.

Phoebe was not in her room.

He glanced down at the travelling bag that still sat by the bed and the sudden thought struck him that maybe the footman had had an accomplice waiting there to snatch her from Spitalfields. His stomach dipped with the dread of it.

'Did Miss Allardyce return safely from her morning sojourn?'

Trenton cleared his throat 'Indeed, sir, but she has gone out again on an errand for Mrs Hunter some fifteen minutes ago.'

'An errand?' Hunter frowned.

'Mrs Hunter is suffering from a headache. I believe she dispatched Miss Allardyce to purchase a herbal remedy.'

'From where?'

'I do not know, sir.'

And neither did his mother.

'Inform me immediately that she returns,' he instructed Trenton, and aside from that there was little that Hunter could do, despite all his unease.

He went to his study to wait, blaming himself for not guarding her better, chiding himself for not realising that she would steal the ring to save him.

Phoebe made her purchase of feverfew and betony and had just left the apothecary shop when she was assailed by a familiar voice.

'I say, Miss Allardyce, how nice to see you on this glorious morning.'

Phoebe felt her heart sink. She was in no fit state for conversation. Her stomach was churning with dread at the thought of what the villains might have done to Hunter. Hunter was tall and strong and fast and she did not doubt that he could best any man, but what chance had he against a pistol or a knife? She would not rest until he had returned, despite all that would ensue. She hid her worries and glanced up to see Lord Bullford's coach stopped by the side of the road and the gentleman himself emerging to stand before her on the footpath.

'Good morning, Lord Bullford,' she said politely and forced a smile to her face.

'You are out and about early this morning, Miss Allardyce…' he glanced around the street paying special attention to the apothecary shop from which she had just emerged '…and without Mrs Hunter?' His expression held all the kind friendliness that it ever had.

'Indeed, sir. I am afraid Mrs Hunter is much distressed with a headache. It is the reason for my journey; I have come to fetch a prescription to relieve her pain.'

'Oh dear,' murmured Lord Bullford with his brow creased in concern. 'Poor Mrs H., how she suffers with her head.'

'Indeed,' said Phoebe. 'Which is why, sir, I must beg your leave and return immediately to Grosvenor Street.'

'Of course.' Lord Bullford nodded. 'But I have a better idea. Please, Miss Allardyce, allow me to convey you home in my coach.'

'Your offer is very kind, my lord, but I should not.' She smiled in earnest to soften her refusal.

'By coach the journey will take but a few minutes. On foot, I imagine a great deal longer. And you did say that Mrs H. is quite unwell… I thought only to relieve the lady's discomfort. But if you would rather walk…'

Phoebe felt a pang of guilt at Bullford's gentle reproach. 'Perhaps you are right, sir.'

'I will have you at Grosvenor Street in no time at all to tend the poor lady.' He smiled, and Phoebe was reassured. He held out his hand and helped her climb up into his coach, and the door slammed shut behind them.

Chapter Nineteen

Hunter stood before the fireplace, thinking of Phoebe. If anything had happened to her... And as he worried, his eye caught the carving on the stone beneath the mantel.

A hunter with a great black dog pursuing evil-eyed foxes and boars and ferrets. It was a picture that had fascinated Hunter since he was a child. He remembered coming to this house and tracing his fingers against each of the figures of the scenes. He had always thought that lone huntsman astride his horse had been hunting with his dog, but now that he had seen the defined colourful mosaic in Obsidian House he could see that the dog was not a dog at all, but a wolf. And he could see, too, that there was something missing from this carving, a small detail that had been clear in the background of the tiled mosaic version.

Lurking amidst the trees of the forest, the backdrop against which the hunter rode, were six wolves' faces— Hunter knew there were six because it had been his habit to count them as a child. In the mosaic there had been seven. Hunter looked where the seventh should have been on the stone carving, and there in its place, clear now that he was looking for it, was a headless wolf.

And the strangest thought occurred to Hunter. From his pocket he withdrew the wolf's-head ring, and the wolf seemed to look up at him, its emerald eyes sparkling in the morning sunlight. Hunter pressed the silver wolf's head into the hollow where the wolf's head on the carving should have been, and turned, and one of the long wooden panels in the mahogany wall of his study popped open. Behind the hidden door was a room all in darkness. Hunter lit a candle and stepped into the secret room.

The candlelight showed a long narrow room empty save for four Holland-covered paintings that hung upon the wall and a large chest in the corner. Hunter pulled the holland cover from the closest painting. The cream linen slid silently onto the floor to reveal his father staring out from the canvas at him. In the portrait his father's hair was as dark as Hunter's and his face only a little lined. He was dressed in the same long black ceremonial robe that Bullford and the men had worn and on his finger was the wolf's-head ring. And Hunter suddenly knew that his father was the 'monk' in the picture at Blackloch. His gaze dropped to read the plaque fitted to the bottom of the gilt frame—*Mr Edward Hunter, Master of the Order of the Wolf.*

The other three paintings showed Hunter's grandfather, great-grandfather and great-great-grandfather; all three men were garbed in the same black robes and each wore the same wolf's-head ring upon their fingers.

Hunter's heart was thudding as he turned to the chest, and his hands shook as he found the letter addressed to *My Son, Sebastian Hunter.* The writing was that of his father, the seal that of his father's signet ring. He broke the seal, unfolded the paper and began to read.

7th September, 1809
My dearest son

If you are reading this letter then I am gone from this world to meet my maker, and you have found yourself on the path to the Order.

Firstly let me say that I love you and have always loved you and been proud of you as my son, no matter the disagreements that we have had. You are a young man, reckless and wild as young men are wont to be; as I myself once was. It is a father's duty to prepare his son, to guide and nurture and train him for the path that lies ahead. And if I have been harsh and hard with you, Sebastian, then it has only ever been with this in mind. As a Hunter your path is already mapped and it is not an easy one.

I am Master of the Order of the Wolf, a secret society founded by your great-great-grandfather in accordance with the instruction of King George II for the good of all Britain, her people and her king, just as my father was master before me, and his father before him...and just as it is your destiny to be. To the Hunters of our line this is the duty to which we are born and must devote our life's work.

Your great-great-grandfather foiled a plot being hatched amongst the nobles against the king and was rewarded with a fortune to rival that of the wealthiest in the land and the honour of establishing and leading this society. The Order exists to work secretly in the shadows to safeguard this great country and her line of monarchs, to fight against tyranny and foreign invasion, injustice and dishonour. We are the hunters that seek out the traitors within. We are the wolves that slay the guilty. There is meaning in our name, indeed, my son.

Forgive me for having deferred bringing you into the Order for so long, but such is the responsibility that I deemed it critical to wait until you had sown your wild oats and calmed your wild ways. And now that I am gone you must find your own way in. But remember always that no man who is not a member may know of the order's existence and live, and this rule is true for you, too, Sebastian.

By virtue of the fact you are reading this then I have already given into your keeping the wolf's-head ring and with this letter I name you my heir and successor. Whosoever wears the ring is Master of the Order, so guard it well.

All that you need know of the Order is written in the book you will find with this letter.

May you fulfil the destiny that is given you as a Hunter.

God bless you, my son.
Your loving father,
Edward Hunter

Hunter wept as he read the words his father had penned only two months before his death. He wept because written in that letter were the words his father had never spoken to him in life—that he loved him, that he was proud of him. He lifted the ancient brown calf-leather-bound book from the chest, and leafed through its pages.

His father was right, everything he needed to know was there. The history and inception of the society, its rules, its purpose, the methods of its operation, initiation ceremonies and trials for new members and much more. At the back of the book were pages and pages of names of men who had been, and still were, members of the Order. The last name entered on the list, written in his father's own hand, made his heart skip a beat, for it was Hunter's own. He took a deep breath, and scanned the list. Linwood was there, marked as an office bearer, which explained his wolf's-head cane, and the viscount's father was listed, too. Francis Edingham, the Marquis of Willaston, Bullford's father, was described as the deputy master. Bullford's name was not amongst them, but Hunter supposed that no one in the Order had had access to the book to add any new members since his father's death.

Hunter knew now why they wanted the ring and he had an inkling why it was Bullford who had been given the task. He took the neatly folded black robes from the chest and then moved back out of the dark chill of the secret room to the sunlit study.

A knock sounded at the study door. He snuffed the candle and, retrieving the ring, slid it onto his finger. The panel pressed easily back into place, the seam of its outline invisible against the rest of the ornate panelling that surrounded it. Then Hunter opened the study door to find Trenton waiting there, a single letter lying upon the silver salver.

'A letter has just been delivered for you, sir. The boy who brought it said it was for your most urgent attention.'

Hunter felt his jaw tense as he lifted the letter and saw his name upon it, for it was penned in the same disguised hand that had been used in all of Bullford's letters to Phoebe. He ripped it open and read the unsigned contents.

If you wish the safe return of Miss Allardyce, then you will leave your father's wolf's-head ring on the gravestone of Abigail Murton in the churchyard of Christ Church, Spitalfields, this afternoon at two o'clock.

He screwed the paper into a ball and threw it onto the

grate in the fireplace. Then he readied his pistols, slipped them into his pockets and rang the bell for Trenton.

Phoebe woke to find herself lying in a dark room. Her wrists had been tied behind her back and her ankles bound together and there was a gag around her mouth. She could hear nothing and see nothing; she remembered the carriage and Lord Bullford removing a small brown bottle from his pocket to drip some of its foul-smelling liquid onto his handkerchief. The warning bells had been sounding in her head, not so much at what he was doing, but at the strange expression upon his face.

She heard his words again: *I am sorry, Miss Allardyce, if only you had done as we asked.* And there had been genuine regret within his eyes.

And she had known, then, who it was that had organised the break-ins in Mrs Hunter's Glasgow town house and at Blackloch, and who had sent his Messenger to threaten her papa.

'You!' she whispered in disbelief and tried to flee, but Bullford was across the carriage and pressing the foul-reeking cloth to her nose and mouth. The vapour of it choked her and burned her throat and lungs, and that terrible suffocating sensation was the last that she remembered.

She shifted, trying to ease her body into a more comfortable position.

'You are back with us again, Miss Allardyce.' The voice was not that of Bullford, but it was one she recognised. This man, whoever he was, was the same one who had held her hooded within his coach.

A flint struck against a tinderbox and she saw the spark catch to the tinder and the flame light a candle. The small flickering light seemed too bright against the darkness and she narrowed her eyes and peered through the blackness to see the identity of the man to whom Bullford had delivered her.

There were two men standing looking down at where she lay, but even if the room had been fully lit she would not have known their identities for both men were dressed in plain long black robes, the hoods of which had been pulled up over the heads to leave their faces hidden in shadow.

The stouter man gestured to the other and his associate bent down and released the gag from her mouth, and as he moved she thought she caught a glimpse of a narrow face and shifty grey eyes and she was sure that he was the Messenger.

'Untie me, sir,' she demanded.

'I am afraid we will be keeping you safely trussed for now, my dear,' said the gentleman from the carriage and she realised with a shiver that his voice was not so dissimilar to Bullford's. There was a small silence as he stepped closer to loom over her in the darkness. 'You told Hunter, did you not, Miss Allardyce? Despite all our warnings.'

'No,' she lied. 'I do not know how he came to be in Spitalfields.' That, at least, was the truth. 'He knows nothing of any of this, I swear it.' She did not know how Sebastian had found her at the marketplace, but she knew with all her heart that she must protect both him and her papa.

The gentleman, whose face remained hidden by the folds of his cowl, gave a small laugh and clapped his hands together in mock applause. 'Very impressive, my dear, but I seem to recall at our last meeting how very anxious you were to protect Mr Hunter from harm.'

'The gentleman is my employer's son,' she countered.

'His welfare affects Mrs Hunter and therefore also, albeit indirectly, myself. I would not see Mrs Hunter's sensibilities distressed.'

'How solicitous of you, Miss Allardyce. If it is not too indelicate of me to say, the gentleman may be your employer's son, but he has engaged your affection, Miss Allardyce, a feeling which, if I am not mistaken, is reciprocated.'

'You are very much mistaken, sir!' she exclaimed, frightened of where this was leading and what it would mean for Sebastian.

'For your own sake, Miss Allardyce, you had better hope that I am not.' There was a chill in his voice as he uttered the soft words.

Her blood ran cold. 'My papa?'

'Your papa remains unharmed and blissfully oblivious to all.' He reached down and stroked a finger against her cheek. 'But what will Hunter give to save the life of the woman he loves?'

She jerked her face away from his touch and stared up at him with defiance. 'He will give you nothing!' It was the truth. Sebastian would not part with the ring even when he had loved her and she had no doubt what his feelings were for her now. A shiver rippled through her at the memory of his face in the marketplace. Whatever Sebastian did, he would not give them the ring.

'Oh, no, my dear Miss Allardyce. I very much suspect he will give us exactly what we want.' She heard the smile in his voice. 'Had we known Hunter would develop such a *tendre* for you, it would have made matters so much easier for us.'

'And if he does not give you the ring?' Her heart was filled with fear and none of it was for herself.

'Let us just hope, for your sake, my dear, that he does.'

And then he gestured to Messenger, who knelt down and fixed the gag in place across her mouth.

Then the two black-robed men were gone, taking the candle with them and leaving Phoebe alone in the darkness.

'Lord Bullford is not at home,' the footman said to Hunter, who was standing upon the steps of Bullford's father's house in Henrietta Street.

'Perhaps you wish to reconsider that reply.' Hunter slipped a pistol from his pocket and held it against the footman's ribs. He had seen the shadowy figure of Bullford outlined against the library window as he called the lad over to hold Ajax.

The footman gave a nod and showed him in to the hall where he pointed silently at the library door before hurrying back down beneath stairs.

Bullford was loitering at the side of the window when Hunter opened the library door and stepped inside.

Bullford took one look at Hunter and the pistol in his hand and the colour drained from his face.

'Hunter, old man,' he tried to bluff, 'what on earth are you doing here and with a pistol at the ready?'

But Hunter had no time for games. 'Where is she, Bullford?'

'I have no idea what you are talking about, old man.'

'Then you had better start thinking and fast.' Hunter aimed the barrel of the pistol at Bullford and began to close the space between them.

Bullford backed away, stumbling in the process, but righted himself to keep edging away.

'You blackmailed her, terrorised her, threatened her father.'

'It was not supposed to be like that.' Bullford shook his

head. 'We did not think for a minute that Miss Allardyce would not accept the bribe. There are not many women who would have walked away from two thousand pounds. We had made no provision for it. Charles, m'father's footman, made the threat out of desperation. They were just empty words uttered on the spot. We never would have hurt Sir Henry.'

'But you did hurt him. When Miss Allardyce visited him that day he had been beaten.'

'I swear upon my very life, Hunter, that no harm came to her father by our hands. Charles did not understand Miss Allardyce's sudden change of heart when she emerged from the visit that day, but he was not about to look a gift horse in the mouth and start asking questions.'

'So you continued to torture her with threats to her father's safety?'

'I am sorry, Hunter, truly I am. But I needed the ring.'

'Why was acquiring the ring your responsibility?'

Bullford shook his head. 'I cannot tell you, Hunter. I am sworn to secrecy on pain of death.'

'I know all about the Order of the Wolf, so start talking, Bullford.'

Bullford's eyes widened; he made to step back farther, but there was nowhere left to go. He shrank against the library wall and looked as if he had just seen a ghost.

'Let me guess,' said Hunter. 'Part of your initiation ceremony?'

Bullford nodded and something of the fight went out of him. 'My father brought me into the society close to the end of last year.'

'Just after my father's death, if I am not mistaken.'

Bullford nodded again. 'My initiation is not complete until I have passed the task I have been set. I cannot become a full member until I bring them the ring.'

'And Miss Allardyce?'

'It was not my idea, please believe me, Hunter. They made me do it, but I swear she is unharmed.'

'Where is she being held?'

'Cannot tell you, old man.' The sweat was glistening on Bullford's temple and upper lip and chin.

Hunter experienced the urge to pistol whip Bullford's face and probably would have, had he not learned his father's final harsh lesson.

Instead, he leaned over Bullford and said, 'Ten months ago I learned that in the end there is always a reckoning for one's actions. Your task is the reason for Miss Allardyce's predicament; it was *your* task and thus *your* responsibility. You may not have envisaged the way she would be used, but you went along with it readily enough. And do not delude yourself for a minute that you are but a bystander swept along with events. This is no game, James. Do you honestly think I will let you play with the life of the woman I love and walk away scot-free?

'The Order was established by men of integrity to recruit men of integrity who would be the moral compass when those around were lost. It is a great responsibility and the tasks set were meant to test a man's mettle. So I give you the chance, Bullford, that I never had. Will you put right your mistake? For I tell you now, you *will* take responsibility for your actions this night, one way or another.

'Do you possess the integrity to join the Order in truth? If you do not, I swear by the responsibility given to me by my father, and the responsibility that a man has for the woman he loves, that you will die.'

Hunter touched the muzzle of the pistol to Bullford's forehead. 'Where is Miss Allardyce?'

He saw Bullford's Adam's apple bob nervously. 'You

are right, Hunter. I knew it was wicked work and I said nothing. She is in the cellar of Obsidian House. In this I will do right, at least. And if they take my life for so doing, then it is just recompense for all that I did to Miss Allardyce.'

'Your first decision worthy of the Order, Bullford, but do you have what it takes to become a member, I wonder?' said Hunter slowly as he lowered the pistol. 'Let us save Miss Allardyce and see if we cannot both complete the initiation tasks set us by our fathers in the process.'

Bullford's brow creased. 'What do you mean?'

'You will take the ring to Obsidian House.'

'That will allow me to join the Order, but how will it help you or Miss Allardyce?' Bullford's puzzlement increased.

'Because I will be wearing the ring when you present it,' replied Hunter with a cold smile.

Chapter Twenty

'Afternoon, sirs.' The footman nodded as Hunter and Bullford slipped into the hallway of Obsidian House.

'Afternoon,' murmured Bullford in reply, then steered Hunter down a corridor and into the first room that was out of sight. There, the two of them pulled the black robes they had brought with them on over their clothes.

'You are sure this will work?' whispered Bullford.

'As sure as I can be,' said Hunter. 'You know what to do…'

Bullford nodded and wiped away the sweat that was glimmering on his face.

Hunter checked his pocket watch, then gave a nod.

They lifted the hoods to cover their heads and slipped out into the corridor to merge amidst the other robed and hooded men walking towards the ceremonial chamber.

The grandfather clock in the corner of the room chimed three and Phoebe knew the deadline had passed. Two hooded men had brought her up from the cellar and tied her to a St Andrew's cross in the centre of a large shadowed hall. High on the wall facing her hung a larger version of Hunter's ring, a great silver-crafted wolf's head. And as the creature's emerald eyes glinted in the flickering wall-candles a stream of black-cowled men filed into the hall to encircle her.

Phoebe strained against the ropes that bound her wrists and ankles to the wood of the cross, but the knots were tight and secure. A wave of panic swept over her at the ever-growing circle, but she was determined to reveal nothing of her fear.

A man appeared by her side. He pushed the hood back and there was the Marquis of Willaston, Bullford's father. The scent of sweet tobacco and sandalwood hit her and she knew that he was the gentleman from the carriage even before he opened his mouth to speak quiet words that were for her ears only.

'It seems you were right, Miss Allardyce. Hunter does not care whether you live or die. He does not deem your life worthy of one paltry ring.'

She closed her eyes. Sebastian was an honourable man. He would not break the oath he had sworn to his dying father. Now that she had seen these hooded men, so many of them, all garbed in their 'monk' robes, now that she knew that even Bullford, who was supposed to be Sebastian's friend, was one of them, and had seen the great silver wolf's head on the wall, she understood that the ring was in some way a part of all this, too. So much so, they were prepared to kill for it. But to Sebastian, who had guarded it so close to his heart for all of the time since his father's death, that small piece of silver with its tiny emerald chips meant something different.

He felt he had failed and disappointed his father and there were no means to prove himself a better son, no way to win his father's love or forgiveness. Death had robbed him of that chance. And, worse than that, Sebastian had carried the guilt for that death all of these months, as surely as he had carried the ring. To break his oath would be to fail his father in the final test. Keeping this faith was the one thing left he could do for his father. Sebastian would not give them the ring, not even to save her life.

Phoebe closed her eyes all the tighter and would not let the tears fall. She understood, yet the realisation broke apart her shattered heart and ground the fragments to dust. Despair wrapped its dark tendrils around her and grew until there was no more light; it no longer mattered that the men would kill her.

'I'll wager that your affection for him has waned, Miss Allardyce, now that you know the truth of him.'

She opened her eyes and looked up to meet the Marquis's gaze. 'I love him.' The words were quiet and certain.

The Marquis looked at her with a strange expression. 'Do you not know what we mean to do with you?'

'I know,' she said in that same calm voice.

He slid a knife from the scabbard that hung from his belt and showed it to her. 'And are you not afraid?'

She slowly shook her head. 'I have nothing left to fear.' It was the truth, for, inside, Phoebe was already dead.

The last of the black-hooded men entered the hall. As the door thudded shut and the footsteps of the footmen echoed away down the corridor, the Marquis sheathed the knife again. He smiled at Phoebe and turned to face the men gathered in the circle around them.

'Welcome, brothers,' he intoned. 'We are gathered here on the matter of the master's ring and the fact that it lies in the hands of one who is not a member. Our latest novice has failed in his task to retrieve the ring and thus we must take matters into our own hands and act for the good of the Order. Remember that whatever takes place here today is a sacrifice we must make for the greater good.' He glanced meaningfully towards Phoebe. 'And thus—'

One of the black-robed figures stepped into the circle and pulled back his hood to reveal himself as Bullford. 'I have not failed in my task, master. I have brought the ring as you required.'

A sudden murmur of voices passed around the circle.

The Marquis gaped at his son. 'You have the ring?'

There was a silence as all of the black-hooded figures turned to face Bullford.

'I do, master.'

'Then bring it to me, boy!' the Marquis bellowed.

Bullford glanced round to his right-hand side and the black-garbed figure stepped into the circle to stand by Bullford's side. He slipped back his hood and the breath caught in Phoebe's throat, for there stood Sebastian, his face pale, his hair black as night and his eyes green and more deadly than she had ever seen.

A gasp went round the circle, and an even louder one when he lifted the black sleeve to reveal his right hand— there on his third finger, for all to see, was the wolf's-head ring.

'Good lord!' exclaimed the Marquis. 'What treachery is this?'

'What treachery, indeed, Willaston?' demanded Sebastian.

'Seize him!' shouted the Marquis.

'On whose authority do you act, sir?' said Sebastian. 'You are not master here. Perhaps you have not noticed, sir, but the ring is upon *my* finger.'

'You are not even a member of our Order!'

'On the contrary, Willaston, I claim my birthright to be not only member, but master.'

'You cannot just claim membership. You must be proposed by one of the office bearers. And have your name written in the book.'

'My name is in the book, written there by my father's own hand.'

'Your father is dead!'

'And I am his successor, named by him. I am the master here, by blood, and birthright and will. I have my father's decree here for any who wish to read it.' Phoebe watched as he pulled out a letter and held it aloft. 'Do any contest my right?' His voice rang out as his eyes roved around the circle waiting for a challenge, but there was not one sound to break the silence.

The Marquis held his hands out in petition to the circle. 'What is wrong with you? Tell him he is wrong. Will you just stand there and let him trick his way in here and take over?'

'Edward always meant to bring him in,' someone said.

'He was wild!' said the Marquis.

'He was young,' came the reply. 'And not that much worse than your own boy.'

'He is the rightful Hunter,' said another.

'He is a damned usurper!' cried the Marquis.

'You are the usurper,' called one of the figures at the far end. And when the Marquis stared in the direction of the voice no one moved. It was as if they were closing ranks against him.

Even Bullford stepped back to resume his place within the circle.

'James?' The Marquis stared at Bullford with shock and anger and hurt.

Sebastian walked forwards to stand before the Marquis. 'You have forgotten the aims of this society and bent the rules to suit your own selfish desires. You have threatened the innocent, and blackmailed and terrorised a woman whose very honour this society should have fought to protect.' He gestured towards Phoebe, his eyes meeting hers briefly across the floor before he turned back to the Marquis. 'As master, I strip you of your office, sir.'

The Marquis gave a hard laugh. 'That is all you can do. You cannot throw me out. Membership is for life. Once one knows our secrets he is either a member—'

'Or dead,' finished Sebastian.

'Are you threatening me?'

'I would not stoop to your level. I mean to rule this Order as my forebears intended and uphold the very values for which it was founded. All that is rotten will be cut away and the Order's integrity restored.' Sebastian held out his hand to the Marquis, as if he were showing him the ring.

Phoebe watched as the Marquis's face flushed puce. He stood there for a moment with such a look of murder upon his face that she feared for Sebastian's safety and then, to her amazement, the Marquis got down on his knees and kissed the ring.

Hunter longed for nothing more than to go to Phoebe, to cut her down from that awful cross, but he knew that he must first ensure the loyalty of all the members; without that he doubted that either of them would leave the hall alive. His heart tightened as he met her eyes and he could only hope that she understood. He stood there and the first man pushed back his hood, dropped to his knees and vowed his allegiance with his lips upon the ring. The circle began to slowly rotate as each dark figure in turn followed suit.

The swearing ceremony was only half-completed when

he heard Phoebe cry out. The circle gave a collective gasp and stopped. Hunter looked up to see Willaston standing behind Phoebe, one hand gripping her hair, wrenching her head back, while the other held a ceremonial knife pressed against her throat. Everything in that moment seemed to slow. Hunter felt his gaze narrow and sharpen. He could hear the call of outraged voices. He could hear the beat of his own heart and that of the woman he loved.

'She knows our secrets,' shouted Willaston. 'And as a woman she cannot be admitted to our order. Therefore Miss Allardyce must die. Unless you wish to tell everyone here how you mean to bend the rules for your own fancy piece, Hunter.'

Hunter's words were like ice. 'The rule states that no *man* may know of our existence and live. Miss Allardyce, as you have just said, is a woman, and she is no fancy piece but the woman who will be my wife.' Hunter turned so that he was facing the Marquis and Phoebe squarely across the chamber. His eyes gauged the distance that separated him from them. Thirty feet of clear space. He could feel Phoebe's gaze, but he did not allow himself look at her. Instead, he kept his focus on Willaston.

'Release her or I will kill you, sir,' Hunter growled.

Willaston was panting heavily; his face was flushed and sweating.

Hunter saw the tiny flicker in the older man's eyes that preceded the movement of his hand. In the space of one heartbeat Hunter had drawn the pistol from his pocket and fired.

There was the flash of the powder in the pan and an almighty deafening roar and through the blue smoke Hunter watched the knife fall away to clatter on the floor. And Willaston crumpled in its wake, a red stain spreading over the arm that had held the knife.

Hunter was across the distance in seconds, grabbing the ceremonial knife and cutting the ropes that bound Phoebe. Relief surged through him and his love was all the fiercer for it. He pulled her into his arms and clutched her to him.

'Phoebe,' he whispered. 'My love.'

'Sebastian.' She clung to him, pressing her face against his chest.

'I am taking you home.'

'No.'

Hunter's heart gave a lurch. And then she looked up into his eyes and he saw the love that was there.

'Not until you finish what must be done here,' she said.

And Hunter wanted to weep for love of her. There had never been a woman like Phoebe Allardyce and there never would be. She had sacrificed her own heart and all chance of happiness for him. She would have given her life for him. She was his heart, his life, his very existence. And their love for each other would burn bright beyond the aeons of time.

He kissed her and, with Phoebe by his side, completed all that his father had asked of him.

The house in Grosvenor Street had been decked in flowers and greenery. The vases in every room were brimful and overflowing. Great garlands festooned the banisters and mirrors and mantels. Outside the sky was a cloudless powder blue and the sun shone in glorious splendour. The events in Obsidian House seemed far in the past, although only two weeks had elapsed.

Phoebe stood before the full-length looking glass in her bedchamber and stared at the woman who looked back with eyes sparkling with such happiness. She looked radiant dressed in Mrs Hunter's gift. The bodice of the new ivory gown seemed to shimmer in a haze of tiny pearls and iridescent beads. Its neckline was square and cut low enough to hint at the swell of her breasts. Its skirt was of smooth Parisian silk that dropped away to hang perfectly and from beneath which peeped the toes of new ivory silk slippers. Her hair had been caught up in a cascade of curls and threaded with fresh cream roses. And on her arms she wore a new pair of long ivory silk gloves.

'You look quite, quite lovely, my dear girl.' Mrs Hunter dabbed a little tear from the corner of her eye. 'I am so glad to be gaining you as a daughter.'

'And I, you as a mother,' said Phoebe and smiled warmly at the woman who had helped her so much.

'You are almost ready to go down to Sebastian, but for one last thing he bade me give to you.'

Mrs Hunter took out a small cream-leather box and pressed it into Phoebe's hands. Within the box was a gold heart-shaped locket with a wolf's head engraved upon it, and when Phoebe opened the locket, there, inside, were two tiny portraits, one of Sebastian and the other of herself.

Mrs Hunter's fingers moved to touch her own dress where her oval locket lay beneath. 'Such things are precious, Phoebe,' she said as she fastened the locket around Phoebe's neck. And the little golden heart lay above the gentle thud of Phoebe's own.

'Quite perfect.' Mrs Hunter smiled.

Phoebe felt the tears well in her eyes.

'Why, whatever is the matter, my dear?' she asked gently.

Phoebe shook her head. 'I was just thinking of my papa and how much I would give that he could be here this day to see me married.'

'You must be brave on your wedding day, Phoebe. It

is what your father would want. And upon our return to Scotland Sebastian will see that Sir Henry's debts are cleared and that he is released.'

Phoebe nodded. 'You are right.' She dried her tears and let Mrs Hunter lead her down the stairs. And as she reached the bottom of the staircase, Mrs Hunter smiled and stepped aside, and there, waiting across the hallway, was her own dear papa, dressed in his best wedding finery. Phoebe ran to him, tears of joy streaming down her cheeks as she threw her arms around him.

'Papa! Oh, Papa!'

'Child!' Sir Henry laughed and hugged her to him as if she were still his little girl. 'Mr Hunter was insistent that a father ought not to miss his daughter's wedding day. And I do believe that he was right.'

Mrs Hunter pressed a posy of flowers into her hands and her papa led her through to the drawing room where two tall dark-haired, dark tailcoated men stood waiting.

The Duke of Arlesford, who was standing by Sebastian's right-hand side, gave her a smile, then looked at Sebastian. Her papa handed her to Sebastian and left her there.

In both Sebastian's and Arlesford's buttonholes was a fine sprig of purple heather.

'From our own moor, Phoebe,' Sebastian whispered as he smiled at her, and Phoebe's heart was flooded with happiness and she thought there had never been a better man in all the world. She faced to the front, where the old priest stood, and she married the man that she loved.

Phoebe and Sebastian had set off back to Blackloch alone the next day. Both had been of the opinion that there was nowhere else in the world that they would rather be for their honeymoon than the beautiful Blackloch Moor.

As their coach travelled over the narrow winding moor road they could see the great dark house that was Blackloch Hall, silhouetted black against the fiery orange glow of the setting sun. On the horizon was the purple haze of the distant islands. The moor was quiet and the breeze gentled in welcome, and the air was sweet and fresh and scented with heather. And when the coach drew to a halt outside the great studded front door Phoebe and Sebastian climbed out.

Sebastian drew her against his chest so that they stood together and stared out over the blushing moorland.

'We are home, Phoebe,' he whispered as he nuzzled her ear.

'To our moor,' she said and the golden heart-shaped locket nestled between her breasts seemed to glow warm as she turned her mouth to meet his.

And Sebastian scooped her up into his arms and carried her, as his dearly beloved wife, across the threshold into Blackloch.

* * * * *